FIA

FIA

Books By James Ramsey Ullman

FIA FIA

DOWN THE COLORADO

THE DAY ON FIRE

TIGER OF THE SNOWS (WITH TENZING NORGAY)

THE AGE OF MOUNTAINEERING

BANNER IN THE SKY

THE SANDS OF KARAKORUM

ISLAND OF THE BLUE MACAWS

WINDOM'S WAY

RIVER OF THE SUN

KINGDOM OF ADVENTURE: EVEREST (EDITOR)

THE WHITE TOWER

HIGH CONQUEST

THE OTHER SIDE OF THE MOUNTAIN

MAD SHELLEY

FIA FIA

A NOVEL

OF THE SOUTH PACIFIC

by James Ramsey Ullman

CLEVELAND AND NEW YORK

THE WORLD PUBLISHING COMPANY

AUTHOR'S NOTE

The setting of this story—like the story itself—is fictional.

True, the islands here imagined bear considerable resemblance to American Samoa. The interpolated words and phrases of native language are, with a few exceptions, Samoan. And I have drawn largely on Samoa for both the physical and social background against which the story takes place.

But—repeat—the locale is fictional. In the atlas there is no Manaian Group, no places called Tiara, Utoia, Apingo, or Maniloa. And the people of the story are in no way intended to represent actual persons on factual islands.   J.R.U.

PUBLISHED BY The World Publishing Company
2231 WEST 110TH STREET, CLEVELAND 2, OHIO

PUBLISHED SIMULTANEOUSLY IN CANADA BY
NELSON, FOSTER & SCOTT LTD.

Library of Congress Catalog Card Number: 62-9045

FIRST EDITION

WP262

TO MARIAN

— talofa —

FIA
FIA

Fia Fia—pronounced feeah feeah—
is a word much used in the South Pacific.
It means Happy Times, Happiness,
Contentment, and it has many more specific
meanings, all of them of a pleasant nature.

Seek ye the way. Though the distance be great, though the way be long, keep thy course, O son. Across the waters is thy path.

—*Old Polynesian chant*

1

IT IS THE SAME, Carr thought. It has not changed; only you have changed. For sea, earth, and sky, eighteen years are an instant. Nothing. For a man they are—eighteen years.

He watched the island growing larger, clearer, between the bare blue planes of sky and sea.

"The hills are big," said the girl standing beside him. "They're almost mountains."

"Not really so big," Carr said. "It's because the island's small and they go up fast."

"Not like Hawaii."

"No."

"Nor even Utoia," the girl said. "Though I didn't see much of Utoia."

"You would have, if a few of those stateside Utoians had had their way. There were some sad-looking bachelor types on the dock when we took off."

Carr smiled, expecting a smile in return. But it didn't materialize. She was a pretty girl (or young woman; he would have guessed her in her middle twenties): slim, trim, with a pert face and hair bright as the sunlight—very much the sort, he had judged, who would be pleased by a whiff of flattery. But—wrong again, he thought. He was usually wrong about women. Instead of smiling, her face seemed to constrict, and her eyes were suddenly withdrawn and opaque.

"I—I hadn't noticed," she said, and looked away again at sea and island.

They were side by side at the ship's rail, but not otherwise together.

Indeed, they had met only the day before in a Government office in Utoia's capital town of Apingo. Carr was with two other men, by name Mel Melnick and Frank Lavery; but Melnick was in the cabin, seasick, and Lavery was beside the captain on the bridge. Carol Loftus was in the care of Leonard Shafter, assistant administrative officer in the Government of American Manaia, who now came up to them along the swaying deck.

"So there it is," Shafter said to her, nodding forward. "Does it look like home?"

"It looks beautiful," said the girl, and her eyes were again bright and young.

"Yes, it does. It is. I hope you'll be happy there."

"Oh, I'm sure I will."

The three stood silently looking ahead, while the interisland motor ship, *Harold L. Ickes,* cut the deep swells of the Pacific. Directly before them the sea was indigo blue, the blue of depths beneath, unseen and unimaginable. Then, farther on, it grew lighter. It became a cobalt blue, a dazzling glinting blue, threaded with green, stippled with sunlight; and beyond this, in turn, showed the scalloped white line of a reef. What was directly beyond the reef could not be seen. There was only the bulk of the island, grown larger now; a looming purple mass between sea and sky. . . . Until it too, like the sea, began to change; the purple brightening, becoming greenish blue, then green; the whole of it sweeping upward in a great green wave. . . . And now it was no longer merely a mass, a shape, but living earth, carved and textured. It was shore line, valleys, ridges, trees, and the trees now were the wave, green and gleaming, rising to the knobs and spires of the island's summit. In all the sky, from sea to sea, there was only one cloud, white and luminous, and that rested poised, motionless, upon the highest spire.

"Now you see how it got its name," Shafter said to Miss Loftus. "Tiara Peak. Tiara Island."

The girl nodded, keeping her eyes on the vision before her.

"They talk of Bora Bora," said Shafter. "And Moorea and Rarotonga. I've never seen them, but I'll take Tiara."

There was perhaps a slight proprietary tinge in his voice; but no more than a tinge. There was more of earnestness and genuine feeling. For Leonard Shafter, Ph.D. (*cum laude* in social sciences, University of California, 1954) was an earnest young man. As he stood now at the rail of the little steamer, looking out at the island—in a way, *his* island—his eyes, behind their horn-rimmed glasses, were as bright as those of the girl beside him; and it was obvious that the work he was involved in meant more to him than a job and a living.

16

"It's the loveliest place I've ever known," he said. "And I think the happiest. I hope to God it will stay that way."

If the comment was directed at the man beyond Miss Loftus, he showed it neither by glance nor intonation. And Carr, for his part, seemed not to have heard. He was standing with arms folded on the rail, his tall body bent, his shoulder hunched, with head thrust slightly forward; and although, like Shafter and the girl, he was staring at the island, neither his dark face nor darker eyes gave any hint of what he thought or felt.

Presently they could hear the rumbling of surf on the reef. A few minutes later came the clank of a bell on the bridge, the voice of Captain Stack shouting orders, the padding of feet of the Manaian crew. And the *Harold L. Ickes* began changing course. First it veered off at an angle to the reef line, then for a while moved parallel to it, and finally, with another clank of the bell, swung again and bore straight in. It had been a six-hour trip from Apingo, on Manaia's main island of Utoia, and, throughout, their progress had been unvarying: a slow rolling and pitching in the deep ocean swell. Now, however, things changed—and fast—as a wave lifted them by the stern and pushed them on. The reef came up with a rush. The rumbling rose to a roar. Ahead and on either side, the breakers, which before had been merely a low scalloped fringe, lashed up in a frenzy of white spume; and in the next instant, it appeared, they would be among them, grinding, foundering. But it did not happen, of course. There was a break in the reef. And now, straight and true, they swept through it, as if through the narrow spiked gate of a castle. Spray beat at their faces; the sea churned; in the white welter, not ten yards abeam, they could see jagged prongs and claws of coral. But they were in free water. Tide and engine carried them through. And in another moment they were past the gate; the roaring faded, then the rumbling; they were riding smoothly, gently, on Tiara's lagoon.

Carol Loftus's hands had been tight on the rail, but now she relaxed them; and Shafter smiled. "That's all," he said. "Bill Stack can do it in his sleep."

This time the girl smiled back, and her face, wet with spray, was fresh and glowing.

The ship moved slowly into the island's welcoming arms. And as it moved, island, like sea, underwent another change. Above them the heights were gone, the knobs and spires hidden behind intervening hills, with only a shred of white cloud projecting beyond them into the bare blueness of sky. The hills were soft, lush, irridescent in the late afternoon sunlight, curving in gentle arcs to the valleys, which in turn curved gently to the lagoon. Around the lagoon, except at its seaward end, behind them, was a line of palm trees, and beneath the palms, rimming the water, a sweep of glittering beaches. As they advanced, palms and beaches on either side grew closer; ahead they narrowed into an apex; and at the apex, presently, could be seen a jetty, a few huts and sheds, and human figures.

"Is that the village?" Miss Loftus asked.

Shafter shook his head. "The village is on the other side of the island. About three miles. But there's no good landing there. This is where boats always come in. And where the hotel will be."

He looked past the girl at Carr. "Over there, do you see?" he said, pointing. "Where they've begun clearing the trees."

Carr nodded but said nothing. During the passage of the lagoon, as before on the open sea, he had been looking quietly, fixedly, out over the rail: first at the island as it took shape around them; then at the lagoon itself, its silken surface, its transparent depths. Through water as clear as air he had watched the white sand of the bottom, the occasional dark pools and weaving eddies, the jagged sunken ranges of the coral heads. For the lagoon was his job. It was why he was here.

Now Frank Lavery, down from the bridge, approached and stood beside him, his red face redder than ever in the flaming sunlight, his paunch bulging solidly against the rail. "They sure as hell haven't got much done," he said, indicating the area of the fallen trees. "Well, one bulldozer'll do in a day what it takes these Johnnies three weeks.

"When we get the 'dozer, that is," he added morosely. "What with that Harry Bridges and his goddamn Reds, it's probably still settin' on the pier in Honolulu."

He spat into the water, and the four at the rail stood silently watching the shores converge. Then the fifth passenger, Mel Melnick, appeared from the cabin and joined them. He was a slight, dapper man in his mid-fifties, with a sallow complexion, dark darting eyes, and an habitual air of nervous tension; but as of the moment, tension, along with much else, had been drained from him by five hours and fifty minutes of seasickness.

"Now maybe you see why you're here," he said to Carr. "My God, with a trip like that the tourists wouldn't want a hotel; they'd want a hospital." He passed a smoothing hand over his custom-made luau shirt that had become wrinkled during his accouchement. " 'Why a plane?' the directors keep asking me. 'Why not ferry 'em by boat, the same as any other island hotel?' Well, now I can tell 'em so they stay told. And the sooner we get that plane here the better."

He squinted out at the lagoon. "How's it look to you?" he asked. "Much stuff in there to foul up landings?"

"It doesn't look bad," said Carr. "But I can't tell for sure until I get out with a boat and a diver. My guess is it will need some blasting of coral heads, especially in here near the shore."

"Well, get after it, boy. Maybe you and Frank here are seagoing supermen, but I want to do my puddle jumping in that li'l ol' seaplane."

Turning to Lavery, the contractor, he pointed to the cleared area ashore and began talking about the Tiara Beach Hotel. The land was now closing in fast. The jetty and the brown waiting figures were near and clear. Again a bell clanked, Captain Stack barked orders, and the *Harold L. Ickes* nosed in alongside the crude landing. Its engine reversed. Ropes spun. The ship nudged the jetty and lay still. They were there.

You are here, thought Mitchell Carr. After eighteen years you are here.

They came down the plank gangway onto the island of Tiara. In the lead was Leonard Shafter, lending a steadying hand to Carol Loftus, and the crowd on the dock stared in fascination at her pink-white face and sunlit hair. Then, in order, came Melnick, Lavery, Carr. And these the islanders stared at too, but only briefly; for though also strangers, they were men-strangers, and these were not so rare as women on Tiara. The crowd itself was motley; men, women, children, perhaps fifty in all: a few dressed in traditional Manaian lava-lava, but most in odds and ends of Western clothing—the women in prints and ginghams, the men in T-shirts and denim trousers, or old khakis cut off at the thigh. They were curious and excited; but they were also well-mannered, and there was no shoving or shouting. Some welcomed Shafter by name, and he greeted them in return. Then at a call from the rear a path was opened to permit the approach of a man of importance.

This was a big handsome Manaian in his middle years, well-fleshed and dignified in bearing, dressed half—below the waist—in lava-lava, half in an old but laundered linen jacket, and carrying the traditional staff and fly whisk of a talking chief. His graying hair was closely cropped, his broad Polynesian face clean-shaven; and the face broke into a smile as he tucked his fly whisk into his lava-lava and shook hands warmly with Leonard Shafter.

"Fahoai, greetings!" said Shafter. Then to Miss Loftus, who stood beside him, "This is our famous Fahoai, talking chief of Tiara."

The girl smiled and extended her hand.

"In a few days," Shafter added, "you'll know all about chiefs and talking chiefs. Here, Fahoai is the talking one and Tafutimo is the other. . . . Fahoai, this is Miss Loftus, one of our supervising nurses, who will be with you for a while."

The chief bowed slightly and took the proffered hand. "It is an honor for our island. May you be happy here," he said in slow, careful English. Then, holding his staff before him, he intoned for a few moments in resonant Manaian.

Shafter then introduced the three men: Melnick, Lavery, and Carr. "They have come for the building of the new hotel," he said. And the chief spoke the same words to each.

"Perhaps you have already met Mr. Carr," Shafter said to him. "He visited here on Tiara during the war."

Brown man and white man looked at each other. Then both shook their heads. "No, I do not think so, alas," said Fahoai politely. "I was not much here during the war, but working for the Navy on Utoia. And there, of course, there were so many—"

There was another stirring in the crowd, then the sound of a motor; and a jeep materialized from among the palm trees. It pulled up at the jetty, and out stepped a tall thin Manaian wearing shorts, a T-shirt, and a khaki cap with a brass insignia. "This is Malele, our policeman," said Shafter. And there were more introductions.

Malele was apologetic for being late. At the last moment before leaving the village, he had had to stop a fight among some boys, and though nothing serious, it had taken time. "Then I call for Miz Mundy," he said. "I say the boat comes, Miz Nurse comes; but she says no, they come tomorrow, and she is still fixing Miz Nurse her room. Miz Mundy is a good lady, a good schoolteach, but not so good with today and tomorrow. So at last I come myself. I come late. I am sorry."

He saluted smartly, and Shafter nodded. His eyes had moved out to the jeep and the road beyond. "And Tafutimo?" he asked "Where's Tafutimo?"

"He is fishing today. Most men in the village, they fish for bonita."

"*He* knew we were coming today—" Shafter paused, annoyed, and looked at Fahoai. But the talking chief said nothing.

"If you are ready now, sir," said Malele, "I will drive you and Miz Nurse to the village."

Shafter shook his head. "No, I can't go yet. I've business with these gentlemen here. Besides"—he looked at his watch—"it's getting late."

"Don't hurry because of me, please," said Miss Loftus.

Shafter considered. "If Mrs. Mundy doesn't expect you anyhow until tomorrow, maybe it makes sense for you to spend the night here too."

"Whatever you think best," the girl said.

"Fahoai—"

"Yes, Mr. Shafter?"

"There's a suitable place here for Miss Loftus?"

"Oh yes," said the chief. "Three huts are now up. There—you see?—in the palm grove, and very nice. There is plenty of room for Miss Nurse, and for you too and the gentlemen."

"In that case," said Shafter—

He looked around. During the conversations the crew of their ship had been unloading its cargo, and now the jetty was piled high with bags, duffels, cases, crates, and bales.

"In that case," said Mel Melnick, who had been waiting restlessly, "let's look things over before it gets dark."

Fahoai gestured with his staff, issued an order, and the watching crowd converged on the stacked baggage. In a few minutes everything was moving inland through the palm grove, borne on the heads of men, women, and children; and the newcomers, with Fahoai and Malele, followed after.

The huts, as the chief had said, were "very nice." They were small quonsets that had been shipped over in sections from Apingo on previous sailings of the *Ickes,* and they had been assembled properly; they were clean; they were sparsely but decently furnished with tables, chairs, chests, and cots. One hut was half dining room, half kitchen, with a smiling cook. Off to one side, among the trees, was a newly built privy, marked GENTS, under which someone—within the past few minutes, presumably—had added AND LADY.

The crowd lingered curiously for a while and then drifted away. Malele saluted Shafter, said, "I leave jeep in back," and rode off on a bicycle. Then, Miss Loftus having excused herself and gone to her room, the four white men, led by Fahoai, moved off through the palm grove. It was only a short walk to their destination: along a shaded path, up a small incline, into the area of felled trees. As Lavery had commented on the ship, the area was not large. No more than two dozen trees were down. And Melnick, surveying the scene with his quick dark eyes, pursed his lips in annoyance.

"I'd expected it to be all clear," he said to Shafter. "What's the trouble, you think: men or equipment?"

Shafter looked at Fahoai, and the chief said, "There is no trouble."

"So what's holding things up?" said Melnick.

"There is no holding up. First the men fix the huts. Then they come to the trees."

"And where are they now?"

"Now it is late. After five. They have gone home."

"And when they *are* here how many are there?"

"About twenty."

"Only twenty?"

"When we receive word from Apingo that there will be a hotel on Tiara and first the land here should be cleared, I make an announcement in the village. There will be many jobs, I say, and good wages. But only twenty-six come. And now it is twenty."

"With yourself?"

"Myself?"

"You're the working boss, aren't you?"

"Working? I?" A tinge of indignation touched Fahoai's placid features, and he flicked with his fly whisk at an imaginary insect. "No, I do not work any more," he said. "I am a *tulefele*—a talking chief."

"And you just talk, is that it?" said Melnick.

"That is correct. I talk."

Shafter was on the point of interposing himself, but Melnick shrugged and turned away. "You'll want a few men too," he said to Carr. "On the lagoon, for diving. How many will you need?"

"Two or three should do it," said Carr.

"All right, you pick 'em in the morning. The lagoon comes first, so we can start using the plane soon as it gets to Apingo." Melnick turned to Lavery. "You'll just have to scratch away for a while, Frank," he told him. "I'll send over what I can from Apingo, and when your Hawaiian gang gets here we'll be in business."

The contractor nodded without enthusiasm, and the two men moved off to inspect the site of the future Tiara Beach Hotel. Melnick, apparently wholly recovered from his seasickness, walked quickly, veering this way and that, pointing, talking. Lavery moved slowly, with professional calm, occasionally nodding again but saying little.

Fahoai had taken his ruffled dignity and gone off through the palm grove. Shafter and Carr stood looking out across the lagoon toward the westering sun. Somewhere a woman laughed. A seabird cawed. Far away, faint and deep, they could hear the rumbling of the sea on the reef.

"In a way, it's a crime to change it," Shafter murmured. "And yet—"

"—change is the way it is," said Carr.

Shafter looked at him curiously. "You were here much during the war?" he asked.

"No, not much. Just back and forth a bit."

"Was it different then?"

"No. There was no base here. It was just a place you could come over to now and then from Utoia." Carr was silent a moment, peering out at the gleaming water. "Yet in the end," he said, "I guess the war changed everything. For some places it came fast. For others it's later."

It was then, or a moment after, that they saw they were no longer alone. A figure had come out from among the trees and was standing by, waiting.

"Mr. Shafter—" the figure said now.

It was a boy—or young man—dressed in the usual T-shirt and shorts and wearing a pair of old canvas sneakers. He was tall, as were many Manaians, but thinner than most, and especially in his face, which was rather long and narrow. His nose was narrow too—unusually so for a Polynesian—and his eyes, though dark, were somehow differently set, and held a different light, from those of the average islander. There was an intensity, a restlessness, in them that reminded Carr—and he smiled inwardly at the association—of the glint in the eyes of Mel Melnick.

"I am sorry to interrupt you, Mr. Shafter," the boy said in flawless English.

"That's all right. Come over," said Shafter pleasantly, and when the boy came he put a hand on his shoulder.

"This is John," he told Carr.

"John?"

"John Koa, sir," the boy said.

Carr put out his hand, and he took it.

"John is one of our bright lights on Tiara," Shafter said. "He just graduated with honors from the high school in Apingo."

"It is four months now since I graduated," said the boy.

"Well, four months then. Anyhow, we're all proud of him."

There was a moment's pause. The boy swallowed. Then he said, "I do not mean to interrupt, sir, but you are here now, and I thought maybe you have heard from Honolulu."

"Honolulu?" Shafter's eyes strayed off toward Melnick and Lavery, for today he was associating Honolulu with the affairs of the Tiara Beach Hotel.

"From the Air Force," said John Koa.

"Oh—of course." Shafter shook his head. "No, there's no word yet," he said. Then to Carr: "John has applied for cadet training with the Air Force in Hawaii."

"It is now four months, sir," the boy began. "And—"

"Yes, I know." Shafter's hand was again on his shoulder. "With the government there's always the red tape; don't I know it? We've done all we can, John, and you'll just have to be patient." As he went on his voice brightened. "Meanwhile there'll be plenty to keep you going right here. With the hotel, the construction: all sorts of good

23

mechanical jobs. . . . Have you been working on the ground clearing?"

"No. No, I haven't—"

"Why not?"

"Because—" The boy hesitated, didn't answer. Carr had been watching him steadily, and now for an instant their eyes met.

"Why are you interested in the Air Force?" Carr asked him.

This time these was an answer. "Because I want to be a flier," said John Koa.

"You mean a pilot?"

"Yes, a pilot, sir. I'm good with engines. At school I specialized in physics and mechanics."

"Hmm— Well, I'm afraid we can't give you much flying here"—Carr smiled—"but, as Mr. Shafter says, there'll be plenty of jobs. Come around in the morning and we'll keep you busy while you're waiting."

The boy did not say thank you. He looked from Carr to Shafter to the ground. Then Melnick and Lavery came back along the slope, returning from their tour; and he silently withdrew.

"He's a pretty special one, isn't he?" said Carr, his eyes following him.

"Yes," said Shafter, "there aren't many like John. Especially on the out-islands."

"It wasn't only what he said but the way he said it. His face. His eyes. The—" Carr searched for the word. "The *wanting* in them."

"Couldn't you see the reason? Or at least part of the reason?"

Carr gave him a sidewise glance. "You mean he's half white?"

Shafter nodded. Then he smiled a little, as they walked back toward the quonsets with Melnick and Lavery. "Yes, even *here* the war made some changes," he said.

The sun set. Day faded and it was night. A new moon, horned and golden, rode the sky. After supper Carr went down to the shore and walked for a while alone along the beach.

On his return he found Carol Loftus sitting on the steps of the mess hut, looking out through the trees at the glinting water.

"Like it?" he asked her.

"Yes, it's perfect," she said. "I only hope it's as lovely over on the other side in the village."

"How long will you be staying there?"

"It's not definite. A few months, probably—until a Manaian nurse is ready to take over."

"That's quite a while to be out here on your own."

"I won't mind," said Miss Loftus. "I want to be on my own."

Carr looked at her curiously. In appearance, and most of the time in manner, she was a wholly recognizable specimen of the genus American Girl, standard brand, attractively packaged—the sort one encounters in their thousands as nurses, airline hostesses, and high-bracket secretaries in metropolitan offices. But occasionally there was a strange divagation. As with her reaction at the rail of the ship, when he had paid her a routine compliment on her effect on Utoian bachelors. As of now, in the declarative flatness of the words: "I want to be on my own."

Ah, Miss Garbo Junior, he thought, half smiling. What he said, however, was: "I can understand that. So do I—mostly. But for a man it's apt to be easier."

"I don't expect it to be easy," the girl said.

She looked away into the moonlit stillness, and for a while they were silent.

Then she said: "And you—you're staying just a few days, aren't you?"

"Yes, just a few days," said Carr. "To blast out the lagoon."

"That's all you're here for?"

He considered a moment.

"Yes, that's all," he said.

There was room beside her on the steps, and the thought crossed his mind to sit down. But, instead, he went on into the hut, where Melnick and Lavery were playing gin rummy.

2

THE MORNING SUN climbed a sky as pure as on the earth's first day. Tiara's cloud cap gleamed. The lagoon was a sapphire in a band of emerald. Within the sapphire, below the surface in refracted sunlight, lay the myriad world of the tropic sea.

It was a world, in part, of stillness: of sandy floors and rocky ledges: of shells and fronds and fish suspended motionless, as if transfixed by shafts of brightness, and coral breathing, building, an inch a century. It was a world of movement, too: movement of light, of shadow, of water: of claw that stirred at last, of swaying stalk, of flickering fin and round black eye. Some movements were slow and undulant, some quick and darting. But all were small—as were all things that made the movements, and all things that stopped them. Life was small. And death, too, was small. Death was minute, delicate, patient. Shark and moray eel were distant on the seaward reefs. Carr's dynamite was still in its crate in one of the huts by the jetty.

Carr himself sat in the stern of a skiff that moved slowly across the lagoon. He was wearing only a pair of bathing trunks, and his bare back and shoulders were hunched, as he peered down from the skiff's side through a small glass-bottomed box. Beside him on a thwart lay a rough sketch chart of his own making; and when he saw something in the water that required closer attention, he called for a halt, peered long and carefully, and then marked the chart with a stub of pencil.

There were two others with him in the skiff. One was the oarsman, a silent heavy-set man named Mahai; and the second, perched on the prow, was a boy. This was not the boy—or young man—called John

Koa (who had not appeared that morning), but a much smaller youngster of perhaps thirteen, named Tuti; and he and Mahai were the only two islanders who had volunteered for the job. They were enough, however, for present purposes—the man for rowing, the boy for diving.

Carr's course was now east to west across the center of the lagoon. And later it would be north to south, so that eventually there would be two coral-free channels, at right angles, to give a seaplane safe waterways in all winds. Thus far, his observation of the previous day had proved right: there were few even minor obstructions out toward the middle. But closer to shore, near the lagoon's apex, were several coral humps that would have to be removed before a plane could taxi in to the jetty. And here most of the stopping and chart-marking was done. At certain points, wanting a better look, Carr let himself over the side and went down with a diver's mask. When deeper or longer dives were necessary, the boy, Tuti, went down and reported back to him. And at points where Carr decided there would have to be blasting, the boy dived again and attached to the coral a length of cord with a floating marker, so that later they would not have to depend solely on the sketchy chart.

Tuti enjoyed the work. He particularly enjoyed the mask which Carr had provided for him, and each time he surfaced after a dive he pushed it up onto his forehead with a professional gesture and announced his findings with zest. "Little rock," he would report. "Is nothing. Can almost push over." Or, at another point, "Big rock. Like a mountain. With many holes, many caves—full of fish."

And when he was back in the skiff, smiling happily: "When dynamite goes, will be something to see. Bang! Boom!" He waved his arms. "Whole island will shake! Whole fountain of dead fish!"

On the shore, nearby, Melnick and Lavery were again surveying what would in time be the grounds of the Tiara Beach Hotel. Of the twenty men the talking chief had mentioned, only sixteen—and half of them boys—were at work, for two had not appeared and two others, Mahai and Tuti, had gone off with Carr. They had only handsaws and used them poorly. The trees went down slowly, leaving great stumps and roots which would later have to be blasted. But Melnick, this morning, had resolved on patience and calm.

"Try to drive hard with a thing like this, and what do you get?" he asked. "You get ulcers, that's what—and that's all. I found that out building the Marina in Acapulco and the Royale in Tahiti. Every gook place in the world it's the same story—labor cheap but lousy. Except that here it's not even cheap. In Mexico, yes. In Tahiti, yes.

27

But let the good old U.S. take over Podunk Island and you might as well be doing business with Jimmy Hoffa."

The calm was cracking. Melvin J. Melnick, promoter, president and minority stockholder of the Pacific Hotel and Development Company, sighed and turned his attention to other matters—initially the fruit fly that had just alighted on his neck. "Labor," he said, slapping, "we can't do anything about till we get back to Apingo. And not much then either, until the stuff comes from Honolulu. . . . Bugs we can do something about. We've got ten gallons of spray. . . . Jesus, those mosquitoes last night! We'll have to spray the whole damn area before we open, or there won't be a tourist who'll stay two nights."

He moved restlessly about, with Lavery following, slow and ponderous. Then, stopping, he took and unrolled the blueprint that the contractor had been carrying under his arm. "So now we're here," he said, pointing. "In the center—right? This is the main building: dining room where we're standing; kitchen there, toward the dock; terrace in front, looking down the slope. The bungalows—" his eyes moved to the left— "they'll be over there where it's still jungle. And straight on down—dance floor, garden, pool, cabanas. This fellow in Waikiki's got something new in cabanas, did I tell you? Sort of Italian style—striped canvas—but underneath he uses a plywood frame, so they can . . . What's the matter? Something wrong?"

Lavery was looking off down the slope toward the water, and his red face was frowning.

"The grade—" he said.

"What grade?"

"Right here in front of us, down to the beach. The center of the whole thing. And it's steeper—"

"Steeper than what?"

"Than the specifications say. The specifications"—Lavery indicated the blueprint—"say an over-all grade of four degrees from up here to the water. And it's at least seven; I'll bet my life on it."

"So, four—seven. Is that the end of the world?"

"Not of the world, maybe, but of a lot of figuring for foundations. The main house, dance floor, pool—everything on the slope."

Melnick was frowning now too. "You mean you'll have to recalculate?"

Lavery nodded. "Whoever surveyed this for you—"

"It was a fellow called Ferguson, last year. An Englishman from Fiji."

"Well, either friend Ferguson wasn't seeing so good, or there's been an earthquake since. Anyhow, it's got to be refigured for fill and foundations."

28

"How long will it take you?"

"Me? I can't do it. I'm a contractor. This takes an engineer."

Melnick's lips were tight with annoyance. Then he had an idea. "They've got engineers with Public Works over in Apingo," he said. "We'll borrow one of them."

"That makes sense," said Lavery.

"But quick. When I go back to Apingo tomorrow. The ship from Hawaii's due in two weeks, and the layout has to be straight, so your construction crew can start cracking as soon as they get here." Melnick started down toward the water, as if he were going to board the *Harold L. Ickes* at that moment. "I've got contracts for my opening," he said. "With Pan Am, the Matson Line, sixteen travel agents; and I'm going to open on time, come hell or a hurricane. I've been working on this deal for five years. This is going to be the best by-God resort hotel in the South Pacific, and I'm not going to have it fouled up before it's started."

The Government jeep bumped along the dirt road that ringed the island. Leonard Shafter was driving, with Carol Loftus beside him, and in the back was the nurse's luggage.

It was only a little over three miles to the village, and Shafter drove slowly, so that she could see something of what they passed. Now he pointed off to the left, at the green valleys sloping up to the hills; now to the right, at the coconut groves and beyond them the beach and the sea. And the girl looked and nodded, but her mind was elsewhere. She was now wearing her uniform. ("It will be better," Dr. Friede, the senior doctor at Apingo had said, "to wear it right from the beginning. It will fix your professional status in their minds.") And she was glad she had, for it fixed it in her own as well. In a uniform one was never wholly a stranger, but a part of the world, with a niche and a function.

Shafter glanced at her. At the fringe of soft yellow hair beneath the white of her cap. At her face, which was soft too, with the fresh smoothness of youth, but at the same time somehow taut and strained in the morning sunlight.

"Don't be nervous," he told her. "There's nothing to be nervous about."

"I'm not," she said. "Not really, that is."

"In a few days it will all seem like home to you."

"I just hope so much they won't resent me."

"They won't. You saw them at the dock. You met Fahoai—"

"Yes. But the other chief—who didn't come—"

"Tafutimo." Shafter was silent a moment. "I'm going to see Tafu-

29

timo this morning. He's a fine man—one of the best chiefs in Manaia —but terribly conservative and opposed to change. He's intelligent though, and not unreasonable. When he understands the situation he'll be all right."

What Shafter did not add was that, as of his previous visit to the island, there had already been much talk of the situation with the high chief of Tiara. Or, rather, of the *two* situations: new hotel and new nurse. Of the two, the matter of the nurse had seemed by far the simpler, because (1) it was temporary and (2) the reasons were self-evident. Tiara, like all the Manaian out-islands, had for years had only native resident nurses, of whom the people were very proud. But the last nurse had suddenly married and left; no other qualified local girls were available for immediate replacement; and since it was essential that so remote a place have someone with medical training on hand, a stateside nurse had to be sent to fill the interval. It was as ABC as that. Tafutimo, no less than Fahoai, had said yes, he understood; the white nurse—the *papalagi* lady—would be welcome. Yet now he had failed to perform the most elementary of island courtesies: the greeting of Miss Loftus on her arrival.

Let alone the greeting of the hotel men. . . .

"I'm sure I can make him feel that I'm here only to help his people," said Miss Loftus quietly.

"I'm sure you can too." Shafter looked at her again—approvingly— and the jeep hit a bump in the road and jounced them.

"Oops, sorry," he said. And then: "You drive, don't you?"

"Yes. Why?"

"Because this jeep will be yours whenever you want it. Melele the policeman will probably be trying to borrow it all the time. But he's not officially entitled to it—just to a bike—so only let him take it when you've no use for it yourself. Mrs. Mundy *is* entitled to it, the same as you. But that's academic, because she doesn't drive, and she wouldn't go anywhere if she did."

"I'm so curious about Mrs. Mundy," said Carol Loftus. "Everyone in Apingo talks about her, but no one seems ever to have met her."

"No, she never leaves the island. At least not since I've been around."

"She must be a strange person. I can't help wondering what it will be like to live with her."

"You'll get on fine, I'm sure. And she'll be a big help to you. She knows everything about Tiara, of course, and speaks Manaian better than a talking chief."

"Is she so very old?"

"About seventy, I'd say. Her husband was a missionary—one of those old fire-and-brimstoners, I gather—but he's been dead a long while now. And she's nothing like that. Not a missionary; not even religious. There's a native parson who runs the church now, and she sticks to the school. A damn good teacher too, from what I've seen. Oh, she's got her old lady's crotchets: a sharp tongue; doesn't take any guff from anyone. But she's good. Better than good. In fact, she's quite a girl, old Mrs. M."

Miss Loftus was about to speak again, but now they rounded a turn in the road, and to their left was a valley deeper than the rest, leading inward and upward toward the heart of the island. Drawn after it, her eyes, too, moved upward, and beyond its highest point, above the sweep of green, she could see domes and spires of reddish rock, and above the rock a crown of dazzling cloud.

"I often think about Mrs. Mundy," said Shafter, following his own train of association, "—and what it takes for a person—a white man or woman—to live in a place like this. I don't mean the way we live: out here for a couple of years, say, for a specific job, and then home again. Nor the beachcombing sort of thing, either. I mean really to live with the people; to make a go of it by one's self. I believe it takes, most of all, an ability to combine, to meld. To keep hold of one's essential self, of what one is, what one comes from, and at the same time to take the new, the different, and make it part of that self." He paused and chuckled. "I'd have gotten quite a mark for that from Professor Kask," he added.

The girl's eyes came back from cloud and mountain.

"Who?" she asked.

"He taught sociology at Cal when I was there. And he turned blue at nice hazy generalities."

"You're a sociologist, then?"

"Yes—if you'll excuse it."

"And you've always worked for the Government?"

"No. After I got my degree I taught for a while. Then I worked for State Welfare in San Francisco."

"Why did you come out here?"

"That's the old question, isn't it?" Shafter smiled. "Well, I suppose I was as susceptible as the next one to the South Sea clichés. And besides, social work back home can be awfully routine. I felt that out here there might be a job that was really challenging; not just Case A and Case B and a sheaf of statistics, but a chance to help a whole people."

Miss Loftus nodded in understanding. She seemed about to speak again—but didn't.

"And you?" Shafter wanted to say. "Why are *you* here?"

But he left the question unasked, for he had already learned that

31

this was a girl who wanted to keep herself to herself. She had been in Apingo only a few months; her work had been in the hospital, where he rarely went; and she had made few appearances at evenings in the stateside homes or at the Coconut Palm Club. One of the few things he did know—and this interested him—was that she had volunteered for this job on Tiara. Whereas most of the stateside women he had met considered Apingo itself the ultimate in exile, this one wanted to get out still farther, still deeper. But the why and wherefore remained a mystery.

"Tiara's going to change a lot," he said. "Soon you'll find it very different."

"With the hotel?" she asked.

"Yes, the hotel. First the building. Then later, when it's open."

"Do you think it's a good idea? For the island, I mean."

"I wish I knew. There's been a lot of argument about it. In the old days when the Navy ran Manaia there wasn't a chance of any commercial enterprise getting in; and since the Department of the Interior took over in Fifty-one it's tried pretty much the same thing. But it can't be run as an isolation ward. Even Manaia's part of the world, of the twentieth century, and eventually it will have to face up to it. About the best we in the Government can do is to try to make the process as painless as possible."

Miss Loftus nodded. "This Mr. Melnick—" she said.

"I don't much care for Melnick. Strictly Waikiki and Miami Beach. But they say he's a first-rate hotel man, and if we're going to have a hotel here it might as well be successful. . . . Incidentally, you're welcome over there any time, you know."

"Yes, he and Mr. Lavery invited me. But I think my work will keep me busy enough."

"They'd be a change for an evening." Shafter smiled. "If you like noisy gin rummy."

They drove for a bit in silence. Then the girl said: "The other one—Mr. Carr. He's quite different."

"Yes, he seems different. I don't know much about him; he doesn't say much."

"He's been here before, hasn't he?"

Shafter nodded. "During the war. In the Navy, I think."

"He said he's just staying a few days."

"To get the lagoon cleared out for Melnick's plane."

"It seems a long way to come for such a short time."

"There's a job to be done. Someone has to do it who knows how."

They rounded another curve. Ahead, the road widened a little, and on either side, in the shade of palm groves, appeared the thatched huts of a village.

"So, journey's end," Shafter said. "Mrs. Mundy's house is right down the line here, next to the school."

They drove slowly on. Chickens scurried, dogs barked, and dark curious eyes watched them from the palm groves. Carol Loftus sat erect in her seat, hands folded in her lap, her face fixed in her too rigid smile.

"Easy does it now," said Shafter.

And the smile became more natural.

"That's the girl," he said. "These are good people. You'll do all right."

It was midafternoon when Mitchell Carr set out on the same road from the lagoon. But he was walking. And he was alone.

He had worked in the skiff from sunrise until about two; then, deciding that was enough for the day, had gone to the quonsets, had lunch, and lain down for an hour. When he rose he had put on a pair of old shoes, khaki trousers, and T-shirt; and now, after threading the palm grove, he had reached the road. He stayed on the road for only a short distance, however. Then, slowing his pace, he searched for a path leading off to the left and, presently finding it, followed it inland.

It is the same, he thought. You have changed. But it is the same.

He walked with a slow long-legged gait, his shoulders a little stooped, his hands thrust into his trouser pockets: the walk of a man who has plenty of time. Near where the path began there were a few huts, with islanders roundabout, and as he passed he called to them, *"Talofa—Talofa,"* and was pleased that he still remembered the Manaian greeting. Beyond the huts were a small taro swamp and a few patches of vegetables. Then all traces of man, except the path, slipped away, and he walked on up the valley through green solitude.

His eyes moved over the greenness, and it seemed to flow like a stream into his mind and spirit. Yes, it was the same, he thought. Still soft, still gentle: earth and earth's covering, its life, and even man, all soft and gentle on a sunlit island. There were such places in the world, and there were the other places, and he had spent most of his life in the other: in ungentle places, among ungentle men. On the carriers and planes of a wartime Navy—not long after he had first, and last, been here. Later, on the spurs of the Andes, in the graveled wastes of Libya and Saudi Arabia, in the foundation pits and construction shacks and steel-girt cubicles of unnumbered buildings in New York, Chicago, Detroit, Cleveland, Pittsburgh. He had been a man of tools, instruments, machines; of the hard ungentle materials that make machines; of the hard ungentle mind that controls them. But throughout it all, in a deep pocket of that mind, he had retained the memory, the image, of a place without steel or stone or tool or machine. And now at least he had returned there.

—With a case of dynamite.

But the case was in a hut by the jetty; and the jetty was behind him. Mel Melnick and Frank Lavery and their Tiara Beach Hotel were behind him. Ahead was only the green valley, and he followed the valley upward, beyond the last of the palms, under the breadfruit trees, past groves of pandanus, of wild orange and lime trees, through banks of rioting croton, hibiscus, gardenia, frangipani; and then the path turned and tilted more steeply up one of the soft green ridges that descended from the central hills. As he climbed, his legs tired and his breath grew short—as they had not in earlier days; but then he had been twenty-four, and now he was almost forty-three. He knew, however, that the ridge was not high. Climbing on, he was soon at the top. And there, for a distance of a few yards, the trees and foliage fell away and he could see about him in all directions.

Behind him was the valley from which he had just come; at its base the huts and the road; beyond it, ringed in long white-fringed arms, the blue oval of the lagoon. Ahead was another valley, indistinguishable from the first, except that there was no road nor lagoon beyond it, but only a green slope rising to another ridge. On the left, above, still high above, were the summit peaks of Tiara, jagged and notched against the sky, with the white cloud poised, as always, just above the topmost spire. And to the right was the sea. Only the sea. For on this side the ridge fell away abruptly, and it seemed there was no land below at all, but that the sea began directly beneath him, sweeping up and away, unbroken, to the far horizon. There was the sea and nothing more. No island showed, near or distant. No mast or stack or sail or wisp of smoke, and in the sky no plane, nor even a bird or cloud. There was the blue of sky, the blue of sea. And in their emptiness all that moved was the soft tide of the trade wind, breathing gently now, with the westering sun, and stirring a soft whisper among the fronds and grasses of the ridge.

Carr felt it too: against his eyes, in his hair, on the flesh of face and body. For a few minutes he stood there, simply feeling it—and nothing else. Then he turned and moved on. Descending the far side of the ridge, he came to the floor of the second valley, and here again he moved on through deep foliage, between tall boles and emerald fronds; and it was the same as the first valley—the same, and yet not the same—for now his progress was different. Now he was not only looking about him, but listening, halting every few moments to catch a possible sound from ahead. And presently he heard what he was waiting for.

The path curved, descending a little; the greenness opened; and before him were the waterfall and the pool. The fall was high but not broad, a long ribbon of silver pouring soft and sheer between mossy walls. And the pool at its base was small, its water dark but clear, its surface seeming to be lighted not by the sun but by a deep glow from within. Around the pool were grassy banks. And on the far bank the breadfruit tree. There were uncounted thousands of breadfruit trees on the island, but this one was *the tree,* the one he knew. Circling the pool, he approached it and stopped, and for a while stood looking at its cool and gentle symmetry. There was no thrust in a breadfruit tree; no Gothic soaring at a distant sky. It was calm, self-contained: its trunk smooth, its fruit plump and bland, its tiered leaves fanning out in lacquered stillness. It was a tree of the earth, for the creatures of earth. It was a tree of life. It fed. It sheltered.

Moving forward, he sat at its base—as he and Lovana had used to sit long ago.

He looked at the leaves above him: the sheltering leaves, broad, firm, each with its five tapered points, that shut out sky and sun. . . . Like hands, he had once said. And Lovana had said yes, they were hands, the hands of the Old Man, and then she had told him one of the ancient stories of the islands. . . . Of how the breadfruit tree had come into being. Of how, ages past, there had been two young lovers, a village fisherman and the daughter of a king. They had loved truly and well; but the king was against them, the whole island was against them, and the young man had been threatened with death if he was so much as seen with the princess. To be alone and secret, they had fled to the woods. But the king's men followed them. They tried to hide, but there was no hiding place. Their pursuers were everywhere, following, closing in, and soon they would be upon them and it would be the end.

In their flight the young lovers came to a glade in the forest. And here they stopped for they could go no farther. There was no way out. For the last time they embraced and waited for what would come. And then it came. For now, presently, they were no longer alone. A figure had entered the clearing and stood beside them. But it was not one of the king's men. It was an old man, and he was not savage and fierce but smiling, and he said to them, "Do not be afraid. I am your friend. I am the Old Man of the Woods, and I will help you." Then he bade them sit on the soft moss, and he stood beside them with arms and hands spread wide, and said, "Now you are safe. You are in the place of happiness; the place of *fia fia*." And there the lovers stayed, doing what lovers do. And when at last they looked up the old man was gone, and where he had been was now a breadfruit tree. His body had become its trunk, his arms its boughs, his hands its leaves; and the leaves hid them, sheltered them, from the king's men when they came; and the men went away.

Ending the story, Lovana had smiled. She had kissed him. "And there they still are," she had said, and with her finger had touched her chest, then his, then the bole of the breadfruit tree. "She and he and the Old Man," she said. "And there they will always be. For no harm can come to lovers in the place of happiness. Of *fia fia.* . . ."

Carr watched the pool and the silver fall. He lit a cigarette and watched the smoke drift slowly out over the water. Lovana had liked to smoke. She had always been asking for a cigarette, and when he had lighted one for her she would draw on it deeply, trying to inhale; for she loved to see the blue clouds come out through her nose. She was rarely successful, however. Usually, in a moment, she was coughing; and in the next moment laughing; and then, laughing together, they would rise—he taking off his shirt and shorts or whatever it was he wore, Lovana unwinding her lava-lava (in the village she had often worn a Western store-bought dress, but here, always, it was a lava-lava) until she stood before him bare, her body brown and gleaming; and then hand in hand they would walk into the pool's living water.

He looked at the sun and at his watch, and it was going on five. It was at this hour that they had usually come here, and it had been their own place, their "secret" place, well guarded both by the Old Man and by the fact that the villagers, though they liked fresh-water bathing, were too lazy to walk so far from the village. Not that secrecy had been necessary, except for his own tastes. The Tiarans had been delighted that one of their girls had acquired a *papalagi* lover—particularly a *papalagi* who wore the two bars of a Navy *lutenanti*—and Lovana herself was so proud of him that she would have been glad, he had sometimes thought, to do their lovemaking in the main street of the village.

No, there had been no problem in Tiara. Tiara did not know what a problem was. The difficulties had been at the other end, in Utoia, where he was stationed, and it had taken all his ingenuity—compounded with deceit, chicanery, and pure lying—to effect most of his visits to the outer island. The first, when he had met Lovana, had been legitimate enough (though he had stayed rather longer than necessary): the establishment of a small fuel depot for planes that might run low on gas short of Utoia. And two other trips, as well, had had official sanction. But the rest—perhaps a dozen in all during his four months in Manaia—had been strictly catch-as-catch-can affairs, under all manner of pretexts, in patrol boats, trade schooners, fishing smacks, once even in an outrigger. And once. . . .

He smiled. As yes, that once. . . .

In those days there had been a stream of planes over Tiara: the few, mostly small and all seaplanes, that came in for refueling, and the many, large and small—bomber, fighter, transport, reconnaissance—that flew past, going toward or from Utoia. And Lovana had loved planes. She had loved them even more than cigarettes. Each time a PBY or other craft had put down in the sheltered bay before the village (for there had then been no need to clear the lagoon) she had stood about watching it, fascinated, as if it were the first she had ever seen; and once she had learned that he, Carr, was a pilot, she had begged him to take her up. He had laughed and told her no, it was impossible. But she had gone on begging: "Please, please, Meesh." (That was his island name, his only name; he had no last one.) "Yes, you can do, Meesh. You are a chief, no?—a *matai,* a *lutenanti.* You can do anything." And he had laughed again.

. . . Until the day when he was alone in a little Seagull scouter, returning to Utoia from a routine patrol, and there ahead was a white cloud and beneath it the island of Tiara. And then he had looked at the fuel gauge, which showed that his tank was half full, and told himself, "No, it's gone wrong; the tank's dry." And he had come down in the bay, close to the village, and there was Lovana on the shore, watching, and he had yelled at her, "All right, come on! Climb in!" This time she was wearing her lava-lava, and she had wanted to go home and change to her store dress for so great an occasion. But he had said, "No, stay as you are. It's better this way." And although she had not understood what he meant, she had complied and climbed in; and off they went, while the islanders gawked in awe along the shore.

She had not been afraid. At first she bounced up and down like a child in the tiny cockpit; then, when they were airborne, twisted round and round, trying to see in all directions at once. Her shoeless feet were tucked beneath her. Her bright lava-lava hiked up with her gyrations until her brown legs were bare to the thigh. For a while she put her head out over the side, and her black hair streamed in the rush of air; then swiveling back, she threw her arms around him, kissed him, laughed; and he was laughing too, as he struggled to keep his hands on the controls. He banked the plane. They swooped over the sea; over the lagoon, the beaches, the valleys. They climbed the ridges, buzzed the peaks, plunged through the white cloud and out the other side, and then he climbed and dove and climbed again, soaring, roaring, while the island reeled wildly below, and Lovana, beside him, clapped her hands and shrieked in delight. . . .

Now he lay by the pool beneath the breadfruit tree, and plane and roar and shriek were far away. Lovana had not shrieked here. Here she had been quiet and soft and gentle, not a child but a woman, with a woman's face, a woman's body, and the only sounds had been her occasional murmurs of pleasure and, beyond them, through them, the deeper murmur of the waterfall. He could hear the water now. It seemed almost that he could hear Lovana, that if he turned a little he would see Lovana, her dark eyes smiling at him, her long hair falling loose over her breasts and waist. It had been a long time since he had seen her thus, thought of her thus—or thought of her at all—for that had been the special, the wonderful thing about their relationship: that in itself, in its own time and place, it had been whole and perfect, but that, outside and beyond them, it had scarcely existed.

He had made love to Lovana. Perhaps, in a way, he had *loved* her. But if so, it had not been in the way men loved—or thought they loved—in the world from which he came. True, he had desired her; desired her greatly. When she had been nearby, and at least potentially available, he had used every trick, broken every rule in the book, to be with her as much as he could. But when he left Manaia, it was over, finished. There had been no residue of longing, no emptiness of separation, of ending, but only a quickly fading memory of what had been perfect in its time and place—and afterward, elsewhere, wholly gone. And it had been the same, he knew, with Lovana. She had loved men before him. And she would love men after him—probably many men; and some loves would be long and some short, some good and some not so good; and theirs had been short and good, and that was that. They had loved not as Westerners love, but as the islanders love: in a time, in a place. The time and place of *fia fia*. And later there had been—he remembered the island word—no *pilikia* to mar it. No trouble. No grief.

The other sort of love had come later. Twice it had come—first with Margaret, then with Helen—and each time, in varying ways, it had brought all the things there had not been in his love for Lovana. Including the trouble and grief. For twelve years—first for seven, then for five—his life had been enmeshed with the two women he had married: his thoughts with theirs, his emotions with theirs, his very existence with their existence, no less than with his work, which, together with them, had given life its meaning. And it had come to—what? To no-meaning. Nothing. To a nothing that had haunted, tormented, driven him—from marriage, from work, from everything he had known and needed; to this place and that place, to stray jobs, stray companions, stray women—until all of living had become a withdrawal, a flight, from what was true and real.

Until . . . Here. Now.

For here, now, at flight's ultimate point, there had, he knew, at last been a change. He had come far enough into the past, and from one world into another, so that the eye of memory saw differently, and it was now no longer that other world that was true and real, but this one, so long lost and forgotten. There was no steel here; no tool or machine. There was no Margaret, no Helen. There was only Lovana, the pool, the fall, the breadfruit tree. The place of the happy time: of *fia fia*.

—And a case of dynamite in a hut by the jetty.

Presently he rose, took off his clothes, and bathed in the pool. Then when he was dry he dressed again and, in the slanting sunlight, followed the path on through the valley.

3

THE HOUSE of Fahoai, talking chief of Tiara, was built *fa'a Manaia*—"in the fashion of Manaia"—and next to that of the high chief, Tafutimo, it was the largest and finest in the village. Elliptical in shape, it had a high steep roof of thatch supported around its circumference by upright, smoothly hewn logs, lashed at the top to other, transverse logs by lengths of plaited coconut fiber, called sennit. The uprights were spaced at intervals of some five feet, and between them, suspended from above, were louvered screens of pandanus leaf, not unlike Venetian blinds. But except in high wind or storm these were kept pulled up under the eaves, night and day, making of the house, in effect, a pillared hall, open on all sides. Raised above the level of the surrounding ground, the floor was of sea-smoothed fragments of shell and stone, covered here and there with mats of pandanus or palm. There were no rooms or partitions; a Manaian *fale* serves in its entirety as living, eating, and sleeping quarters, depending on the time of the day. But the preparation and cooking of food was done in a small shed out back, and the house itself was neat and immaculate.

Not, to be sure, that this required much doing, for its furnishings were sparse. In addition to the floor coverings there were mats of finer texture for sleeping; but when not in use these were kept on shelves up under the roof, as were the clothing and other possessions of the family. In a household purely *fa'a Manaia* there would have been no further furnishings. But Fahoai's habits, and philosophy, were such that he was not averse to a few Western appurtenances. To one side, near the enclosing pillars, was an iron-framed bed, complete with mattress, quilt, and cushions. On the other side was a table with a pressure lamp, near it a sewing machine of the old treadle variety, and near that in turn two slat-backed chairs. But the chairs were used principally by the women when at the sewing machine, or—like the bed—for the comfort of an occasional *papalagi* guest.

In this home there lived six people, and, as in many Manaian households, the relationships were complex; or at least would have seemed so to a Westerner. At its head were Fahoai and his wife, Polu. But no blood children of their own lived with them; of the four they had had two had died, and the two who remained, a son and a daughter, were married and living on other islands. In their stead were two nieces and a nephew of Fahoai's—the girls by one sister, the boy by another, both long since dead. And also there was an old uncle of Polu's who had been a widower as long as anyone could remember. Perhaps half the families of Tiara, as of all the islands, were made up of such components; but what was unusual about this one was that there were no small children.

In the late afternoon of the day following the arrival of the *Harold L. Ickes* five of its six members were at home. Fahoai, who had spent the previous evening with friends on the lagoon side of the island and most of the day strolling leisurely home, with other visits en route, was taking his ease on the mat reserved for the *matai*: the head of the household. He had removed his linen jacket, which was his garment of office on public occasions, and was wearing only a lava-lava, above which his brown midriff bulged comfortably; and he puffed with satisfaction at a Filipino cigar which Captain Stack of the *Ickes* had bought for him in Apingo. Polu, his wife, a short moon-faced woman of much greater bulk, had just gone to the cook shack to see to the evening meal. And at her call the older niece, tall, heavy-limbed Mena, rose to help her. On a mat near the bed the other niece, Va'ina, a lithe and handsome girl of perhaps nineteen, was bent with concentration over a small hand-mirror, oiling and brushing her long black hair. At the far end of the *fale,* against a post, sat the old uncle, Kalamakoa, a skeleton covered with hanging flesh; and now, as throughout each day, he was rolling coconut fiber into sennit against his bare and tattooed thigh.

The absent member of the family was the young nephew, John Koa.

A moment or two passed in silence. Then, before the niece Mena could join her, Polu reappeared from the cook shack carrying a wooden bowl of taro tops and coconut cream. "It is lumpy and has no flavor," she said accusingly.

"I am sorry," said the older girl meekly. "Shall I—"

"I will take care of the lumps. But it needs salt, pepper—"

"We have no pepper," said Mena.

"Then go to the store and. . . . No, you have the fish to clean." Polu turned to Va'ina. "Go to the store," she told her, "and get some pepper from Asimo."

Fahoai cleared his throat. "I don't see why it is necessary—"

"If you can afford cigars, we can afford pepper." Polu turned back to Va'ina, who had not moved from her mirror. "Well?" she asked.

"I will go when I am finished with my hair," the girl said.

"Finished? When are you ever finished? With your hair, your face, your eyes, your nails? All you ever do is look at yourself in that mirror. And all *you* ever do"—this to Mena—"is go to church." Polu sat down and thumped the contents of her bowl with a mallet. "Church and mirrors and cigars," she said. "While I work myself into my grave."

This had been heard often before, and no one replied.

"And shall I tell you why it is—what is wrong with this family?" she went on. "It is that there are no children. On all the island we are the only family without children, and will you give me a reason? Two girls who are old enough to have many babies. Even John, he is old enough to be a father. And what happens? Nothing. My own son and daughter, they have children, yes—they do the natural thing; but they are away, and what good does it do here? A family must have children to help, to do errands, so that old people do not work themselves into the grave. To laugh, to cry, to run about, so that a house is a home."

This, too, had been heard before.

"Young Patali, the son of Tafutimo," she said to Va'ina, "—he comes to see you last night; he asks you to go walking. And you will not go. Will you tell me why, please?"

The girl did not answer. Bent over the mirror, she was twining a hibiscus blossom into her hair.

"Will you tell me *why?*"

Va'ina looked up at her placidly. "Because I am a *taupou*," she said.

"So you are a *taupou*. You are supposed to be a virgin—hah!—to stay one until you marry. But does that mean you will never marry? Not even when the son of the high chief comes to call on you? . . . And you—" Polu veered back to Mena. "You do not even have a caller. You who are not a *taupou* and do not even have to pretend to stay virgin. You do not so much as have a man for a night, let alone one to marry you."

"Aunt, please—" Mena said, still meekly.

"She is already married, didn't you know?" said Va'ina. "To Jesus."

"If you were closer to Jesus, sister—"

"Stop this chatter, all of you!" Fahoai commanded. "It's got so a man can't enjoy a minute's peace in his own home."

"If it's peace you want," Polu began—

"—I shall one day move right out of this house," he said, "and live at the other end of the island." He drew a deep breath on his cigar. "The other end is where everything will be from now on, anyhow. With the hotel people here—"

Va'ina looked up with quick interest. "They have come then?" she asked.

"Yes, with the boat yesterday. That is why I went across the island, in my duty as talking chief."

"Chief Tafutimo did not go," said his wife.

"No. Because he is stubborn and foolish. And so it is even more important I go, to show the manners and courtesies of Tiara."

"How many *papalagi* have come?" said Va'ina.

"Three. For the hotel, that is. Then there was also Mr. Shafter and the new nurse."

"Yes, I saw Mr. Shafter and the nurse," said Mena. "They came to the village this morning and are now at Miz Mundy's, where she will live."

"And the other three—for the hotel; what are they like?" asked her sister.

"Like?" Fahoai shrugged. "They are men. They are American." He considered a moment, stroking the plump bulge of his jowl. "One of them—he is the chief, I think—I did not too much like. He was not courteous. The others I know nothing about, except that one was here during the war."

"They too will come to the village, do you think?"

"No. Why should they come? It is as I say: everything will now be on the other side of the island. And it will be like nothing we have seen before."

"Or should ever see." It was the thin, quavering voice of the old man, Kalamakoa, now looking up for the first time from his rolling of sennit. "Is it not enough that such things should happen in Tahiti and Samoa and other islands of the sea, but that they must happen now to us?"

"Progress happens everywhere," said Fahoai. "And it must come to Tiara too, no matter what you and Tafutimo say. We cannot live forever like our ancestors, but must ourselves become people of the world."

The old man slowly shook his skull-like head. "We must live our own way," he murmured. *"Fa'a Manaia."*

"You will see: the lives of all of us will be changed. And much for

43

the better, if we are wise and careful. Until now we have had enough to eat, yes, and shelter in storm, for our island is bountiful; but we have little money to buy the things of civilization. Now we will have money. Our young men will have work and earn it. You will see soon with John."

"John?" said his wife, still engaged in her thumping.

"He came yesterday to where the hotel will be. He talked with the men. That means he is working there now and at the end of the week will come home with twenty dollars."

"How can he be there when he is also here?"

"Here? What do you mean?"

"He came home late last night and was here all day. He went out just before you came."

"Out? And he was here?" Fahoai showed his bafflement. "I do not understand. Where has he gone—do you know?"

Polu shook her head. "I know nothing. He says nothing any more."

Va'ina looked up from her mirror and laughed. "But I can tell you that before that John works," she said, "he will want to be *matai* of the whole hotel."

"Be quiet," her uncle told her. "I did not ask for your opinion."

"No, from a *taupou* one does not want opinions," the girl said. "One wants only husbands and babies and pepper." Finished with her hair, she rose and smoothed down her print store dress over her breasts and thighs. "So I shall be a good *taupou* and go to the store—and maybe on the way home I can also find some babies."

She laughed again and went out, swaying her hips; and Polu, rising with her bowl, looked after her angrily. Then she turned on Mena. "Go now and clean that fish," she snapped, "—or we will all starve together in this crazy house."

Mrs. Haskell Mundy's Christian name was Birdie, and its aptness would have pleased anyone who knew it; for she was wholly bird-like—in her beaked nose, her quick dark eyes, her tiny body—indeed in every way except in mind and heart. But it was so long since she had been called by the name that she had all but forgotten it herself. In Tiara she was Miz Mundy, or as a variant, Miz Schoolteach. And, with no dissenters save an occasional pupil lately fallen from grace, she was beloved on the island.

Greeting Carol Loftus that morning at the door of her schoolhouse, she had first extended a yellowed claw of a hand; then suddenly said, "My, no, that won't do," and rising on her toes, kissed the girl on the cheek. That done, she had led her in, with Leonard Shafter following, and the children in the single room rose and solemnly sang a song of welcome in English to the tune of "My Maryland."

"Two of them wrote the words themselves," Mrs. Mundy announced when the song was ended. Then she waved a hand at the children, and, solemnity gone, they rushed out.

"Oh, you shouldn't have," Miss Loftus protested. "Not because of me."

"Yes indeed, because of you," said the teacher. "Do you think we have a new arrival every day; or even every year? . . . And besides"—she smiled—"it will get you off on the right foot, my dear. Since you've been responsible for a holiday, they may feel it ungrateful to run away when they see you with a pill or a needle."

Leaving the school, they crossed the road to where stood the only Western-style dwelling in the village: a one-story bungalow of white clapboard with a green roof. "Remember, this is not just my home; it's *your* home now too," Mrs. Mundy said, as she led the way in.

Two of the bigger schoolboys trailed in after them with the baggage from the jeep, and Shafter, excusing himself, went off into the village. The old woman showed the young one her room, then the rest of the house, which consisted of one other bedroom, bathroom, living room, and kitchen. "As you see, Miss—" She smiled. "I may call you Carol, mayn't I?" she said. . . . "Please," said the other. . . . "As you see, Carol, it's small and very simple. But we have electricity and running water. I did without for most of my life and never missed them, but during the war in they came, along with everything else."

She opened drawers and closets, explaining as she went. Her dentures clicked, and her eyes sparkled behind old-styled rimless glasses. Then, when she had covered the bungalow, she opened a door in the kitchen and led the way through into an annex. "And here, my dear," she said, "is your own private preserve."

It was a dispensary—a small whitewashed room equipped with desk, chairs, sink, and examining table, its walls lined with shelves and cupboards—and although Carol had known that such a place was being built for her, she had had no idea that it would be so close at hand.

"The old one was at the other end of the village," said Mrs. Mundy. "But by the time Tulipa—that's the old nurse—left, it was falling apart. It was my suggestion to build the new one here, so close and convenient for you. Your patients, of course, will use the outer door, but you can just go back and forth through the kitchen, and you'll find it a blessing during the rains."

She pointed to a stack of boxes and cartons. "Those are your supplies and drugs. And here"—she opened another door, revealing a

45

cubicle with a single cot—"is your hospital. All ten-by-eight of it. It's only for emergencies; anything serious is sent as soon as possible to Apingo. But of course you know more about that than I do."

Carol nodded. Through the past two days, since leaving Apingo, she had been exposed to an almost dizzying succession of new scenes and new faces; but here in her own world, her own dispensary, she was again, solidly, competently, Miss C. Loftus, R.N., and she looked about her with professional appraisal.

"It looks fine," she answered. "So much better than I expected. And I can't tell you how grateful—"

The old lady made a tut-tutting sound, said, "Now I'll leave you for a bit so you can get yourself acquainted," and re-entered the dwelling quarters. Carol busied herself setting up her new domain. And when she in turn went back to the living room she found that Shafter had returned and was talking with Mrs. Mundy.

"—and he'll be all right," he was saying; then looked up as Carol entered. "I've just been with Chief Tafutimo," he told her. "He and the other *matai* will hold a welcoming ceremony for you tomorrow evening."

"A ceremony? Oh dear—"

Shafter smiled. "You can't get by in Manaia without ceremonies. They'd rather do without food and drink. . . . Anyhow, the old boy was all right—perfectly reasonable—and you've nothing to worry about." He turned back to Mrs. Mundy, and the smile was gone. "But with the hotel," he said, "it's another story. He wouldn't quite come out and say so, but that's obviously the reason he didn't meet us yesterday. Not because of Miss Loftus, but because the hotel men were coming too."

The old lady nodded. "He's so conservative," she said. "So *fa'a Manaia*. Fahoai—that's the talking chief, dear," she said to Carol— "is very different; he thinks the hotel is a fine idea. But Tafutimo wants everything just the same as it's always been."

"Very few of the men have reported for work over at the lagoon," Shafter said. "Do you think that's his doing?"

"I'd say it's partly his influence. And partly—well, you know how Manaians are about regular jobs. Over in Utoia, I gather, it's changed a lot, what with so much going on and the high wages. But here it's still the old island story: why work if you don't have to? There's always the fish and the taro, the breadfruit and coconuts."

They talked on for a while. A housegirl, named Falima, appeared and went into the kitchen. And a little later there came, as luncheon guest, the village pastor, Solomona. He was a graying middle-aged

46

man, short and thin for a Manaian, dressed in clergyman's black and with a pompous manner; and his conversation during the meal was heavily embellished with scriptural quotation.

"I'm afraid Solomona is rather of the old school," Mrs. Mundy said when he had left. "But it was Mr. Mundy, you see, who trained him." She smiled a little. "And so was he."

"I suppose the island has changed a lot since you've been here," said Carol.

"Yes, it has. And what hasn't? My goodness, when I left the States with my husband there wasn't such a thing as radio, let alone television, and the women were marching around demanding the vote."

"And here—are things better, do you think?"

"I would say so—on the whole. I don't think I'm a prude, but in the old days the sexual morals *were* shocking. And then in your field, of course, there's been wonderful progress. The islands used to be full of dreadful diseases: hookworm, yaws, filariasis, leprosy. But now they're mostly well controlled."

"Thank goodness."

"With the hotel coming, of course," said Mrs. Mundy, "there'll be bigger changes than ever. And of a different kind." She looked at Shafter. "What do you think about it all, Leonard?"

"I think it's inevitable," he said. "But I'm afraid, too."

"Afraid. . . . That's what I've been wondering: if it's something just to be afraid of, or if something good can come of it too. My Lord, it's hard to imagine Tiara with boats in and out—and planes too, I suppose—and people all over with money and cameras, and heaven knows what not! I can't imagine how I'll keep any of my pupils in school."

"You'll keep them all right. As far as Tiara's concerned, you're the President of the United States. But the rest of us—" Shafter shrugged. "Well, I'll struggle along with Tafutimo. And any help you can give us there. . . ."

After a bit, he went out again. Mrs. Mundy lay down for a nap, and Carol returned to the dispensary. Then, in the cool of the afternoon, the three walked through the village. Besides the bungalow and the schoolhouse there were only two Western-built structures: the church, a squat building of coral rock erected in the last century by the predecessors of the Reverend Mr. Mundy; and the store, a decrepit box of a place, used during the war for the storage of aviation gasoline. All the rest, scattered through the coconut groves, were huts in the old island style, with spaced wooden pillars and thatched roofs. And only an occasional article within—a bedstead, a washtub, a kerosene lamp, a sewing machine—gave evidence (and even that anachronistic) that this was mid-Pacific America in the second half of the twentieth century.

Dark, curious eyes watched them, as they had when Carol entered the village in the jeep; and a crowd of children was soon following them. But this time there were more than stares, for at almost every hut Shafter or Mrs. Mundy greeted people and introduced them, and each time there was a welcoming smile and a murmured *"talofa."*

Two huts at which they did not call—and, indeed, carefully circum-navigated—were those of the high chief Tafutimo and the talking chief Fahoai; for a visit to either, by Carol, before the next day's ceremonial welcome, would have been a Manaian faux pas of major proportions. But in the neighborhood of Fahoai's they encountered the first person to approach them of his own accord: a young man who appeared suddenly from among the trees and stood before Leonard Shafter.

"Well, hello there," said Shafter. And he introduced John Koa.

"I'm sorry to bother you again, sir—" the boy said.

"What is it, John?"

"It's a small thing, sir. A favor." He held a slip of paper in his hand. "When you get back to Apingo would you please send this off for me?"

"Send it off?"

"Yes. It's a cablegram. Please. It's to the Air Force Headquarters in Hawaii." With the other hand he took three dollar bills from his pocket.

"Will this be enough to pay for it?"

Shafter looked at bills and message but didn't take them. "John, John," he said, shaking his head, "you're still such a kid."

"A kid, sir?"

"So impatient. So impulsive." The boy started to speak but he forestalled him. "Look—your application is being processed, I promise you. These things take time; big organizations move slowly; and I won't have you throwing your money away on something that will do no good."

"But it's been—"

"Yes, I know—it's been three months."

"Four months."

"All right, four. That's not a lifetime. The Air Force will still be there even a year from now."

John stood before him, money and paper still extended. "Please," he said. "If they get a cable at least they'll know that—"

"No, I won't let you waste your money." For an instant Shafter's

48

voice was sharp; then he softened it. "We've done everything we can in Apingo, John," he said. "The director of education wrote a fine letter; I know because I've seen it. Now there's nothing to do but be patient, and the best thing is for you to take a good job with the hotel people and keep busy. I promise you'll hear from us the minute *we* hear."

The boy stood silent for another moment; then he turned away. And Shafter and the two women walked on toward the bungalow.

"Poor John," said Mrs. Mundy. "He's so eager, so intense."

Shafter nodded.

"He was like that even when he was a little boy and I used to teach him. But now, since he's back from high school, he's even more so." She mused for a bit. Then she said, "I do hope he gets what he wants. What sort of chance does he have?"

"I don't know," Shafter answered. "We've really pressed his case, but it's an unusual one. There's all sorts of machinery set up for college scholarships, if a boy can make the grade. But an Air Force cadet is something else again. There's never been an application from a Manaian."

"He's such an attractive boy," said Carol Loftus. "He seems so bright."

"Too bright, I sometimes think, for his own good."

"And somehow different from the others I've seen."

"He is. He's half white. . . . Not that there aren't a lot of half whites in the islands; the war saw to that. But most of them don't look it, or even seem to feel it. John does."

Mrs. Mundy nodded her old head in agreement. "Yes, John feels it," she said. "He never forgets it."

The sun was setting as Mitchell Carr came down the last valley toward the village. The tops of the palm trees along the shore before him rose into a sky of flame and glory.

Before reaching the village he stopped. He had decided that at some such point as this he would cut over to the shore road and follow it back to the lagoon. But he did not do it at once. Nor, in the end, did he do it at all. An impulse stronger than decision gripped and held him, and presently he moved on toward the huts in the palm grove.

If he met Lovana—well, he would meet Lovana. Or, more likely than not, they could pass by within arm's length and neither would recognize the other.

Dogs picked him up first, barking. Then small boys picked him up. Arriving on foot, without uniform or status, he was not, like Nurse

Carol Loftus, an object of awe, and their greeting was unshy and voluble.

There were few adults moving about. Most seemed either to be taking their ease in their open-sided huts or to be gathered around cook fires in shacks behind the huts. When he reached the road it was empty, and he walked along it toward the church. He recognized the church. As he drew closer he recognized, nearby, the shed he had helped build for the storage of gasoline; but now apparently it was the village store, for there were lights and people inside. A bit farther on he could see a green and white bungalow, with the Government jeep parked outside, and he knew that this must be where Carol Loftus would live, and that Shafter was still there. Shafter, he further knew, was planning to drive back in it that evening to the lagoon, whence it would be returned to the village in the morning by Malele, the policeman.

Good enough, Carr thought. He would get a ride back; he had had enough walking for one day. . . . And he had had enough of the village. He did not want to see more of it. Or to see Lovana—if she was still there. He had seen the Lovana he had known in his memory, beside the pool in the valley. Here, not in memory but in flesh and blood, she would be a woman of almost forty. At forty, Polynesian women were old. They were fat. She would have grown children, probably grandchildren; even a husband. . . . He walked on, quickening his step a little, toward the bungalow and the jeep.

And then he stopped, because he saw Lovana.

He was passing the door of the shed-that-was-now-a-store, and the door opened and she came out, carrying a package. Her hair was black and lustrous, with a pink flower in it, and although she was wearing a store dress—as she usually had in the village—it did not hide the arch of her breasts or the soft swelling of her hips and thighs. She came out, and she was smiling. She was smiling at him, as she had always smiled, and her teeth were white, her lips were red, her eyes were dark, and in their darkness, shining, was the smile of Lovana.

"*Talofa*," he said.

She replied, "*Talofa*," and came closer. And she was the age of Lovana remembered.

"Who are you?" he asked.

"I am called Va'ina," she said. "Who are you?"

Now he too was smiling. "I am called Meesh."

"You are with the hotel?"

"Yes, sort of."

"It is good there will be a hotel. It will then not be so dull here."

"You find it dull now?"

"Yes, now it is dull. I think there is no place so dull in all the world." Her lips had pouted, but now they smiled again. "When the hotel comes, though, it will be different," she said. "All people and lights and nice clothes and music for dancing. When the hotel is open I will come there."

"Yes, you must," said Carr.

"Maybe I will come even before, while it is building, and see how it is getting on." Her eyes flicked across his. "You have a cigarette, please?" she asked.

He brought out his pack, gave her one, and lighted it.

"Thank you." She inhaled, blowing the smoke out through her nostrils. Then her eyes met his again, and this time held them. "Why do you look at me so?" she asked.

"I'm waiting for you to cough," he said.

"To cough? What do you mean?"

He smiled again. "I don't mean anything. I'm afraid I was thinking of someone else."

"Oh?"

"But you needn't be offended. You're as pretty as she."

The girl's face was puzzled. Then her own smile returned. "I am glad you think so. You are nice, Meesh," she said. And with a little nod she moved slowly away and disappeared into the palm grove.

For a few moments Carr stood where he was. He lit a cigarette of his own. Then he started toward the green and white bungalow, but stopped before he reached it and sat down on a palm stump beside the road. He looked back at the store. He looked at the sky above it, now heavy with dusk, and beyond it, past the palms, at the beach and the bay. The beach still gleamed whitely, as if with an afterglow of the vanished sunlight, but the bay was indigo blue, the blue of night. It was at a point on the water just a little to the left of the store that he had brought the little Seagull to a stop and Lovana had climbed aboard.

Lovana. . . .

Now—what was it? . . . Va'ina.

Va'ina, who smoked and did not cough.

Again, as by the pool that afternoon, his mind moved back—past Helen—past Margaret—through the years. And when at last it returned to the road before him, an old woman was going by prodding a pig with a stick.

"*Talofa,*" she said.

"*Talofa,*" he replied.

After that, for a while, there was no one. Then another figure

51

approached—a man, or tall boy—walking slowly with eyes on the ground; and this one made no greeting, nor even raised his head.

"So here you are," Carr said to him.

John Koa looked up and stopped. "Good evening," he said.

"We were expecting you at the lagoon this morning."

"I—couldn't come. I was busy."

"Perhaps tomorrow, then?"

"I am busy tomorrow too."

"It isn't just cutting down trees, you know," Carr said. "I'm working out in the lagoon itself, to clear the coral. I could use you for diving."

"Yes, I know," John Koa said. "The native boy diving for pennies."

Carr's lips tightened. His voice changed. "You've forgotten about inflation. These days it's for dimes."

The boy was silent.

"If you change your mind," said Carr, "—and you think you can watch your manners—come on over. We'll have work for you."

He rose and walked on toward the bungalow, and as he reached it Shafter was just coming out to the jeep.

4

A SAMPLE FOLDER for the Tiara Beach Hotel had arrived with the last airmail, and Mel Melnick held it up with a flourish. Opposite him, behind a desk in Apingo's Government building, sat Russell Gorman, senior administrative officer in the Department of the Interior.

The folder was of heavy, smooth paper, printed in four colors, and on its cover, against a background of sea and palms, were the words, YOUR TROPICAL PARADISE. . . . "Paradise. That's the punch—the gimmick," said Melnick. "It's been proved over and over as the sellingest word in the business. We'd have called the place the *Paradise* Beach, except that the people in the East would get it mixed up with the one in Nassau. And with jets on the way we're expecting plenty from the East."

Gorman nodded noncomittally and took the folder. He was a plump balding man of about fifty, inclined to perspiration and rumpled clothes; but his eyes were cool and detached, and so was the mind behind them—the mind of a civil servant of twenty-eight years' standing, well attuned to the verities of grade and tenure, but also to the conscientious performance of duty. From the beginning he had been against a hotel on Tiara. Not against one somewhere in the islands; for he was well aware that Manaia needed a source of income other than Government handouts. But he believed that the main island of Utoia was the proper place for it. Utoia was sufficiently—to use Shafter's Ph.D.-ism—acculturated, already far enough along in Western ways, to take such an innovation in stride. But an out-island like Tiara, as he saw it, was nowhere near ready, and he had fought stub-

53

bornly against the granting of a franchise to the Pacific Hotel and Development Company.

He had fought and lost; for neither Melnick's outfit nor any other hotel people would consider building on Utoia. It had too much rain, they claimed. It's beaches were inferior. The harbor stank. Apingo and the countryside were still littered with debris from the war. And in the end the Government capitulated to the fact that either the hotel would be on Tiara or there would be no hotel at all.

Gorman had lost. But still he had been right—or so, at least, developments were indicating. The Tiaran representative in the local legislature, while all for the money the hotel woud bring to his island, had vehemently protested against the blasting of the lagoon. According to Shafter, the chief Tafutimo had been anything but co-operative. And scarcely a day passed on which Melnick was not in his office, beset by some new problem of labor or supply.

It was therefore with no great enthusiasm that he took the folder of the Tiara Beach Hotel and thumbed through its lush pages. "Looks like quite an installation," he conceded, as he handed it back.

"You couldn't be righter. One million dollars' worth," said Melnick. "Granted these architects' drawings are always half pipe dream; still it's going to be something. The best by-God resort in the South Pacific."

At this point Leonard Shafter came in, said good afternoon, and sat down. "Are you set with the engineer?" he asked.

"We will be any minute," the hotel man said. "Frank Lavery's over at Public Works right now."

"And if they can't spare one?" said Gorman.

"Not spare one? For a job as important as this?"

"Well, we'll see." Gorman glanced at his desk calendar. "The ship with your construction crew is due on the eighteenth, right? Today's the ninth. And I gather the engineer will need about a week before construction starts."

"That's what Frank says."

"So your schedule's tight. If you don't want your men sitting around doing nothing."

"You're damn right I don't."

"At least the clearing's going on," said Shafter.

"Slow," said Melnick. "Slow as hell."

"How many men are working now?"

"It was down to fourteen yesterday, Frank said."

Gorman nodded and glanced at Shafter.

"With twelve more," said the latter, "going over from here tomorrow."

54

"If they show," said Melnick.

"They'll show all right. And they'll do a good job. This Tom Taki you're getting is the best foreman on the island. He'll do as much for you in a week as—"

"That's another thing," Melnick said to Gorman. "What's this he was talking about no Saturdays or Sundays?"

"Just what he said, I guess. They work a five-day week."

"And the other two just sit on their cans?"

"If they want to. If they want to work they get time-and-a-half."

"Jesus Christ!" Melnick shook his head. "Eighty cents an hour, and *then* overtime. When I built the Royale in Tahiti—"

"This isn't Tahiti," Gorman said. "This is Manaia, U.S.A."

There were steps outside and Frank Lavery appeared. Melnick looked up eagerly, but the contractor was shaking his head.

"What?" said Melnick.

"No deal. Public Works says they've got just two engineers and they're both busy."

"Busy? Doing what, for God's sake?" Melnick had jumped to his feet, and now he swung around on Gorman. "If we can't get any co-operation—"

"We're giving you all the co-operation we can," said the administrator blandly. "You can hardly expect the Government to go out of business because you're building a hotel."

"I'll talk to the Governor."

"That would be a little difficult, with the Governor in Washington."

"Then I'll—" Melnick broke off and, with an effort, composed himself. "And you," he said. "You won't help out on this?"

"Public Works runs its own show, the same as every other department. If they say they don't have a man free, they don't have him."

Melnick seemed about to explode again. Then he drew a deep breath and walked to the window and back. "So there goes another couple of thousand," he said to Lavery, "getting a man down from Hawaii."

"How about from Fiji?" Shafter put in. "It would be a lot cheaper."

"No sir—no Fiji. Not after that Ferguson we had last year." Melnick took another deep breath, let it out as a sigh, and turned back to Lavery. "So it's a cable to Honolulu, I guess—"

"Looks that way," said the contractor. "Unless—" He thought for a moment. "Well, I've had one other idea."

"What's that?"

"Carr."

"Carr?"

"Who's he?" said Gorman.

"He's the other fellow who came with us," Melnick said. "To fix the lagoon. I picked him up in Honolulu, and he said he knew planes and demolition work, but—" He spoke to Lavery again. "How do you know he's an engineer? What did he say?"

"He hasn't said anything. At least not right out. But a few comments he made—and the way he handled that blasting—"

"Where is he now?"

"At the hotel, I think. He was there an hour ago."

"You mean here?" said Shafter. "In Apingo?"

Lavery nodded. "He came over with me this morning. The lagoon's finished and he's set to go."

"Let's send for him," said Melnick.

He looked at Gorman, and Gorman looked at his watch. "Well, if we can make it quick," he said.

He tapped a bell, a Manaian clerk appeared, and he gave him instructions. Then he leaned back and said to Shafter, "I've an idea that by the time this hotel opens you and I are going to be night clerk and bus boy."

They waited. Gorman made a phone call about other matters. Melnick lighted a cigar and paced about, then took Lavery to a corner and talked in a half whisper. Leonard Shafter looked out the window and the harbor and the sea beyond and pondered the adjustments which would soon have to be made on the island of Tiara. For he knew, no less than Gorman, that the changes about to come would involve far more than real estate and package tours. Along with the cranes and bulldozers and construction crew, all the intangibles of the outer world—its ways and means, its forms and values—would roll in on the island like a tidal wave, and its people would know greater change and dislocation than in all the years since the first Western sail came up on the horizon.

Some ten minutes had passed when Mitchell Carr came in. He was wearing a white shirt and linen trousers, and the week on the lagoon had burned his face as dark as a Manaian's.

Melnick introduced him to Gorman, and Carr smiled. "Deportation papers in order?" he asked.

But the hotel man was in no mood for pleasantries. "Frank says you're an engineer," he said.

"I said I *thought*—" Lavery began. But Melnick gestured him into silence. Carr sat down, crossed his legs, and seemed to think the matter over before answering.

"Well—yes," he said.

"What sort of engineer?"

"Different sorts at different times. But mostly structural."

"That means buildings?"

"Yes, buildings."

Melnick puffed on his cigar with satisfaction. "Where are you heading from here, Mitch?" he asked.

"I was thinking of Pahukahuka," Carr said.

"Of *what?*"

"Pahukahuka. It's another island."

"You've got something very special there?"

"No, nothing special. I just like the name."

"Like the—" Melnick swallowed. "Look, Mitch—"

"What are you getting at?" asked Carr.

"What I'm getting at is that we'd like you to stay on here. The surveying over at the hotel has been loused up—Frank's probably told you about it—and we'd like you to straighten it out."

"How much of a job is it?"

"Well, Frank's construction gang gets here in nine days. It'll take about another week to get everything over to the island."

"And after that," Lavery put in, "I'd say we'd need you about another two weeks while the job's actually under way."

"Call it a month in all," said Melnick.

Carr was looking at the ceiling.

"And as far as the fee is concerned, I think you found me fair on the lagoon job. We can talk details later." Melnick's pitch of voice changed slightly, so as to take in the two Government men. "But I can promise you the Pacific Hotel and Development Company is a solvent outfit."

Carr didn't seem to be listening. His glance moved from the ceiling to the window, and his dark eyes squinted into the glare of sunlight.

"I'll have to think about it," he said, rising.

Melnick's face showed disappointment. "If it's the fee, we can go over to the hotel right now and—"

"No, it's not the fee."

"We're under a lot of pressure, Mitch. If you don't do it, we've got to cable Honolulu and—"

Carr nodded. "I'll let you know tonight," he said.

"Before the cable office closes?"

"Yes, before it closes."

Crossing to the door, he went out.

"Well, that's a character you've got yourself," said Gorman, pushing his chair back. "Pahukahuka, no less—wherever that is. Because he likes the name. . . ."

Carr walked down the glaring main street of Apingo toward the

57

Admiral Nimitz Hotel. Along the street were shops, other Government offices, a garage, a movie house, a flyblown soda fountain: compared to Tiara, this was metropolis itself. Compared to its own former incarnation of eighteen years past, however, it was only a sleepy South Seas village. Then it had swarmed with the men and machines and installations of America at war; with ships in the harbor, planes in the sky, soldiers and sailors and marines overflowing the streets, the town, and almost bursting from its palm-girt shores. What remained were relics—and memories. A jeep went by carrying a fat Manaian, his wife, three children, and two pigs, and on its tailboard, barely distinguishable, were the words U.S. MARINE CORPS—SHORE PATROL. The garage been built as a supply dump for Navy Ordnance. The soda fountain had been a PX. The Nimitz Hotel had been the club for Air Force sergeants.

Entering it, Carr was immediately in the dining room; for the Nimitz was actually not a hotel at all, but a boarding house, maintained by the Government for the accommodation of Manaia's few transients. There was no lobby, no bar, no clerk—nor even a guest in sight, as he walked down the hall to his small screened room.

It was hot in the room: even hotter than in the sun-glare of the street. Stripping, he lay down on the bed and tried to think; but such thoughts as he had were, like the ceiling, only dimly perceptible through a haze of sweat. Presently he rose, dressed again, and leaving the hotel, went down the street to the Apingo Bar. It too was empty, except for the barman, a fat half-Manaian who was dozing behind the counter; and waking him, Carr ordered a beer.

Two years, two months, two weeks before, it would have been a whisky. Indeed, two weeks before, in Honolulu, it *had* been a whisky —and then a second and a third and a fourth—after he had left Mel Melnick at the Royal Hawaiian and walked into a bar on Kalakaua Avenue. "I'll have to think about it," he had said to Melnick then too. But the thinking had been drinking. Sitting at the bar, he had flipped a coin, but it had fallen to the floor and he had laughed and let it lie there. Then later he had slept; in his sleep he had dreamt a confused drunken dream of Tiara and Lovana; and when he had answered Melnick's call in the morning, hung over and still half asleep, he had heard himself saying yes, he'd go.

Now at least he tried to think. But he was little more successful than on the bed in the hotel, for his thoughts twisted back on themselves, like snakes swallowing their own tails. He had made his decision to join Melnick not by thinking but through drink and dream. And it had been a good one; he did not regret it. . . . Or did he? (Another twisting back.) . . . He had not liked the blasting of the lagoon: the shattering of life and mirrored stillness and the boy Tuti's "fountains" of dead fish. But that had been the necessary concommitant. The rest—the island itself, the sea, the beaches, the valleys, the pool, the breadfruit tree—had all been as he had hoped it would be. The white cloud, Tiara's tiara, had been as pure and radiant in fact as in memory. It had been good. Right. It had, for the time at least, brought him an inward peace that he had rarely known; a peace in which he could now, quietly, drink a beer, not whisky—nor even want a whisky. It had been good . . . and yet (another yet) at the same time not good . . . for his was a journey not only in space but in time; into the past, to what was dead and gone; and this, he knew, was the most obscure, the most dangerous, of all journeys that a man can make.

"Another beer?" the barman asked.

Carr shook his head.

Paying, he went out into the sun-baked street, and as he stood there one of Apingo's three decrepit taxis went by and he hailed it.

"To the airport," he told the driver, and off they went on the Belt Road that ringed the island of Utoia.

On Apingo's outskirts they passed the hospital, the high school, and the Coconut Palm Club, and beyond these the bungalows that had used to house service brass and were now the homes of Manaia's civilian officialdom. The road, unlike Tiara's, was paved, but still bumpy. With the town behind them, huts in the native Manian style appeared among the groves of palm and breadfruit; but there were also many shacks of frame and wallboard, with tin roofs glaring bald in the sunlight; and scattered about were abandoned quonsets, dismantled jeeps, and heaps of rusted machinery. It was not hard to see, Carr thought, why Melnick had insisted that his hotel be built on Tiara, and not here.

Three miles and perhaps ten minutes brought them to the airport, and he got out at a still-functioning quonset that served as operations building.

"Wait for you, boss?" the driver asked. But Carr shook his head and paid him, and when the cab was gone he walked slowly off around the edge of the field.

He had been there, of course, the week before, when he came in from Honolulu, but then he had been talking with Melnick and Lavery and had paid little attention. Not that there was much to see when you *did* pay it. In the old days there had, at any time of day or night, been scores of planes around the field, and, further back among the palms, a whole small city of quonset huts. Now there were no planes, and perhaps a dozen of the huts, apparently used for storage. He found himself trying to fix the site of the hut, now gone, which he had occupied for four months; then thought the hell with it—what on earth did it matter? The runways of crushed coral, though planeless, looked the same as ever; and presently he reached the head of No. 1, where they had used to turn and rev up before takeoff, if the wind was the usual southeast trade. Those had been good flights, with no sweat on the hands, no hollow in the stomach, for there had been no combat missions from Utoia. They had been training flights or patrols. Including, one day, a patrol to Tiara. . . .

But no, that had been from the seaplane base, over in the bay.

The combat missions came later: out of Tarawa and Kwajalein. And from the decks of carriers. But he had had a lucky war—both in Manaia and afterward—although he had been in it early when the going was toughest. As a boy, he had loved machines and known how to handle them. At fifteen he could not only drive a car, but strip and reassemble it; and by mid-college, thanks to much hanging around small airfields, he had learned to fly. From as far back as he could remember, he had been resolved that he would be an engineer, and college had led straight to engineering school, and engineering school to—the Pacific. Pearl Harbor had come during the first term of his final year; that same week he had applied for a commission in the Navy Air Arm; and a few months later he was in Manaia.

In early, he had been out early, with no worse than a smashed kneecap from a ditching in a choppy sea. And he had been sent stateside direct from Kwajalein, with no stop at—or even thought of—the way station of Manaia. The Navy had kept him on for six months as a flight instructor, then let him out to complete his schooling. In June of 1945, with two years of postponement behind him, he emerged as Mitchell Carr, C.E. And in the same month he married Margaret Sherwood.

Now he had circled the airfield and was back at the operations shack. Since there were no planes, there were no taxis, but it didn't matter. He was not going anywhere—until tomorrow.

And then?

To Hawaii? . . . To—what was it—Pahukahuka? (He had made that one up fast.) . . . Or back to Tiara?

Through the now late afternoon he walked slowly along the road toward town.

He could not recall if he had ever mentioned Tiara to Margaret. (Certainly he had not mentioned Lovana.) In those days Tiara had been as remote as—well, as Margaret was now. He was looking forward then, not backward, and forward meant work and plans and the establishment of a career. Margaret's father was a building con-

60

tractor, and a rich one, partner in the huge construction firm of Sherwood-Monaghan; but that was coincidence and had had nothing to do with their marriage. Or so he was convinced at the time. For this had been what he called his "bridge in Bolivia" phase. Most of his contemporaries, back from war, were on a great security jag, wanting only to stay put, strike roots, raise families. But his taste of far places had affected him otherwise; he had other ambitions. And while there had been no actual bridge in Bolivia, there had, over the years, been a dam in Peru, a mill in Cuba, a power plant in Casablanca. Margaret had traipsed dutifully along: at first with enthusiasm, then with less, finally with none at all, but only a growing need for a settled life, for a home and children. "There's plenty of time for that," he used to tell her. And in those days, to him, it seemed there was.

Eventually, of course, he had gone to work for her father. There was a home in New Jersey, then one on Long Island; a first-rate job and swelling income; everything was going right. And at the same time not right at all. For there were still no children. His life was split into two hermetic parts: that at home with Margaret, which was boring and sterile, and that of his profession, which increasingly took him about the country to where Sherwood-Monaghan was erecting buildings—and on these trips Margaret did not accompany him. In time came the inevitable misstep with another woman. A while later, a second. And although, back home, he tried hard, as did Margaret, to make something of their marriage, it was no good; whatever she had had for him (other than a father in the construction business) was gone. She was a placid reasonable woman—which in a way made it easier, for there were no scenes or explosions, but in another way made it harder, for it increased his feeling of guilt. Their relationship simply petered out. And in 1952, while he was on a job in Pittsburgh's new Golden Triangle, she went, by agreement, to Nevada and got a quiet divorce.

For a while he stayed on with Sherwood-Monaghan, for his ex-father-in-law knew a good engineer when he saw one and was reluctant to have him leave. But more than his marriage, he now realized, had gone wrong, for he no longer got zest or satisfaction from his work. One after another, the great buildings went up: office buildings mostly, in the centers of great cities: monuments of steel and concrete, chrome and glass, to the industry and prosperity of postwar America. But they were all alike. Or at least the jobs, as he was given them, were all alike. The plans and decisions were made in the offices of board chairmen, of bankers, of Arthur Sherwood and his senior partners, and by the time it was his turn the work was as routine as on a Detroit assembly line. . . . And what do you expect? he had asked himself. You are only in your thirties. You are what you wanted to be: an engineer: a worker in steel, stone, rivets, cement: a man of machines. Stick to your machines. . . . But talking to himself had not helped. He had lost his zest and his satisfaction.

He had taken his problem to a psychiatrist. And the psychiatrist had asked him about his own father. "My father died when I was a child," he told him; and the doctor nodded and said, "Yes, I rather thought so. I would say that a large part of your problem is that of a search for a father. Subconsciously you hoped you had found him in the father of your former wife, but now guilt feelings have entered in, and subliminal resentments." "That could be so," he conceded. "But what has it to do with my work in itself?" "You will perhaps find that out in analysis," said the psychiatrist.

But he had not gone into analysis. He had left Sherwood-Monaghan, and New York as well, and for a year gone back to his old life: working first for the Government at Wheelus Air Base in Libya, then for an oil company on the Persian Gulf. And in Paris, on the way home—wherever home was—he had met Helen Mears. Helen was a successful fashion writer for women's magazines, and she was tiny and intense, brilliant and mercurial. She was a very different sort of woman from any he had known before—as he was different from men she had known—and their response to this strangeness had been immediate and electric. The second night after meeting they were lovers. And a month later husband and wife.

Helen could no more have lived in Libya or Arabia than in a crater of the moon; and soon they were back in New York. She went on with her own work. He formed a small firm of his own. But soon it was no longer so small; it was highly successful; and presently, as its head, he was concerned with all the facets of enterprise and decision that in earlier days had been beyond his province. Engineering meant building. Building meant real estate. In time, he was deeply involved in corporations, holding companies, equities, loans and mortgages; more a businessman than an engineer.

For a while he was content, for success was heady. And his life with Helen was as stimulating as that with Margaret had been dull. They enjoyed each other; they desired each other. When they were among people, which was often, her talk, sparkling like her eyes, brought a glow of pride and pleasure to his own. When they were alone, at night, her lithe small-breasted body was as deft an instrument of sex as any lover could have wished. There was only one lack, one irony, and this was that now, a man of forty, it was he who wanted the fruit of sex—a child—and his wife who did not.

Sometimes he smiled, recalling the psychiatrist, and thought, "Then I was a son in search of a father. Now I'm a father in search of a son." But beneath the smile was a deep wanting, a needing, and he spoke increasingly of it to Helen. For a long time she fended him off. She was not the mother type, she said. She had her career. She was so small through hips and pelvis that no baby could fit through. But he persisted. And at last he won out, and she allowed herself to become pregnant. From the third month on she was ill almost constantly. She was unable to work, unable to go out, forever restless, nauseated, and in pain, as she idled miserably about the house. And in the end, when the Caesarian section was performed, the baby was born dead and she herself barely escaped with her life.

Irony had become tragedy, and their marriage was never the same again. Always high-strung, Helen was now a living bundle of nerves and neuroses. The least disagreement would cause a scene. Often he would wake in the night to find her sobbing in her bed. And when he tried to make love to her, the body that had once welcomed him joyously now stiffened, rejecting him in fear and revulsion. She, in turn, went to a psychiatrist; indeed, underwent a year's analysis. But the effect on their relationship was negligible. More and more she turned away from him, back to her work, her own world and activity. Higher and higher grew the wall between them. She went to Paris for the fashion showings, and stayed in Europe for two months. He went to Chicago on a job, and stayed for three. And at last, after five years of marriage, she too followed the sad worn trail to a Nevada ranch.

He had been alone again. He had worked compulsively. Involved now in all sorts of projects and transactions, he gambled high and recklessly. On the quick construction and sale of a New York apartment house he made a small fortune. In a development scheme in Florida he lost it—and more. He scarcely cared. Money came. Money went. He had no wife to support, no children to think of, but only himself. And he was very tired of himself.

He remembered a day in winter, a day of thin, cold wind and dirty snow, when he had walked alone in New York's Central Park, struggling for a point of view, an appraisal. What had gone wrong with him? His marriages; his work? Least of all he understood what had happened with his work: why it had changed as it had, why ambition and success had twisted it, why success, no less than failure, was savorless and empty. The beginning had been engineering. It had been steel, stone, plans, computations, machines. And although the computations and machines were often complex, the rest was simple, the fundamentals were simple: a man building, placing on the earth a thing that had not been there before: a thing that was part of man's world, of his civilization. . . . Was it that, at the core, that had gone wrong—civilization itself, and its values? Certainly there were points to be made for it in the seventh decade of the twentieth century. . . . But had there been a day in all history when men—some men—did not think their world was out of joint? There were always lost generations, beat generations, angry young men, embittered old men. Men who were themselves out of joint because they *were* men, not God.

And the solutions?

Ah yes—solutions.

There was CMF, of course. That had been the contribution of Jack Osterman, one of his roommates of college days. "CMF—Christ, Marx, Freud," he had used to say. "The Holy Trinity, gentlemen—and always in that order. Then with the three behind you, you go out and earn a living."

Well, he had had his brush with each. As a child, with formal faith and churchgoing. As a college boy of the thirties, with the chimeras of communism. More recently, with psychiatry. And he had earned his living, and here he was, and what was left? A drink was left, for one thing. And leaving the park, he had had one, and then another, and some more; in the months that followed he had many many more; for the first time in his life he drank heavily and steadily; and it was childish, that he knew—it was stupid and feckless and solved nothing and led nowhere—but nowhere was where he wanted to go. Or at least somewhere where he wasn't. And now he was in New York, now in Chicago, Denver, Los Angeles, San Francisco, living on what remained of his capital, working occasionally at odd jobs, with no purpose, no direction—except that, for some reason, the direction was always west, toward the Pacific Ocean.

In San Francisco a phone call had caught up with him. A call from an old friend, George Swanson. George was starting a new construction company to specialize in New York office buildings; he had already formed a partnership with a red-hot finance man named Bromley; and they wanted it to be Swanson, Bromley & Carr. Many thanks, he had said. But no thanks. And though George had argued, all but pleaded, with him, he had made the no stick. That was precisely what he was getting away from: the stale, flat—and profitable.

"So it's true what we heard: you've gone nuts," George had said.

"Quite likely," he had conceded.

"Well, when you recover let us know. We want you, boy. We really want you."

And that had been that. From San Francisco he had gone on to

Hawaii. He had lived in a furnished room in a cheap suburb of Honolulu. He had sat on beaches. He had sat in bars. Until the day had come when he was sitting in the lobby of the Royal Hawaiian Hotel, listening to a dapper, sharp-faced man in natty sports clothes who bore the improbable name of Mel Melnick. . . .

He walked on. As he had walked a year ago in Central Park. But now he was seven thousand miles from Central Park. He was on the Belt Road near Apingo, Utoia, Manaia, Pacific Ocean; and before him were palm trees, beyond them beach and bay and sea; and beyond the sea, invisible but close, in the sinking sun was the island of Tiara.

He was here. But why? On the surface it was simple. Mel Melnick, a hotel, a lagoon that needed blasting. But it was more than that. It was more than the drinks and the dreams after the meeting with Melnick. From the very beginning—from the time he had left New York and moved west, to California, the Pacific, Hawaii—it had been Tiara that had been pulling him. He knew that now. Even before Melnick had spoken its name, it had been re-emerging into memory, from the forgotten and lost. . . . Why? What did he want of it? What could it give him? . . . He had not come back for Lovana; the very notion was absurd. Nor was he so naive as to believe in any vague "recapture" of the past—or in the imagined therapy of the "simple life." His life had not been simple, nor would it ever be. For it was the life of a man of his time and place, full of uncertainty and doubts, conflict and contradiction, and, now, a man in his forties, he was not going to be reborn.

He pushed the *whys* away. . . . The question now was staying on. And if he stayed, to what purpose? . . . For himself, perhaps, only to know for a little longer the inward peace that needed no farther wandering, and no whisky; to sit for a while again beside a pool, beneath a breadfruit tree. To know again the peace of *fia fia*.

And for others (for was it perhaps not time, at last, to think of others?), what could he bring to them, to this speck in the ocean, this island of Tiara that had given to him so greatly? He brought certain skills and knowledge. He could help build a hotel. And a hotel: was that good? If it was good by the standards of the West— of Western "progress"—it was, judging from the lack of response, not good by those of most of the islanders. His thoughts went back to his days in Libya and by the Persian Gulf; to the men of Africa and Asia standing around the construction sites; the dark men watching the encroaching white men with dark eyes full of hate. There were dark men here too, and he thought of them, watching. He thought of the boy, or young man—what was his name?—John Koa—

65

whom he had seen once at the hotel site and again in the village. He remembered his face and his eyes. But these eyes had been different. It had not been hate that shone in them, but desire—and frustration.

John Koa wanted to leave Tiara. He, Mitchell Carr had wanted to return there. Each wanted what he had not, and perhaps that alone was the Law and the Prophets.

He took a coin from his pocket, as he had in the bar in Honolulu two weeks before. Heads, Tiara, he thought. Tails, Pahukahuka (or some such). And then of course there was the third choice: back the way he had come. To Hawaii, California, New York. To picking up the pieces. To a firm called Swanson, Bromley—and Carr. . . . He smiled thinly. . . . That would be if the coin stood on edge.

As he walked, he flipped it—this time not dropping it—and when he had ten heads and ten tails he put it away. The sun had set when he came to the outskirts of Apingo, and it was dark when he reached the Admiral Nimitz Hotel. Melnick and Lavery were already at table in the dining room; and Melnick was holding up a piece of grayish meat on his fork and asking the Manaian waitress if it was shark or rhinoceros.

5

On HER WAY to the reception at the *fale* of Tafutimo, Carol Loftus had been taut with nervousness. But whatever unpleasantness she had feared failed to materialize. True, the high chief of Tiara was a formidable figure of a man: tall and spare, with a gray leonine head, a harsh-planed face and somber eyes. But he had bowed to her as she entered with grave courtesy; and Fahoai, the talking chief, who presented her, had kept smiling reassuringly and held his big hand firm on her elbow.

There had been no conversation in the usual sense. The first presentation over, everyone in attendance—some twenty men, no women except Carol—had sat on mats against the enclosing pillars of the *fale,* with Tafutimo at one end, herself at the other, and the rest ranged between them according to rank. Fahaoi, in his official capacity, holding staff and fly whisk, had made a speech of welcome in Manaian. A junior talking chief had replied on her behalf. And several others—though not the high chief himself—had risen to speak their roles in stylized ritual. Then younger men had brought in a great bowl, with water and the clublike roots of the *tugase* shrub; kava, the ancient ceremonial drink of Polynesia, had been prepared and passed; and as each received his cup, he drank down the milky, faintly peppery liquid to the accompaniment of ritual words and rhythmic clapping. At her turn Carol, coached by Fahoai, spoke the only two words required of her: "*Manuia*" (blessings) as she raised her cup, "*Soifua*" (it is blessed) as she set it down. And then the ceremony had been over, and Fahoai had led her out.

"I hope you were pleased, Miss Loftus," he said to her. "For it is unusual, and a great honor, in Tiara that kava be drunk for a woman."

And she had smiled and said, "Oh yes, I'm so grateful," and inwardly given thanks that the ordeal was over.

In the days that followed she became rapidly acquainted with the village and its people: with their faces, names, family connections— and, of course, their ailments. As Mrs. Mundy had said, there was little left of the old South Seas scourges. (Leprosy, for instance, was gone entirely, and of elephantiasis there were only a few cases among the very old.) But two of the white man's legacies, tuberculosis and syphilis, were widespread, and almost everyone had a variety of skin infection or intestinal parasite. The children, in particular, needed care and watching, and these she saw first every morning at her clinic in the dispensary. Then came the women; then the men; by which time the morning was gone. And in the afternoon she wrote up her records and made her home visits—on foot if they were in the village, in the jeep if they were farther afield.

Also, there were meetings with the village women on matters of diet and hygiene. And other meetings with the "Sanitation Corps," a trio of young men who had had training in Apingo and whose part-time function was to wage war on mosquitoes and supervise the water supply and latrines. Penalties for breach of hygiene were severe. But the Tiarans, Carol had been happy to find, were a naturally clean people, and Malele the policeman had no culprits in his one-room jail. Nor any other prisoners, either, for there was no disorder, no criminality, in the village.

Thus far, whatever the outer world had brought it, Tiara seemed able to take it in stride and go quietly on its immemorial way. The sun rose. Cook fires smoked. The women carried wash to the pump and tended the taro patches; the young men went fishing or into the woods for logs and fruits; the old men sat cross-legged in their *fales*, talking and rolling sennit against their thighs. Dogs, pigs, chickens, and small children moved endlessly through the palm groves, and when school was out were augmented by the larger children. Then the sun sloped down. There were cook fires again. There was quick darkness, and perhaps the sound of a guitar or singing voices, and then only darkness and a vault of stars.

Here was paradise (and not Mel Melnick's), a sentimentalist could have said. But it was not paradise. There were the diseases, for one thing. There was the quietude that may have seemed like peace, but was all too often lethargy. And from the lethargy, here and there, sprang a restlessness, a discontent, that clawed like the sea against the crumbling cliffs beyond the beach. Atop those very cliffs, through many hours, a boy sat, staring out at the sea and wishing only that

68

he were beyond it. In a *fale,* a girl was bent over a small mirror, combing her hair, her pretty face sullen with boredom. And in the rear room of the shack that was the village store, one Tuu Asimo, a squat, barrel-chested man of perhaps thirty-five, lay drinking himself dully into unconsciousness.

Hard liquor was forbidden in Tiara. Stateside beer was legal, but too costly for all but a few. The drink of those who drank was bush beer, made of the fermented juices of wild fruits; and of this Asimo, proprietor of the store, was both the chief purveyor and consumer. "A sad man," Mrs. Mundy had called him, speaking to Carol Loftus. "Not a bad one. Just sad—unhappy." And Carol had nodded sympathetically; but after a week she had not been so sure. On her first visit to the store he had, though obviously a little drunk, been meticulously helpful and polite. On her second, she had not seen him, a young boy at the counter having announced that he was "resting." But the third time, though he had again been polite and quiet, his voice had been thick, his dark eyes glazed, and from behind the glaze he had stared at her, steadily, unwaveringly, from the moment she entered to the moment she left.

Asimo's, to be sure, had not been the only stare. On her rounds of the village she was often conscious of eyes watching her, following her; sometimes the eyes of men, sometimes of women or children; and although she had expected this, and knew it to be inevitable, she still found it hard to banish a disquieting self-consciousness. It was only when she was actually at work, absorbed in her nursing, that she was wholly without it, wholly at ease . . . no, more than at ease, for when the change came it came absolutely . . . and then she was no longer a strange and bewildered young woman in an alien world, but a trained and effective technician, with a role and a purpose, fulfilling that purpose with an almost fierce dedication. She was Carol Loftus, R.N., and she knew exactly why she had come to this place and what she must do here. She was the daughter of Dr. John Norman Loftus, and she knew that, if he were alive, he would be proud of her.

In the dispensary, the patients came and went. The babies with coughs and rashes. The children with running sores. The pregnant women; the women with tumors and chancres and bloody sputum. The men with these, plus legs torn by machetes and hands by fishhooks. And then, one day, the parade was over: the last of her patients had gone, and she was preparing to close up and join Mrs. Mundy for lunch, when she saw that she had been wrong, that there was still one patient left: a boy—or young man—sitting beneath a tree close by the door and watching her.

Going to the door, she said, "All right—come in." And as the boy rose and came toward her she saw it was the one she had met on her first day in the village when Leonard Shafter and Mrs. Mundy were showing her about.

"Why, you're—"

"John Koa," he said.

"Yes, of course, John. I haven't seen you around."

"I'm not in the village much."

"You mean you're working over at the hotel?"

He shook his head. "No." Then he added, "Manaia is not like America, Miss. We do not have to work to live."

Carol smiled. But the boy was not smiling. His thin fine-featured face was expressionless, giving no hint of what lay behind the words; and although he had certainly not been drinking, she was conscious of the same vague discomfort as when Asimo had stared at her in his store.

"So come inside," she said with professional cheeriness. "What can I do for you?"

"Do?" Then he understood. "Oh. Thanks, but there's nothing."

"Nothing?"

"I was just looking at the new dispensary."

"Well, come on in and look more."

She led the way, and he stood glancing around him. "It's nice, isn't it?" she said. "Small but nice."

He nodded. "Much better than when we had only a Manaian nurse."

"Only? What do you mean, 'only'?"

"For Tulipa—she was the old nurse—the old dispensary was good enough. But now for you there is a new one."

"For goodness sake, it isn't for *me,* John. It's for the people here. Don't you think they're entitled to it?"

"I do not mean this personally, Miss Loftus," the boy said, "but there are many here who feel they are also entitled to a Manaian nurse. It is a proud thing for people like us to have nurses and doctors of our own."

"Of course it is. And you'll be having one again, as soon as she's qualified by the Health Department."

"In Fiji," said John Koa, "they have the Central Medical School that takes young men and women from many islands and trains them. There are many qualified. But in Manaia—"

"Manaia is much smaller." Without intending it, Carol spoke almost sharply. "Dr. Friede and his assistants are doing fine work, both with the hospital and with training."

70

John's eyes had gone to a row of bottles on a shelf, and she took a few down to show him. "You see, even here we have all sorts of drugs. . . . Penicillin, of course. The sulfas. Streptomycin. . . ." She smiled, regretting her sharpness. "When the new nurse comes you can feel free to catch anything you want."

For a moment John said nothing. Then he looked up from the bottles.

"You have been much in the Pacific, Miss Loftus?" he said.

"In the Pacific?" The sudden change of subject threw her off balance. "What do you mean?"

"Have you been to many of the islands?"

"Well, flying out here I was in Hawaii, of course. And then in Fiji and Samoa."

"Did you see much of them? I don't mean the airports and hotels and Government people. I mean the people who live there—who are part of them—like the earth and trees."

"No, I'm afraid I didn't. I hadn't much chance to."

"And here in Manaia, too: you were not much away from Apingo before you came here?"

"No. I was very busy in the hospital."

"So you probably think of the people as strange and queer. Almost savages, maybe. Like something out of Captain Cook or a book about cannibals."

"Nonsense!" Carol's voice was sharp again. "I know perfectly well—"

"What, Miss Loftus?"

"—that you're people, just like ourselves. Nurses and doctors: students and teachers; almost anything you can think of. . . . Including fliers," she added.

She was putting the bottles back on the shelf and aligning them carefully. Again the boy was silent, and she had the sensation that he was looking fixedly at her back.

"I think it's wonderful that you want to be a flier," she said, turning.

Still John did not speak.

"I couldn't help hearing what you said the other day to Mr. Shafter, and I know how awful it is to have to wait around. But I'm sure that everything possible is being done."

"Are you?" he said.

"Of course it is. You can't mean you think that Mr. Shafter—"

"No, I think Mr. Shafter has done all he could. And Mr. Lebolt too—the director of education. But I wonder, in Hawaii, in Washington. . . ." There was another pause.

Then, suddenly: "Would you fly with me, Miss Loftus?"

"Fly with you?"

"If I were a pilot, in a plane. Would you feel safe with me? Would you think I knew what I was doing? . . . Or would you think, 'No, he doesn't know. He's not a pilot, not a real one, but just a savage, a gook—' "

"John!"

"Or at best a half-savage, a sort of bastard—"

"John, John—you mustn't talk like that!"

"Aren't there plenty of people who—"

"No, there aren't. And those there are are stupid and nasty." The boy was standing close beside her, his body and thin face tense, his dark eyes holding hers. One of his hands was pressed flat and tight against the counter below the shelves, and impulsively she put her own upon it. "John, truly, you mustn't—"

He seemed about to speak again, but didn't. Instead, his eyes moved down to the counter, and after a moment hers moved down too: to her small white hand and his beneath it, long and brown.

She raised hers gently and said, "John, believe me—"

But he turned and ran from the dispensary.

In the evenings Mrs. Mundy talked about this and that. And one evening it was about how Tiara had got its name.

"It was from the French, of course," she said. "No one but a Frenchman would have thought of it, even though it seems so natural afterwards. The Spanish would have called it Santa-something, the British New-something, the Americans—well—maybe Cloud Island. Or John Paul Jones. . . . Even the Manaians accepted the name, and that's unusual, because they're so proud. On many islands the people don't seem to care at all about their old ways; but the Manaians are different—they care very much. Yet you never hear the original name of the island any more. It was Palikoa. I suppose part of the reason is that Tiara at least *sounds* Polynesian."

Her teeth slipped. "Damn," she said. Then, "Excuse me, my dear, but it's very annoying. I've been promising myself for five years to go over to Apingo and see the dentist, but—"

"You mean," said Carol, "you haven't been off the island in five years?"

"No, it's about that. Oh. I suppose I should go off sometimes: not only for errands—just to go. But—well—Tiara's home to me now, you see. And as one gets older that's what one wants: home." She paused and looked at the glowing young woman who sat opposite her. "Not that that sort of thing is for you, dear," she said. "You must get around as much as you can—at least over to the hotel—or you'll get dreadfully bored."

"Oh no, I won't be bored," said Carol. "I'm very happy here."

"Work going all right?"

"Yes, I think so. I was afraid that a lot of the people wouldn't come to me—that they'd be afraid or too shy—but it hasn't been that way at all."

"You never can tell," the old lady said. "Sometimes it's one way, sometimes another. But at least it's easier with the Tiarans than with most other islanders."

"You haven't always been here then?"

"On Tiara? Oh no, only twelve years or so. Before that we were in Samoa, Tahiti, the Cooks, the Marshalls. It was—let's see—1912, I think, that we first came out to the islands."

"You must have been very young then."

"Yes, I was young. Younger even than you."

"And you must have had a wonderful life."

Mrs. Mundy looked down at the veined claws of her hands and seemed to be thinking it over. "Yes, in many ways it's been wonderful," she said. "Full of experiences, certainly, and always with a chance to help people who need it."

"You've taught, always?"

"Yes, always. Except when I was having children of my own." The old lady looked up. "As you've probably gathered, my dear," she went on, "I'm not a very religious person—at least not in the fundamentalist sort of way my husband was—and so our relationship, I suppose, was a rather strange one. I don't mean that I didn't love him. I did. I admired his sincerity, his courage. To this day, if I hear a white man talking down the old-style island missionary—granting all his faults—I simply ask one question: 'How would *you* like to step ashore on one of these islands if no missionary had ever stepped there first?'"

"How long ago did Mr. Mundy die?" asked Carol.

"Eight years now. No, it must be nine. His grave's just down the road there, behind the church."

"And when—when he was gone—you had no desire to go home?"

"Home? After half a century where would that be? Except here?"

"You said you had children. Aren't they in the States now?"

"No," said Mrs. Mundy. "There were two boys, and they're gone too, like their father. They were shot by the Japanese when we were in the Marshalls during the war."

After a moment Carol rose and, walking over to her, put a hand on her bony arm. "Do you know what I hope?" she said.

The old eyes looked up at her brightly through their rimless glasses. "No, my dear. What do you hope?"

"That I can bring to this island just the tiniest bit of what you've brought."

"Thank you. That's sweet of you." Mrs. Mundy threw off the past as easily as if it had been a shawl on her shoulders. "And I'm sure you've already brought a great deal. Everyone in the village is very fond of you."

"I can think of—" Carol hesitated, stopped. "It's nice to think so," she said.

"You've had no trouble with Tafutimo?"

"No, I haven't seen him since the kava ceremony. But I've seen the other one—Fahoai—several times, and he's very easy to be with."

"Yes, they couldn't be more different. But it isn't only themselves, you know; it's their positions, too, that make a big distinction. Tafutimo is a paramount chief, and they're always very conscious of dignity and tradition. Fahoai is only a talking chief." Mrs. Mundy smiled. "It's a nice title, don't you think?—meaning a sort of executive officer. And the talking chiefs in Manaia have always been the ones to handle negotiations, both with their own people and outsiders. You might call them the island politicians. And they take much more easily to new people and ideas."

"Fahoai's been very friendly. He's asked me to his home for tea."

"And he'll do it well. Partly in Western style and partly *fa'a Manaia*. It will be interesting for you."

"I'm sure it will."

"And his family too. For it's a strange one, you know; not like the others in the village." Mrs. Mundy began counting its members on her fingers. "First there's Fahoai himself, of course—so anxious to be modern. His wife, Polu, seems the same as most of the other women; but then there's her uncle, old Kalamakoa, and he's just the opposite of Fahoai—even more old-fashioned than Tafutimo. Also there are the two nieces—have you met the nieces—?"

"I've seen them," said Carol.

"Well, they couldn't be more different. Mena, that's the older one, is very pious; Pastor Solomona says she's the best church member in the village. But the younger one, Va'ina: the pretty one—" The old lady shook her head. "She's the village *taupou*; do you know about *taupous*? . . . In every Manaian community there's a sort of traditional village princess who serves as a special tribal symbol and leads the ceremonial dances. She's always from one of the leading families and is supposed to remain a virgin until she marries. . . . Anyhow, Va'ina is the *taupou* here, but—well—she has her own way of being one.

Not that I blame her much. It's all part of the pattern: everything changing: the old ways going. And who can say which is better? In the old days it was blood feuds and leprosy and drowning unwanted babies. Now it's a whole new set of problems."

She sighed.

"Like John's—" she added.

"John's?"

"John Koa. The boy who wants to be a flier. He's part of Fahoai's family too—didn't you know?"

Carol shook her head.

"If you can call John part of anything, that is."

"He seems so intense, so disturbed—"

"Yes, he's disturbed all right. Some of it comes from his being half white, of course; and the rest from—well, I'm afraid from being too well educated, too bright. It's a sad thing, you know, what can happen sometimes in the islands with the best young people. And it's not just lack of opportunity either. Take another example right here: Asimo the storekeeper. . . . You don't know about Asimo, do you? . . . Back before I came here he was the shining light of Tiara: a high school graduate like John Koa. He wanted to be a lawyer— eventually a judge or a political leader. And he had his chance too; he was awarded a Government scholarship to Stanford University for four years of prelaw study. But he couldn't make it. I suppose the pressures of life in the States were just too much for him. Like so many of these people when they leave here, he wasn't one thing or another—neither an American in America nor an islander on an island. Anyhow, he began to drink, flubbed his studies, got in trouble. In less than three years he was back here, broken and ashamed, and— well—you see him now."

Mrs. Mundy took off her glasses, wiped them, and put them back on her small beaked nose.

"With John Koa, of course," she said, "it's not the same, and won't be. Yet really it *is* the same, because the problems are. I've spent my life teaching young people out here, and sometimes I wonder if it hasn't all been a mistake; if they wouldn't be better off just learning how to fish and climb a coconut tree." She sighed again, a little. "No, I don't mean that; not except when I'm very discouraged. We *have* to teach them—bring them into the world that we've forced on them. What else can we do? What else justifies our being here? Without that, my dear, we all belong in the cannibal pot where they used to put us in the first place."

She talked on for a while. And at nine o'clock, as always, she rose, kissed Carol on the cheek, and went off to bed. Left alone, Carol

75

tried to read, then to sew, but she could keep her mind on neither. Her thoughts kept reverting to Tuu Asimo and John Koa; to Mrs. Mundy's two sons, dead from Japanese bullets on a distant island. And then suddenly she had risen and was going through the kitchen into the dispensary. Snapping on the light, she looked about her, and it was bright, neat, ready. She almost wished that an emergency patient would appear out of the night. But no patient came, and she again went back to the living room.

It seemed hot to her—hotter than usual—and, opening the screen door, she went out on the stoop. But there was no air outside either. A low black sky was clamped like a lid over the island, and no wisp of breeze touched the fronds of the palm trees. In front of the bungalow stood the jeep, and the thought crossed her mind of getting into it and driving: along the coast road, where it might be cooler—possibly even to the lagoon and the hotel site. "Come over any time," the men had said. But then she remembered that they were in Apingo. And the only one that had seemed interesting, the tall thin one named Carr, was gone for good.

The one with the dynamite. . . . He hadn't seemed the sort she would have associated with dynamite. . . . Yet even here, three miles away, she had heard the sound of its detonations as he blasted out the lagoon.

Anyhow, she did not want to go. That was not what she was here for. She was here to—

Suddenly she turned her head and her body tensed. She had had the sensation of being watched. But looking into the darkness, she could see only the jeep and the road and the palms, and scattered among the palms, a few dim lights from the village. She had been wrong. . . . Or had she? She couldn't tell. She didn't know. . . . And at that moment it was borne in on her, like a tide through the darkness, how little she knew of this place she had come to. How ignorant she was. And how alone.

Something close to panic rose within her; but she fought it down, struggled her way to calmness. . . . If she was alone, it was from choice. "I want to be on my own," she had told the man named Carr. "I don't expect it to be easy." . . . And besides, she was not *really* alone. There was Mrs. Mundy. There was her father. In the black lonely night she thought again of her father, and how he had lived and died, and now he was beside her, and she was not afraid.

She re-entered the house, went to her room, and prepared for bed. It would have been nice, she thought, as she waited for sleep, if her father and Mrs. Mundy could have met.

It was two days afterward that she went, in the late afternoon, to the home of Fahoai. Since it was a social call she had changed from her uniform into a cotton print, and she was glad she had, for the family made an event of her visit. The talking chief himself came out to meet her as she approached through the palm grove, and when he had led her into the hut the others rose—including the old man, Kalamakoa—and greeted her in turn with the traditional *"Talofa."* In the center of the hut two old straight-backed chairs had been placed, and Fahoai held one from behind for her to sit down.

"No," she protested, "I'll sit on a mat. They look so comfortable."

But Fahoai was insistent. "On a mat the knees get stiff, if they are not used to it," he said. Then he added, smiling: "Besides, I like to sit in a chair myself, and this gives me a good excuse."

So she sat on one of the chairs, and he on the other, with the rest of the family around them, cross-legged on the pandanus mats. Fahoai was wearing his ceremonial dress of linen jacket and lava-lava; the old man simply a lava-lava; but the women were in Western clothing—Polu, the wife, and Mena, the elder niece, in long sacklike dresses like Mother Hubbards; Va'ina, the younger niece, in a fitted cotton print similar to Carol's. There were only the five of them. Carol glanced around carefully to make sure she had not missed a sixth. But John Koa was not there.

It was pleasantly cool in the large wall-less hut—much cooler than in the bungalow—and she commented on it. "We are in a good place here; there is always a little breeze from the water," Fahoai said. And he went on to comment at length on the vagaries of Tiaran wind and weather. Indeed, he did all the talking. (After all, he *was* a talking chief, Carol thought.) And when he had disposed of the weather, he discussed, in order, the copra crop, the fishing prospects, the condition of Tiara's roads, and the happiness of his people at having Miss Loftus in their midst. The others sat silent on their mats—the old man staring into space with sunken eyes, the wife and older niece looking decorously at their laps. But the younger niece, Va'ina, looked steadily at Carol, and Carol began to find it disconcerting. When now and then Fahoai paused, she tried to think of something to say that woud make the conversation general. But before words came to her he would be talking again.

Then at last he stopped. His wife raised her eyes and he nodded, and the three women rose and went about serving tea. Tea there actually was. "We get it from Fiji," Fahoai said. "They are British there, of course, so it is full of tea." But there was much else besides: bowls of fruit and taro and dried fish and coconut cream, plus a jar of peanut butter and a tin of corned beef. And Carol accepted only a minimum helping of each, so that she would not give offense by refusal, but also not gorge herself to the bursting point.

Fahoai watched her solicitously. "You enjoy our island food?" he asked.

"Oh yes," she said. "It's delicious."

"But you do not take much. And I know why." He laughed. "It is because here in Manaia we think a woman should be fat like a *fau* tree, but in America, no, she must be thin like bamboo."

He himself ate enormously, dipping into all the bowls with practiced fingers. But Carol noticed that the old man, Kalamakoa, ate nothing at all; and she asked him politely why not.

Kalamakoa seemed not to have heard her, but Fahoai said, "No, he will not eat. Only a few mouthfuls each day of breadfruit and coconut milk. That is why he is so weak and his skin hangs from his bones."

"I've some good pills in the dispensary. Vitamins. They'd be very good for him if he'd take them."

Fahoai shook his head. "He would not take them. He will not take anything. In this family there are two people who do not eat: the old one and this one." He pointed at Va'ina. "This one thinks she is an American, that she must be like bamboo. And you see her clothes—they are like an American's too."

"It's a pretty dress," Carol said to Va'ina.

"Do you like it? Thank you," the girl said. "And yours too is pretty. Does it come from New York?"

"Oh dear no. I got it in a little town in Ohio. That's where my family lives."

"In the States, then, you can buy nice clothes anywhere. But in Manaia, no. In Apingo are only things from five years ago; and here at the store nothing."

"Va'ina will not wear a lava-lava at all," Fahoai said. "The only time she wears Manaian costume is when she dances."

"She is a *taupou*," said the older niece, Mena. "And the best dancer in Tiara."

"And Mena," said Polu, "is the best singer. Every Sunday she leads the choir at the church, and her voice is an angel's."

Mena covered her face with her hands, like a child. And Fahoai laughed. "So you see what a talented family we are," he said. "And how good at boasting. When the hotel opens and the tourists come, we will go over and be famous."

His wife was again passing the bowls of food, and he dug his fingers in deep. "That will not be so long now either," he added. "I was over at the lagoon this morning. With Malele the policeman"—

78

he bowed to Carol—"in your jeep that you were so kind to lend him. And the boat is now back. There are many workers from Utoia and the three hotel gentlemen and—"

"Three?" said Carol.

"Yes. There is the little one—the *matai*—Mr. Melnick. The red one, Mr. Lavery. And the tall one, Mr.—" Fahoai groped.

"Meesh," said Va'ina.

"No, that is not it." Fahoai eyed his niece. "What do *you* know about it?" he asked.

"I have met Mr. Meesh," she said primly.

"It is not Meesh. It is—Carr."

"It is Meesh."

"There's a Mitchell Carr," said Carol. "Mitchell is his first name and Carr is his last."

"Anyhow, I have met him," Va'ina said. "When he made a visit here to the village."

"Here? He wasn't here."

"Yes, Miss, he was. The same day you came with Mr. Shafter. Perhaps you did not see him, but he spoke with me."

"But—" Carol was confused. "But even so; he was staying just a few days—not coming back—"

"Perhaps he changed his mind," said Fahoai.

"Yes, changed his mind," Va'ina echoed. "I am glad. He is nice, I think, Mr. Meesh Carr."

She smiled, and for a moment her eyes met Carol's. Then, taking up two of the bowls of food, she offered them to her.

"No. No, thanks," said Carol.

"You do not like papaya? Or breadfruit with coconut cream?"

"If Miss Loftus wishes more she will take it," said Fahoai. "If not, we will not force her."

He began talking again. About the hotel and what it would mean to the island. About changes on the island, past and future. Perhaps fifteen more minutes passed; then Carol felt she had been there long enough for politeness, and rose and expressed her thanks. The others, rising too, said, *"Talofa,"* and Fahoai said, "It was our honor. You must come often," and escorted her out.

Hospitable as he had been, she had felt strain and awkwardness and was glad to be alone. But she was not alone long, for almost at once a figure appeared from behind the palm trees and approached her.

"Good evening," said John Koa. "May I see you home?"

"Why John, you've been waiting there!" she said. "Why didn't you come in?"

"I—I wasn't hungry." There was a moment's pause. "You don't mind if I walk with you?" he asked.

"Of course not. It's very sweet of you."

They walked through the grove, and the slanting sun threw long bars of light and shadow across their path.

"What did you do today?" she asked him.

"Nothing," he said.

"Nothing?"

"I walked. I went to the beach."

"The beach is lovely, isn't it? I hope to go swimming a lot, but I have to be careful at first or I'd get a bad burn."

The boy didn't say anything, and they walked on a way. Then, turning, she saw that he seemed to be looking at something on the top of her head.

He looked away quickly. "I'm sorry," he said.

"Sorry? Why—what is it?" She smiled and raised an exploring hand. "Was it a bug?"

"I was looking at how the sun shines. In your hair, I mean. It's so bright."

"Oh." Her smile changed a little. "You're just not used to blondes here," she said.

They came out of the grove onto the road. Ahead were the school-house and the bungalow, and she quickened her pace a little.

"And I'm sorry, too, about the other day," John said.

"The other day?"

"When I came to the dispensary. When we talked and I was rude to you."

"You weren't rude. You were just—upset. I understood."

"I'm sorry anyway."

"Well don't be," she said. "Forget about it."

Now they had reached the bungalow and she was about to say goodbye. But he had put his hand in his pocket and was holding something out to her.

"What is it?" she asked.

"It is for you," he said. "Maybe you will find some use for it."

With a quick movement he put the thing in her hand; then turned away and in an instant was gone. Looking at what she held, she saw that it was the shell of a small turtle that had been cleaned and polished until it gleamed like dark jade.

6

IT HAD BEEN some time since Mitchell Carr had used level and transit, and those he had succeeded in getting hold of in Apingo looked as if they might have been left there by Bougainville or Captain Cook.

"Let's be patient with the workmen," he told Frank Lavery, as he struggled to get accurate sightings and readings, "or they may start making a few cracks about the engineer."

But now at least there was less need for patience, for, with the arrival of the work crew from Utoia, things were going more smoothly. Each day trees came down by the dozen along the broad sweep of the hotel site. A gang was turning the path to the jetty into a road wide enough for heavy machinery. And on a hill up behind another detail was clearing the vegetation for what would become the quarry for coral building rock. Tom Taki, the foreman, was, as Shafter had said, a topnotch man; both a driver and a worker, he seemed to be everywhere at once. Short and scrawny, he had the dark skin and hair of a Manaian, but his eyes were gray and his nose snubbed—as, presumably, had been those of his stateside father. He was a half-caste, however, who made no burden of his ancestry. "They ask me who your old man," he would say, grinning. "He Navy? Merchant Marine? Some damn fancy *capitani*? An' I say how I know? They say, well your mama knows. No, she don't know neither, I say. An' they say how come? An' I say on account of she never seen him with clothes on."

Then, slapping his thigh and hooting with laughter, Tom Taki would get back to work.

The men from Utoia lived in the newly built quonsets and had their own mess. Carr and Lavery remained in the same quarters they had had originally; and for the time being there were just the two of them in charge, for Melnick was busy in Apingo. Work began at seven o'clock each morning, continued until noon, and, after a midday break for lunch and siesta, went on again from three until six. Then there was a swim in the lagoon. There was the evening meal, beer, and the blaring of the radio that had come over with the work crew on the *Harold L. Ickes*. At this time, many of the Tiarans, invisible by day, when work was in progress, would materialize from the palm groves and sit about on the cleared slope while the magical sounds filled the air.

The number of local workers had leveled off at about a steady dozen. John Koa was not among them. Nor did he ever appear among the evening radio audience.

The talking chief, Fahoai, however, appeared several times, accepted beer from Carr and Lavery with gracious thanks, and commented approvingly on how the work was going.

"It would go a hell of a lot better," Lavery told him, "if you'd get more of your people to help."

But at this Fahoai shook his head a little sadly and said, "Would that I could, sir. But that is the trouble with these outer islanders: they do not have the energy or ambition of the men from Utoia."

"I've met one with plenty of ambition," said Carr. "And he's one of your family, I think."

"Ah yes, John." Fahoai's jowled face brooded. "He is a special one, that John. Full of ideas and fevers of the blood."

"He could damn well sweat out his fever swinging an ax," said Lavery.

"If he would do it, yes. But he will not." Fahoai sighed. "Often I have told him that I too am for progress, for the advancement of our people, but that such things do not come from wild ideas but from hard work. As with the trees, yes: that is what he should do. Chop chop." His big brown arms swung an imaginary ax. "Chop chop—like that; hard work all day. And soon there is a fine hotel and a new Tiara."

Resting from his exertions, he drained his can of beer. "Ah, good. Yes, cold and good," he said. . . . "Another? Well—hmm—perhaps one; one only. . . . Thank you, gentlemen." He drank again and wiped his lips. "There is nothing like cold beer, I say. But for cold-ness there must be refrigeration; for refrigeration there must be money; for money there must be work. I am ashamed of my people who are so foolish and lazy. If they would work on the hotel like the men from Utoia there would soon be fine cold beer for all Tiara."

A workman ripped his hand on a saw, and Carol Loftus came from the village to treat him. Two days later another accident brought her back. And thereafter she came every second or third day, as a matter of routine. Arriving in her jeep about the time the workday ended, she set up an impromptu dispensary in an unused section of one of the huts, ministered to the ill or injured with cool deft competence, and, when her work was done, returned to the jeep and drove off. More than once, Carr and Lavery suggested that she stay on for an evening swim and supper; but each time she thanked them and said she had to get back to the village.

"A real cold fish, that one," Lavery commented, one night after she had left. . . . Then a few nights later, as amendment: "Warm her up a bit, though, and she'd be a damn cute tomato. I wouldn't mind driving her home one of these days, if I had some way to get back here."

"Your own jeeps will be here soon," Carr reminded him.

"Yeah, sure—plus twelve guys from Honolulu. All of them full of beans, and not one past forty." The contractor sighed; then he looked at Carr quizzically. "You're not much past it yourself, eh Mitch?" he asked.

"Enough," said Carr.

"You don't look it. Got all your hair. No pot. No wife you been latched to for twenty-three years. . . . You know something? I bet you could make time with that gal if you want to."

"What makes you think that?"

"The laws of nature—that's what makes me think it. And the way she looks at you sort of sideways sometimes before she goes. . . . Don't be chicken, boy. Some night when she's getting in that jeep, whyn't you just go up and say, 'Move over, honey, I'm coming with you.' "

Carr laughed. "So *I* can walk back," he said.

"Yeah, so *you* can walk back. But you got longer legs."

Almost as if she had overheard the conversation, Carol Loftus did not appear the next evening. But another female visitor did: a girl with golden skin and long black hair, who, as Carr came up toward his hut from a swim in the lagoon, emerged from the grove beside the path and approached him, smiling.

"Good evening, Meesh," she greeted him.

"Good evening," he said.

83

"You do not remember me?"

"Yes, I remember you. You are—Va'ina."

"I thought maybe you would not know. For both times we meet it is almost dark and hard to see."

"Have you come to listen to the radio?" Carr asked.

"The radio? No. I have heard the music is sometimes nice, but I do not come for that. It is to see Mr. Melnick that I come."

"Melnick?"

"He is the chief of the hotel, is he not?"

"Yes, he's the chief." Carr smiled. "The talking chief."

"So I have come for talking with the talking chief. About dancing."

"Dancing?"

"Yes. I am the *taupou* of Tiara and dance the best of all on the island. Mr. Melnick will see, and he will want me. When the hotel is built, I will dance for all the people who come there."

"Oh." There was a pause and Carr looked down at her. At her upturned face and the blossom in her hair; at her curved young body in its sheath of bright cotton, so like the again-remembered body of Lovana. "I'm sorry," he said to her, "but Mr. Melnick isn't here."

"Not here?" Her face fell.

"He's in Apingo."

"But he will come back?"

"Yes, he'll be back. When the men and machinery come from Honolulu."

"Then I will come back too," said Va'ina, brightening. She looked around her—down at the lagoon, now shimmering in dusk; then up toward the huts, from which came the wink of lights and the sound of the radio. "Maybe I will come often, for it is nice here. In the village it is dull; at night it is dark and quiet; but here there are lights and music." Now, again, her eyes were on Carr. "You do not mind if I come?" she asked.

"Mind? Of course not. A lot of your people come every night."

"Yes, I know. And Miz Loftus, she comes too, no? In her jeep."

"Miss Loftus comes to take care of the workmen when they have accidents."

"And there are so many accidents, it is a shame. But it is lucky there is Miz Loftus to take care. . . . She is so nice, do you not think?"

"She's a good nurse. And serious about her work."

"Yes, serious, that is how she is. You can see in her face. And her face is pretty, no? With the skin white like unripe breadfruit and the hair yellow like broken eggs." The girl broke off, and her voice changed. "Why do you look at me so?" she demanded.

"How am I looking?"

"You are laughing."

"No."

"Yes, you are laughing. At me. Why do you laugh at me?"

"Would you rather I frowned?"

"You think I am a silly girl. Miz Loftus, with her pills and her hair like eggs, you think she is serious. But I am silly."

"I didn't—"

"I am only a brown girl from a village who cannot give pills or drive a jeep. . . . But Mr. Melnick will not think I am silly when I dance for him. When I dance at the hotel, they will not say I am silly, but clap their hands and cry '*Malo! Malo!*'"

Anger had touched her voice, but not her eyes. Her eyes were mocking, laughing back at him. And she said, "Only you, I think, would not cry '*Malo! Malo!*' Because you too, Mr. Meesh Carr, are very serious, no? Like Miz Loftus. Like my sister, Mena, who does not dance and has no boy friend but only Jesus."

"Perhaps I should meet your sister," Carr told her.

"Yes, you must meet her. You will go to the village and take her to church—and Miz Loftus too. And I will come here and dance for Mr. Melnick."

She paused and stood listening, and through the palm grove, muted by distance, came the sound of music from the radio at the work camp. "It is the music of Manaia," she said. "The music I dance to. . . . So," she said. "And so." . . . And as she spoke she moved slightly. An arm moved, and a shoulder. Then her waist, her hips, her thighs. For a moment the whole of her was moving, save only her bare feet on the earth of the path and her dark eyes fixed on Carr.

"And so," she said once more—the girl, Va'ina—the girl, Lovana. And then she stopped. She had lowered her eyes demurely. "I am sorry, Mr. Meesh Carr," she murmured.

"Sorry?"

"That I keep you here. That I take the time of a serious man with such foolishness. But forgive me; I cannot help it. *Laititi a'u. Fia siva.*"

"What does that mean?" Carr asked.

"It means, 'I am young and like to dance.'"

There was another pause, and through the stillness the drifting music. "So I will come again when he is here and dance for Mr. Melnick," the girl said. Then she laughed. "And you will go to church with Mena and Miz Loftus."

She turned away.

"Va'ina—" he said.

"Yes?"

"Wait. There's something I want to ask you."

"No, I waste your time. I am a silly girl," she said. "I go now."
And she was gone.

Word came through the radio that the ship from Hawaii had
reached Apingo. But it would be a week or more before men and
machines could be transshipped to Tiara.

Meanwhile, the *Harold L. Ickes* appeared and reappeared on its
routine ferryings; and from its deck, one day, the figure of John Koa
stepped down onto the jetty.

"So you've been to Apingo," said Carr, intercepting him.

The boy nodded.

"And sent your cable?"

The boy was taken by surprise. "How did you—"

"Mr. Shafter told me you wanted to send one. To the Air Force
in Honolulu."

"Yes, I sent a cable," John said.

"You don't have to be defiant about it. It's all right with me."

"I—I'm sorry, sir. It's just that—"

"Yes, I know—that Mr. Shafter didn't want you to. He said it
would be a waste of money."

The boy said nothing.

"And was it?"

"I don't know."

"Meaning you got no answer?"

"No."

"After waiting how long?"

"For three days."

"So you see, Mr. Shafter was right. They'll answer when they're
ready, and not before."

Again the boy said nothing. Instead, he turned to go, but Carr
called him back. "Now that your money's gone," he said, "hadn't
you better earn some?"

John shook his head. "One does not need money on Tiara."

"Your uncle, Fahoai—he'd like to see you work."

"Yes, he's for everyone working. Except himself."

"Is it this other one then—Chief Tafutimo—who's put you up to
this?"

"No. It is myself only. After twelve years of school that is not
what I want: to cut down trees—to carry rocks."

"Only to fly, eh?"

"Yes, to fly. Is that wrong of me?"

"Because you're so mad at the world you want to drop bombs?"

"No," said the boy, "I do not want to drop bombs."

86

"You want to be a fighter, then?"

"No, not a fighter."

"In the Air Force," Carr said, "you either fight or drop bombs."

"I do not plan to stay in the Air Force, sir."

"Oh?"

"Without money, it is only as an Air Force cadet that one can learn to fly. Many pilots have done that. And then when I have learned—"

"What?"

"Then I will fly with a great airline. I will be a man in the world, like other men, and not a gook on a little island."

There was a pause. Carr's eyes were fixed on the young brown face, half boy's, half man's; half fearful, half defiant.

"Have you ever been in a plane?" he asked.

"No, sir," said John Koa.

"What do you know about them?"

"What I have read. What I have studied. While I was in school in Utoia I went often to the airfield to watch and to talk with the fliers."

Carr stopped.

The question was, "How did this start? Where did this come from?" But it remained unasked. He was unable to ask it.

Instead, it was the boy who put a question: the same he had put before and to which he had received no answer. "Is it wrong of me?" he repeated. "*Why* is it wrong of me?" And now, for the first time, the shell of his reserve cracked wide and the words broke out in tumbling urgency. "I am not some sort of savage. I am an American. Manaians have been Americans for sixty years, and I am even more than most, because—"

"Hey, Mitch!"

Frank Lavery came up the jetty.

"Did the power saw come?"

"I don't know," Carr said. "I haven't seen it."

Lavery shouted up at Captain Stack on the bridge of the *Ickes*; Stack shouted back; and by the time Carr looked around again John Koa was moving away.

The contractor looked after him too. "If a few of the gooks like that would get off their asses," he said, "we wouldn't be needing any damn power saws at six hundred each."

The radio had given its last bleat and fallen silent. Outside, over palm grove and lagoon, there was moonlit stillness, but in the quonset the mosquitoes (fortified by Melnick's insecticide) droned and dove, and Lavery snored rhythmically in his adjoining cubicle. Carr turned and slapped and punched his pillow. Then he got up. Putting on a few clothes, he went out and sat on the steps; but the mosquitoes were there too, and after a bit he rose and went down the path toward the jetty. The *Ickes* was gone again, and there was no one around. Nor was there anyone on the nearby road.

The moon, now full, gave ample light to see by, and he walked on down the road. He was not going anywhere, but simply walking; away from the drone and the snore: away from the two figures, a girl's and a boy's, that emerged from enclosing darkness whenever he sank off toward sleep. On his left, inland, were Tiara's hills; on his right, a strip of palm grove and the sea; and ahead, moon and palm fronds swathed the road in a web of black and silver. For perhaps half a mile it was the same. And beyond that still the same— except that now, presently, there was a different, heavier shadow in the pattern ahead, and he came to an empty jeep that stood at the roadside. At this point, the sea was only a few yards away beyond a line of palms, and passing between them, he came onto the beach and saw Carol Loftus.

She was sitting on a slope of sand, wearing a light cotton dress, with bare feet extended before her, and she was looking out at the white line of the reef and the ocean beyond. Suddenly conscious of his presence, she turned, and he said quickly, "Don't be afraid. I'm not a ghost."

She watched him as he approached, and the thought came to him that it was she, rather, who might have been the ghost, for, against sand and moonlight, her face was spectral white, and her hair seemed no longer yellow but of silver. Standing beside her, he saw a small pile of shells close by one of her hands, and he said, smiling, "Working the night shift too?"

"There are some lovely shells along here," she said. "With the full moon they're as easy to find as by daylight."

"Do you come often?"

"Now and then."

"If you drove a half mile farther you'd be at the lagoon, and we'd be glad to have you any time."

"Thank you. But there haven't been any accidents lately, and I've been very busy in the village."

"In the evenings?"

"Evenings I try to get my records up to date. Then there's Mrs. Mundy too. I don't like leaving her alone before she goes to bed."

"By now she must be pretty used to being alone."

"Well, yes. But—" Carol left the "but" hanging. "It was Mrs. Mundy who told me about the shells," she said. "She says that sometimes one of the Tiarans finds a golden cowrie, but I've had no luck yet."

Carr stood for a few moments watching the lap of the wavelets a few yards beyond them. Then he sat down on the sand.

"Do you mind?" he asked.

"No. Why should I mind?"

He smiled again. "You're the girl, I recall, who wants to be on her own."

"Oh."

He picked up a few of the shells, turning them in his hand, and for a little while neither spoke. Nor had they spoken much when they had met on her nursing visits to the hotel site. She had commented that he was back. He had asked if there was anything she needed professionally and seconded Lavery's invitations to stay for supper. And that had been the extent of it. He knew no more about her than on that first night when they had talked briefly on the quonset steps.

"And how is it?" he asked her now.

"How is what?"

"Being on your own."

"My work is very interesting," she said. "And I hope I'm being of some use."

"And for yourself?"

"Myself?"

"Is it going the way you hoped? Are you proving what you want to?"

"I don't know what you mean."

"Yes you do," he said. "You volunteered to come here, didn't you?"

"To Manaia? Of course."

"Not just to Manaia. To Tiara: back of beyond. At least now, until the hotel's up. . . . Isn't that playing it against the grain?"

"The grain?"

"Against nature. How old are you?" he asked.

"Twenty-five."

"Yes, twenty-five. You're young—attractive—"

"What has that to do with it?" she asked, almost belligerently.

"It has a lot to do with it. I've been in a good many out-back places in my life—in Africa, Latin America, here and there—and and there's always been one thing the same about the women you find there. Not the native ones. And not the married ones. I mean the single women, the career ones—the ones you find working for the Government or corporations or whatever—and some are damn fine people; but those who are attractive, *as* women, you could count on one hand. They're always the homely ones, the frustrated ones, the rejects. Those who couldn't make a go of it at home, couldn't find the husband, have the children, and are trying to make a life for themselves another way."

"And a—what you call an attractive woman can't make a life for herself?"

"Usually she doesn't need to. Not that way. That's why I'm curious about you, and why you've come here."

It was a while before the girl spoke. She looked at him, and he saw that her eyes too, like her hair, were different in the moonlight; not young and blue, as they usually were, but gray—a withdrawn opaque gray—and he thought back to the day at the ship's rail, coming to Tiara, when he had first seen that there was something strange and special about her.

Then she said: "I could ask you the same thing, couldn't I? As to why *you* are here."

"I came," he said, "to blast the lagoon."

"That's done now. Why did you come back?"

"To do some surveying for the hotel."

"Is that what you do usually—surveying?"

"Among other things."

"What other things?" When he hesitated, she smiled a little, for the first time. "Now it's my turn to ask questions," she said.

"Sometimes I build things," said Carr. "And sometimes I tear them down. I make and lose money. I get married and unmarried. I do what the world expects of me—which is most of the time what I expect of myself; and then suddenly I stop; I ask, what's going on here? why am I doing this? And I pack my dynamite and come to Tiara."

"*Back* to Tiara."

He nodded.

"You were here during the war; Leonard Shafter told me. When we were on the boat coming over I saw you there at the rail, looking at the island, and the way you looked, I thought no, you couldn't just be thinking of dynamite; and then when I heard about the war I understood. Something must have happened to you here, I thought, something good, that had meaning. That made you need to come back."

"You seem to know a lot about me," Carr said.

"No, I don't, of course. But—" She paused. "But still—well—something, perhaps. . . . You see, my father did the same thing," she said.

"Your father? He was *here*—in Tiara?"

She shook her head. "No, not here. His island was called Mbinga. It's in the Solomons."

"He was there during the war?"

"Yes."

"And he went back?"

"Yes."

There was another pause.

"Go on," he said.

"There's no point. Why should I?"

"Because I'd like to know about it. And you'd like to tell me."

For another moment she hesitated. Then she went on.

"My father was a doctor," she said. "We lived in a town called Hillsboro, in eastern Ohio, and he was the youngest of three doctors there. When the war came he was the one to go—into the Army— and they sent him out to the Solomons. He had a strange sort of war there apparently. Hardly any combat, and no medals or things like that. Most of the time he was on assignment on this little island of Mbinga, taking care of the native people.

"Then when the war was over he came home. He and my mother had never got on too well, and now, with those three years' separation, they had more trouble than ever. In fact, I think they'd have broken up right then if it hadn't been for me and my older sister. I was only about ten at that time, so of course I didn't know too much; but I did know that he'd been happier out in the Solomons than he was back at Hillsboro. He used to tell me stories about his life in Mbinga. About how wonderful the people were—kind and simple and decent—but also how poor, diseased, and ignorant, and what he had done to try to help them. As I say, I was just a little girl. I suppose I understood only about half of what he told me. But there was no mistaking how much the years out there had meant to him.

"Anyhow, back home, things between him and mother went from bad to worse. And though he was successful enough in his work, I think all it meant to him was just earning a living. Finally everything just—well—broke up, and he left. A while later he came back for a day to see my sister and me, and told us he was going back to the Solomons—to Mbinga. And off he went. For two years we had letters from him almost every month, telling us about his life there, and his work. Then the letters stopped. Three months went by. And at last we had another letter—not from him but from the Governor of the Solomon Islands. It told of the fine work he had done and expressed the thanks of the Government. But it was all in the past tense, of course, for he'd died on the island of blackwater fever."

She stopped and looked out at the sea. And for a while there was only the gentle sound of the sea.

"Well—that was eight years ago," she went on. "I was seventeen and a senior in high school; but already, for as long as I can remember, I'd known what I wanted to be, and that was a doctor, like my father. I'd loved him terribly, of course—I suppose that's obvious—and at first it was just one of those childish things. But I didn't lose it; instead, it grew stronger all the time, until it wasn't childish at all, but the very center of me—what I *knew* I had to do with my life. My mother thought I was crazy. She had it all figured out the way it should be: that Edith, my sister, should be the working one—in fact, she was already working in an office in Columbus—and I was the get-married one. The pretty one. Oh, I was supposed to marry so wonderfully well—

"We argued and fought, but my mind was made up. And I went off"—she paused and glanced at Carr—"on my own. I enrolled at Ohio State for premed courses and was there two years. And then the facts of life caught up with me, and I realized I wouldn't be able to make the grade. It was a frightful disappointment, of course. For a while I hardly wanted to live. But then I pulled myself together and decided to do the next best thing, which was nursing. I got my R.N. all right. I worked in a hospital in Columbus and then in Cleveland. Once I'd got over my disappointment, I loved nursing. But—"

She paused, looking down at the shells on the sand beside her.

"But it was—well, something like what you said before: about what people *expect*. My mother, my friends, everyone; even the doctors and interns in the hospitals. No one would take me seriously as a nurse, let alone as a doctor. I was playing at nursing, they thought. I was the 'cute little blonde' waiting for Mr. Right to come along and just passing the time in the meanwhile. I'd hardly ever be given a really responsible job, in the operating room or on a serious case, and all anyone seemed interested in was what I was doing on my night off.

"I thought of my father, and how he had lived—and died. Then I looked at myself, and I hated myself. And suddenly I knew what I had to do. I had to live as my father lived, work as he worked—where I was wanted, where I was needed—where I wasn't just playing at nursing but giving something of what I have to give. And I wrote to the Solomons. They wrote back that, yes, they remembered my father well; that he had done great work there and Mbinga would never forget him; but that now, as a British colony, they were taking only British subjects on their staff. So I wrote to Washington about

92

American islands. I knew that places like Samoa and Manaia wouldn't be like the Solomons; that the people would be better off, healthier, less primitive. But still, I thought, they were places where I could be of *use*, where I could be something more than the little blonde number in Ward Three. I filled out forms and took exams and had interviews. And at last it happened: I had word that a position was open in Manaia, and a few weeks later I was in Apingo."

"But even that wasn't right?" Carr asked.

"Oh, I know it must sound—"

The girl broke off. Her face and voice hardened. "No, it wasn't right," she said. "It was the same thing all over again. The first night, at the Coconut Palm Club. In people's homes. Even in the hospital. 'What are *you* doing here? What are *you* good for?' everyone seemed to be asking; or if they didn't ask they thought they knew. At least the men did. . . . I was sick of it, so sick of it. . . . And when they needed a nurse here, I volunteered. The other nurses thought I was crazy. Dr. Friede and Leonard Shafter think I'm crazy. All right, let them—"

The hardness of her voice had sharpened. There was no apology in it, no gentleness or femininity, but only a cold fierce pride wrenched up out of her inwards. "All right, then I'm crazy," she said. "Crazy like my father. Crazy because I won't play at living; because I've something to give—that I must give. . . . Can you understand that? . . . Can you understand that just because I'm young and a woman I'm not a doll, a fool, a nothing? A nothing with blue eyes and yellow hair, good for nothing but bed and babies. My father could have understood. Yes, I know it. But no one else can. No one, ever—ever—"

The pride and hardness had risen. Now, as suddenly, they crumbled. Her eyes, a moment before gray and hostile, fixed on Carr softly, almost pleadingly; then looked down and away; and her face, white in moonlight, seemed no longer that of a woman but of a child.

"I—I'm sorry," she murmured. "I don't know why I've gone on like this."

Carr smiled a little. "Perhaps because I'm—fatherly," he said.

"Do you think I'm crazy? Yes, of course you do. You must."

"No, not crazy at all. Just very upset. And very lonely." He felt, rather than saw, her face change again, and his smile deepened. "You've heard that 'lonely' part before, haven't you?" he said. "But this time don't worry, I'm staying fatherly. I won't lunge at you and scatter your shells."

She looked at him, uncertainly. Then she, too, smiled. They were both smiling; and then, in the next instant, she was laughing. The

93

sound of her laughter filled the stillness—at first soft and gentle, but then changing, then less soft, more highly pitched—a wild high laughter, growing, swelling, until it broke, until it was no longer laughter at all but something far from laughter. And then that too broke, it faded, and at last it stopped, as with a great effort she caught herself, held herself, and sat again in silence, head bowed, on the moonlit beach.

Carr extended his hand and put it on hers. "It's not a lunge," he said. And she let it remain there. And, side by side, they sat watching the black and silver sea.

"When I think—" she began.

"Don't" he said. "Not now. It's against the law here after ten o'clock. You're supposed to concentrate on how beautiful it is."

"It *is* beautiful," she murmured.

He nodded, but didn't answer. Instead, after a few moments, he began to hum softly, and then his lips were moving with half-spoken words.

The girl looked at him. "What?" she said.

"I was crooning a tune . . . 'neath the moon . . . on the tropic lagoon. Where
      no
        one
          has
            a
              care. . . ."

He paused.

"That's from a musical show," he said, "that I saw in New York when I was a schoolboy. I think it ran three nights, but I thought it was wonderful."

Presently he helped her up, and she put her shells in her handkerchief, and they walked up the slope of beach and through the palms to the jeep. She asked if she could drive him back to the hotel site, but he said no, he'd walk, and she said, "Good night—and thank you," and drove away toward the village. When she was out of sight he turned and went in the other direction. As Lavery had said, he had the longer legs of the two of them; but it didn't matter, for he walked slowly with his eyes on the road.

7

BENEATH THE DUST of the road was coral. Beneath the coral was the rock of earth's crust. And the rock plunged down through the pit of ocean, through the floor of ocean, into immeasurable depths of pressure and dark fire.

A million years ago—or two, or three, or five—these depths had heaved upward. Earth and ocean had convulsed, and from the convulsion, out of fire and sea, had risen an island. For ten thousand years—or twenty, or fifty—the fire was not dark, but flaming. It spewed up in volcanoes, through fissures and craters, into the ocean night. Then slowly it subsided. It withdrew again into darkness. The island stood black in the sea; and the sea gnawed at it; waves and winds and rains lashed and battered it, crumbling its lava, boring in toward its fireless core. For ages they did this, trying to wear it away.

But it did not wear away.

For in the warm shallow water that ringed the island, there was life. This was the life of coral polyps, in their untold trillions, and each of the trillions as it died, over the ages, left its tiny calcified skeleton on the shores and shallows. As, above, erosion diminished the island, so, from below, the coral augmented it: with reefs that held off the surge of the sea; with platforms that buttressed the cliffs and thrust up the beaches. The living elements destroyed. The dying coral built.

And the island did not wear away.

Coral, to be sure, was not the only form of life—or death—on the earth. Beyond, in the ocean depths, a whole kingdom of life had been born; and on greater land masses, far away, other kingdoms of terrestrial creatures. Out of the plant world had come the animal world, and it grew and flourished and multiplied—and died. The

95

dinosaur came and went. The mastodon, the saber-toothed tiger, the Pithecanthropus. They came and went and vanished, but the coral had its own way. Like the rest, it died, but it did not vanish. It built on.

In time, other builders appeared on earth. Builders not with their bodies but with wood and stone and metal. They built shelters and paths, and then towns and roads, and then cities and bridges and ships and machines; and they fashioned marvelous tools for building. And for destroying. They fashioned clubs and spears and swords and flintlocks; and then rifles and siege guns and shells and bombs; and with shell and bomb, in due time, they ranged even to the coral seas. Under the impact, the coral splintered here and it crumbled there, but it gave back as good as it took, and continued on its own way.

The coral engineers built on.

At first they had been alone in their building, but later other forces had joined in. A seed drifted across the ocean and found lodgment on the island's shore. A coconut drifted in, a pandanus fruit, a root, a tuber. A bird passed and left its droppings. Then more seeds came; more fruits and roots and birds, in endless accretion. And as the years passed the island was no longer black but green; it was no longer made of dead lava but of living earth; and in its sheath of life it stood in splendor between sky and sea. . . . And so still stands. . . . As far as man's time on earth is concerned, it is complete, finished: born out of fire and ocean, coral and seed.

Alone, lost in the miles, it is wrapped in stillness. Under its white cloud cap, under sun and stars, it lies in a caul of enormous peace. . . . But the peace is fragile, transient. Out of its very core, suddenly, comes violence. Violence of cloud turned black, of wind rising, screaming; of wind and rain and roaring sea; of the sea heaving upward, drowning beaches, flooding valleys, cracking palm trees. Or, now, violence below; of things that live and die; of fin and tooth, the circling shark, the coiled moray; the flash, the strike, the rending, the patch of red that glistens briefly on blue water. . . . And then it is gone. Scream and roar and patch of red, they are all gone, and there is stillness. There is peace again, immense and shining.

From a skiff on Tiara's lagoon, Mitchell Carr looked down into the heart of peace.

The lagoon was cleared now. A plane could come and go. But no one, unless he had known exactly where to look, could have guessed that a few brief days before it had been wracked by dynamite. Its surface was of silk, its depth of crystal, and through the crystal rose the coral, still living, still building. Where the fountains of dead fish had risen were now live fish by the myriad thousand; sleeker, brighter, stronger with life for having fed on those that had died.

With mask and flippers, Carr moved deep through this world below the world. Through rays of slanted sunlight. Over beds of shining sand. Into rainbow mazes of coral, past towers and grottos and forests and drowned cities. And the roar of dynamite was remote and lost. . . . Or, leaving the lagoon, he would go to the seaward beach and at low tide walk out on the flats that shelved to the reef. All was stillness here. Beach and flats were deserted: a skeletal realm of sunbleached, long-dead coral. Yet in the stillness there was movement everywhere. In the sea, here broken into streams and rivulets, seeping through grooves and funnels and tunnels as it advanced or withdrew. In the march of crabs and mollusks, forging their threaded tracks in the sand. In the fish darting in the tidal pools: so quick and tiny that they seemed only flecks of sunlight and vanished even as he saw them. . . . And then, perhaps, he would move out farther, to the reef itself, to where the white surf broke rumbling on the island's parapets. Here, at embrasures in the reef, protected from surf, he would look down the walls beneath the parapets, the outer cliffs of the island fortress falling away into the ocean abyss. . . . And then at last he would turn and head homeward— perhaps picking up a shell for Carol Loftus's collection as he crossed the beach toward palms and road.

At this point his work was easy, almost nonexistent. For he had done his sighting and calculating, and, except for a few supervisory chores, there was no more for him to do until the construction crew arrived from Apingo. Tom Taki and his Utoians went on with the ground-clearing. The few Tiarans who appeared swung their axes lazily and watched the power saw (which was for Utoians only) with fascination. And Lavery gave orders to Taki, who gave orders to his own crew, who gave orders to the Tiarans, who paid no attention.

Twice in five days Carol Loftus came over from the village. Each time Carr gave her a shell or two, and she thanked him; but that was all the conversation they had, as she went professionally about her work and then drove off again. "That's a queer one all right," Lavery said, looking after her. "A real honest-to-God queer one."

The next morning Tiara's cloud cap darkened. Other clouds moved in. And for two days rain fell, wind blew, and work at the hotel site all but stopped. The day following was the one on which the men and material from Apingo were due; but word came on the radio that the storm had slowed things up over there as well and that there would be a forty-eight-hour delay. Carr and Lavery played gin rummy. Carr returned to lagoon and beach. And from the beach, on the second day, he found himself walking, not back along the road toward the quonsets, but on the path that led inland to valley and hills.

Again he followed it through the green bowers, up the ridge, to the high bare promontory. And again he stopped there, looking out to sea, feeling the trade wind soft and cool on his sweating flesh. Sitting, he smoked a while, and when the cigarette was gone he still sat, breathing in space and solitude. His mind went back to other solitudes he had known—in the Arabian desert, in the Andes of Peru; times when he had been alone not accidentally, but, as now, by choice: not in body only but in the core of him: when a huge need had driven him, for a few days or a night or an hour, away from the clatter of men and machines. Then to the more recent solitudes of New York, of the city nights: total and absolute. With Margaret gone, Helen gone, money gone, desire gone. With only a street ahead, and a bar; the next street, the next bar; bars on strange streets where he would know no one, where he would be alone in the multitudes; alone in the street again, in the night, in his room, his bed, his drunken dreams.

But that aloneness had been different. That had been the way down. This—perhaps—was the way up. At least (making allowances for Melnick and dynamite) it was why he was here: to walk off alone; to breathe deeply alone; to pull away from the clatter and clutter and fever of his usual life and take stock of where that life had brought him. There was nothing that could be accomplished from without. Like Margaret and Helen, CMF was behind him, and a church, a political manifesto, a psychiatrist's couch were, for him, no more The Answer than a bottle of whisky. "My salute to you, Lord Jesus. My respects to you, Messrs. Marx and Freud. But, great men though you are, you cannot help me. I alone can help myself. By myself. On my own."

He smiled, thinking of another who was "on her own." . . .

And when the smile had gone he still thought of Carol Loftus— half purposeful dedicated woman, half lonely romantic child—and of what he could conceivably have said or done that night on the beach when she had bared herself to him. Of what he *had* done: putting a hand on hers. Of what he had said: "I won't scatter your shells." (Very funny.) And then the tired old tin-pan alley jingle.

And yet . . .

Yet neither, he knew, had been out of context. The girl, above all else, was afraid of—just that: being a girl. And the jingle had not just been an aberration; it had somehow *fit*. Not helpfully, to be sure —not gently or prettily—but it had belonged to that time and place, no less than sea and moon themselves. For it had been not only sea and moon that were there, but he and Carol Loftus as well, and it had been they, the human ones, who had supplied whatever meaning there was. Nature did not know beauty. Nor did it know the cliché that can make a mockery of beauty. Both were human concepts, fashioned by humans out of their endowments and experiences, and on Tiara's beach that night, both had been true and valid. For man, no place, no situation, is simply what it is—a thing in itself—but also what he brings to it in his mind and heart.

There was the hope and frustration that Carol Loftus had brought. There was the bitter tiredness that he, Mitchell Carr, had brought. Always, wherever you went—however far, however high or deep—there was the baggage you brought with you.

In the silver darkness she had thought of her father. He had thought of two other, distant beaches, long ago. Of Margaret, on a beach in Mexico (there had been sunlight then, not moonlight, with the sea gleaming in its glory), turning miserably to him and saying, "Mitch, when you've finished this job can't we please, please, go home and settle down and have our children?" Then of Helen, on a beach at Cannes (early evening then, and the Mediterranean aflame with sunset), suddenly covering her face with her hands and murmuring wildly, "Oh Mitch, I can't go through with it. I'm afraid—so afraid—" And with them, too, he had extended his hand; he had touched theirs; and that was all he had done, without even a joke about shells or a music-hall jingle. These women had not been strangers—they had been his wives—yet he had been unable to help them, to resolve the desires and fears they brought with them to the peace of the beach and sea. He had been able only to hurt them. To reject—not coldly, not harshly, but none the less ruthlessly—what *they* wanted for what *he* wanted, only to find that when he had it he did not want it at all.

He looked down at the shore and the sea, then up at Tiara's cloud cap and the golden sun. And he thought: What you bring with you is self. In moonlight or sunlight, on beach or hill, in Cannes, in Mexico, on a Pacific island—that is your baggage: self. And he was sick of self. Was it not time, at last, to think of others? he had asked as he walked, meditating, from the airport to Apingo and made his decision to stay on in the islands. And it *was* time, surely. It was past time. And he knew it.

But knowing was one thing, doing another. What could he, Mitchell Carr, do for a girl in love with a dead father? Or—now the other image came to mind—for a brown boy who roamed like a ghost through the palm groves; who was born to climb coconut trees but wanted to climb the sky in a roaring plane?

He had traveled a lot. He had lived a lot. And he knew that the hardest of all journeys was that into another's inward self. A shaking hand extended, to find the way in darkness, was worse than no hand at all.

He rose and walked on. As on his first time in the hills, three weeks before, he descended from the promontory by a second ridge, entered a second valley, moved on between tall boles and emerald screens. And as before, too, he felt, as he moved on, a deep and gentle easement of spirit. The screens shut out the flaming sun and wide horizons. The boles enclosed him like a pillared temple. Slowly he followed the aisle through shadowed stillness; and then ahead there was the temple's sanctuary—the waterfall, the pool, the breadfruit tree—exactly as they had been three weeks, and eighteen years, before.

He sat under the tree. Leaning against it, he closed his eyes and listened to the soft sound of the fall; and it was as if it had never left his ears, as if in all his life he had never left this place; and when he reopened his eyes there would be Lovana, standing before him, smiling.

Then he opened them. He looked at the girl, Va'ina. And Va'ina, smiling, said, "Good afternoon, Mr. Meesh."

He blinked. He smiled back at her. Then he laughed.

"Another part of the forest—" he said.

"What does that mean?"

"It means you never can tell what's going to turn up next."

"It is a small island," said the girl. "And also the Old Man of the breadfruit tree does not like it when one sits under him alone."

She came nearer and sat down a few yards away. For the first time since Carr had met her she was wearing not a dress but a lava-lava, a length of red and white cotton wound about her and tucked in at the top, that reached from her knees to just above her breasts. Her shoulders were bare and golden under the black hair that fell over them, and in the hair, this time, gleamed two white gardenias.

"You know the story of the Old Man?" she asked.

"Yes," said Carr.

"It is a foolish story, of course. I do not think it can really happen, for a man to become a tree. But also it is a nice story. And nice to sit with a friend under his arms."

She readjusted one of her flowers.

"You and I, we are friends, Meesh?" she asked.

"I hope so," he said.

"Or perhaps you were not really alone under the tree? Perhaps, when I come, you are waiting for another friend?"

"Another—?"

"For Miz Nurse, maybe? What is her name?—Miz Loftus. With her nice skin like green breadfruit and her hair like broken eggs."

He grinned. "No, I'm not waiting for Miss Loftus."

"For me, then?"

"Yes, for you."

She nodded, satisfied, and looked away at the pool and waterfall. And he too looked at them for a while—and then at her.

"I haven't seen you in a lava-lava before," he said.

"You like?"

"Yes, I like."

"I do not wear it in the village. There I am always *sao tamaitai*."

"What's that?"

"That is a perfectly complete lady. Like a *papalagi* lady, with the dress, the shoes, even the things for underneath. But when I come to the hills I come so. Like—how do you say?—a sovagi."

"A savage."

"Yes, a savage." She touched the top of her cotton sheath. "Only when we were really savage we did not wear the lava-lava so high, because we did not yet know that a woman's body makes God angry."

She looked at her legs. "I like too to go sometimes with bare feet. And God does not mind that," she said. "It is good; it is free." Then, glancing at Carr's sneakers: "You cannot go without shoes, no? With a *papalagi* the feet are too soft."

Carr nodded.

"And the rest, it is soft too, maybe? Like the legs. You are not used to climbing hills, and the legs are tired, so that it why you sit down here."

"My legs are all right," he said.

"No, they are tired. I can see." An idea struck her. "But I will fix. I will fix good," she said. Beside her lay a small knotted pouch of flowered cloth, and opening it, she produced a bottle. "Is coconut oil," she said, "that I bring for bathing, and I will give you a *lomi-lomi*."

"A what?" he asked.

"*Lomi-lomi*. It is the massage of Manaia. When it is finished you will want to run up and down the hills like a goat."

"An old goat."

"No, a young one. One that says 'Maaa, maaa' and goes so with his horns."

She jerked her head up and down and laughed. Then, ignoring his protests, she pulled off his sneakers and socks and, holding his feet in her lap, kneaded them slowly with strong fingers.

"There, you have feet like a goat," she announced when she had finished. "Now I give you a head like a goat." And moving behind him, she went to work on his scalp and the back of his neck. "In the head," she said, "a *papalagi* much needs the *lomi-lomi*. He is always thinking, thinking, and that is bad for the head."

"Very," he agreed.

He had again closed his eyes. No longer thinking; no longer protesting. Head bowed, he sat in the soft shade of the breadfruit tree, while the strong deft fingers moved through his hair and around the rim of his skull. And then he was lying flat, first prone, then supine on the green mattress of moss; and he had let Va'ina, with much giggling, pull off his shirt and trousers; and now her hands, warm with coconut oil, moved over his body, kneading firm and deep. Only once she spoke, saying, "You are thin, Meesh. Sometimes I almost break my fingers on your bones." And then, for the only time, he opened his eyes and saw her bent over him, her black hair framing her face and falling in a cascade on his chest. And she smiled and threw her hair back over her shoulder and went on with the massage, and he lay still, eyes closed again, until she had finished.

"So, now you are all a goat," she said, "—and we go swim." And rising, she pulled him up and led him to the edge of the pool. He was wearing his undershorts, she her lava-lava; but as the water closed around them she released his hand and lowering the sheath of cotton, rewound and tied it about her waist. "It is easier so for swimming," she explained. "And in the water God does not see so good."

Another giggle. And she dove. Black hair and golden body arched through the depths, with lava-lava trailing after like a mermaid's tail. And then she surfaced. She beckoned to Carr and splashed water at him, and as he approached she laughed and dove again, this time coming up near the base of the waterfall. Her hair was spread around her like a dark cloud, and the two gardenias that had been entwined in it were drifting away across the pool. While still on the bank she had anointed her own flesh with coconut oil, and her face and shoulders glistened with clinging drops of silver.

Again, as he came near, she moved away. As he followed, she circled about. Then he was no longer following, but had turned on his back and was gently floating, his eyes on the overhanging foliage that lay patterned against the sky. His eyes were smiling. His mind was smiling. And his mind thought: so here you are. So here it is. The tease. The chase. Brown flesh and white shadow in the South Sea glade; in the old cliché, in the tinkling jingle. And he spoke the jingle. He sang it. He sang it, smiling; he sang it, laughing; and Va'ina clapped and cried, "*Malo!* It is beautiful." Then, still laughing, he rolled over—his body, and his mind with it—his new goat's body, and his goat's mind—and they lunged through the water; they lunged and rolled and dove through shining brightness; and if the brightness was a cliché, well enough; if pool and fall were, well enough; if the golden girl was, well enough, and let tin-pan alley make the best of it. He laughed. The girl was laughing. She was closer now, and he could see the bright clichés that were her mouth and eyes.

They swam side by side. The floated. They drifted under the fall, and silver rained on their faces and shoulders. They were close now. Sometimes their hands touched, sometimes their legs, and once her breasts brushed against him, cool and firm in the crystal water. Then hand in hand they came up out of the pool and sat on the bank beneath the breadfruit tree, and the drops shone like diamonds on the girl's oiled flesh.

"You are not mad, like God," she asked, "that I do not pull high my lava-lava?"

"No, I'm not mad," he said.

"And you do not want I should go away so you can think?"

"No. No more thinking today."

"Good. So it is a happiness time we have. A *fia fia.*" She smiled, looking up at him. "You know what it is, Meesh—a *fia fia.*"

"Yes, I know," he said.

"So you will kiss me, please."

He kissed her. And she kissed him back. Then she looked at him earnestly.

"Is it all right?" she asked.

"Is what all right?"

"How I kiss."

"No complaint," he said.

"With the kissing I am sometimes not sure. My people, from the old days, they did not kiss so; they only press with the noses. But I like better with the mouth, like the *papalagi* do—like I see in the movies in Apingo; so I practice and hope I am all right."

"You're all right," he told her.

"The movies I like much when I see them. Not the ones with the horses, but the ones with the love, and I try to do what they show." Va'ina clasped her hands about her knees and looked thoughtfully up at branches and sky. "Because do you know what I think?" she said. "I think that sometime I will be in the movies myself. . . . No, do not laugh when I say it, for it is true. From this little island of Tiara I will be a star in the movies. . . . And do you know how I will do it? With the hotel. With Mr. Melnick. I will dance for Mr. Melnick and he will hire me for the hotel. When the hotel is open I will dance for all who come. I will dance for big men from the movies who will come, and they will clap their hands and say '*Malo!*' and take me to Hollywood, and there I will dance the dances of Manaia for all the world to see."

She paused, eyes bright with the vision. Then, in the next instant, she was on her feet. She was dancing. . . . "So—and so—and so," she said, as she had that evening on the path near the quonsets. . . . But her dance was not like that other. Then her movements had been deliberate, chosen: one here, one there, the mere suggestion of a dance. Now all movement flowed together—of arms and legs and body, of breasts and belly and swaying hips—at first slow and sinuous, then faster, wilder, in orgiastic abandon. And now she *was* a savage: in body, in face, in every cell of her flesh and spirit. And her dance was not for Mel Melnick; it was not for the big men from the movies; it was not, in its essence, even for Mitchell Carr—but for itself alone; a thing of the blood, of the genes, of a thousand ancestors. Her body spun, her shoulders quivered, her hips writhed. Her knees spread wide, thrusting the pelvis forward. Then they were deeply bent, they touched the ground, and thighs and trunk arched back in jerking rhythm, her loose black hair sweeping the earth beneath them, bare breasts and belly heaving higher, higher. . . .

And then, as suddenly as she had begun, she had stopped. Still on her knees, she was facing Carr, smiling, and the smile was half that of a little girl and half that of a savage. "Do you like?" she asked. "My dance of the *fia fia,* of the happiness time?"

Again her body undulated. Fresh with water, smooth with oil, it coiled closer, snakelike, and the nipples were erect on the golden breasts. Then she flung herself forward. She was on the moss beside Carr; she was drawing him down. With a quick movement of one hand she loosened the wet strip of cloth from around her waist and lay naked against him along the length of their bodies. And now her other hand moved too; more slowly, but unhesitantly. It moved as only a savage's can, without constraint, without shame; and what it wanted it took, what it took it held; and holding each other, they met and mingled, tightly, deeply, without constraint, without shame. The moment came and held and raised them, and was done. For the thousandth, ten thousandth, millionth time the most ancient of all acts had been performed under the tree of *fia fia,* and a man and woman lay close and tight, close and spent, in each other's arms. And the Man of the West, who had said, "No more thinking today," allowed himself just one thought, and the thought was, "Dear God, it can be so simple." And the Woman of the Island sat up, picked a burr from her hair, and said cheerfully, "Now we eat."

Rising, she rewound her lava-lava about her waist; then standing on tiptoe, plucked a breadfruit from an overhanging bough. Though without a knife, she got its skin off with nail and tooth and broke the fibrous white inwards into even crescents. Carr, still lying at full length, merely nibbled at his share as she forced it on him, but she devoured hers with gusto and, when it was gone, picked another fruit from the tree.

"Is good for you," she said. "After the love the breadfruit makes you strong again." And under her urging he took a few more bites, while she munched on busily.

When she had finished she went to the edge of the bank and, lying prone, drank from the pool. Then for a few minutes she disappeared among the trees, and when she returned she had with her two fresh gardenias which she was twining into her hair. Sitting beside Carr, she completed the operation and, when it was done, leaned back with a contented sigh, her head resting on his stomach.

"Yes, is *fia fia*," she murmured.

He nodded.

"And that is nice. Do you not think so?"

"With you it's nice," he said.

"Pastor Solomona, he does not think this sort of *fia fia* is ever nice. In church he talks about it, and he says it is lewd and las—lasc—"

"—ivious?"

"Yes, ivious. He says it is not ivious only when you are married. But who wants to get married?"

She looked at Carr again. "You—are you married, Meesh?" she asked.

He shook his head.

"That is good. And I am not either. My people, they want me all the time to get married: to Patali, the son of Chief Tafutimo, who is a jerk. But I say no, I will not, I will marry no one. With marrying, what would it be with my dancing, with the movies, with making love with who I like? If I am wife to Patali and am here with you, he comes whoosh swoosh after with a knife. . . . No, with marrying it is like with thinking: it is only *pilikia*, only trouble. But without, it is nice, it is *fia fia*. Like this—" She kissed his cheek. "And this—" She kissed his lips. "And if it is ivious," she said, "I do not care."

Again they did not speak for a while. He had propped himself to a sitting position, with his back to the tree, and she nestled against him, her head on his shoulder. His hand lay on hers. He was looking down at the hands. And now he was thinking of the other hands . . . the hand of Carol Loftus on the moonlit beach . . . of his wife Margaret, his wife Helen, on the other beaches . . . the white hands of white women lying tight and tense beneath his own. He had wanted his touch to mean something to those hands. He had wished for words that could help and comfort. But there had been a hand on a hand, and that was all. No touch, no word could find a way through to the inward self: the self that each had brought with her as her baggage—even as he too had brought his own.

Va'ina's hand was brown. It was not tight and tense; it needed no comfort; she needed no words. And as for her baggage—well, there it was. All the intangibles, all the problems and doubts and fears and frustrations of a more complex world, could flow and ebb, rise and fall—and there it would still be, as it had been before them. . . . The baggage of *fia fia,* in the shade of a breadfruit tree; in the world of no *pilikia,* of no trouble at all.

Carr looked up at the tree. And it too: there it was. Eighteen years before, he had sat beneath it, exactly as he sat now, and in the time between he had seen it often in his mind, cool and gentle, calm and still, beside the hidden pool. The girl, Carol Loftus, had been right. Something had happened to him here that "had meaning," and he had searched for the meaning in the tree itself. At many times, in many places, he had searched; but now at last, back beneath it at last, he would have to search no longer. For now at last he knew. Whatever meaning there was existed not in the tree but in himself. The tree had no meaning. It needed no meaning. Like the sky beyond it, like earth and sea and building coral—like the brown hand in his and the dark head on his shoulder—it was simply there. It *was.*

And that was all. And enough.

But now the dark head moved a little, and Va'ina's eyes were looking up at him. "You think again, Meesh," she said.

"Just a little," he answered.

"That is all right. Because I think too."

"That's bad, isn't it?"

"How I think now is not bad. It is nice. I think that maybe you and I we have a baby."

Carr sat up straight.

"*What?*" he said.

"A baby. Like so—" She made a cradling movement with her arms. "Yes, I would like, I think. It would be nice."

"But—"

"Many of the girls in the village they have babies. When they are nineteen like me, they have already one, two, three, and I have yet none at all."

"But if you don't want a husband—"

"A husband, no." She made a face. "But a baby, that is different. That is good. A little baby that I will come and play with. And when I am away—when I am busy with love and dancing and movies—then my mother will take care."

There was a pause. Then—

"Your mother?" he said.

"Yes, Polu, the wife of Fahoai. My aunt-mother."

"Not your real one?"

"No. My real one she is dead."

There was another pause. And out of it, presently, Carr heard the sound of his own voice.

106

"And she—your mother—" he said, "was called Lovana?"

The girl looked at him in surprise. "How do you know this name?" she asked.

"I—I heard it somewhere. From someone who said that you look like her."

"Yes, they say that. That Lovana was pretty too. Like me." Va'ina made the statement simply, as a declaration of fact. "But she was not my mother," she said. "She was the sister of my mother."

"And is dead?"

"They are both dead. It is long now. They die at the same time in a how-you-say, epidemic, while there is still the war. My sister Mena and I are babies; and Lovana has just had my cousin John; and so—"

"John?"

"Yes, John Koa. You have seen him, yes? He is the son of my aunt Lovana, from a *papalagi* who was here in the war. But then she dies; my mother dies; John and Mena and I, we have no mothers. So Polu she is aunt-mother and takes care of us. Like she will take care of my baby and—"

She stopped, her eyes questioningly on his face. "What is it?" she asked. "Why do you look so? You do not want the baby?"

Carr didn't answer.

"You think it is *pilikia*. But no, it is not. For me there are Polu and Mena to take care. And for you it will be nothing. You will not ever see it. Like the *papalagi* father of John, who is poof, here—poof, gone—and does not even know there is a son at all."

Carr had risen. And now she too rose, standing close beside him. "Meesh, please," she said. "Do not be angry, please—"

He shook his head.

"You are not? . . . Good. . . . But you are now not happy. You think again, you make *pilikia,* and that is bad." She put her arms around him. "Instead, we will make *fia fia*. We will be happy, yes? Like before. Like when I kiss you, so—and so—and so—"

And she kissed him. She pulled him down. They were lying again on the moss beneath the breadfruit tree, and her soft face and flowered hair were close above him, and beyond them the tree, the foliage, and the shining sky.

"Now we are ivious again," she said, smiling. "Yes, Meesh? We have *fia fia* and are happy, the same as before."

And he nodded. He said, "Yes." He smiled back at the niece of Lovana and the cousin of John Koa.

But the time of *fia fia* was gone.

8

THE CORAL engineers built on. . . .

But now they had competition.

Through the break in the reef and across the lagoon came the
Harold L. Ickes, towing two barges behind it, and from them, in
massive array, the twentieth century spilled out upon Tiara's shore.
There were trucks and jeeps. There were tractors and a bulldozer.
There were pumps, generators, tanks, pipes, girders, cables, cement,
lumber. And there were nails, screws, wallboard, flooring, stoves, re-
frigerators, basins, bathtubs. Tiarans who had lost interest in the
hotel site in its phase of tree-felling and road-widening now flocked
by the hundred to watch the show, and the route from wharf to
cleared slope was like the midway of a carnival. Everything that came
ashore received its share of staring—and, if possible, of touching. But
the show-of-shows was the rumbling concrete mixer, on its yellow
caterpillar mounting, and the twenty-four gleaming toilet bowls, pre-
maturely uncrated, that presently stood ranged like monuments before
the hillside quonsets.

As various as their tools and trappings were the men who came
with them. Their trades were mason, carpenter, fitter, joiner, roofer,
plumber, painter, electrician. Their names were Johnson, Ashimoto,
Fu San, Goldberg, Carvalho, Spitz, Hamalua, O'Neill. The *Ickes*
and its barges disgorged them with their mountains of gear and
lumbered back to Apingo for more. And the Tiarans stared at them
no less than at concrete mixer and toilets. Especially did they stare
and wonder at Fred Hamalua, seven-eighths Hawaiian and master
fitter for the Diamond Head Pipe and Joint Company, who was at

one and the same time obviously a *papalagi* of full status and a man of the islands such as themselves.

"He is perhaps the King of Hawaii," ventured an old woman who could conceive no other explanation.

But her husband, who had been around more, set her straight. "No, stupid one," he said. "It is that in Hawaii every man is king, because they are all Americans. Here we are not yet Americans, but only belong to them."

The men filled the quonsets. Machines and supplies filled the groves and shorefront. To the disappointment of the onlookers, the dazzling toilet bowls disappeared into a shed; but the mixer and the trucks and the yellow cats not only remained in view but began to function, and each hour, each day, new wonders were unveiled from out of opened sacks and crates and bales and boxes. Enough firewood was now at hand so that no one would have to chop for it for weeks to come. And enough beer, too, so that a little spilled over into the public domain. Responding to such lures, Tiarans reapplied for jobs, until there were some thirty of them at work; Tom Taki's crew of Utoians had more than doubled its original number; and, including the "Hawaiians," there was now a labor force of more than eighty. By day, the birthing of the Tiara Beach Hotel began in earnest, to an obbligato of shouts, rumbles, thuds, and grinding gears. At night, the radio blared, the empty beer cans multiplied, and the stakes of the poker game in the foremen's quonset crept up from a ten- to a fifty-cent limit.

Mel Melnick had returned on the *Ickes* and, once his stomach had settled, moved restlessly about from shore to crest of slope, from pile of earth to hole in the ground, replete with energy, orders—and a clip-board of notes. With the main work of construction now in full swing, he was in a euphoric phase, and was presently even able to forget that the laundry in Apingo had ruined three of his luau shirts and two pairs of slacks. But his war with Tiara's mosquitoes was yet to be won; and each evening he prowled the premises on solitary patrol, armed with spray guns of insecticide.

Frank Lavery, too, was everywhere, but in his own fashion—slow, calm, heavy-footed—and whereas Melnick's speciality was posing problems, his was solving them. He was a dull man, a stolid matter-of-fact man, whose spirit was a fleshy as his red face and bulging paunch. So far as Carr knew, he had never once, during his weeks on Tiara, had the curiosity to leave the hotel site; and after working hours his sole interests were poker (with gin rummy as occasional variant) and beer (which might or might not be laced with bourbon). But come the next morning, he was always totally on the job, totally competent and in control of what went on. Mitchell Carr knew his sort: from a hundred jobs in a hundred construction camps and city lots. And it was the sort to have where men were building. The Frank Laverys of the world had, perhaps, little to contribute to its wisdom or graciousness; but without them there would be no cities, no factories, no bridges or dams or tunnels—and no Tiara Beach Hotel.

Carr himself was now mainly involved with the masons and foundation workers; with the holes in the ground and what went into them. And along with Melnick and Lavery he took part in general supervision. For the first time since the blasting of the lagoon he was busy all day, every day. And he was glad of it. He sank himself into it. Like Lavery, he drew his boundaries around the shore, the slope, and the world that was taking shape there, with the world beyond excluded and gone. There was no forest path, no pool and breadfruit tree, no golden Va'ina.

. . . Or cousin of Va'ina. . . .

At least not in the days. When night came, and he lay alone in his cot in the quiet darkness, it was another matter.

Toward the end of the first week after the invasion two visitors appeared in official capacities. The first was Talking Chief Fahoai, in full regalia of office, to extend a formal invitation to all on the hotel project to a ceremonial welcome at the village a few days hence; and this time—Melnick's mood being still euphoric—all was smooth politeness, with no ruffled feathers. The second visitor, appearing the following morning, was Leonard Shafter, who arrived on one of the return trips of the *Harold L. Ickes.*

Shafter too, it soon developed, was involved in the village welcome. For he had, he said, discussed the matter at length during his last visit there, and was obviously pleased that the invitation had finally, if belatedly, been extended. For some time he spoke with Melnick, Lavery, and Carr about the touchiness of Chief Tafutimo, the conservatism of the older villagers, the importance of dealing with them tactfully. And he asked them to pass the word on to the newcomers from Hawaii.

"No trouble yet," Melnick assured him, "and there's not going to be. So long as they treat us right, we'll treat them twice as good." And he went on to list—not for the first time—how many he could use, once the hotel opened, as waiters, maids, dishwashers, cleaners, gardeners. "If they'll get off their asses I'll make them real pros," he said. "And they'll be earning more in a month than they ever saw before in a lifetime."

Later, alone with Carr, Shafter pursued the subject further.

"You've been here a while now," he said, "and I think you've—

well—the feel of the place more than the others. I'll be coming over often from here on, to hear complaints and try to settle problems—and there'll be plenty, you can count on that. But between times, if there's anything you can do, or at least keep me posted on—"

"I haven't been off the place lately," Carr told him. "And not to the village since the first day."

"You haven't met Tafutimo then?"

"No."

"Or Mrs. Mundy?"

"No."

"What about Miss Loftus? How's she getting along?"

"All right, I'd say—though I don't know much there either. She comes over every day or two to look after the workmen, and she's a first-rate nurse, no question of that. But she does her job, goes back to the village, and that's all we see of her."

Shafter mused for a moment. "She's a strange sort of girl," he said. "Especially for such an attractive one. I was talking about her to Dr. Friede over in Apingo the other day, and he doesn't get her either; says he doesn't know what makes her tick."

"She wants to be on her own," said Carr. "She has something to prove to herself."

"I suppose so. . . . Well, let's hope she's proving it. . . . Meanwhile, as Friede says, I guess we should be grateful there's someone who *wants* to be out here."

They were walking toward the Government jeep, in which Malele the policeman was waiting to take Shafter to the village. And for a few moments they said nothing further.

Then Carr asked: "Have you heard anything from the Air Force?"

"The Air Force?"

"About the boy here. John. John Koa."

"Oh. . . . No," said Shafter. "No, we haven't."

"Do you think there's any hope?"

"No, not much."

"Why?"

"Well, for one thing, it's the first application from Manaia, and you know how the Services hate 'firsts.' Also, the Air Force likes college degrees when it can get them, and when it can't, at least accredited high schools. The school in Apingo does a decent job on what it's got to work with, but it's a long way from being accredited."

"But if a boy's outstanding—"

"It's pretty hard to be outstanding when the ones you want to see you are five thousand miles away." They had reached the jeep, and

Shafter climbed in beside Malele. "Has John been working here?" he asked.

Carr shook his head.

"Or been around?"

"No. I haven't seen him since the day he came back from Apingo after sending that cable."

Shafter looked at him curiously. "You seem interested in him, though," he said.

"Yes, I am."

"Well, I'll be seeing him in the village and have a talk with him. Lord knows I want to help him if I can."

The jeep drove off, and Carr walked back to the headquarters hut. Arriving, he was greeted with the news that ground water was seeping into the foundation hole for the main building, and that kept him busy for the rest of the day. But on his cot that night, in the darkness, it was again another matter. And again he heard Shafter's voice saying, "I'll have a talk with him. I want to help him."

So would he, Mitchell Carr, have had a talk with John Koa—if he had known how to help or what to say.

In the house of Tafutimo, high chief of Tiara, the *matai* and elders of the village were gathered in council. Tafutimo, lean-bodied, lion-headed, sat cross-legged before his chiefly post, with Fahoai, plump and smooth, in the position opposite, and the others, numbering perhaps a dozen, in between. All were wearing lava-lavas, with Tafutimo further adorned by a necklace of red pandanus fruit, as was proper to his rank on such occasions. And all were rolling sennit against tattooed thighs—save only Fahoai who, instead, held a fountain pen and sheaf of papers.

It was he who was in charge of arrangements for the reception that would be given the hotel builders two nights hence, and for some time now he had been checking with the *matai* on what the family of each would supply for the feast. The list was long and various. Some of the men doubted they could supply all that was required of them. And a few were reluctant to supply anything at all.

"In their storehouses," said one, "these *papalagi* have enough for a hundred feasts, but I do not see them giving one for us."

"What has that do to with it?" asked Fahoai. "And why should they? It is we of the island who are the hosts, and they are our guests."

"Not guests," said another *matai*. "Invaders."

"Soon the island will not even be ours, but theirs. They will take it from us."

"And why should we give a feast for such as these?"

Thus far, Tafutimo had taken little part in the talk, but had sat looking down at his roll of sennit, a brooding expression on his heavy features. Now, however, he raised his head and spoke, and the others were silent.

"The feast will be held," he said in a slow, deep voice. "Strangers have come among us, and we will do our duty by the laws of Manaian hospitality."

Fahoai nodded. And so did the old man of his household, Kalamakoa, who sat hunched and skeletal beside him. "*Fa'a Manaia,*" the old man murmured. "So it must be: *fa'a Manaia.*"

"And each family," said the high chief, "will provide what is required of it."

He looked at the others, and now they too nodded. Fahoai made check marks against his list with his pen and turned to another sheet in his sheaf of papers.

"And now there is the matter of drink," he said.

"Drink? What about drink?"

"There is kava and coconut milk. What more is needed?"

"I was thinking we should perhaps have beer," said Fahoai.

"Beer?"

"Yes. The *papalagi* always like beer. And there is some on hand at Asimo's store."

The *matai* exchanged glances: some undecided, some shaking their heads.

Then Tafutimo spoke again.

"No," he said, "there will be no beer. For a thousand years we have had our feasts without such things as beer, and so we shall continue to have them—in the old way of our people."

A murmur of assent ran through the gathering. And old Kalamakoa nodded. "*Fa'a Manaia,*" he said again.

"They will bring their own anyhow," said one of the others.

"And whisky too, probably."

"Yes. When the *papalagi* come, there are always two things they bring with them: their machines and their whisky."

"What? You mean they will bring their machines too? Here—to the village?"

"Of course."

"The yellow monsters—the things that shake and roar and tear—they will all come."

"They will knock down our houses, crush the taro and yams."

"Do not talk like fools," said Fahoai, "Such machines are for digging, scraping, building the hotel. They will not bring them here to the village."

"Not some, perhaps. But others, yes. You do not think they will walk here, do you? Or all ride on Malele's bicycle?"

"There will be all the jeeps."

"And the trucks."

"And they will roar down the street killing pigs and chickens."

"Nonsense," said Fahoai. "I tell you—"

But he was interrupted at once.

"Already," said one *matai*, "I have seen chickens dead on the coast road."

"Soon," said another, "there will be none left to eat."

"And with the fish it is even worse."

"Yes."

"With the noise and shaking of the earth, the fish are afraid and leave their feeding grounds. Yesterday my two sons and I, we fish for six hours off the reef, and in all that time we catch two *anae* and one *malauli.*"

"And even the squid—"

"And the crabs—"

The voices were growing louder. But now they, in turn, were interrupted, as a sound came from beyond the *fale* and a jeep pulled in off the road and stopped beneath a nearby tree. At the wheel was Malele the policeman; beside him, Leonard Shafter; and as the latter got out and approached, the council sat in waiting silence. They were not taken by surprise. The administrator was expected. But now, *fa'a Manaia,* the meeting would continue in different fashion.

Shafter knew the rules too. Stopping just beyond the hut's encircling pillars, he addressed himself to Tafutimo and asked, "May I have the honor of joining the council?" And when the high chief answered, "It is our honor, and you are welcome," he came on in. In accordance with custom, the *matai* did not rise, but remained as they were, seated against their posts, while he went the rounds shaking hands in order of precedence. Meanwhile, at a signal from Tafutimo, one of the lower ranking men brought a chair from a corner and set it in the center of the hut. But, the handshaking over, Shafter declined it with thanks and, instead, selected a vacant post midway between Tafutimo and Fahoai and sat cross-legged upon a mat, as did the others.

From the moment of the jeep's arrival a crowd of villagers had surrounded it and now most of these, augmented by others, had gathered around the *fale* to watch the proceedings. None spoke, however, and none ventured beyond the ring of pillars, until, presently Tafutimo clapped his hands and two young men came forward carrying a bowl and the ingredients for kava. Squatting on the pebbled floor, they prepared the ceremonial drink. Fahoai, rising, made a formal speech of welcome, and Shafter replied briefly in slow, careful Manaian. The cup was passed and raised and drained. The *manuias* and *soifuas* were said. Then Shafter produced cigarettes, which were accepted by perhaps half the council—including Fahoai but not Tafutimo.

Shafter mentioned the weather. It was good, all agreed.

He presented greetings from the Governor, Mr. Gorman, and others in Apingo, and these were accepted and returned.

How, he asked, was the copra crop shaping up? Very well, he was told. . . . The fishing? That was good too. . . . The new village pump? Excellent. . . . And Miss Loftus? All was well with Miss Loftus? Yes, Miss Loftus was excellent too.

A short silence followed. Shafter glanced at his watch and, seeing that he had now been there the requisite time, cleared his throat.

"And with the welcoming feast?" he asked. "Is everything going smoothly?"

Chief Tafutimo nodded. "Very smoothly," he said.

"There are no problems?"

"No."

"The hotel people are grateful for your hospitality. They want very much to have a good relationship with the village."

The chief nodded, without speaking.

"And if there's any way they can help you—or if they're causing any difficulty for you—they'd like to know about it, so they can do what's necessary. Feel free to speak to them about it at any time. Or better yet, tell me, and I'll pass the word on."

The chief nodded a third time.

"There is nothing now?" Shafter asked.

"No."

"Nothing at all?"

Tafutimo considered for a long moment. Then he said: "Yes, there are a few things."

"What?"

"There are the men who work at the hotel. Before, there were only a few; now there are many. It is three miles from here to the hotel, and they do not like to walk so far twice a day. So they stay there. They sleep in shacks by the lagoon and do not come back at all. And the women are unhappy."

This was a valid complaint. Shafter thought it over and said, "Yes, six miles a day is too far, and the hotel needs many workmen. I'll speak to them over there and see if they can't send a truck back and forth."

Tafutimo's face was noncommittal. But a few of the *matai* nodded, and Fahoai said, "Yes, a truck, that is what is needed. . . . And then later, when the hotel is open, perhaps a bus."

"A bus?" The high chief looked across at him challengingly. "And why do we need a bus? Especially after the hotel is open and the work is through."

"Because when it is open even more will go there. Not only men but women. Mr. Melnick has given me a list of all he will need: for waitresses, chambermaids, and at night of course for the dancing. And these, with the men, will make—let me see—"

He consulted one of his papers, but Tafutimo did not let him go on. "Waitresses—chambermaids—dancing?" he said. "I have heard nothing of all this."

"It is—"

"It is one of the things I have come to speak about," Shafter put in quickly. "When the hotel is open it will be a busy place. A large staff will be needed to run it, and it is the hope both of the management and of the Government that many will be people of Tiara."

"Many? You say many. And with all these at the hotel, who will be left here?" Tafutimo demanded. "With the women, who will cook? Who will wash and tend the taro and take care of the children? And with the men, who will fish, pick the coconuts, dry the copra?"

His voice had risen, and his eyes flashed angrily. "I am the high chief of Tiara," he said, "and I must know, I must understand such things before I let them happen. Will you explain please, Mr. Shafter?"

Shafter took a deep breath that was almost a sigh. But before he could speak again there was an interruption from the crowd that still stood, watching and listening, around the edge of the *fale*. "And there is another thing too," a voice said, "that you will please explain—"

All in the hut looked up as John Koa stepped in between two of the posts.

"What are you doing here?" said Fahoai sharply.

But John, ignoring him, addressed himself to Shafter. "There is much talk, sir," he said, "of what will happen when the hotel is built. How many will work there, at this, at that; as maids and waiters and cooks and cleaners. But may I ask this: What else will it bring to the people of Tiara? Besides wages, which we do not need. . . . Will we own the hotel? No. Will we run it? No. That we do not expect. . . . But answer this, please. Will we even be allowed in it, except as servants? Will it be our hotel, too, that we work and change our lives for, or only for tourists—*white* tourists— while we are outside—the natives, the gooks—and not fit to come in?"

Shafter had raised his hand. "John, John—" he was saying.

Fahoai had risen to his feet.

But it was the voice of Tafutimo that now sounded through the *fale,* harsh and loud.

"Quiet, boy!" he commanded. "How dare you come here and disturb our council? . . . Go! Go now, or I will have you whipped before the whole village."

John turned to him, courteous but uncowed. "Yes, I will go," he said. "I meant no offense to the council or to Mr. Shafter. But what I have said must be said. Change will come to Tiara. If we are not fools, all of us know it. But the important thing is not a matter of machines, but of men—of *us.* How will it be for us in this new Tiara, Mr. Shafter? Will we be free and equal men on our own island? Or gooks and savages: fit to wait on the white man, but nothing else. Not to enter the hotel; not to eat or drink or swim with the *papalagi;* not to vote or speak our minds or touch the white man's power or fly the white man's planes or—"

Fahoai had seized his shoulder.

"Out! Get him out!" said Tafutimo.

But John did not wait to be ejected. Slipping from his uncle's grasp, he moved quickly across the *fale,* between the posts, through the gaping crowd—and was gone.

There was a silence. Then Fahoai, visibly shaken, turned to Shafter and the high chief. "I am sorry," he said. "Most humbly I apologize for this exhibition. The boy is wild, crazy. Since he is back from Apingo—"

His voice trailed off. Returning to his place, he sat down, composed himself, and reclaimed his pen and sheaf of papers. "Now, where were we?" he said. "At beer? No, we were finished with beer. . . . Ah yes, at buses. . . . Mr. Shafter, you were saying there would be a truck, and perhaps later a bus, so that our people . . ."

In the house of Fahoai, across the palm grove, the women of the family were not idle. Polu, his wife, sat at the sewing machine, her bulk billowing out from one of the flimsy chairs, as she stitched the hems into new store-bought lava-lavas. Mena, her elder niece, sat on the floor nearby, weaving a pandanus mat and humming "Rock of Ages." Perched on the bed, off to one side, Va'ina was inspecting her *taupou's* costume which she would wear for her dancing at the welcoming feast.

For some time there had been no conversation; only the whir of the machine and the murmur of Mena's voice humming the hymn. But now Va'ina glanced in annoyance at her sister and said, "Can't you, for God's sake, think of something else?"

Mena stopped and said primly, "There is no reason to use the

Lord's name so. But yes, of course, I know many songs. Would you perhaps like 'A Mighty Fortress' or 'Mine Eyes Behold Thee'?"

"I would like—let me see—'Yellow Dog Whammy,' please. The way Mr. Elavis Presaley sings it on the radio."

Mena did not bother with a reply, and Va'ina supplied the humming for herself. As she went on, her beat grew faster, she began to sway to it, and then, holding her costume against her, she jumped from the bed and began dancing about the *fale*.

Then John came in.

He did not speak to his aunt and cousins, but went silently to a far side of the hut and sat down against a post. After a few moments he rose again and made as if to leave; then changed his mind and resumed his place, staring across the hut with unseeing eyes and rubbing his thin face with his hand.

Va'ina glanced at him and interruped her performance. "I know another nice song—just for you," she said. "It is called 'You Are My Sunshine.' "

John looked away from her and said nothing.

And she sang:

You are my sunshine, my only sunshine,
You make me happy when skies are gray.
You'll never know, dear, how much I love you;
Please don't take my Miz Loftus away—

John jumped to his feet. Polu looked up from the sewing machine and was on the point of speaking, but then thought better of it and put a new length of cloth under the needle. Mena had stopped her humming, but went on with her weaving, as John crossed the hut and confronted Va'ina.

"You are very funny, aren't you?" he said.

"Yes," she agreed, "I am funny. A *taupou* she is an entertainer, you see. She must dance and sing and make funny sayings, so that for everyone there will be *fia fia*."

"I do not—"

"No, you do not like the *fia fia*, my poor cousin. I know. You like only the *pilikia* and to make your long face longer, like a fish with a toothache."

"If you speak of Miss Loftus again—"

She raised a pert face. "So? If I speak of her, then what?"

"Then I will speak some myself. About your *papalagi* friend—this man at the hotel—"

"Ah, Mr. Melnick, yes. I have not yet met Mr. Melnick, but I am sure he *will* be my friend. I will dance for him at the feast, my

118

taupou dances"—she held up her costume—"and he will clap, he will say '*Malo!*' and—"

"I am not talking about Melnick."

"No?"

"I am talking of the other one, the tall one, whose name is Carr."

"Carr?" Va'ina wrinkled her forehead. "Carr?" she repeated. "I do not think I know anyone of that name."

"You know him all right. You've been seen going up in the hills, and he too, at the same time, and if you do not keep your mouth shut about—"

He stopped abruptly, as a sound came from beyond the *fale,* and turning, he saw Fahoai and Shafter approaching through the palm grove. His cousin forgotten, he wheeled about. He squared his shoulders and stood waiting. . . .

But suddenly he had a change of heart. He took a step sideways, then backward. His eyes darted about: toward his aunt, his cousins, the two approaching men. Then quickly he turned and ran out through the far side of the *fale.*

He walked for an hour. For two. For three. He went to the hills, the cliffs, the beach, and at low tide walked out to the reef beyond the beach and along the coral ramps beside the booming surf. He let his feet lead him wherever they would—except back to the village.

It was not that he was afraid of his uncle and Shafter. Or of Tafutimo either. It was simply that to confront them would be useless, hopeless: a rush of words from them: from him defiance, or penitence; which, it didn't matter, for in the end it would all lead to the same result—nothing. That was all Tiara was for him now—nothing—and every moment of the five months since he had returned to it from high school in Apingo, he had been bored and stifled. In the family *fale,* with his uncle's speeches and the women's chatter. With the young men of his age, who talked of nothing but fish and coconuts and what girl they hoped to sleep with that night. With the girls, who did not talk at all, but only giggled. With the blankness of days and nights in a rundown barnyard, to which the only alternative was chopping down trees for the white man's hotel. His outburst at the council had been prompted not by a hope of accomplishing anything (for he had well known that he would be thrown out) but by the seething within him that had long been building up toward explosion.

All right, he could explode. He could pour out what he thought and felt, without care for the consequences, but what good did that do? And now he was not only rotting away, he was being badgered and harried. And about that he could do nothing. He had talked—what?—three or four times with the nurse, Miss Loftus (the first time with an explosion he had regretted, the other times quietly, pleasantly), and not only his cousin but the whole village was full of gossip and jokes about it. Half the people, headed by his Uncle Fahoai, condemned him for not working at the hotel; the other half, of Tafutimo's stripe, for not becoming a fisherman or copra drier. And now, apart from any official punishment—he cared nothing about that—he would never hear the end of his performance before the council. Already that afternoon, as he had tried to slip unnoticed from the village, Patali, the son of Tafutimo, had seen and accosted him with a smirk, saying, "I hear my father is resigning so that you can take over." And it had required every ounce of his self-restraint not to punch the jeering face.

Even now, alone on the reef, his hands were balled into fists, as if he were about to strike out at the foaming sea. Looking down at them, he forced them open, forced himself to breathe slowly and deeply, and thought, "I am not a child any more. I am a man, and must act like a man. . . . But how?" The next thought followed swiftly, bitterly. By doing what? What *could* he do? . . . What besides waiting, waiting, for a message from over the ocean that did not come? That he knew now, in his heart, would never come.

As the tide rose he returned to the beach, and from the beach to his familiar perch on the cliffs beyond. Here, in happier times, he had sat by the hour looking out at the sea, and his heart had swelled with the vision, the promise, of what lay beyond it. But now there was no vision, no promise. The sea was the monstrous wall of his prison. And he looked away. He looked to his left, and there was the village; to his right, and there was the lagoon, and beside it the cleared, scarred break in the shore line that would soon be the new hotel. And he thought, yes, you are between them, that is exactly where you are—between—and you belong to neither, you are part of neither, and never will be. . . . Suddenly his hands were fists again. His body was trembling. Even in this place, the place of old happiness, of solitude and dream, there was no longer refuge; he was no longer safe. . . . And, still trembling, he rose and plunged blindly down through the brush.

He waited until it was night before entering the village, and even then avoided the road, cutting circuitously through the palm groves between the *fales*. But as he passed by the rear of the old shed that housed Asimo's store, a voice spoke his name, and in the dim light he saw Asimo sitting on the ground nearby, his back propped against a tree. Murmuring an answer, he was about to pass on. But the storekeeper spoke again, saying, "Hey, what's the rush? Can't you stop and be friendly?" And something in the voice must have held him, for he did stop, and after a moment approached Asimo, as the latter beckoned.

"Don't look leery. I'm not one of those that's going to chew you out," the storekeeper told him. "I hear you spoke your piece today, and I say nice work. I'm going to drink to you."

He reached for a calabash that stood beside him, tilted it up, and drank deeply. "Now you," he said, holding it out.

"No. No thank you," said John.

"Go on," said Asimo. "It'll put hair on your chest. You want hair on your chest, don't you?"

John hesitated for another moment. Then he took the calabash, raised it, and drank. It contained bush beer, made of fermented orange juice, but the orange flavor was only vaguely perceptible in the tide of alcohol. John had sampled the island home brews before, but in small sips, surreptitiously, with other boys of the village, and now, taken at full swallow, the thick syrupy liquid seared his throat like a flame.

He coughed. And the storekeeper laughed. "Tuu Asimo's magic health tonic," he said. "Guaranteed two hundred proof and nationally advertised." He patted the ground beside him. "Sit down, boy," he urged. "Take a load off and tell me all about it."

John sat beside him, and Asimo drank again and passed the calabash. "So you gave it to 'em," he said. "By God, that's good. Right in Tafutimo's teeth—the old bastard. And Shafter's too. Another bastard."

"I didn't mean—"

"Yeah, I know. Shafter seems all right outside, with all that mush-mouthed professor stuff. But don't buy it. Inside, he's a *papalagi* bastard, the same as all of them." Asimo took the calabash back and leaned forward across it, so that his face was less than a foot from John's. "Maybe you don't know that yet," he said. "But I do, and I'm telling you: they're all the same. You haven't been off these islands. I have. I've been on their own grounds—three years I was there, in California—and they fixed me good. Look at me. And now they're here, and they're going to fix this place too. But good. The island and the village and heap big chief Tafutimo and that uncle of yours and all the rest of 'em. And it's fine with me. They got it coming to 'em."

He raised the calabash. "Here's a toast, boy," he said. "To the brown bastards and the white bastards, and the hell with both of 'em."

He drank again. So did John. And once the liquor was past his throat, it was no longer burning but warm and pleasant. As Asimo talked on, they passed the calabash back and forth.

9

THERE WAS the eternal sound of sea on reef. There was a new moon and a sky of stars. But in the first hour of darkness, two nights later, they were scarcely to be heard or seen from Tiara's coastal road. The rumbling of motors filled the ear, the beams of headlights stabbed the eye, as a procession of trucks and jeeps made its way from the hotel site toward the village.

In two of the trucks were Tom Taki's men from Utoia, squatting on the floorboards, with beer cans bouncing beside them or jiggling in raised hands against their lips. And in another smaller truck, plus a jeep, were the men from Hawaii. They too had beer—plus whisky—plus cameras and flash bulbs and fresh shaves and luau shirts—and they were not depressed at the prospect of their first night away from the hotel site since their arrival in Tiara.

In still another jeep, behind, were Melnick, Lavery, Shafter, and Carr. Carr was driving, Melnick sat beside him slapping at bugs, and the other two bounced behind them, with Lavery holding a bottle and a cigar.

"Wonder if that Loftus chick is gonna be there," the contractor mused. "Yeah, sure she will. She's gotta be. And this time I'm gonna get more'n a hello-goodbye out of her, if it's the last thing I do."

"If it's the last thing you do," said Melnick, "get that grader over here and fix up this road. The tourists will yell bloody murder if they have to take a beating like this—"

"She's a real queer one, I'm telling you. Cold as a fish and—"

"—Though the big deal, of course," Melnick went on, "won't be them coming here, but the village coming to the hotel. . . . Did I tell you my idea? . . . After things are going a bit, we build a regular little village, maybe right near the dock—just like their own place only smaller, and without all the dirt and crap. Then we get the natives to come over two or three times a week and make like they're living there. In the daytime they do weaving, carving, mix stuff in bowls. And then at night—twice a week, say Wednesday and Saturday—dancing. That's the big thing, of course: the real honest-to-God South Sea dances. In the real costumes. Except that their own costumes will be so crummy we'll have to have them sent from Honolulu. . . ."

"You know what I think's wrong with that dame, Mitch," said Lavery, leaning over Carr's shoulder. "I think she's a lesbo, by God, that's what I think."

In the dispensary in the village, Carol Loftus, still wearing her uniform, sat at her desk under the single electric light bulb that hung from the ceiling. There was a patient in the adjoining cubicle that comprised her one-bed hospital: a ten-year-old boy suffering from diarrhea whom she thought it best to keep close by for observation. But the last of those who required treatment that day had long since gone, and she was writing her weekly report to Dr. Friede in Apingo. She had already covered developments in the more serious cases: those of TB, advanced filariasis, major intestinal and skin ailments. There had been one death—that of an old woman, from the multiple factors of senility. And no births, though one was expected shortly. She was sending two patients, both ambulatory, to Apingo: one for dental treatment, the other with a suspicious cough that warranted chest X rays.

While she had been dealing with specifics the report had gone easily. But now, as she reached General Comments, it was another matter. *Regarding co-operation and basic attitude of the people,* she wrote, *there is great variation. In fact, it is impossible to* . . . And there she stopped; for that was exactly it. She did not know what to write. In most ways she was satisfied with how things had been going. She had the practical aspects of her work well under control, and the results had been all that could be expected. But when it came to *attitude*—to what the people she dealt with truly thought and felt—she was at a total loss. For the contradictions were endless and unfathomable. It was all very well to say—as did most outsiders—that the islanders were "simply children," moved by a new emotion every five minutes. But she knew that there was far more to it than this; that the roots and causes were subtle and deep.

Again and again, during the past weeks, she had thought of her father, and of what he had said and written of his experience in the Solomons. She had, of course, been only a child then, and he had told his stories on a child's level of outward action and incident; but even so it was plain that he had been among an extremely primitive and simple people. The people of Tiara, on the other hand, were in some ways primitive, but in others far from it. And once you were an inch beneath the surface, they were not simple at all. Indeed, in each of them there seemed to exist not one individual but two: the first so modernized and Westernized as to seem no different from a person in a village back home; the second still wholly embedded in the heritage of his stone-age ancestry. The first warm, friendly, outgoing toward her, as a stranger on the island; the second withdrawn, suspicious, implacably hostile.

There had been the case of a young mother who had voluntarily brought her coughing child in for examination, but, as Carol produced a tongue depressor, suddenly snatched the baby away and ran screaming into the bush. There had been a middle-aged man with skin lesions who had submitted gratefully to her treatment of salve and dressings, only to be found, an hour later, minus dressings, caking his wounds with mud from the village street. There had been three younger men, theretofore highly circumspect in behavior, who one day slaughtered a pig directly outside the dispensary, with the obvious purpose of trying to upset her.

And then of course there was still another young man: the young man—or was it the boy?—called John Koa.

With him, to be sure, it had been very different from the other cases. But these others had been only single incidents, while in John's case there had developed a continuing relationship in which she never knew what would happen next. It had begun with his outpouring of bitterness that day in the dispensary. But almost immediately thereafter he had made her the gift of the tortoise shell. Then he had come twice again to see her—not as a patient, simply to talk—and both times the talk had been easy and pleasant—about things of the village, his family, her shell collection (to which he added more contributions)—until, once each time, she had tried to bring the conversation around to the things that were bothering him, at which point he had instantly closed up and found an excuse for leaving. And since then, when she had seen him on her village rounds, he had alternated between greeting her warmly and going out of his way to avoid her.

Now, sitting at her desk, she thought of possible means by which she might get him to talk again about himself: not wildly, foolishly, as he had that first time, but with calmness and reason. If she possibly could, she wanted to help him. And for him to talk would in

124

itself be a help. . . . As it had been for her, that night on the beach, with Mitchell Carr. . . . At the time, and even more later, she had been astonished that she had poured herself out to him. And embarrassed as well—to the point where she had tried to avoid him on her subsequent visits to the hotel site. But still it had helped: to look backward a moment, to put things in perspective. Even though he had been able to offer no more than a silly jingle and a touch of the hand. Even though he had been almost a total stranger—and for that matter was still a stranger, for she had done all the talking—she still knew nothing about him, except that—

She brought her mind back to John Koa. It was he, not Mitchell Carr, she was thinking about. Or had been. . . . And simultaneously she was conscious of the fact that this same sort of thing had happened before: that thoughts of one often led to thoughts of the other. . . . Partly, of course, it was because they were the only two people on the island, other than Mrs. Mundy, with whom she had had any personal relationship. But there was something else besides; something she had felt but not been able to define. Now she groped for it. And groping, she became aware that there was somehow, somewhere, a certain *likeness* between the two; an almost physical likeness, implausible though it seemed, between the engineer from New York and the brown boy of Tiara. Was it simply that they were built alike: tall, thin, and angular? Or was it more than that? The timbre of their voices, perhaps, or the way they held their heads when they were listening. . . .

She heard footsteps coming through the kitchen from the dwelling part of the house, and Mrs. Mundy appeared in the doorway, wearing her best flowered-print dress.

"My goodness, you haven't changed yet," the old lady said.

"Changed?"

"For the party. It's time to go."

"Oh. I won't be going," Carol said. "I thought I told you."

"Nonsense—of course you're going. Get up this minute and put on your prettiest dress."

"I have a patient." Carol nodded toward the hospital. "I can't leave him."

"Of course you can." Mrs. Mundy poked her head through the door. "He's tight asleep, and he'll stay that way. And besides, Falima will be here all evening."

"No, Falima should go and—"

"She doesn't want to go; says she'd just have to work in a cookhouse all night. And if by some chance you *are* needed, she can come and get you in two minutes."

Carol shook her head. "And—I have my report," she said.

"Fiddlesticks! You've been writing that report for three hours." Mrs. Mundy came closer and rattled the back of Carol's chair. "Come on now," she commanded. "Up with you."

Still Carol did not respond. And now the old lady moved around until she was facing her, and both her voice and manner changed. "Look dear," she said gently, "you're being silly, plain silly. You can't work *all* the time, you know. And when you're not working you can't be alone all the time."

"I'm not alone," said Carol. "I'm with you."

"Me—bah. I don't count. I mean getting away from here. Going places, seeing people. It's not right, not healthy, the sort of life you're living."

"It's the sort of life you live. And you're healthy enough."

"I'm an old woman. You're not."

"And the sort you lived when you were young, too."

"When I was young? You mean I was out here then in these islands—living hard, working hard—the way you are now? Yes, that's true." Mrs. Mundy paused. Then she said with great earnestness: "But with a difference, my dear—a tremendous difference. For I was married, you see. I had a man."

Her upper denture slipped, and she said, "Damn," and pushed at it with her thumb. Then she went on:

"Oh, I won't say my poor Haskell was the Lord's gift to the female sex. I had my troubles with him; plenty of them. . . . But I was no great gift either. I wasn't pretty like you; I was lucky to have a husband at all, and I knew it. And oh my dear, my dear, I'm telling you this and don't you ever forget it: a woman with a man and a woman alone are two *very* different things."

She paused again and chuckled. "Don't look so nervous now," she said. "We're not going out to find a man for you tonight. Just some *men,* in the plural, and some lights and music and fun. Come on now: one, two, three—"

And she went on. She cajoled. She scolded.

And she won.

As Carol rose at last she stood on tiptoe and kissed her, and Carol smiled and kissed her back, and said, "You should have been around to show my mother how to do it."

Then, going to her room, she changed from her uniform into a green cotton dress. She spoke to Falima, the housegirl, about the sleeping patient. And a few minutes later she and Mrs. Mundy left the house and turned into the main road of the village. A truck and a jeep had just pulled up in an open space nearby, and they were greeted at once by shouts and waving beer cans.

"Hey, there's Blondie!"

"Blondie, hell. It's Marilyn."

"Hiya, Marilyn!"

"Hiya, Grandma!"

"C'mon gals, we're off to Buffalo—"

Arms were twined in theirs. They were swept up and along. Ahead was the hum of a great crowd, and torches gleamed through the palm grove.

"Here's mud in your eye, boy," said Tuu Asimo, raising his calabash. "—No, the hell with that. Here's mud in *their* eye. The *papalagi,* the gooks, the whole lot of 'em—" And he drank and passed the orange beer to John Koa.

Tonight it was too crowded in the village to sit outside under a tree, and they were in the back room of the store, with doors closed and windows shaded. From outside they could hear the sounds of the gathering crowd and the rumble of trucks and jeeps coming in from the hotel site.

"And I got another toast," said Asimo. "Here's to the graduating class of Apingo Central High School, rah rah, and may they all learn to drink their bush beer like ladies and gemmen."

These two particular graduates (at an eighteen-year interval) had now been together for about an hour. And this time it was not by accident that John had come, but of his own desire, for he had found in the storekeeper a strangely kindred spirit. He had known him, to be sure, for many years. But only as a boy knows a man, and even thus not well; for Asimo's alternating boisterousness and sullen apathy had never encouraged intimacy. John had of course heard something of his history, and it had interested him. But he knew of his drinking, too, and that had frightened him. . . . Until that hour, two nights before, when he had stumbled upon him in the darkness and discovered their bond of brotherhood.

Now he took the calabash from his new friend and drank deeply and with satisfaction, for in this too there lay a new discovery. Previously he had thought that drinking brought only befuddlement, sickness, trouble. But now he knew that these were lies that had been told him. For what it truly brought was strength and clarity, and a deep, pervading self-confidence that he had never known before.

Indeed, these two sessions with Asimo had been his only endurable hours since the village council. After the first one he had gone home, thinking it was late enough so that everyone would be asleep. But his uncle Fahoai had been waiting up. And he had stormed at him: first for what he had done at the council, and then, when he saw him close and smelled his breath, for his drinking.

"I am ashamed," he had shouted. "I am disgraced before the village, that a son of mine—"

But John had not taken it.

"I am not your son," he had snapped back. With that he had run out and away and spent the night on the beach and cliffs. And there he had not slept, but sat through the hours, brooding, and over and over he repeated to himself what he had said to Fahoai:

"I am not your son. . . . I am not your son. . . ."

It had been the first time he had ever said it aloud. But not the first nor the tenth nor the hundredth that he had thought it in the secrecy of self; for all his life, as far as memory reached, he had known that his true father was a *papalagi,* an American who had come to Manaia during the war. In his early years, as a small boy in Tiara, it had scarcely concerned him at all. Fatherhood, in Manaia, was often a vague affair anyhow; during the war there had been hundreds of half-white children born in the islands; and no one had thought much of it, including himself. It had been when he went to Apingo, to high school, that the change had come for him. Among the white teachers, speaking only English—in a world of Western literature, Western history, Western politics and economics and mathematics and science—he had, month by month, year by year, felt less and less a Manaian, a Polynesian, and more and more a Westerner: an American, like his unknown father. It had been at this time that he had changed his name from Ioane to John (a change back to the original, really, for it was as John that it had come to the islands in the missionaries' gospels). And he would have changed his last one as well, had he known the name of his father.

He felt no resentment of this unknown man. For centuries white men had come to the islands, mated with their women, and disappeared back to their own world; and, like everyone else, he had accepted this as being in the natural scheme of things. But the rest he had not accepted. He had burned with curiosity to know who and what his father was. Almost the only thing he did know—or that anyone on Tiara seemed to know—was that he had been a flyer; indeed, that he had taken his mother (whom he had also never known) on a flight over the island. And it had been this, of course, that had first turned his thoughts to planes and flying.

Nor had it been just a childhood fancy. At high school he had concentrated on math and the physical sciences, and won honors in them. After hours he had haunted the airport, talking his way into hangar and machine shop, crew room and control tower, until he was sure he knew as much about planes and their operation as any nonflyer who ever lived. . . . Yes, he well knew that there had never yet been a Manaian pilot: not even a private one, let alone with the Air Force or a commercial line. But it had not been long ago that there also had been no such thing as a Manaian doctor or lawyer, or even a college graduate. . . . There had to be a first of everything. And he, John Koa, would be the first to fly. That was what he had been born for, what he had lived for, what had sustained him through the years until . . .

Now.

And now it was gone. Finished. Dead.

Now it was an unanswered cable. A shake of the head by Leonard Shafter. A chance to cut down trees for a hotel for people with white faces and full pockets. . . .

In the early morning he walked out from the beach to the reef. And from the reef he plunged into the ocean beyond. He would swim out, he resolved, until a shark got him or a current carried him away. But no shark came. The tide pushed him back toward the reef. He had not even the power to put an end to his misery, and feckless, hopeless, he returned to the beach.

Back in the village—apart from punishment—he would be set to work with the other young men killing pigs and cleaning fish for the feast. So still he stayed in the bush. He ate fruits and shellfish. He spent the next night out, and the next day, and not until evening of that day, with the feast about to start, did he make his way back to the village—and Asimo's store—and Asimo's orange beer. And here again, at last, there was companionship and refuge.

Or at least there *had* been companionship. While the calabash passed. While Asimo talked on: of his days in America, his disgust with it, his disgust with Tiara, with everyone in it—"except of course you, my fellow alumnus, my colleague in learning, who along with me are destined for higher things. . . ." But now the beer was working differently on the storekeeper. His voice grew thick and became a mumble. He began to speak and forgot what he was saying; reached for the calabash and couldn't find it. And then his eyes closed. His head lolled forward on his chest. He rolled over and lay prone.

And John was alone again.

He could find the calabash all right. He took it, held it, drained it. He too, he had decided, would drink until he could drink no more; until his eyes closed and his head fell forward; and then he too would roll over and sleep—and sleep.

129

But it did not work that way. As he drank, he did not grow sleepy. His head felt not heavier but lighter; and his body, too, felt light, his limbs strong, his perceptions quick and clear. He was again conscious of the sounds from outside. Lights gleamed and flared beyond the shaded windows. The stir of the crowd assembling for the feast flowed into the quiet room like an electric current. For several minutes he sat motionless, listening, feeling, until sound and current seemed to envelop him in a mighty tide. Then, rising, he crossed the room, his step light and steady. He opened the rear door and looked about. He went out, closing the door behind him.

Instantly the crowd absorbed him. Surging toward the *malae*— the central open space of the village, where the feast was to be held— it was a crowd of shadows, a weaving, blending mass rather than an assembly of individuals, and he was easily lost in it. Even as he came closer to the *malae,* where ranks of flaming torches gave a brighter light, everyone was too concerned with what lay ahead to pay him any attention. . . . And even if they did, he thought: what of it? . . . In the center of things, giving orders, welcoming their guests, Tafutimo and his Uncle Fahoai would be far too busy to notice him. . . . But if they did, what of it?

He was not afraid of them. Or of anyone.

Past him now went a group of young men carrying a huge roasted pig on a shoulder pole, their half-stripped bodies glistening with the sweat of their exertion. Among them, he saw to his satisfaction, was Patali, the son of Tafutimo. And that was where he too would have been, if things had been otherwise, As Patali passed, he was seized with the impulse to put out a foot to trip and send him sprawling— pig, pole, and all. But he managed to suppress it, and moved on.

Then, to the other side, he saw three of the *papalagi* from the hotel. The three who were not newcomers: the ones called Melnick and Lavery and Carr. Carr was the tall thin one; the one who had something going on—or so he had vaguely heard—with Va'ina. And also the one who had been after him—that night on the road, that day on the dock—with his job talk and his questions and the queer look in his eye. . . . Even now, he suddenly saw, the man was looking at him. The other two were continuing straight along toward the center of the *malae,* but Carr had slowed his pace and was staring— yes—straight at him. He seemed about to come toward him. . . .

And John moved quickly on.

Ahead, now, were other *papalagi*: the new ones from Hawaii. They carried bottles and beer cans, cameras and cigars. They were shouting and laughing. And at their center, with arms in theirs, carried along by the surge of movement, were Mrs. Mundy and Carol Loftus.

Then they were gone too. He moved on again. And he thought, "The hell with them. The hell with them all. Here's mud in their eye—"

They meant nothing to him. Nothing meant anything to him. Nothing except the strength and sureness that filled him as he moved now, lightly, ever more swiftly, through the crowd. For all depression, all misery was magically gone, lost, forgotten. His mind danced to the light of the torches. His heart leapt to the beat of the drums that now came through the palm groves in the spangled darkness. His feet seemed barely to touch the earth. He was walking on air; flying in air. He was a bird in the sky—a flyer in his plane—high and soaring, high and free. . . .

10

THE FEASTING TABLE stretched for perhaps thirty yards down the center of the *malae*. In strict accuracy, to be sure, it was not a table at all; it was a great strip of mats laid end to end on the ground, with narrower mats on either side for the seating of the feasters. But it was as richly laden as the banquet board in any palace of the West.

At intervals along its length, the carcasses of full-grown pigs, fresh from their all-day roasting in underground ovens, rose in vast massifs, like reddish-brown mountains. Between them, by the dozen and score, were lesser mountains of piglet. And between these, in turn, rising from green bases of leaf and frond, were the foothills of the meal's other components: chicken and fish and shellfish; breadfruit and yams and taro and fruits and berries. Some were cooked, some raw; some were served plain, and others in sauces or juices or latherings of coconut cream. And there were scarcely two items in the array that were identical, for each had been made from the special ancestral recipe of the family that had provided it. For drinking, there were wooden bowls of kava and rows of young coconuts with their tops knocked off. And for the guests, though not the hosts, there were knives and forks—if they could be found among the welter of food. On either side, behind the seating mats, a file of tall brush torches, planted in the ground, ran the full length of the "table," enclosing it in a golden oblong of light against the night beyond.

At one end sat High Chief Tafutimo, at the other High Talking Chief Fahoai, each wearing a lava-lava and the pandanus necklace of his office. And between, ranged in two rows, were the lesser hosts and the guests, numbering together some five dozen. There were no young men among the seated Tiarans; only the *matai,* who were the heads of families, and others whose age and background gave them almost equal status. And there were no women, other than Mrs. Mundy and Carol Loftus. The women, girls, and youths of the island—however high their family standing—were the fetchers and carriers, moving in and out between the torches to serve, clear away, and replenish, and between times joining the swarming children, dogs, and village nobodies in outer darkness.

At such a feast, *fa'a Manaia,* there were no speeches or formal kava ceremonial. At the beginning Pastor Solomona intoned grace in the island language; but thereafter all conversation was informal and in English—and with most of it by the guests—for their hosts, also *fa'a Manaia,* concentrated single-mindedly on eating. The mountain ranges of pork crumbled and vanished. The hills and hummocks of other food were leveled, built up again, and releveled to their bases of frond and leaf. For such edibles, in such quantity, were no common thing on the island, and it was old tradition—no less than sound self-interest—to get the full benefit while the getting was good. Nor was the feasting, after the first few minutes, confined to those at the official board. All over the *malae* the other villagers, between their bouts of labor, were soon squatting on the grass and eating too. The *papalagi* did their best. And some, among them Frank Lavery and several of the "Hawaiians," were men of girth and capacity. But they were no match for even the smallest of the Tiarans, who ate and ate, beyond the dreams of white men, and then licked their lips and fingers and rubbed their stomachs and reached for more.

Not only the two chiefs but all the official diners were seated according to protocol: the *matai* and other elders in their traditional places, and the guests spaced between them—though in the case of the latter, and especially the newcomers, there had been some Tiaran puzzlement as to order of precedence. As senior Government representative, Leonard Shafter sat at Tafutimo's right, with Pastor Solomona beyond him. Mrs. Mundy and Carol Loftus were on the high chief's left. Melnick, Lavery, and Carr were at the far end, near Fahoai. And the others were in between—with the "Hawaiians," as *papalagi,* in the positions nearer the chiefs, and Tom Taki's Utoians in the less prestigious middle. It was from this sector, as the feast progressed, that most of the noise came. And presently beer cans had begun to sprout on the terrain where before there had been only kava bowls and coconuts.

At Carr's end most of the conversation had been between Melnick and Fahoai. Or, more accurately, from Melnick *to* Fahoai (on the

133

intricacies of the hotel business), with the talking chief, his mouth full, nodding agreement. Carr himself had talked little, for both Lavery on his left and the *matai* on his right were also absorbed in food; and he too, for a usually moderate eater, had not been neglecting it. Halfway through the meal, Lavery produced his bottle of bourbon from where it had been cached under his thigh, and, receiving Fahoai's permission, passed it around. Melnick took a small drink, and Carr a medium one. The nearby *matai* declined. But Fahoai, after a long-range glance toward the far end of the table, permitted a generous pouring into his now empty coconut shell, and soon after, full mouth or no, began holding his conversational own with Mel Melnick.

At intervals Carr peered out between the torches to where the villagers ate and watched and milled about. But he saw no more of John Koa. Nor had he seen Va'ina at all since his arrival. His guess was she was preparing for the dancing that would come later; and this was presently confirmed by Fahoai's calling their attention to the sound of distant drumming, and saying, "It is the young ones practicing the *siva-siva*."

But where John had gone he had no way of knowing.

The feast moved on toward its end. Then it crept on. Then at last it reached it, and hosts and guests walked out on the *malae,* while women and girls closed in to clear away the remains. Now Carr was alone with Melnick and Lavery, and Lavery passed his bottle again, and Melnick was talking about the feast, and the food and service, and how they would have to do something of the sort once a week over at the hotel.

"—Only better, of course," he said. "Real Waikiki luau style, with a few Manaian gimmicks thrown in." An idea struck him. "Know what I'm going to do? I'm going to get a real *kaukau* chief down here from Honolulu. Someone like Freddy Hoapola at Don Beachcomber's—or, by God, maybe even Freddy himself, if I can pry him away—"

He made a note on a slip of paper. Lavery took another drink and said, "Excuse me now, gents; I got a date with a blonde tomato over there." And Carr, watching him go, saw him join the group of "Hawaiians" that again were surrounding Mrs. Mundy and Carol Loftus.

"Do you know what that Freddy can do?" said Melnick. "He can even make that goddam poi so you can eat it."

Then Fahoai came up. Then a *matai,* and another, and a small lost boy, and two dogs. There was moving, shifting, interweaving, shreds and patches of talk. . . . And then Melnick was elsewhere.

The others had drifted off. And Carr too was drifting: around the *malae,* through the crowd, past a group of women at a cook shed (who wanted him to eat some more), past a group of Utoians (who gave him a beer): finally toward the knot of "Hawaiians," awash in talk, laughter, tilted bottles, and popping flash bulbs. . . . Mrs. Mundy was no longer among them. Indeed, Carr had seen her a few moments before talking to some village women and girls. But Carol Loftus was still there in their midst. And Lavery was making good on his resolve; for there he was at the center, too, one arm about her, the other holding his bottle, while a "Hawaiian" made ready with camera and bulb.

Lavery grinned. Carol managed a smile. The bulb popped. Then Carr moved forward and said to her, "I'm sorry to interrupt, but I have a message for you."

For a moment her face was startled, almost frightened. Then with an "I'm sorry" to the others, she let him lead her away; and when they were off together on the *malae* she looked up at him anxiously.

"The message," he said, smiling, "is that I thought you might like to be rescued."

"Oh," she said, relieved. Then she returned the smile, and it was a better effort than she had made for the camera. "Thank you," she added.

"You seemed rather in danger of becoming Miss Party Girl of Tiara. And that would be strictly out of character."

"Yes, it would, wouldn't it? Anyhow, it was nice of you." She looked up at him for a moment, and then away, and he could feel her unease and embarrassment. "And now I shouldn't be keeping you any longer—" she said.

"Keeping me from what?"

"From the party. From getting around and enjoying yourself."

"And you?"

"I—I really should be looking for Mrs. Mundy."

"Mrs. Mundy's doing all right," he told her. "Can't I be a relief chaperone?"

Their eyes met again, but only briefly. "Thank you," she said. "But—"

"But what?"

"I should think you'd have had enough of me the other night."

"Enough of you?"

"The way I talked, on and on. It must have been for hours."

"It was about ten minutes."

"Even so—I've felt awfully about it. I don't usually behave like that."

"I'm sure you don't. That's why, perhaps, it was good for you."

Again she looked at him—gratefully. But also uncertainly. "Anyhow," she said, "I won't repeat the performance." She glanced at her wristwatch, then around the *malae*. "And besides, the feast's over, and it's getting late and—"

"You're a big girl now. Maybe not a party girl, but a big one, and you can stay up after dinner."

"I—I really should—"

"Yes, of course. . . . Which way do you live?"

"Just down the road." She nodded. "In that direction."

"That's good to know," he said, and led her in the other.

Around them now there was even more sound and movement than before, for the festivities were entering a new phase. The remnants of the feast had been wholly cleared away; a horde of women and girls had brushed off the serving and seating mats and were rearranging them in a great semicircle; and young men and boys were uprooting the torches and replanting them in a corresponding arc behind the mats. The center of the *malae* had been the banqueting ground. Now it would be the dancing ground. From all sides the crowd was converging on the impromptu amphitheater—men and women and children, chiefs and *matai* and guests and nameless shadows—and in the grove beyond, the beat of drums, which had been rising and falling in broken rhythm, grew swiftly louder and nearer. The Manaian *siva-siva* was about to begin.

The mats, forming a curved front row, were reserved for the chiefs, *matai,* and *papalagi* guests; and Carol Loftus made no further protest as Carr led her to a vacant place and they sat down. Next to him, on the other side, was Melnick, beyond him Shafter and Mrs. Mundy and Lavery and the "Hawaiians," and, farther on, Tafutimo, Fahoai, and the other senior hosts. In the row behind were the men from Utoia, lesser village dignitaries, and a few of the ranking Tiaran women, such as Fahoai's wife, Polu, and the wife of Tafutimo. And behind them in turn, and spread out to both sides around the whole circumference of the dancing ground, was almost the whole remainder of the population of the village and, indeed, the island. Pacing before them in a long circuit was Malele the policeman, wearing his cap with brass badge and carrying a cub of polished *toa* wood. But the crowd, though excited, was happy and well-behaved, and his only official acts were occasionally to order back an overeager spectator who was crowding in too closely on the VIPs.

Mrs. Mundy waved at Carol. Lavery glowered at Carr. Carr inquired of Carol if she still thought it was too late for her to be up, and she conceded that she did not.

136

Then the entertainers appeared.

First came the drums, thrusting their way through the spectators at the far side. And there were four of these: three small ones, borne by the drummers themselves and pounded by hand, and a fourth so huge that it was carried on slings by two boys, while the drummer marched behind, thumping with padded sticks. Then the dancers came. First a troop of small children, not more than ten or twelve years old; then, separately, two files of adolescent girls and boys; finally two more files, also separate, of full-grown young men and women. All wore grass skirts, of varying colors, that swirled and glinted in the torchlight, with headdresses of flowers and necklaces of shell or sharks' teeth. Apart from these, all the men and boys and the younger girls were bare above the waist: but the older girls wore halters of tapa cloth or woven fronds over their breasts.

As they appeared, they fanned out into long rows and sat cross-legged on the ground facing the center of the audience. The drummers had established themselves to one side, and it was they who provided the first phase of the performance, setting the tone and mood of what was to follow. There were no other instruments, neither wind nor string, but only the drums and their beat: the small ones sharp and staccato, the big one deep and throbbing, and all increasing in volume and tempo as their overture built toward its climax.

The dancers sat motionless. Or almost motionless, for some of the younger ones were looking about, and a few waved to watching mothers or Mrs. Mundy. Carr's eyes moved along the ranks of the older ones, but he knew that Va'ina would not be there; that, as *taupou* and *première danseuse,* she would make her entrance later, alone.

And John was not there either.

The drums reached climax, paused, then began again. And the children were the first dancers. Their tiny figures were almost overwhelmed by the tide of thumping and booming that swept over them, but they went bravely at it, swaying, whirling, stamping their feet: first the boys alone, then the girls alone, then both together—though still not intermingling; each moving as a separate file, a separate team. Halfway through, a photo bulb flashed in the ranks of the "Hawaiians," at which one of the smallest boys stopped, howled, and ran off—to the delight of the crowd. But the rest kept on to the end, finally returning to their seats in a salvo of clapping and shouts of *"Malo!"*

Then the adolescents came on. Then the young men and women. As with the children, there were male, female, and mixed numbers

137

(with the sexes still divided as teams), but as age increased, so did the repertory and the intricacy of step and rhythm. There were sword and ax dances by the men, and, by the girls, a weaving, swaying sequence not unlike the Hawaiian hula. There was a dance of hands slapping against thighs and biceps; another of paddlers in a tribal canoe; still another in which the performers remained seated throughout, moving only their arms and torsos. Through the kaleidoscope of variety, however, one element persisted, and that was the ever-heightening tempo from one number to the next. Dance by dance, the drumming grew faster. Feet and legs and arms and bodies moved faster. Partly it was because of the nature of the dances themselves, but even more because of a gradual change in those who were doing them: a warming to the business at hand, a throwing off of self-conscious restraint, a submission to the beat and rhythm that soon enveloped them like a kinetic force.

In all the night, now, there were only the weaving bodies; only dance and fire and drumbeat. The earth itself seemed a drum, pounded by naked feet. And as they launched into their final number—the traditional closing dance of courtship and love, in which, at last, men and women were not separated—not opposed teams, but partners—the dancers, in mood and movement, reached a peak of frenzy. They were no longer in the twentieth century, Mitchell Carr thought, watching. No longer on an American island in a plane-spanned sea, with trucks and jeeps parked nearby, performing for an engineer, a sociologist, a hotel man, and assorted experts in the construction trades. They were back in the ancient night of Oceania, dancing as their immemorial ancestors had danced, to fire and drum. And at the end, like those ancestors, savage and unashamed, they would fall to earth where they stood, locked together, man and woman, in the act of love.

It would be so. There could be no other ending. . . .

But of course there was.

The drums stopped. The dance stopped. The centuries rearranged themselves, the crowd clapped and cried *"Malo!"* and the young villagers who had been entertaining them bowed awkwardly, grinning or giggling, and retired to their seats at the rear of the dancing ground.

Then Va'ina was there.

She did not seem to have come from anywhere, but simply to have materialized, standing alone before the others. And now, alone, she moved forward. The drums started up again, but slowly, softly, and she too moved slowly, with a soft gentle rhythm. After the orgiastic excitement of the group finale, an attempt at emulation by a single dancer would have been sure anticlimax. But she attempted nothing of the sort. Her body, save for her gliding feet, was almost motionless. The drums merely murmured. And the crowd responded to the contrast with utter silence.

Like the others, she was grass-skirted (hers had a silver sheen), but she wore it in the style of Tahiti, fastened not about her waist but lower, across her hips, leaving belly as well as midriff bare. Covering her breasts was a strip of halter, also silvery. But she had no necklace or other bodily adornment, except for thin strands of pandanus leaf about wrists and ankles. It was on her head that she carried her ornamentation—and her badge of rank—in the age-old ceremonial headdress of a Manaian *taupou.* Her black hair was swept up and piled high, and into it had been woven an elaborate superstructure of small sticks, which in turn supported a great plume of red parrot feathers and a myriad of tiny fragments of mirror glass. Over-all, it added more than a foot to her height. The plumes nodded and swayed with her slightest movement. And the bits of mirror shone and glinted in the torchlight—as did the bare oiled flesh of her arms and body.

She carried herself like a queen. (Which indeed now, symbolically, she was.) Her head, under its gleaming tower, was held high. Her face was proud, contemptuous. And as she began to dance it was as a queen might dance: poised, aloof, controlled. For a time she moved only her hands and arms. Then only her feet. Then only her hips—slowly, sinuously—while all the rest remained still. It was by almost imperceptible stages that the rhythm grew faster; that the thump of the drums behind her grew gradually louder and more insistent. Outwardly, all was still regal decorum. It was only when the glare of a torch brushed across her, or a photo bulb flashed, that one could see that her face was changing, that the queenly hauteur was disolving, that the eyes were mocking, laughing. And then one knew that in the next instant, or the next, the façade would fall and another figure would emerge: unqueenly, wild, barbaric, as if ignited by the flames that lapped around her.

When it came, it was all at once. Her body went taut. The drums thundered. From the rear, the other dancers, rising, leapt forward, forming two lines behind her. And in an instant even the memory of the *taupou*'s measured ritual was swept away in the tide. As if there had been no interval at all—no grinning and giggling of village boys and girls—the chorus plunged back into the frenzy of its last climax. Brown bodies leapt and whirled. Brown legs and arms and hips and shoulders jerked and vibrated to the drumbeat, as again a wild and savage exuberance rose up from the past through bone and blood. And out in front, Va'ina danced with them, matched them, excelled them—for the wildness, the savagery, the exuberance, she had in as full measure as they; and beyond it, she had a thing which they did not, and this was a mastered, matchless style. With leg and shoulder, thigh and hip, she did as much as the rest, and more. She leapt higher, spun faster, writhed more sinuously, with even more abandon. But at the same time the mocking light was still in her eyes. Her full lips smiled. They seemed almost to be saying, "Look—look at me, you hungry ones. I am the maenad gone wild. I am sex incarnate. . . . But remember please, I am also a *taupou*. I am a *sao tamaitai,* a perfectly complete lady. . . . See how I keep my tall headdress straight, even as I whirl—so—and shake—so—"

And she whirled. She shook.

And the headdress stood straight.

The chorus, this time, did not carry through to a climax, but, as the drums pounded on, withdrew rank by rank into the background, leaving Va'ina again as the only dancer: a single quivering figure framed by the torchlight against the blackness beyond. And her response was a sequence wilder, more fevered, than anything that had been before. Any moment, it seemed, her movements would rip the strip of halter from her swelling breasts, send her silver skirt flying, whirling, from her writhing hips. And her eyes promised, "Yes, it will happen. . . . Wait. Wait some more. Any minute now. . . . Well, at least it *might* happen. . . ."

And she danced on. The maenad. The dervish.

Faster . . . faster . . .

And then stopped. The drums stopped. For a long moment she stood motionless in the deep stillness of their echo, her silver skirt and halter gleaming, her mirrored headdress reflecting the surrounding flames as if it were itself a burning torch. . . . Until again the drumbeat started. But now softly, slowly. And then she too, again, was moving—softly, slowly—in a dance the very opposite of the wild whirl of a moment before. . . . But she did not return to the mannered poise of queen or *taupou*. For now she was neither *taupou*-queen nor maenad-dervish, but only woman, and this, with her other roles discarded and done with, was her woman's dance of love. Soft and slow though it was, it was not a subtle nor a gentle thing. By the standards of a more reticent world, it was brazen and obscene; for the love it portrayed had but one aspect, one end. Yet as the girl performed it, as with her whole body, fully, wantonly, she gave and asked for love, it seemed, in that time and place—in the timelessness and placelessness from which she evoked it—to be as simple, as natural, a part of the scheme of things as the rise and fall of the sun, the flow and ebb of the sea. She had, to be sure, no partner. Nor did she need one. Every man watching her was her partner—her lover—and moving around the firelit circle, she paused, now here, now there, before this or that one in outer darkness, to bestow the favors of her untouched flesh.

Then at last, her circuit ended, she was back at its center. She was moving forward, toward where the guests of honor sat, for the final phase, the grand finale. Reaching the edge of the mats, she danced sideways before them: passing Tafutimo, Fahoai, and Pastor Solomona as if they had been invisible: pausing briefly before the "Hawaiians," whose cameras and flash guns were now frozen in their hands: past Lavery, Mrs. Mundy, and Shafter, until she reached the point where Carr and Melnick sat side by side. . . . And they were not invisible. She stopped again. She danced. And if Carr thought she danced for him, he was right; and if Melnick thought it was for him, he was right too; for the *taupou* of Tiara was both loving and practical. . . . At first she danced standing; then, still dancing, sank gradually to her knees, and from her knees swayed slowly backward—as she had that day under the breadfruit tree—until her tall headdress touched the earth; and even now she danced, her belly domed, her thighs spread wide, in final ecstasy, in immolation. . . .

Then slowly she swung upward. She was again on her knees. On her feet. The plumes and mirrors soared high. Beneath them, for an instant, her face was that of a savage—dark, wild, lustful. But for an instant only, and then it changed. It smiled. The eyes were smiling, and the lips; and the lips moved, as if to speak; and this time they *did* speak. They said one word. They said, "ivious—" And then an eye winked, a hip twitched; she moved away.

"What? What was that?" Melnick demanded, jerking his head toward Carr. "What did she say?"

Carr shrugged. "Something in Manaian, I suppose."

"It sounded like—"

"No, it was Manaian. It probably means 'hello' or 'good evening.'"

"Well, whatever it was, she's something. By God, yes—that dame's something!"

His voice was lost as the drums flared up again. Back in the center of the arena, Va'ina had stopped and raised her arms. She stood unmoving, transfixed, while the crescendo rose and roared about her: again the queenly priestess, the *taupou* triumphant, framed in night and fire. . . . And then it was over. The drums were still. Her headdress swung forward and brushed the ground, as she made her bow. And in place of the drumbeat there was now the roar of applause and shouts from everywhere of *"Malo! Malo!"* . . . Loudest of all the *malos* were those of Mel Melnick, president, executive manager, and entertainment director of the Pacific Hotel and Development Company; and as the future *première danseuse* of the Tiara Beach Hotel now blew him a smiling kiss, he blew one right back to her. "You know," he said to Carr, "with a bit of coaching, a little polishing up, say with some Arthur Murray teacher—"

And producing paper and pencil, he made a note.

Now Va'ina had vanished, and the other dancers as well, and in their place was the crowd, again swarming about, filling the *malae* with movement and sound. But the white guests—or at least all except Shafter and Mrs. Mundy, who were old hands at such occasions—remained for a while seated motionless on their mats, still under the spell of what they had seen. Throughout the performance, Carol Loftus, beside Carr, had not spoken a word; indeed had not moved or even seemed to breathe. But now at last she took a visible breath, a deep one.

"My—" she murmured. "My goodness."

Carr smiled at her. "You survived it?"

"I—I think so."

"Nothing like that in Hillsboro, Ohio?"

She smiled back, pulling herself together. "Only Saturday nights, at the church socials . . . And even then," she amended, "we haven't many Va'inas."

"She *is* pretty special, Va'ina."

"And I'd never have guessed it: seeing her at home and around the village. I'd always thought she was just a simple young girl. Wouldn't you have said so?"

Carr appeared to give the matter mature thought. But the best he could come up with was, "Well—you never can tell."

Around them, now, many things were happening. The drums were thumping again. But, in addition, there was the sound of guitars and a concertina, and the open space where the show had been was now quickly turning into a general dance floor. When Carr first looked up there were perhaps only a dozen dancers. But a few moments later they had doubled—then doubled again, and again—until, in no time at all, the center of the *malae* was once more a whirling, seething turmoil. All the performers in the show, except Va'ina, seemed to have returned, and were now picking up where they had left off; some with one another, some with young people who before had been merely watchers; dancing in couples, in teams of four or eight or whole phalanxes, a few bounding off, as fancy took them, to stomp and whirl and leap alone.

But it was not only the young men and women who were there.

The children were back too. Other children had joined them. And villagers of all ages, all ranks, from adolescent to graybeard, from the lowliest of chore boys and kitchen maids to the highest of the *matai* and their billowing wives. Even Tafutimo danced briefly: his lion's face stern and somber, but with feet and body moving rhythmically to the beat of the *siva-siva*. Fahoai and his wife Polu danced longer, and with gusto, until the ground all but rumbled under their careening bulk At one point, suddenly, an old crone burst with a whoop into a quivering solo hula. A hunchbacked dwarf leapt and spun like a brown Nijinsky.

This was dancing by people who had learned it in their mothers' wombs and would not forget or renounce it before the grave.

On the sidelines, among the "Hawaiians," the bulbs were popping again. The bottles and beer cans were going the rounds. And presently, paper cups had come down the line as well, and Carr and Carol Loftus were each holding one and drinking. For the girl, Carr noted gratefully, had at last relaxed. Her face, which earlier had been tense and preoccupied, as if any moment she would rise and flee back to the refuge of her dispensary, was now smiling and animated. Her eyes were bright in the torchlight. Between sips of her drink, which she had taken almost without protest, she was trying to look everywhere at once: pointing, exclaiming, borne up and on by the excitement.

Time flowed unnoticed—except by a scattered few. Glancing about, Carr saw Tafutimo and wife taking their leave. The pastor was already gone. And Mrs. Mundy was no longer to be seen. But, for the rest, minute and hour had ceased to exist. There was no beat of clock but only of drum, of thrumming string, of pounding foot. And as the music grew faster, wilder, so too did the dancing. By now it was obvious that liquor, of some sort, was circulating not only among the guests but among the Tiarans as well; and here and there in the crowd there was a glazed eye, an ominous lurch. But there was no general drunkenness. Nor would there be, at least from alcohol. For here were those who could draw deep from their own more potent brew of blood and gene.

Carr watched and drank. Beside him, Carol Loftus watched too: silently, raptly.

Then she murmured, "How I envy them. How lucky, how wonderful, to be able to throw off everything like that—"

"They have less to throw," said Carr. "They haven't collected as much junk on the way."

"Junk—" She looked at him and smiled. He smiled back. The smile became a grin.

"Yes, junk," he said. Setting his drink down, he suddenly sprang to his feet. "Come on— *we*'re going to throw some off."

She looked up at him, startled.

"Oh no. No, I couldn't—"

"Sure you can."

He seized her hand. He pulled her up. And they were out on the *malae,* dancing. A salvo of applause and whistles came from the "Hawaiians," and he bowed in acknowledgment and swung off into the crowd. . . . He had not, he assured himself, lost his mind completely, and he did not try to dance the *siva-siva.* . . . Not that he had never danced it, for he had. Right here on this island of Tiara— in this village, on this *malae*—he, Mitchell Carr, lieutenant junior-grade, aged twenty-four, had danced the *siva-siva,* with the help of ten drinks and a girl called Lovana. . . . But he was not twenty-four now. He had not had ten drinks. (Only four.) And this was not Lovana. . . .

This was not Va'ina. . . .

She was all right, though. For a non-Polynesian, non-child-of-nature, non-*fia fia,* complex, confused, neurotic, ambivalent, post-Freudian, post-Marxian, keyed-up, loused-up creature of the Age of Female and Nuclear Emancipation—she was all right. She had spirit. She had honesty. She had guts. After the first shock had worn off, she even danced all right—she danced damn well—light and lithe in his arms. Her green dress and yellow hair flashed brightly, and her eyes, too, were bright, as for a moment she raised them to his. And he said to her, "God knows what we're doing, but we're getting by," and they danced on, spinning, whirling, through the whirling crowd.

Soon they were no longer the only white dancers. Some of the "Hawaiians" were now also out on the *malae,* whirling or stalking or stumbling (according to talent or alcoholic intake) with assorted village girls. And others still on the sidelines were obviously priming themselves for the plunge. Presently a large bulk barged forward, not toward a Tiaran couple, but straight at Carr and Carol; a big hand touched Carr's shoulder, a friendly voice said, "Share the wealth, comrade"; and Carol was gone in the arms of one Eddie O'Neill, master mason. A backward glance assured him that she was not upset—indeed, had taken the cut-in quite in stride and was whirling with O'Neill as if there had been no change of partners at all.

As he made his way to the sidelines, the thought re-recurred: No, you never could tell.

He wandered. He found a drink. When that was gone he found

144

another, and when that was gone cut back in on Carol Loftus, who, after three or four intervening partners, was now dancing with Howard Spitz, electrician. "All right?" he asked her. "Oh yes, it's a grand party," she told him. And that was all the talk they had time for before Frank Lavery cut in and he was back on the outskirts.

He had another drink. He watched the dancers. Most of the Tiarans were now gyrating so fast that figures and faces were no more than a blur, and even if John Koa were there—which he didn't know; he hadn't seen him since that first moment of arrival—he could not have picked him out in the turmoil. . . . But one familiar face he *did* see. Va'ina was back. . . . Her tall headdress was gone, and she was not as conspicuous as before. But conspicuous enough; in her silver skirt and halter, the most vivid figure on the *malae,* she danced, whirling, glinting, laughing, with Mel Melnick.

His cup was empty. It was refilled by a "Hawaiian." He cut in on Carol and Lew Johnson, plumber, and was cut in promptly by Saul Goldberg, roofer. He watched the dancers again. . . . Still no John. Now no Va'ina. . . . And then a voice beside him said, "Good evening. Do you maybe remember me, Mr. Meesh Carr?"

The *taupou* of Tiara looked up at him quizzically. Her hair flowed in a black cascade over her back and shoulders, and two fresh gardenias glistened above her ears.

"Is it maybe too much trouble that you dance with me?" she asked.

He grinned at her. "You and your new boss were in conference," he said. "I didn't want to interrupt."

"Mr. Melnick he liked very much my *siva-siva.* Like I told you, he says '*Malo! Malo!*'—and yes, that I will dance at the hotel."

"Good girl," said Carr.

"But you, you did not like it? You like only this Miz Nurse, with her pills and hair like eggs. To sit with her—dance with her. Because she dances better than me."

"No, not better. All right for a *papalagi.* But not like you."

"I am not so bad, then?"

"No, not so bad."

"Good." Va'ina grasped his hand. "So now we dance together—"

She had him out in the crowd. In the torchlight and the tide of music. But at first it was not the two of them who danced, but only she—circling about him, her arms raised, her trunk swaying, in the first sinuous movements of the *siva-siva*—while he stood still, watching.

"So, you do the man's part," she said. "With the legs, the hips."

"I can't," he told her.

"But yes—"

"No."

"Yes."

She smiled up at him. Her golden body beckoned, invited. And in another moment it might have happened. With another drink—or two, or three—it *would* have happened. And there he would have been: flailing his legs and hips, jerking his shoulders, leaping like a demented goat—trying pitifully, ludicrously, to recapture a past that was gone, a night when he had been young and wild and drunk with a girl named Lovana—but now no longer young, nor even wild, but only drunk—a drunken, middle-aged, back-to-nature *papalagi* making a public fool of himself for the delight of the village. . . .

It was a close thing. Va'ina's magic was potent.

But she spared him.

Suddenly laughing, she said, "No, I frighten my poor Meesh. So, no *siva-siva*. We dance the *papalagi* way; that, too, I like—" And coming close, she let him hold her, and off they went into the dancing tide.

They danced fast, until his breath grew short and his head dizzy from whirling. Then slow—in half time, quarter time; sometimes, in the press of the crowd, scarcely moving at all. And now her body moved in and was flush against his own; it clung to him with thigh and breast and belly, soft yet firm, soft yet thrusting; while a hand slipped from his shoulder to his neck, and then the other hand, until both arms were around his neck, and her head was back, and her eyes smiled up at him.

A sound that might have been a sigh escaped her. "Is nice, no?" she murmured.

He nodded.

Then, a little later:

"I feel—"

"Yes, I know."

"What do you know? How do I feel?"

"Ivious." He looked down at her. "Don't you ever *not* feel ivious?"

"Sometimes," she confessed.

"Such as when?"

"Such as—" She thought it over. "Such as afterward," she said.

Her eyes shone up at him: laughing, mocking. Then, with a quick movement, she broke away from him, taking his hand and pulling it. "Come," she said. "We go now. It is time."

"Go where?" he protested.

"I will show. Come."

"It's too far to—"

"Yes, is too far to the pool. Too dark. But there are other places. . . . See—" She indicated the crowd around them, which had at last begun to thin out. "They go now: the young ones, the lovers. They go to the trees, the dark places. Like we go. . . . Come."

She led him on across the *malae*.

"But—"

"It is a nice place, you will see. No things that stick. No pigs and chickens."

"But—"

"You talk too much—when talk is no good." They had reached the edge of the *malae,* and she pointed into the darkness ahead. "We go here now," she said. "Like so—and so—"

And she led him on.

Carol Loftus was still dancing.

She had not danced so much since she was a girl; since the days of high school proms back in Hillsboro. Nor had so good a time, either.

For she *was* having a good time. A wonderful time. Some of the men from Hawaii had been excellent dancers, and all, even the drunker ones, had been pleasant and behaved themselves. Frank Lavery had danced with her and managed not badly. Mel Melnick and Leonard Shafter had had their turns too. Which totaled everyone there—or at least all the white men—and later some of the Utoians and a few of the bolder young Tiarans had also cut in. These last had been marvelous dancers, and had not expected her to do the *siva-siva,* but only the sort of steps she knew; and whirling about with them, she had enjoyed herself even more than with the men from the hotel. After the second time, Mitchell Carr had not reappeared. The last she had seen of him, he had been dancing with the *taupou,* Va'ina. But she was grateful to him that he had started her off; that he had made her enjoy the party, in spite of herself. While the others, though good partners, were at the same time strangers, he was by now—well—more than a stranger. And she hoped he would return again before the evening was over.

. . . Which would now not be long, she realized, looking about her as she danced with the fourth or fifth of the village boys. The torches circling the *malae* were at last burning low. The crowd was thinning, with men and women, boys and girls, going off toward the palm groves hand in hand. And she too would have to be leaving soon, whether Carr returned or not.

Then she thought she saw him: a tall angular figure coming toward her in the flickering half-light. But as it came closer, she saw it was not he. A hand reached out, touching her partner, and the partner was gone. And she was dancing with John Koa.

"Why John—where have you been all night?" she asked him.

But he said only, "Around—I've been around," and then concentrated on the dancing.

He danced wonderfully well. She would have expected him to be shy, awkward, ill at ease—especially with her. But he was none of these. He was easy, graceful, sure of himself: a poised, flashing partner carrying her along at his will. Alone among those she had danced with, he did the patterns of the *siva-siva*. Not expecting her to—allowing her her own steps, her own movements—but now and then breaking loose, backing away, then circling her: arms wide, feet stamping, his body arching, jerking, in primeval rhythm.

Only once did he speak again. "Tonight I'm the native boy," he said. "All that's missing is my grass skirt and nose ring." And then before she could answer, or even more than half hear what he had said, he had swept her up again; he was leading her, spinning her, circling, returning—on and on, faster, wilder—until at last the drums crashed, the music stopped, and she stood beside him panting and dizzy.

"Oh John," she was barely able to murmur. "What a dancer you are! I'd never have guessed—"

"There'll be another," he said. "I'll do better."

"Better! You'll have me tumbling right over. I almost am already: I've been dancing for hours—" She looked around again: at the guttering torches, the departing figures. "In fact, it's time to stop. Truly. If I dance any more I won't be able to stand up tomorrow, let alone do my work."

He seemed on the point of arguing or pleading. But he didn't.

"Really, I must go," she told him. "It's awfully late."

"Then I'll take you home," he said.

"Oh no, thanks—there's no need to. It's just a few steps and—"

"I'll take you," he said.

And he went along as she crossed the *malae*: walking straight and silent beside her . . . a little too straight, it presently seemed to her; almost unnaturally straight and stiff (though that was perhaps only in contrast to the supple ease of his dancing) . . . and a little too silent; darkly, heavily silent (though that too could have been contrast after the tide of music) . . . and she wanted to break it, to speak; she tried to think of something to say—but couldn't; and now they had left the *malae* and were on the road under the palms.

What was left of the torchlight was now behind them, and the night was thinned only by the sweep of stars above the overhanging fronds. They were alone on the road—yet not alone—for from the darkness around them, from within the groves of trees, came occasional sounds: of movement, a whispering voice, a ripple of laughter.

John Koa took Carol's hand.

"Do not be afraid," he said.

"I'm not afraid," she answered.

"It is only the young people of the village who are together . . . Do you know what I mean, together?"

"Yes, I know."

She did not look at him. Instead, she quickened her step—or, rather, tried to—but the boy's hand tightened on hers and held her back.

"I must get home," she said.

"We will get home later. First let us stop, like the others."

"John—"

She tried to pull away, but he held her. "Please—please," he said. "You will see: I am not a boy but a man. I am not a savage, but half white."

"John, stop—"

"And I will make love like a white man."

He had her close now. He put an arm around her. And she struggled.

"Let me go," she said. "Please—let me go?"

She broke away and tried to run from him, but he caught her quickly. And now he held her in both arms.

"John, stop it!" Her voice was louder. "Do you hear me? Stop!"

She strained back with her body and wrenched at his arms. Then Malele the policeman came up the road on his last round of the night, swinging his club of polished *toa* wood.

11

"I COULD USE a few days off the rock myself," said Frank Lavery, standing on the lagoon dock the next morning with Mitchell Carr. "But I guess I'm stuck till the job's done."

A few minutes before, they had seen Melnick and Shafter off on the *Harold L. Ickes,* and now they watched as the ship moved out seaward toward the break in the reef.

"Anyhow, it could be looking up a bit from here on," the contractor consoled himself, as they turned and headed back toward the hotel site. "That was a blowout last night, eh, Mitch?"

Carr nodded.

"Even our blonde icicle, Miss Carol L., warmed up some, you notice? Can't say she went exactly on fire, but at least she was halfway human. . . . And that island babe, the one with the hootchy-kootchy: say, what about her? She was something, wasn't she?"

"Unh-huh," Carr agreed.

"Real chatty this morning, aren't you?" Lavery gave him a sidelong glance and his red face grinned. "But of course you don't know from nothing about 'em, do you? Old Mitch Carr—scared to death of the dames. . . . Well, at least you got back for breakfast. . . ."

As they moved up and across the slope, the new world of the hotel enveloped them. What had been the path was now, for half its length, a road of crushed coral, and along the other a grader and roller were snorting their way on. The straggling palm grove was gone; there were only files of trees along the road and others spaced about in ornamental groups; and the bulldozer was nudging out the last of the unwanted stumps. On all sides, grass and undergrowth were gone. Greenness had become brownness: the scarred and ragged brown of scraped earth, mounds of earth, holes in the earth. From many of the holes wooden forms and concrete blocks were already emerging, and near the largest of them, where the main building would soon stand, the cement mixer ground out its rumbling rhythm. "Hawaiians," Utoians, and Tiarans were everywhere, bare to the waist above shorts or blue jeans, busy with hammers, saws, drills, and the controls of machines.

Lavery took himself to the office hut, where Paul Carvalho, master carpenter, was waiting with a problem about warping wallboard; Carr to the excavation for the main building, where the shorings he had designed and Tom Taki's men had installed had still not wholly solved the problem of seepage. Through the rest of the morning he was busy there. At noon, when the men knocked off for lunch, he headed for the mess hut. But before he reached it he was intercepted by a young Tiaran woman—tall, heavy, with a flat timid face and shapeless dress—who approached him hesitantly and said, "Excuse— you will excuse me please—"

And pausing, he asked her what she wanted.

"I look for Mr. Shafter, please."

"Mr. Shafter's gone," he said. "He's left for Apingo."

"Apingo—oh." The young woman clasped and unclasped her hands. She looked as if she were about to cry.

"What did you want to see him about?" he asked. "Perhaps I can help."

She hesitated. "I—I am called Mena," she said. "I am of the family of Fahoai, the high talking chief."

"Yes?"

"And it is about my cousin that I come. My cousin, John Koa."

"John Koa—"

"Yes."

"What about John Koa?"

"He is in jail."

"Jail?"

"Yes."

"What for?"

Again she hesitated. "It is from something after the dance last night," she said. "I was not there; I do not know. But it was something with Miz Nurse and—"

"Miss Nurse? You mean Miss Loftus?"

"Yes, Miz Loftus. And there was some trouble and—"

She went on, the words running together and scarcely audible. Then Carr broke in.

"Where's he in jail?" he asked. "In the village?"

"Yes, in village—"

Again Mena went on. But now he was no longer even trying to listen. He was not looking at her, but past her, to where one of the jeeps was standing before the mess hut.

Then, out of confusion, came decision.

"Don't worry, it will be all right," he mumbled, not knowing what he meant. And then he had left her. He was at the jeep. He was in it. He was driving off through the hotel grounds, down the slope, along curves and potholes of the coast road.

He drove fast. In a minute or less he was passing the strip of beach where he and Carol Loftus had met, that night some two weeks past. And now—composing his thoughts—he was trying to imagine what could have happened to her, with John Koa, on this night just past. When he had last danced with her she had been doing fine; indeed, was relaxing and letting herself go for the first time in their brief acquaintance. When he had last seen her—before leaving with Va'ina—she had been dancing with assorted "Hawaiians," apparently still going strong. . . . And then what? Then John Koa. . . . He had not seen John since the very start of the evening. Where had he been? When had he appeared? And—repeat—then what? He could well imagine Carol's having a problem with one or another of the island men. In fact, it was inevitable, sooner or later. . . . But with John. John Koa. . . . He was not even a man, but a boy. Not even a creature of flesh and blood—at least not as he, Carr, had known him—but a sort of wraith, a shadow, walking in palm groves, along dark roads, appearing, vanishing, like a wandering ghost.

—Well, he wasn't wandering now, evidently. And if he was a ghost, he was a ghost in jail.

In another few minutes he was in the village. It had been his first plan to go direct to the jail; his second to stop first at Fahoai's *fale* to speak to the talking chief. But now he changed his mind again and drove on to the white-and-green frame house where Carol Loftus lived with Mrs. Mundy. Apparently it was the school lunch hour, for he saw the old lady through the window as he drew near, and it was she who came to the door when he knocked.

"I expected *somebody* would be coming," she said, greeting him. "The coconut radio beats the new kind all hollow."

On meeting her for the first time, the previous night, Carr had been struck by the brightness of the old eyes behind their rimless glasses. They were no less so now—keen, smiling, almost youthful, in the sharp, withered face—and he took it as a sign that nothing too drastic could have happened to Carol.

He told her of Mena's trip to find Shafter.

"Yes, she's a good girl." Mrs. Mundy nodded. "Carol would have done the same herself, if she hadn't known Leonard was gone." Then, seeing his glance move about: "She's in the dispensary. After a night like yesterday's there's always sure to be some extra patients. . . . But she'll be through soon. There are only one or two left."

"She's all right, then?"

"Oh yes. Upset, of course—as who wouldn't be? But I think really more about the poor boy than herself." The old lady shook her head. "It's just a shame, you know. Just a plain rotten shame. . . . Do you know John?" she asked.

"Yes," said Carr. "That is, I've met him."

"He's not a bad boy. Not bad at all."

"Just a da—"

"—damn fool," she supplied. "You can say it. I'm not a missionary; just a backslid widow of one. . . . Yes, that's exactly what he is: a damn fool. . . . The trouble is," she added, and now her usually chirrupy voice grew soft and sad, "that it's so easy to say, isn't it?— and so hard to know what to do, how to help."

She had made Carr sit down; and now, excusing herself, went into the kitchen, returning in a few moments with a sandwich and cup of coffee. "Carol and I have had our lunch," she said, "but I'm sure you haven't. And this is left over, just as if we'd been expecting you."

Brushing off his thanks, she too sat down. And then he said: "You know John well, I suppose."

"Well, yes—in a way," she answered.

"For a long time, at least."

"Since I came to Tiara in forty-nine. He was—let's see—about five then, and he was in my school for eight years."

"Was he always a problem?"

Mrs. Mundy thought it over. "He was always—different," she said. "Always the brightest, the most ambitious. And then of course he's half white, as you probably know, and he was always terribly conscious of it."

A question—a dozen questions—hovered on Carr's lips. But she went on:

"Yet he was a well-behaved, a good boy. No, not a problem. Except, I'm afraid, to himself. . . . A teacher doesn't often have a pupil like John, and I've thought about him a lot. For a long time. . . ." She paused. Then asked, "Have you been to Tahiti, Mr. Carr?"

"Tahiti?" The sudden veering threw him off, but he managed to shake his head.

"Yes, I know, that must seem quite a jump. But when I think of John I often make that jump to Tahiti; or, more particularly, to Gauguin. My husband and I, you see, lived there for several years before the war, and I collected many Gauguin prints—you can hardly help it in Tahiti, even though Mr. Mundy never much cared for them—and the one I especially remember was called *D'où Venons Nous? Que Sommes Nous? Où Allons Nous?* It's one of his famous ones; perhaps you recall it? A great magical thing with many figures, full of the mystery of these islands. But what stays with me, in terms of John, is the title. Gauguin was thinking of all Polynesia, of course. Or of the whole world. But what I see when I hear it, when I visualize it—right in front, right in the center of those figures—is John. John asking, *Where do I come from? What am I? Where am I going?*"

She mused for a few moments. Then she said:

"A thought I've always had is that if Gauguin had lived longer he would have seen it the same way. With his own children. He had two in Tahiti, you know—half white, half brown—who were living there when I did. And if he could have known them as they were later, he would have realized that his vision and his words applied to them even more than to the pure Polynesians he painted. For it's half-and-halfs, like them, like John, who are the real lost ones.

"Oh, it's not an exact parallel, of course. Emil Gauguin—that's the son—could never have been much like John. For years now he's been a town loafer around Papeete; more like Asimo, perhaps, who runs the store here. In some ways, I suppose, it's been worse for him: having a great and famous father he couldn't conceivably live up to. But on the other hand. . . . Well, I don't know." Mrs. Mundy shrugged her frail old shoulders. "In a different way, I sometimes think it may be harder for John. For better or worse, Emil at least knows one of the answers to: *Where do I come from?* John hasn't even got that."

A door opened and Carol Loftus came in from the dispensary. What with quick step and trim uniform, she seemed to Carr none the worse for whatever experience she had had, and as he rose she greeted him with a smile.

"Mr. Carr has heard about last night," said Mrs. Mundy, before he himself could explain his presence.

"Oh." The girl's smile faded, but she did not lose her composure. "Then—then it's—"

"Yes, it's gotten around."

Carr told her of Mena's coming, and when he had finished she nodded. "I suppose it was bound to be that way. I'd have talked to Mr. Shafter myself, if he'd still been here. . . . Not that I want it all over, Lord knows, but he'd have been the one to get poor John out of jail."

"You're not angry, then?"

"Angry? . . . Oh no. At least not that way. I was upset, yes. I still am—and so sorry it happened. But angry? Wanting him in jail? That's just awful."

154

"Would you tell me about it?" Carr asked. "I'm not just curious. I'd like to help if I can."

She hesitated—but only for a moment. Then briefly and simply she told him what had happened after she and John had left the dance. "It was frightening, of course," she added. "So dreadfully sudden and unexpected. But I'm sure he didn't mean any real harm. He couldn't; he's not that sort. I suppose he'd been drinking, though that didn't occur to me then. But it wasn't just that either, I'm sure." She paused, feeling her way through her uncertainty. "He—he's such a strange boy, John," she said. "So intense. So sort of boiling inside."

"And after the policeman came?" Carr asked.

"That was frightening too. It was awful. He yelled at John to let me go, but John paid no attention—he was just wild and crazy—and so Malele swung his club and hit him. Thank God it wasn't too hard; it must have just glanced off his head and stunned him a little. Anyhow, he stopped holding me, and then Malele took hold of *him* and told me to go on home. And I couldn't think of what else to do, so I went."

"And that's the last you've seen of him?"

"Yes. At the time I was too upset to do much thinking about it; but if I thought at all it was that Malele would just make John go home too. It wasn't until this morning that I learned he was in jail."

"Have you been there?"

"Yes, I went right away. At least to the little police office next door. I didn't want to see John; I thought it would be too difficult for both of us, so soon after it had happened. But I talked to Malele. I asked him to let John out, but he wouldn't. I begged and pleaded, but it was just no use, and then I had to come back and open the dispensary. Truly, I feel worse about the jail part of it than anything else."

Carr shook his head. "The crazy kid," he murmured. Then to Carol: "You wouldn't mind then if I see what I can do?"

"You?" She was obviously surprised. "Oh no," she said. "I'd be so pleased—so grateful."

"I think perhaps a man could do better," Mrs. Mundy put in. "I was planning to go over after school, but I'm afraid a woman—even a white one—doesn't carry much weight with the Manaians."

"I've no official status, of course," Carr said. "But I'll give it a try."

"It's good of you," said Carol. "To bother—to take the trouble." She paused and looked at him curiously. "Do you know John?" she asked.

"I've met him a few times."

"He's a fine boy, really. Just—as I say—so confused, so churned up."

"Well, I'll talk with him, anyhow." Carr went to the door. "And speaking of being grateful"—he looked at Carol admiringly—"he damn well should say his thanks to you."

The two women came outside with him and pointed out where the jail—or what passed for it—lay, down the road beyond the *malae*. And a few minutes later he entered the adjoining shack that served the island policeman as office. Malele was at a battered desk, writing laboriously—presumably a report on John Koa, Carr thought, for he gathered there were no other prisoners—but rose as he came in and politely offered a chair.

"I've come about the boy," said Carr.

"Ah yes," Malele shook his head. "A bad case, sir. A real bad case, this one."

"I want to get him out."

"Out? I am afraid that will not be easy, sir. This is a serious offense."

"Not all that serious, I wouldn't say."

"He is charged with assault and attempted rape."

"Nonsense. He'd just had a bit too much to drink—like a lot of people last night."

"When I came upon him and Miss Loftus—"

"You've had no formal complaint from Miss Loftus, have you?"

"Formal? No, but—"

"In fact, she came here this morning and begged you to let him out."

The policeman rallied his defenses. "Assault and attempted rape are felonies," he said. "In the case of a charged felony no complainant is needed; the accused is held for trial by the arresting authority." He held up a mimeographed booklet that lay on the desk. "Here is the penal code and manual of procedure, sir. If you will look at page twenty-six—"

Declining, Carr took another tack. "All right, I see your position there," he said. "So let's arrange the bail."

"Bail, sir?"

"Yes. He's not charged with murder, so there must be provision for bail. . . . Unless you operate here under some sort of Russian laws?"

Apparently Malele had not had previous experience with such matters. As he hesitated, Carr took the booklet, thumbed through it, and found what he wanted. "Yes," he said. "Bail—here it is. Read it." He handed the booklet back to the policeman and, taking his wallet from his back pocket, produced five ten-dollar bills.

Malele looked at the money. He looked at the booklet, then at another booklet, then through a mildewed sheaf of typed and mimeographed papers that he pulled from a drawer. He nodded. He shook his head. He scratched his head. And for the next half hour, while Carr paced and smoked, he assembled blank forms, studied them, filled them out, discarded them, refilled them, signed them, sealed them, reread them—and at last, reluctantly, pushed them across the desk. Carr signed here and he signed there. He received a receipt for the fifty dollars. He waited another ten minutes while Malele read over everything again. And then, still reluctantly, the policeman rose, took a ring of keys from a nail on the wall, and led the way from the shack.

The jail, next door, was simply a concrete box with a single door, a barred window in the door, and a square cubicle beyond; and as Malele turned his key and pushed, Carr saw John Koa lying on a mat on the floor. The boy rose. The policeman, entering, spoke to him briefly in Manaian. And then he brought him out.

"I have told him what you have done," he said to Carr. "And also that he is still under arrest and will behave, or he will quickly find himself back in jail."

Then he went back to his office.

"And so here we are," thought Mitchell Carr.

The boy did not look at him, but stood half turned away, his eyes squinting in the sunlight. His hair was rumpled and his thin face seemed almost haggard.

"Come on," said Carr.

John glanced at him questioningly, but did not speak; and as Carr walked to the jeep he followed and got in beside him.

"How's your head?" Carr asked.

"My head?" John repeated.

"I understand you got hit on it."

"Oh. . . . It's all right. It wasn't anything much."

"Sure you don't want your friend Miss Loftus to have a look at it?"

"No," John murmured. "No, it's all right."

Several villagers, passing by, had stopped and were watching them curiously, and Carr started the jeep and drove off. Neither of them spoke as they moved along the coast road. Then, when they were well out of the village, he swung off the road and stopped in the shade of a palm grove. But even then he did not speak: sitting silent and unmoving, looking at his own hands as they rested on the wheel. . . . *So here they were.* The unspoken words echoed back. *So here it was*: the moment he had been awaiting . . . and avoiding. . . .

Through the past days and weeks John Koa had been almost constantly in his thoughts. Sometimes at their very center, as he sought consciously and rationally for understanding, a point of view, a course of action. Sometimes peripherally—as the boy himself had been peripheral: a figure appearing, vanishing: an emanation of the past—perhaps of the future as well; but as of the present, the living here-and-now, without reality or meaning.

The boy of here-and-now was named John Koa. The boy who appeared and vanished was named John Carr.

This was the first time he had more than glimpsed him since he had learned from Va'ina that he was her cousin—Lovana's son. That, of course, had been the moment of revelation, of truth. Or so it had seemed at the time. But looking backward, he realized that it had been less revelation than confirmation of something he had known, or half known, before. He had recalled his previous meetings with John: on the dock when he had returned from Apingo; on the village road at dusk; first of all, on the day of arrival, when the boy had materialized from the palm grove by the lagoon and asked his question of Leonard Shafter. And he had recognized that from the very beginning he had had a presentiment, an intimation.

Or had it been from even before the beginning; before he had so much as set eyes on John Koa, or known of his existence? Had he perhaps surmised his existence? And had that surmise, unconscious, undefined, played its part in bringing him back to Tiara? "You are a son in search of a father," the psychiatrist had told him years ago; and if it had been true, he had not known it. Could he not then have become, in reverse, a father in search of a son—and not known it? In search of the son he had never had by either of the women he had married.

His mind shied away from such speculations; returned; shied off again. It was a pragmatic mind, an engineer's mind (or at least so he believed, so he desired), and it distrusted surmise and presentiment, the vague, formless, and undefined. . . . What, after all, did he *know*, even now, about this boy, John Koa? That he was the son of Lovana. That his father was a white man who had been here during the war. That his age was such that he, Mitchell Carr, was very possibly that father. . . . Very possibly, yes. But still not certainly. There had been plenty of wartime visitors to Tiara, both before and after him, and Lovana was of a world in which women took their lovers as they came.

No, he did not *know*. Not yet. Not quite. As of this moment, only John Koa factually existed. John Carr was still a shadow, a phantom. But—

He was not aware that his eyes had moved, but they must have, for it was no longer at his own hands that he was looking but at those of the boy beside him. And they were not the hands of a phantom. They were big, brown, long-boned, like his own. The knees on which they rested jutted high and angled against the dashboard— like his own. Then, as he still looked, the boy stirred, moving forward slightly, so that he could see his profile obliquely, the line of jaw and nose and forehead; see them not as he had before, not merely outwardly, casually, as the features of a stranger; but with penetration, with sudden inwardness. . . . And yes, he knew all right. He knew now, at this moment, once and for all. . . . The facts an engineer's mind craved might not yet be all in place, to produce the ultimate Q.E.D. But he had something beyond the facts. He had the truth.

And now?

Yes—what now?

Did one say, "Permit me to introduce myself. I am your father"? Or perhaps first give an introductory lecture on the impropriety of attempted rape?

But it was John who broke the silence.

"Malele told me you gave him money," he said. "I don't understand."

"He wouldn't let you go," Carr told him, "without bail."

"Yes, I know that. I mean *why* did you do it?"

"Mr. Shafter's gone back to Apingo. Miss Loftus herself tried to get you out, but the policeman said no."

"Miss Loftus?"

"Yes."

"She's not angry?"

"No. She's upset, of course—damned upset. But not angry. When you tell her you're sorry it will be all right."

The boy said nothing.

"Or maybe you're not sorry? Maybe you wish you'd really raped her?"

There was no answer.

"—so you could spend the rest of your life, instead of just a night, in jail."

"Perhaps I'm better off there," John murmured.

"Meaning you're really set on making a mess of your life?"

John shrugged.

"Is that it?"

"What does it matter to you? Why should you care?"

Carr was silent a moment before answering. Then he said: "Because I have a son about your age, and he has his troubles the same as you. I've tried to help him when I could, and I'd like to help you too."

"Your son is white. The world belongs to him."

"And because you're brown—"

"Not brown. Not white. Not anything."

"Not even a man?"

John Koa winced, his thin face tightening as if he had been struck a blow. "Oh yes, of course—a man," he struck back. "A man who goes to jail if he tries to touch a white woman. Who wants to fly planes, but is told to chop trees or pick coconuts."

"And because everything doesn't go his way sulks and mopes like a child."

The boy started to speak again, stopped, and lapsed into sullen silence. Carr, too, was quiet for a few moments, looking out through the windshield at the sea beyond the palm grove. And when he spoke again his voice was soft, without edge.

"Tell me more about the flying," he said.

"There's nothing to tell. It won't happen. It's finished."

"That remains to be seen. What I want to know is the part up to now. Why you applied to the Air Force. Why you want to fly."

"I've told you before. I planned it all through high school. I used to go to the airfield."

"And how—"

Here it was. The question that had hung on his lips that day on the lagoon jetty; that he had not been able to ask. . . . But that now he did.

"And how did this start?" he asked. "Where did this come from?"

"Come from?" said John.

"It's hardly a usual thing. At least here in Tiara. It must have come from somewhere—or someone."

The boy didn't answer.

"Such as your father," said Carr.

He felt the thin frame stiffen. The dark eyes met his for an instant and moved away again. "I have no father," John said.

"But you *had* one. And he was an American, wasn't he? An American here during the war."

There was another pause.

"Tell me," said Carr.

"Why? Why should I tell? What does it mean to you?"

"I want to help you, John—and I think by now you know it. But to help I have to know something about you."

The boy looked at him again, but this time longer—and steadily.

"Yes," he said at last, "he was an American in the war."

"And a flier?"

"Yes."

"What else do you know about him?"

"Nothing."

"He left here before you were born?"

"Yes."

"And never came back?"

"No."

"But you heard from your mother—"

"Not my mother. I never knew her either. I heard from my family, and around the village."

"And ever since you've wanted to be a flier too."

It was not a question. And John made no reply. For a while, again, they sat without speaking; then the boy said suddenly in a hard, flat voice: "But now, as you say, I must be a man, not a boy. And as a man I know it is foolish, hopeless, the dream of a child. It's not a flier I'm going to be, but a gook in my village. A catcher of fish. A drier of copra."

He got out of the jeep.

"Where are you going?" Carr asked.

"To catch fish. To dry copra."

"No you're not."

John looked at him, uncomprehending.

"You're coming with me," said Carr. "To the hotel. To work there." The boy started to speak, but he cut him off. "Three times I've asked you to come. This time I'm not asking. You're just coming. You'll get the same pay as the other unskilled labor, which is sixty cents an hour, and if you get skilled at something it will go up."

John stood still. His face was expressionless. "You can't force me—" he murmured.

"No, that's right, I can't force you. This is a free island that's part of a free country—whatever you may think about it—and you can go back to your village if you want to. You can be stepped on by the chiefs and laughed at by the rest. You can make an ass of yourself again, go to jail again, do any fool thing you want to. . . . Or, after all the talk that you're a man, you can try *being* one for once. You can go to work like one—even if it's not exactly what you want from Santa Claus. You can hold your head up with some self-respect, knowing that at least you're doing a day's work in the world. And you can take my word for it that I want to help you."

He swung the jeep around so that it faced the road. Then, stopping, he moved from the driver's to the adjoining seat. "Come on, get in," he said.

John stared at him.

"It's not a plane, but it's a machine. You say you're good with machines; let's see what you can do with it."

John approached, stopped, hesitated. . . . Carr waited. . . . Then the boy got in behind the wheel.

"This is the gas," said Carr, pointing. "This is the brake, the clutch, the gearshift."

John looked down through the wheel and put his foot on the clutch, and Carr eased the gearshift forward.

"Now you're in first," he said. "Release the clutch slowly and just touch the gas with the other foot."

John followed instructions, and the car moved out onto the road.

12

ON THE NIGHT of the feast, Lou Johnson, Honolulu plumbing contractor, had several times while dancing with Carol Loftus turned away to sneeze. When she had commented on it, he had said, "Aw, it's nothing. Just allergic to coconuts, I guess." But it was a "nothing" with consequences, for within two days half the village was sneezing. Then came coughs, running noses, headaches, backaches, chills and fevers. It was only the common cold; Carol was sure of that from the beginning. But the people of Tiara had, over the years, had so little exposure to it that, in extent and severity, it amounted almost to a minor plague.

No one died, to be sure. No one, in strictly medical terms, was even seriously ill. But more rampantly than the virus, fear raced through the village, filling the dispensary with clamorous pill seekers and the *fales* with supine figures convinced that they would never rise again. By the end of the third day it was obvious that a physician was needed—for morale if nothing else. And the next morning, in response to a radio message from Carol, a doctor came over from Apingo on a special sailing of the *Ickes*.

It was not the medical chief, Dr. Friede, but a young staffer named George Harris, a few months out of his internship in a Los Angeles hospital. As Carol had foreseen, there was little for him to do but dispense routine medication and good cheer, in the same fashion as herself. But his prestige as a male and an M.D. was, as also foreseen, helpful, and within a few days the near-dead were back to life again and the epidemic was over.

"You're a good nurse, honey—and a cute kid," Dr. Harris told her on his last night in the village, as they sat on the steps of Mrs. Mundy's cottage watching the moon rise through the palm grove. And then he had put an arm around her and tried to kiss her.

A few nights later Frank Lavery appeared and suggested a jeep ride—which she declined with thanks. And during the following week the invitation was repeated by three other "Hawaiians." One, who kept nervously turning the gold band on his third finger, seemed actually relieved when she refused. But another argued at length, and the third, who was drunk, she had almost to push bodily from the house. For the dedicated daughter of the late Dr. John Norman Loftus—no less than for the villagers—there was a price to pay for the night of revels.

Mitchell Carr, the one caller she would have liked to have, did not appear. And when she saw him on her periodic visits to the hotel site it was for only a few minutes during the intervals in their work. It was just as well, she told herself, as, with the others disposed of and Mrs. Mundy in bed, she sat at night in the cottage living room. For, whatever men might think, she was not a fool, and she knew it was no accident that it had been to him alone, of all men, that she had revealed something of her inner self. Or that it had been he, rather than any other, for whom she had stayed at the dance. With others, of whatever age, whatever sort, she was forever boringly, hatefully, the "blonde number," the "cute kid." But Mitchell Carr had treated her as what she was—a human being, a grown woman. And the woman in her had responded.

Yes, she thought: she would have liked to see him more. . . . But at the same time, no: it was better this way. . . . For this phase of her life, at least, she was Carol Loftus, R.N., no more and no less, and thus she was going to remain until her work was done. There would be no more moonlit beaches. And no more dancing. The dancing that had produced the train of importunate jeep drivers. And the mess with John Koa. . . .

She had seen John only once since he had gone with Carr to the other side of the island. And that had not been to speak to. One day at the hotel site, as she was driving off from a routine visit, she had noticed him working alongside the road with a crew of other men; and he had seen her too, she knew, for he had raised his head, and for a quick instant their eyes had met. A few yards farther on she had, on sudden impulse, stopped the jeep, with the resolve to go back and speak to him. But when she turned she found that John had again bent to his work, while the whole rest of the crew was staring. And she had been unable to get out. She had driven on: back to the village, the cottage, her dispensary, her work.

Even with the cold epidemic over, there was plenty of work, and she threw herself into it with all her mind and strength.

Mitchell Carr's work, on the other hand, was at an end. Or at least the work he was there for; for now the excavations were all done, the foundations laid, the buildings rising into what would soon, recognizably, be the Tiara Beach Hotel. The engineering phase of construction was over, and the rest would be in the hands of Frank Lavery and his subcontractors.

Still, Carr stayed on. There was plenty to be done: in supervision, in consultation, in the dozens of problems which kept arising in every aspect of the job. A tropical island—as he well recalled from the war—is the implacable enemy of anything not an integral part of itself. It hates a straight line, a clean angle, an unwarped plank, a shiny tool, and wages valiant battle against them with its massed resources of rain and mud and mold and salt sea spray. If inorganic forces weaken, it can call on legions of ants and termites; and if these in turn face defeat, there are always the final shock troops of native human inhabitants. The Tiarans who formed the basic labor force for Mel Melnick's dream of paradise could foul a drill or mis-mix cement or short-circuit an electrical connection as adeptly as if they had been trained all their lives for these specific purposes. And Carr was, if anything, kept busier than before, as he moved day by day from crisis to crisis.

Lavery, who had expected him to leave when the surveying was done, was grateful for his help. "You're sure as hell nuts," he said, "staying on this rock any longer than you got to. But just stay that way, will you? Just a few weeks more. For Chrissake, don't walk out on me now."

So the days passed. Then a week. Then another. . . . And Carr stayed. . . . Each third or fourth day the *Harold L. Ickes* came and went, and at each departure he imagined himself aboard. Tiara would sink away behind, Utoia rise ahead, and he would arrive in Apingo. There would be the Government offices, the Nimitz Hotel, perhaps the Apingo Bar. Then the airfield. And from the airfield he would be off to—where? He could fly back the way he had come: to Hawaii, California, points east. Points past. Or he could fly on through the islands: to Fiji, Samoa, Tahiti. . . . To—what was it?—Pahuka-huka. . . . That was what he had said, that day in Apingo, when Melnick had asked where he was going next. There was no such place. The sounds had simply come to his tongue as the most implaus-ible name he could think of. But if Pahukahuka didn't exist, other

164

islands did; other pinpricks in the sea, no less remote, no less implausible.

Nor more implausible, he thought now, than a certain pinprick called Tiara. Than a certain boy called John Koa, now working on the grounds a few yards distant, who was his flesh-and-blood son.

On the day he had brought John to the hotel he had turned him over to Tom Taki, who put him to work as a general laborer and assigned him quarters in one of the workmen's huts. The next morning he had half expected him to be gone, but the boy had worked through that day as well, and at quitting time he had picked him up in the jeep and given him a second driving lesson. John had learned quickly. By the end of a week he could handle a car better than any Manaian on the job, and by the end of a second he was driving the bulldozer and other tractors. At that time, on Taki's recommendation, he was advanced from the sixty- to the eighty-cent wage bracket.

Carr had given all the lessons with the jeep. When the boy moved on to the bigger machines he stopped off occasionally to give instructions or advice. But that had been the extent of their contact, with no approach to a more personal level. What was in John's mind, apart from the machines he handled, Carr could not remotely guess. And what was in his own was still too confused and unformulated to be transposed into speech or action.

This is my son. This is my son. . . . The words repeated themselves endlessly in his mind. But they were only words, without meaning or reality. Over and over he asked the question he had put to himself that first day in the jeep. . . . "What now? For the love of God, what now?" . . . But he could find no answer.

He backed away, seeking perspective. He was not, he was perfectly aware, the only wartime American in the Pacific who had fathered a half-Polynesian child. Indeed, some islands, notably Bora Bora, over toward Tahiti, were said to be swarming with such children. . . . And what had these other fathers done? . . . Most likely, the majority—like himself for eighteen years past—knew nothing about it. Their island girls, their Lovanas, were long since gone and forgotten, and it had never occured to them that their remote, casual trysts under palm or breadfruit tree might have had such consequences. Others, no doubt, knew—or surmised—but did not care. A brown-skinned barefoot half-caste on a distant speck of an island bore no conceivable relationship to their postwar back-home lives, and if there was any concern at all it was in keeping the knowledge of his existence from wives and stateside children. There were a few, he had heard, who knew and had kept vaguely in touch, sending occasional money and

165

gifts from half a world away. And an even tinier few who at war's end had returned to the islands, to make their homes and become full-time husbands and fathers.

But he was none of these. Not the first—any longer—for now he knew. Never the second or third. And scarcely the last—after eighteen years. He had thought of John Koa as a sort of ghost; but was it not he himself, rather, who was just that: a revenant from the past, intruding into a world that was his son's but not his own?

He took a closer stance, trying another perspective: the perspective of self. . . . How would he, Mitchell Carr, aged seventeen, have felt if, one day, a total stranger had appeared and announced himself as his father? . . . Like John, he had not known his father. The stranger who had been called Stanley Carr had been killed in the First World War, in France, less than a month after he had been born. But that was a father who was demonstrably dead, with name and serial number on a cross in Belleau Wood, and not a ghost who could return. The psychiatrist had told him that, even as a grown man, he was subconsciously in search of a father; that he had tried to find him in his first father-in-law, Henry Sherwood. And that was understandable. Just as it was understandable that John's passion to fly was in origin, in core, a form of father search.

But . . . again *but* . . . always *but.* . . . His first wife's father had, at most, been a symbol. Not a ghost. Let alone a unique and inexplicable ghost who could, in a word, in an instant, become flesh and blood. . . . What would happen when, or if, that instant came? When he spoke that word—those four words: "I am your father"—what would the boy feel? What would he say and do? Would the words perhaps mean nothing to him; be simply words and no more? Would he be stunned, disbelieving? Or resentful? Was there any reason on earth why a son should *not* be resentful of a father who had ignored his existence for all his lifetime, only to appear suddenly, meaninglessly, out of nowhere with a fatuous "Here I am"?

The questions mounted, multiplied.

But not the answers.

He had, as he saw it, three alternatives. He could tell John. He could withhold telling, but still try to help him, to play a part in his life. Or he could simply pull out. If he chose the first, there were the answerless questions—and far more than he had already asked. For instance, *how* would he help him? He could take him from the island, or leave him. But take him where? Leave him to what? Should the boy be encouraged to fly? Should he be given money? Sent to college? Or was he better off in the world and life he had known, rather than being plunged by a stranger-father into a world and life wholly alien?

If he chose the second, it would be the same—plus a masquerade. Only the third alternative posed no question. It posed a fact. If he went away, saying nothing, doing nothing, it would be again the boy, not he, who would be the ghost: a ghost who would follow him through the years of his life.

Mel Melnick's spray guns had won the day; the mosquitoes were gone from the quonsets. But Carr was nevertheless often wakeful at night, and again took to walking alone through the neighboring palm groves and along the road by the sea. Two or three times he went out onto the strip of beach where, on an earlier night, he had found Carol Loftus; but he did not find her again. Nor see her jeep on the road.

"I take it you've given up shelling," he said to her one day when she was at the hotel site.

She had just finished treating an injured workman, with her mind still on salves and dressings, and she looked at him uncomprehendingly.

"Your collection of shells," he said. "Have you lost interest?"

"Oh . . . No," she answered. "I've just been so busy."

"At night, too?" When she hesitated, he smiled. "Or at night are you back to locking yourself in the nunnery?"

She half returned the smile, but didn't answer, and he walked with her toward where her jeep was waiting.

"I gather, too, that you've had some callers," he said.

"Yes, a few," said Carol.

"And not welcome."

"It—it isn't that. It's just that I've been—"

"—so busy."

"Yes."

"And tired at night—from all that dancing."

Reaching the jeep, she got in, but made no immediate move to drive away.

"I'm the one who made you dance," he said. "And I'm sorry it led to trouble."

"It's been nothing, really."

"The John thing wasn't nothing."

She shook her head, almost imperceptibly. "How is John?" she asked.

"He's doing all right," said Carr. "At least he's working and learning."

"I've seen him a few times when I've been over here. At a distance, I mean, I've been wanting to speak to him, of course, but it's seemed better to let some time go by."

He nodded.

Then he said, "You mustn't worry about John, you know."

"It's not really worry," she said. "But I *am* concerned about him. I want him to be happy—to find himself."

"I don't mean that sort of worry. I mean your feelings about yourself."

"Myself?"

"Yes. I've an idea you feel *you're* somehow to blame. By dancing with him. Being nice to him. . . . And that that's why you've closed up inside yourself again."

There was a pause. Then for the first time he could recall he used her first name.

"Look, Carol—" he said.

"Yes?"

"My name is Mitch."

"Yes—Mitch?"

"I know a little about you. You've told me—and I've watched. I know this thing you have about men, and about 'being on your own,' and I even think I half understand it. But don't—and I'm serious—please don't let it foul up your life for you. For a man to make a pass at you isn't the end of the world. Even for a brown seventeen-year-old boy to make a pass isn't the end of the world. With a woman like yourself—and you know it—it's the one who doesn't make a pass that's the peculiar one."

Carr smiled again. "Like me," he added.

Carol stared at him.

"Don't think that you're somehow hurt and cheapened by being attractive to men," he said. "That it makes you any less yourself. Or your father's daughter." He waved a hand. "That's today's lecture. Now get back to the nunnery and lock yourself in tight."

He heard her speak his name as he turned away, but he merely waved again. And she drove off.

She was a complicated girl, he thought.

And he was getting very tired of ghostlike fathers.

He was lying half awake, half asleep on his cot in the quonset when he became aware that the door had opened; and groping, he snapped on the light.

"I think I am very angry," Va'ina announced.

"All right," he said, "but don't be too loud about it Everyone's asleep."

"For two weeks I do not see you. You pay no attention. It is like I am your wife."

"I've been busy."

"Busy, hah! I know how you have been busy. With that nurse, yes? With the breadfruit face and hair like eggs." Ignoring his denial, she put a hand to her own hair. "You like?" she asked. "Is new so. Is not like eggs but is nice, do you think?"

The hair was twisted and piled high and smooth on her head, in what might or might not have been the *dernier cri* from Arden or Rubinstein. And she was wearing a bright, tight-fitting dress that obviously had not come off the family sewing machine. Looking down, she passed her hands over its curving lines and said, "Is new too. Is very so—soph—"

"—isticated."

"Yes, isticated. In a lava-lava I am only ivious, but now I am isticated too. That is the way Mr. Melnick likes."

"Mr. Melnick's not here now."

"Yes, I know. If he was here, I think I go to him instead, because you treat me so bad."

Carr had pulled himself up and was sitting on the edge of his cot. Va'ina glanced briefly around the bare room, found nothing of interest, and sat down beside him.

"Is nice bed," she said, bouncing up and down. "Not so soft as under the breadfruit tree, but there are no things that stick you. I think I will like."

She bounced harder, and the springs squeaked. "Yes, I will like," she confirmed. "We will have the nice music while we make love, and the others will think, poor Meesh, he is having the bad dreams."

She giggled.

"Look—" said Carr.

"Yes, I look."

"It's very late and—"

"Yes, is late. Is time not for talk." Swinging her legs around, she turned her back to him. "You will help please," she said.

"Help?"

"With the lava-lava it is easy to take off. With the isticated dress there are many hooks. You will unfix please."

"Oh Lord—" he murmured.

"What do you say?"

"I say you come right to the point, don't you?"

"The point? I do not understand. There are no points in the dress but only the little hooks."

Putting a hand behind her back, she guided his fingers over the hooks. "So—and so," she said. "Now I hang my dress so it will be nice in the morning. And you will please be careful not to spoil my new hair."

Carr watched her as she rose and put the dress on a hanger. She was *not* a complicated girl, he thought. And there wasn't a ghost in sight.

Two days later he reached a decision. It was late afternoon, toward the end of the working day, and leaving the office hut, he drove in one of the jeeps toward the far end of the hotel grounds, where he knew John was operating the bulldozer. He would drive off with him. They would stop in some secluded place. And he would take the plunge. Whatever came of it, it would be better than the status quo.

The bulldozer was where it was supposed to be: at a red gouge in the earth that would presently be a tennis court. But no one was on it. No one was around at all—except a native boy climbing a coconut palm in a nearby grove. It was a tall palm, and when he first saw the boy he was high up on the tapering bole. Presently he disappeared into the clump of greenery on top; a coconut fell; and then the boy reappeared, climbing downward. He moved with the agile grace of an animal, his arms and legs working in perfect rhythm, seeming to cling by some tactile magic to the smooth column, from which a white man, however able, would have fallen in an instant. It was not until he was almost halfway down that Carr saw that it was John.

He watched without moving as the boy continued the descent, taking the last ten feet in a light leap and then retrieving the coconut. As he picked up a stick, sharpened its end with a few strokes of a knife, and, fixing one end in the ground, split the coconut shell on the other —all as deftly and casually as if he were opening a candy wrapper. As he sat down to drink—but not as a Westerner would sit—not really sitting at all, but squatting, rump on heels, with head thrown back, mouth wide, pale liquid flowing down. . . . And still Carr sat and could not move, but only look. At the brown, barefoot, almost naked figure beneath the palm tree. At the island boy in his island world. . . .

And when at last he did move, it was merely to wave as the boy looked up, and then drive away.

The Tiaran sun was hot, and it was two or three times a day that John climbed a palm for a coconut and a cooling drink. He liked the climbing too; it was a welcome change after hours in the jolting seat of the bulldozer. And at the top, in the shading fronds, there was always the breath of the trade wind, the sweep of island and sea. For years past, the top of a palm tree had been, in his imagination, his soaring plane in the sky.

Now, to be sure, he had another plane, of sorts. The bulldozer. It was ridiculous, of course, to compare the grinding, lumbering, earth-bound thing to a machine that could fly, but still he had only to close his eyes for an instant to make an inward leap into the air. For, like a plane, it *was* a machine. It responded to his touch. Under his hands and feet he could feel the power he controlled—just as he had always dreamed he would feel it at the controls of an aircraft.

The jeep had been the first machine he had had a chance at. The bulldozer was the second. But he not only knew how to drive them; he understood them. When the American, Carr, raised the hood of the jeep and showed the workings of its engine, it had seemed to him wholly simple and understandable. When, later, the bulldozer suddenly took to stalling, he had not had to call one of the Utoian mechanics, but had himself found and corrected the trouble.

"Good boy," Carr had said to him, obviously pleased. And then added, smiling: "A little thing like a jet should be a pushover for you, when you get around to it."

He thought a lot about Carr. And the more he thought the less he understood. The first time he had ever seen him he had begun asking questions. Then he kept offering a job. Then there was the whole jail thing: the talk, the driving, the bail to Malele. . . . But why? He had no idea why. . . . Carr had said he had a son his age, but what had that to do with it? That he wanted to help him. But still—why? Sometimes it almost seemed as if the man wanted something of him; in some way *needed* him. And that was the strangest, the most confusing, part of all.

Anyhow, he was grateful. Carr had taught him to drive. He had given him the top job of any Tiaran working on the hotel. Best of all, perhaps, he had, after that first day, never once mentioned the jail—or what had led to the jail. For that, above everything, was what he, John Koa, wanted not to talk of, not to think of. It had simply not happened. It was a bad dream. Carol Loftus did not exist.

Or so he wished. So he decreed fiercely.

. . . and hopelessly . . .

For she existed all right. In his daytime thoughts, cold with shame. In his nighttime dreams, hot with desire. And it was this last that was the worst of it: that the desire was still there: that it had not been just the wild and drunken impulse of a moment, but a thing that gnawed deep in bone and blood. The more he tried to push her from mind, the more she filled it. And as if the burden of thoughts was not enough, she, in her own self, kept appearing and reappearing, cool and white in her jeep, driving to and from the hotel-site infirmary, passing him as he worked on road or lawns. Half of him wanted to speak to her; to tell her he had been wrong, a fool, and that he was sorry. But the other half—the deeper, stronger half—held him prisoner. It could not face coming close to her, speaking her name, meeting her eyes.

So he turned away. . . . But still she was there. . . . In his mind. In the jeep. In the jokes and winks and laughter of the other workmen. With the Utoians this was only moderately bad, for they knew little about him or, except in vague terms, of what had happened. But the Tiarans, his own people, were merciless, taunting him to the point where he would have quit the job, had he not known that it would be even worse back in the village. This made him doubly glad when he was transferred to the bulldozer, for there he was no longer part of a gang. But at night, in the mess and sleeping huts, the ordeal continued; and also there were others, from outside, who would not let him alone. Malele the policeman appeared, to see if he was "behaving himself"; Solomona the pastor, to inquire if he was "repenting his sins." And his uncle, Fahoai, came from the village not once but several times—primarily, he suspected, to drink beer with the "Hawaiians," but never without stopping off to remind him of the disgrace he had brought to the family.

He set his jaw. He veiled his eyes. He had done a stupid thing and he knew it; a wrong, crazy thing, and he must pay the price. But then the day came when the price rose too high; when Patali, the son of High Chief Tafutimo, came by as he was working on the tennis court with the bulldozer. He had never liked Patali. It was one of his few points of agreement with his cousin Va'ina, and for years he had snubbed, taunted, or fought with him, as opportunity offered. But now it was Patali who held all the cards. And he played them with gusto. "Ah, the great lover—the leader of men and conqueror of women," he said by way of greeting. And for the next half-hour, while John went on working, he lounged close by beneath a palm tree, delivering volleys of comment on Carol Loftus and her charms.

John tried to ignore him. He tried to think only of his job, hear only the sound of the grinding engine. But Patali knew how to make himself heard. In desperation, John moved from the inland to the lagoon side of the court, where there were still piles of loose earth to be moved and distributed. But Patali followed leisurely, found a new shade tree, and continued the barrage. John leapt down from the bulldozer. Striding over, he confronted Patali, and Patali rose, and they stood nose to nose exchanging threats and insults. His arm ached to strike out, to smash the sneering, taunting face of his tormentor. But he held it back—for what was the use? A fight would bring others running. It would only cause more talk, more taunts and jokes, more trouble and humiliation.

So, abruptly, he turned away. He went back to the bulldozer, flung himself into the seat, and wrenched at the wheel with tight, shaking hands. The right-hand tread of the tractor ploughed the piled earth. And the earth was soft and loose. Beyond it, from the edge of the court, the slope of the ground fell away toward the lagoon; and the earth silted down; the bulldozer sank and tilted. John swung the wheel in reverse, but could not pull out. And the machine went over. For an instant, all at once, he saw the pouring earth, the slope, the lagoon, and, above, the sky, a palm tree, and the loutish face of Patali. And then he saw nothing. . . .

He awoke to whiteness—and to pain. The pain was in his head and shoulder and down the right side of his body. And the whiteness was everywhere. It was above and below and around him, as if he were under water, in a white sea; and some of it was still, and some of it moved; and then the moving part took shape, it became a human form, a woman's form; and he knew who it was.

He tried to sink back into the sea, but couldn't. For there was no longer any sea. There were the white sheets of a bed, the white walls of the quonset infirmary, and above him, white and trim in its uniform, the figure of Carol Loftus.

"Well, how's our patient?" she asked, smiling.

And he mumbled something.

"Does anything hurt?"

And he mumbled again.

Then, for what seemed an eternity, she went about taking care of him. She examined his head, shaved a patch of hair away, and applied a bandage. Pulling down the sheet, she examined his body, washed it, made him change from his khaki shorts to pajamas, and bound his shoulder and ribs in a sort of elastic strap. She gave him a pill. She brought him food. She was white and cool and efficient and cheerful. And throughout it all he lay in frozen silence, trying not to see or feel her, never meeting her eyes, wishing, praying that the sea would again rise around him and carry him off.

At last it did. The pill took effect, and she faded; the pain faded; and he slept. When he awoke it was dark, and there was no one there. And then he slept again, and on his next awakening it was morning. Once more there was someone in the room, but it was not Carol; it was Mitchell Carr. And when he asked him how he felt, John said all right; and as far as his body was concerned it was almost true, for the pain was much less.

"That skull of yours has been taking quite a beating," Carr said. "But it must be made of iron. Nothing's smashed." And John learned that, as the bulldozer toppled, he had apparently been thrown clear, bruising head and shoulder and ribs, but with no serious injury; and that the bulldozer itself had scarcely been damaged at all.

Carr made light of it. He spoke no word of blame. Presently he left, with a friendly wave, and John was alone again. . . . And then not alone. For Carol Loftus was back. . . . As on the previous day, she examined him, treated him, cleaned him, fed him. And as before, too, he lay silent and still—except that now it was worse, for at least before there had been the pain to distract him. Without the pain, too, there would be no pill, no rising sea to blot her out; and there was no choise but to lie there in torment, in shame, unable to speak or look at her, pretending that they were only patient and nurse, and that nothing had ever happened.

She pretended too. But for her it seemed easy. Busy, competent, professional, she was all nurse—scarcely a woman at all.

"You were a lucky boy," she said when she was finished with him. "Everything's coming along nicely, and in about two more days I'll let you go."

Brisk, smiling, trim and white, she turned to leave. But as she reached the door he spoke at last, in a voice that he himself could scarcely hear.

"I—I'm sorry—" he said.

She turned back to him.

"What, John?"

"I'm sorry for—"

He couldn't say it. But she understood. For the first time her professional manner dissolved, as for a moment she stood still, hesitant, and then returned to the bedside.

"I know you are," she said. "And it's all right."

It had been a mistake. Another mistake. Now, suddenly she was no longer a nurse but again a woman, and as her eyes met his he looked away. He couldn't meet them. Nor could he speak another word. Presently he felt something touch his hand, and he knew it was *her* hand. It rested on his softly, lightly, as it had on that first day when they had been together in the new dispensary. And, well as she meant it, there was now, as then, no comfort in it, but only more hurt, more torment; and still he could not speak or move or turn his eyes, but only lie there, silent, rigid, thinking bitterly: Yes, she touches me. It is all right for her to touch me. But the other way: for me to touch her. . . .

Then she was gone.

But not gone. . . .

For he must have slept again, and dreamed, and she was still there.

She was standing cool and white beside him, but this time it was not
in the whiteness of her uniform but of her naked body; and this time
he *did* turn to her, *did* touch her—and she screamed. He could not
hear the scream; he could only see her opened mouth, her wild eyes.
But others heard and came running: first Malele with his club; then
Solomona with his Bible; then Fahoai and Patali and all the village;
and some were angry and cursed and hit him, and some were pointing and laughing as if their sides would burst. He turned and ran.
Seizing Carol, he ran to the bulldozer, mounted it, sent it lurching
again into piles of earth. Again the earth poured down, but now not
only on him. It poured on Carol too; on her whiteness, her nakedness.
And soon the nakedness was no longer white, but soiled and brown.
It was browner than his own; it was mud-brown; it was black. And
holding the black woman, he hit back at his attackers, he laughed
at the laughers; then, righting the bulldozer, raced off down the
road, down the runway, touched the levers, soared upward . . . and
awoke, sweating and trembling, in his bed.

The hours passed. One of the boys from the mess hut came in with
food. Then Carol returned. Then Carr. But each time he pretended
he was sleeping, and they went away. Actually, he slept no more; he
would not let himself, for sleep meant dreams. The pain was all but
gone now—no more than a remote, dull ache in his head and shoulder.
And his mind was clear. Clearly, coldly, bleakly, he knew at last
what he must do.

He had made his try at being a *papalagi*—at entering into the
white man's world. First through the front door, as a would-be flier,
and the door had not opened an inch. Now through the back door,
as a workman, and it had opened and let him through—but to what?
To more doors ahead, locked and barred. To walls he could never
climb. So far but no farther, said the white man to the brown man.
Come with us, but keep your place. We may touch you, but you
may not touch us.

He had tried and failed. He had turned from his own people and
found, instead—nothing. He had hoped for the sky and found piles
of crumbling earth; touched the untouchable and reaped frustration
and shame. Like Asimo the storekeeper, he was routed, beaten. And,
like him, he would go back where he had come from. The village
would make it hard for him at first, but no harder than here; and
after a while it would forget—just as it had long since forgotten that
Asimo had ever gone away. Even he, too, would forget. Carol Loftus
would soon leave, and a Manaian nurse would come in her place.
And that was the way it would be: the way of Tafutimo and old
Kalamakoa: of *fa'a Manaia* forever.

He sat up in bed. He could not stand another two days in this place; he would go now, this moment. But then he realized that he would be seen and stopped; for gangs of workmen were all over the grounds, and they would like nothing better than to give him a fresh going over, now that there was his accident added to all the rest.

So he waited for night. Time crept. At last the mess boy came back, bringing supper, and by the time he had finished eating it was dark outside. But still he waited, because now the radio was blaring over the loudspeaker, and the usual crowd had gathered to listen. He took the bandage from his head and the strapping from his shoulder, and for a while he shifted and kneaded the shoulder, working out the last of the soreness. Then he lay quietly listening to the music—until it stopped and did not start again. And after another few minutes he got out of bed. At first his legs were rubbery and his head swam; but after he stood for a bit they were better; he was able to walk. His khaki shorts were hanging from a hook on the wall, and, stripping off the pajamas, he put them on. Then, after a careful look from the window, he went out. As he had figured, the radio listeners had left, and there was no one around. The only lights came from the huts occupied by the white men a short way across the slope.

Avoiding them, he made for the road. Halfway there he paused, dizzy again, and he knew he could not make it all the way to the village. But that did not matter. He would sleep nearby in the bush tonight and go on in the morning, when he was rested. What mattered was to get away—out of the domain of Carol Loftus, out of the world of the *papalagi*.

Yet when he reached the road he slowed and stopped. And this time it was not from dizziness, but because there was one remaining thing in that world that he knew he must do. . . . "Are you a child or a man?" Carr had asked him that first day when he had taken him from the jail in his jeep. And he had answered angrily, "I am a man." . . . But was he being a man now, in what he was doing? Not in the leaving itself—for that he had to do—but in leaving like this; like a frightened boy running away. He looked back at the lights from the quonsets. Then he turned and went toward them. He was not afraid of Carr; he would tell him what he was doing. And Carr would know, once and for all, that he was not a child but a man.

He came to Carr's hut, and his room was one of the lighted ones. But the shade was drawn on the single window and he could not see inside. At the door he paused, hand raised to knock. But the hand remained poised, for in that instant he heard a voice—a voice from within—and it was not Carr's. It was another voice that he knew: not a man's but a woman's, not speaking but softly laughing. And as he heard it, something happened inside him. His head spun again, his body tensed, his raised hand trembled. It did not knock, but seized the doorknob; his body lunged forward; he was through the door and in the room, and there were Carr and Va'ina on the bed.

Carr stared at him. Then he got to his feet.

"What the hell is this?" he said.

John didn't answer. He stared back: from Carr to Va'ina, from Va'ina to Carr. The girl made a sound that was half cry, half giggle, and covered her bare body with a sheet.

"Get out," said Carr quietly.

John didn't move.

"You belong in the infirmary. Go back there. Get out."

John's chest rose and fell. His trembling hands were fists. The words seemed to stick in his throat, but now suddenly they welled up, flooding out of him. "Yes, I am getting out," he said. "That is what I have come to tell you: that I am getting out. But now I will tell you something else too. You and this whore—" His voice cracked. His eyes blazed. All the hurt and humiliation and anger he had known through the past weeks rose like a flame within him, swelling, raging, as he lashed out at this man who was his cousin's lover. "You are the Great White King, aren't you? His Majesty the American, the *papalagi*, who comes to live among the savages and take what you want. For us, if we look at a white woman, it is a crime, we go to jail. But for you it is different. For you it is fine to take the brown woman: to sleep with her—to make little gook bastards— always more little bastards—"

"Stop it," said Carr.

"No, I will not stop. I will go on. I will talk as one of the gooks, one of the bastards. And I will tell you what you can do, Mr. American King—you can eat *kae*, that's what—and you can—"

His English failed him and he continued in a torrent of Manaian. Carr tried to break in, but he didn't stop. Carr moved toward him, grasped him, began pushing him toward the door. And he struggled against him.

"Will you for God's sake get out," Carr said.

But he was wild now; he was crazy; crazier even than on that drunken night when he had put his arms around Carol Loftus. And as Carr still pushed, he jerked away. As Carr approached again, he leapt forward, head down, fists flailing.

Then Carr hit him, and he fell.

13

THERE WERE six men in Russell Gorman's office in the Administration Building in Apingo. Gorman himself was at his desk, with Leonard Shafter seated off to one side. Ranged opposite them were Congressmen Davis, Schramm, and McAleer of the United States House of Representatives. And at the window was one Api Mindolo of the Department of Public Works, repairing the air conditioner which had failed to turn on that morning.

Minus conditioning, there seemed to be no air at all in the small room, and faces and voices alike had a tendency to blur in the sticky heat. And, further, conversation was not greatly helped by an accompanying obbligato of hammer and wrench.

"Perhaps you'd better come back later," said Gorman, with an annoyed glance at Mindolo.

"No, is okay, boss. Finish quick," Mindolo assured him.

And Gorman sighed, patted face and neck with his handkerchief, and returned to the business at hand.

"—Yes, the balances are unfavorable, of course," he conceded to Congressman Davis, who held a sheaf of reports on his lap. "But as I'm sure the Governor pointed out, the deficits are only slightly more than last year's, and considering the higher costs in all departments—"

"Costs. That all we hear—costs. Never anything about revenue. What sort of an economy is that?"

"The unfortunate fact, sir," said Gorman, "is that these islands *have* no economy. At least not in the way we use the term back home."

"You grow things here, don't you? Coconuts and so on?"

"Yes. But the yield is small."

"And fish. Why can't something be done about the fish? Over in Samoa they've got a cannery."

"Samoa is bigger than Manaia. And even there, as I'm sure you saw, the commercial fishing is done by Japanese on contract."

"Meaning these island people just don't work?"

"Sometimes yes, sometimes no."

"They're working pretty well now over at the new hotel," said Leonard Shafter.

"Yes, there's the hotel," Gorman agreed. "That should bring income, if it's run right. And attract more investment capital."

"Income, investment, capital—that's all very well," Congressman Schramm put in. "But I submit again, gentlemen, that these islands cannot be measured by the yardstick of dollars and cents. How, I ask you, can these poor people be expected to function as citizens of a modern Christian community when they are denied the very fundamentals of spiritual uplift and enrichment?"

The air conditioner wheezed, then clanked. Congressman Davis was reimmersed in his sheaf of reports. Congressman McAleer pulled his damp luau shirt away from his ample paunch and shook it gently between two fingers.

"For two years now," Congressman Schramm continued, "the good people of the United Brethren Church have been trying to establish a mission in the village of Ak—Aka—" He glanced at Gorman.

"Angatumu," Gorman supplied.

"Yes, Akatoma. And for two years—so I am informed by some of the finest people in my constituency—they have met with only rebuff and prejudice from the authorities here. I have said to the Governor, and I now say to you, sir, that this is in direct violation of the Constitution of the United States of America, which guarantees freedom of worship to—"

"There's no question of the right of free worship. It's the people of Angatumu themselves who feel they don't want to make a grant of community land to still another church."

Leonard Shafter nodded. "It's a matter, as we see it, of the proper rate of adaptive acculturation."

"I beg your pardon?" said Schramm.

"Mr. Shafter is a sociologist," Gorman explained. "He means that the people get confused if too much is shoved at them too quickly."

"*Shoved* at them?"

"There are already four missions in the area," said Shafter, "Congregationalist, Catholic, Mormon, Seventh-day Adventist. And with less than a thousand people in the whole Angatumu district—"

179

Congressman McAleer snapped his fiingers. "Apatingo—that's it," he said. "The stewardess on the plane was talking about it yesterday. Said it was the best place for grass skirts."

"The Mormons!" Schramm snorted. "There's not an island in the Pacific they haven't got into. But when the United Brethren want the—"

"Was she right?" asked McAleer. "They got some good ones there?"

"Most of the villages have some handicrafts," said Gorman. "Tapa cloth, wood carving, shell necklaces—"

"I don't care about that stuff; it's a grass skirt I'm after. A red one. Patsy—that's my twelve-year-old, and a damn good dancer—she says it's got to be red. Like the one that actress, whatshername, wore in that picture, you know—"

"Mr. Shafter will be taking you around the island this afternoon," said Gorman, "and when you stop at the villages he'll inquire—"

His words were lost in a rain of hammer blows from the window. Gorman waited until they ended and said, "Aren't you almost—?"

"Yes, boss, finish two minutes," said Mindolo. "Whoosh, comes the air in. So cold you go brrrr."

Congressman Davis looked up from the papers in his lap. "This isn't a financial statement," he said. "It's a petition in bankruptcy."

"I wouldn't go that far, sir," Gorman protested. "If you'll look at the analysis in Section Five of the Governor's report, you'll see that—"

"What I see is what the figures tell me. And that is what my committee will hear from me when Congress reconvenes. Deficit, deficit, deficit. And for what purpose? What are we doing in these islands anyhow?"

"May I point out that during the war—"

"The war ended fifteen years ago. The Navy and Air Force have been out for ten. If this place had any conceivable use for defense, it would be another matter. But they haven't. The focus isn't on the South Pacific any more, but on the North—the islands up toward Russia and China. This is a backwater, a nothing, a parasite living on handouts from the American taxpayer; and I shall submit to the Congress that—"

"That we can save a few cents a year out of hundreds of billions?" Schramm inquired. "No, gentleman, our role is not to walk out on these poor people, but the opposite—to give them more. And I am not speaking only of money but of spiritual things; of organizations like the United Brethren Church and—"

"How about this new hotel?" said McAleer. "That should buck things up some, shouldn't it?"

180

Gorman nodded. "Yes, we're confident that when tourist money begins to come in—"

"Tourist money!" Davis broke in. "And where will that go, may I ask? With the archaic tax structure, the loopholes and dodges—"

"I'd like to have a look at this hotel," said McAleer. "Might be a place to take the wife and kids sometime."

"I'm afraid it's not possible," Gorman told him, "with you gentlemen staying only thirty-six hours. It involves a boat trip to another island and—"

"Why's it on another island? Why not here on the main one?"

"This is where we ourselves would have preferred it. But the hotel people claimed that Tiara—"

"And there's no plane to Tarara?"

"There will be when the hotel opens. In fact it's due in on the *Mariposa* next week. But right now—"

"Hmm—that might be a thought for the United Brethren," said Schramm.

"Excuse me?"

"On this other island—Tahala: are all these other churches in there too?"

"No, only one. But—"

"The building of the hotel," said Shafter, "has caused a rather special situation on Tiara."

"With the Government, no doubt," said Schramm, "footing most of the bills."

There was another interruption from the air conditioner: this time a growling, grinding sound followed by a blast of hot air. Gorman took the opportunity to glance at his watch, and when a voice could be heard again said, "If you gentlemen are due at the Governor's for lunch—"

The congressmen checked their own watches and rose, and it was arranged that Shafter would pick them up later at the Nimitz Hotel for their tour of the island. Davis announced that he wanted also to stop off at the Government accounting office. Schramm inquired as to what department would have the vital statistics on the Mormon mission. And McAleer said he would leave it to Shafter to pick the best place for grass skirts. "Come to think of it," he added, "I'll want a—you know—something for up here too." He patted his luau shirt with cupped hands and chuckled. "My Patsy's getting to be a big girl now."

They went out. At the window, Mindolo rose and headed for the door. "Two minutes, boss," he said. "Get new little piece, come back."

Gorman sat down heavily and remopped his damp forehead. "That's just what we need out here," he muttered. "Bigger and better junketing congressmen."

Shafter shook his head glumly.

"And next week we've got those five brass hats from Interior."

"*Next* week? I thought—"

"They've pushed it up."

"I'm due to go over to Tiara," said Shafter.

"Well, you'll have to postpone it. You know what these things are: reports, surveys, twelve conferences going on at once. . . . Anyhow, things are all right over there, aren't they?"

"It's hard to tell from this distance."

"Melnick hasn't been in all morning, so the hotel can't have fallen down. And Doc Friede says the epidemic's over. He tells me young Harris did a good job on it—and that blonde nurse too."

Shafter nodded. "She's a good nurse, Miss Loftus."

"What about that trouble she had?" Gorman asked. "With some drunk wasn't it?"

"That's one of the reasons I want to get back there: to find out more about it."

"Who was the man? That storekeeper fellow?"

"No, that's one of the queer things. It wasn't a man at all, really—just a boy—and one of the best."

"Well, best or not, we can't have our nurses being chased around as if these were still the Cannibal Islands. The kid's in jail, isn't he?"

"He was. Now he's out on bail."

"Bail? Who's got bail money to put up over there?"

"The police say it was this Mitchell Carr."

"Who?"

"The engineer who's working for Melnick. He was in here once, remember? He came to blast out the lagoon, and they got him to stay on for some surveying work."

"And what's surveying got to do with this boy?"

"I don't know—except that for some reason he's interested in him. He has him working now at the hotel."

"Hm. . . . Well, at least it should keep him away from the nurse. And she won't be there much longer, will she?"

"A few weeks. The training school will have a local girl ready by early next month."

"Just as well, too. When you get a blonde bombshell type like that out on her own, there's always sure to be trouble."

Shafter sighed and rose. "If I'm going to be spending the afternoon on red grass skirts," he said, "I'd better get my desk cleared."

He went out, and Gorman turned to the papers on his own desk.

Presently Mindolo, of Public Works, reappeared, said, "Fix now, boss; fix good," and again squatted by the air conditioner. His hammer thumped. His wrench squeaked. Then a Manaian clerk came in and said, "Outside there is the gentleman from—"

But Mel Melnick was there before he had finished, his sallow face taut, his thin frame quivering with agitation.

"That rain last night—" he said.

It occurred to Gorman that he would have preferred even a return visit by the congressmen, but he managed a pleasant conversational tone. "It didn't help much, did it?" he commented. "Today's hotter than ever."

"Oh, it helped all right, it helped fine. Five tons of it came through the roof of the warehouse where all my stuff is stored."

"With much damage?"

"I don't know. I can't even find the labor to open the crates for a look. But the whole housekeeping setup's in there—furniture, rugs, linen, the works—and I damn well want them out before the next cloudburst."

"The man to speak to is the superintendent of—"

"The superintendent's out fishing. The assistant superintendent's wife is having a baby. That tin can *Ickes* boat goes over to Tiara half empty while a hundred grand worth of my equipment sits in that bathtub. And then who shows up again? That customs joker, that's who."

"What's on his mind now?"

"Mind? What mind? He's a certified lunatic. Ten times it's been explained to him about those made-in-Japan labels on the kitchenware. That sure they were made in Japan, but so what? That they went from Japan to Hawaii, where the duty was paid by the importers—and then they get shipped down here, and this jerk expects me to pay duty again."

"Have you the bills of lading?"

"Yes."

"And the Honolulu customs receipts?"

"Yes."

"Then if you just tell your manager to—"

"Manager? What makes you think I've got a manager?"

"I thought he was arriving on yesterday's plane. The same one as the congressmen."

"*Was,* yes. But didn't. Instead comes a cable that he's having trouble with a wisdom tooth." The proprietor of the Tiara Beach Hotel made a sound midway between a snarl and a guffaw. "By now I should have here"—he counted on his fingers—"one manager, one assistant

183

manager, one maître d'hôtel, one chef, one housekeeper. And what have I got? Me."

"When will they come—next week?"

"God knows. Except for the maître d', who's not coming at all. . . . And do you know why not? This is better than a wisdom tooth. . . . Because he says he's just bought a new Thunderbird, that's why, and he's afraid the roads here aren't good enough for it."

There was a gap in the conversation while Mindolo whacked the air conditioner. Then Gorman said, "There's a plane going out tomorrow. Maybe you should get yourself up to Honolulu and straighten things out."

"Sure I should. But how the hell can I, when I'm running this goddam kindergarten over at the Nimitz?"

"You mean training the help?"

"Help—hah! I got thirty-five of them there, straight down from the trees, and if I leave them for ten minutes, back up they'll go. . . . This is what my stateside staff should be doing; that's why I wanted them here early. But who's doing it? Me. . . . Teaching 'em to make beds, no less. How to clean a john. How to carry a tray rightside up."

Since he had been there Melnick had twice sat down and twice stood up again. Now he looked at his watch, groaned weakly, and made for the door. "Now comes advanced dishwashing," he said, "and you'll hear 'em smashing all the way over here."

At the door he turned, recalling why he had come. "This warehouse guy, will you for God's sake find him?" he pleaded. "And talk to that customs jerk?" He breathed in deeply, squared his sagging shoulders, and taking a bottle from his pocket, shook out two tablets. "A man can't even get Miltown in this dump," he muttered bleakly, putting them into his mouth. "Something called Relaxo they hand out to me at the drugstore. Whoever the hell ever heard of Relaxo?"

When he was gone Gorman tried also to take a deep breath, but there seemed nothing to breathe. The air conditioner gave a wheeze, then a sigh, then was silent; and Api Mindolo, after pulling gently at his ear for a few moments, picked up his tools and again started to leave.

"All right now?" Gorman asked.

"All right, boss. Almost okay," said Mindolo cheerfully. "One more little part is need, thasall, but no have it in shop. I tell super, he send stateside, then goes fine."

He went out. The Manaian clerk returned.

"Phone broke now for while," he announced. "But messenger come, bring these." And he put three Government memos on Gorman's desk. The first was from the principal of Apingo High School, to

184

the effect that the main building's front steps had been washed away in the previous night's rainstorm and that there were no funds for their replacement. The second, from the Governor's office, suggested that the village of Kumi, rather than Angatumu, was the best possibility for Congressman McAleer's red grass skirt. And the third, a routine daily report from the Police Department, recorded that a five-year-old boy named Ipao Davali had been killed by a truck on the coast road of Tiara.

In Tiara's village, in the council house by the *malae,* the air conditioning functioned as usual. The trade wind, flowing in over sea and beach, rustled high in the palm fronds and moved gently through the pillared hut where a dozen men sat cross-legged on pandanus mats. There was no sound of wrench or hammer. No one mopped a forehead, plucked at a damp shirt, or brought forth a bottle of either Miltown or Relaxo. Yet these men were no more at ease than those who came and went in the office of Russell Gorman. No less than administrator, congressman, or hotelier, they had their problems.

As with men everywhere, facing problems, there was disagreement. But these were patient men, geared not to clocks and calendars but to the slow cycles of earth and sea; and thus far at least, there had been few raised voices, few interruptions, as each of the *matai* who formed the council had his turn at speaking. Other villagers, of less than *matai* rank, were not permitted to speak or even enter the council hut. But still there were many ringed around it, listening, for they knew that this day's meeting was no ordinary one.

Now it was Fahoai, the talking chief, who held the floor, and he said, "Yes, of course, it is a sad and evil thing, this death of one of our children, and our deep sympathy goes to the bereaved family of little Ipao Davali. But still we must be fair in placing, or not placing, blame. It is the fact, reported by all witnesses, that the child ran suddenly from behind a tree in the path of the truck, so that the driver could do nothing. Also, the driver was not a *papalagi* but one of our own people. So how can it be said it was all the fault of the *papalagi*?"

"No one is saying they wished the child's death," said one of the *matai*. "Nor even that they were directly involved. But it is the fact that without them there would have been no death. It is they, not we, who brought the trucks to our island."

"And all the rest, too."

"Yes, all the rest. The machines that roar and scrape our land away. The dynamite that shakes our lagoon. The drunken strangers. And soon there will be more strangers, more cars on our roads, fouling the air, killing more children."

185

The old man of Fahoai's household, Kalamakoa, had sat through most of the meeting with head bowed on his skeletal chest, as if asleep. But now the head went slowly up, his eyes glowing like coals beneath the hooded lids. "Yes, killing, destroying," he murmured. "That is all the *papalagi* knows. Why does he not bring his bomb and have done with us all?"

"There will be no bomb here and we know it," said Fahoai in annoyance.

"But other things," said a councilman, "almost as bad."

"Too many things," said the high chief, Tafutimo. "Already there are too many."

He shook his grizzled lion's head slowly, looking out from the *fale* toward the beach and the sea. Then, returning his gaze to the others, he continued in a deep, measured voice. "The child's death was bad, but so too is everything that now happens on our island. Others have been injured by the machines of the *papalagi*. Almost all were struck by the sickness they brought among us. . . . And there are further illnesses too: not of the flesh but of the spirit. . . . Is it not illness that many people of our village are gone? Men who should fish and make copra now work for this hotel. Men and women both have gone to Apingo to learn *papalagi* ways, so that later they will work for it. Families are broken. Even those still here do not stay in their homes at night, but go to the hotel place to hear the radio. And at the feast—"

"Yes, the feast—" chorused some of the others.

"It was a disgrace."

"A shame."

"At the feast for these strangers," Tafutimo continued, "there was conduct such as has not been seen on this island before. The *papalagi* drink; always they drink. But now our people drink too. They are drunk. There is Ioane Koa, who is the worst, and a shame on the village. But there are others as well. With such things we will soon be a village of drunkards, like Asimo the storekeeper. And you know why it is so with Asimo: it is because he went to live in the world of the *papalagi*."

There were nods from around the listening circle. Then one of the elders said, "There is also the case of the *taupou*."

"Yes, there is the *taupou*, Va'ina." The high chief's face was somber. "There is her dance at the feast, which all know was not the true dance of a *taupou*, but of a wanton. Not for the honor of her village, but for the favors of strangers."

"And it is not only the dancing."

"No—she *gets* the favors. And gives them."

"She no longer lives here, where she should, but at the hotel place.

And at night, they say, she goes to the hut of this *papalagi*."

"The red-faced one?"

"No, not him. The other. The tall one, who also brought her cousin from the jail."

"This from a *taupou* who should be virgin until marriage—"

"We should do with her as in the old days," croaked Kalamakoa, rousing himself again from seeming sleep.

"How is that, old man? What do you mean?"

"I mean with the stick. With the sharp stick from the *fau* tree into her secret place, here on the *malae* so all can see. If the stick is bloodied, then we know it is all right, she is a virgin. But if not, if it comes out clean, she is no *taupou* but a whore of the *papalagi,* and then it is we, in vengeance, who make the blood—who punish her *fa'a Manaia,* in the way of our fathers."

A few of the others called *"Ai—ai"* in agreement. But from most came a chorus of protest.

"We are Christians, old man," boomed Pastor Solomona. "Would you have us return to heathen abominations?"

Kalamakoa did not answer. As if drained by his outburst, he sat silent again with head bowed. But those who agreed with him took up his cause. Others shouted them down. For the first time emotion had risen to the point where decorum was shattered, and now the council argued and wrangled, while beyond the enclosing pillars the watchers stood in awed stillness.

Then the high chief's voice cut through the babble. "Enough. Enough of this," Tafutimo commanded. "The pastor speaks right—we are not heathens or savages. And there will be no trial by stick."

"Forgive my kinsman that he talks such foolishness," said Fahoai. "He is but an old man and knows no better."

"His years forgive him," Tafutimo agreed. "But for certain of your other kinsmen it is another matter." He was silent a moment, his dark eyes fixed on his subordinate chief. "It has perhaps occurred to you," he then went on, "that the two who have caused most trouble, in these days of trouble, are of your own family. And is there not, perhaps, reason for this? Is it not, perhaps, because you, of all who live here, have taken most to *papalagi* ways? Because in your home—except for this old man—there is least respect for the things of Manaia, so that the boy Ioane Koa and the girl Va'ina have come to do the things they have done?"

Fahoai's plump frame stiffened. "If the high chief will permit," he answered, "may I point out that I am not one of my savage ancestors, of whom the old man is so proud. Nor do I intend, in my home, to live like one."

"So you allow these young ones to run wild, to flout all custom and decency. This boy who is too good for us all and tries to rape *papalagi* women. This girl, an honored *taupou* who could have had my son Patali for husband, but is instead a whore." Fahoai tried to break in, but Tafutimo raised a hand. "Let us not argue it. It is not for these two, anyhow, that I am concerned; they are beyond that. It is for the others among us, for all the young ones not yet corrupted, but who soon will be, if steps are not taken."

"*Ai—ai,*" came the agreement of the council.

"Now," the high chief went on, "there are but a few outsiders on our island, but soon there will be hundreds. Everywhere there will be strange ways. There will be the curse of money, of machines, of drink—of all that is against our way of living. This hotel will be like the *ma'ua,* the inkfish with its eight legs, that reaches out taking everything, until all our old ways are gone, with nothing given in return."

"There will be much in return," said Fahoai. "There will be a whole new world that it is time we knew and lived in. There will at last be money for our people—yes—and what, I ask, is wrong with that? There will be employment, many jobs—"

"As servants."

"No, not only as servants. Already Mr. Melnick, of the hotel, has said he will want many for dancing, for handicrafts, and that he will build a village for us by the hotel."

"So the tourists can come and look at us, as at fish in a trap."

There was a silence. Tafutimo again looked out toward the shining sea, and his lion's face was scowling.

"You try to live in the past," said Fahoai. "But you cannot. . . . You try to stop the world from changing. But you cannot."

"No, we cannot stop it," Tafutimo conceded, his voice low and distant; and for another long moment he continued to look away, deep in somber thought.

Then his eyes moved back to the council. His voice came out firm and hard.

"But we can leave it," he said.

"Leave it?"

It was not only Fahoai who spoke. The words ran like a murmuring echo through the council house and the crowd of villagers beyond its pillared walls.

"This island has been our home," said Tafutimo. "Now it will no longer be ours, but that of the *papalagi,* of strangers. And I say to you we must make another home. We must go."

"Go? Go where?"

Again it was not a single voice. It was scarcely a voice at all, but rather a common breath, an emanation, from all who watched and listened.

"I have thought much of this," said the high chief slowly, measuredly, "and here is what I propose to you, my people. . . . You know the island of Maniloa. It is a low island, an atoll, about two hundred miles to the east of Tiara. Some of you have been there, on the trips of the Government boat when it goes for coconuts. In years past Manaians lived there, but now for long it has lain empty, with no one, waiting for those who might come again. . . . I say to you it is we who should come; who should leave this place that is no longer ours and there make ourselves new homes and new lives."

He paused; and this time there was neither echo nor whisper. The only sound was the rustle of air in the palm fronds. The men of the council sat rigid, and the faces of the villagers hung like a sculptured frieze around the circumference of the hut.

"To leave here will be hard," Tafutimo continued. "But to remain would, in the end, be harder, and we are a people who have never shrunk from doing what must be done to preserve us. In the old days our ancestors journeyed thousands of miles to find their homes: across oceans, through horizons, without weakness or fear. For us it will be but a short journey; and if we have not the *mana,* the strength of spirit, of those who went before us, at least we have the *mana* for that. So I say to you, come! Rouse yourselves! Let us show the *papalagi* that we are still men, still Manaians of old Polynesia. That they can take our lands, our homes, do with them what they will— but that they cannot take *us*. We will go on as our fathers did. Across the seas—through the horizons—to Maniloa—"

"To Havaiki!"

This was a single voice. The voice of Kalamakoa. And as all eyes turned to him, his shriveled form seemed to grow and straighten, and the dark flame gleamed again in his sunken eyes.

"From Havaiki our people came," he cried. "To Havaiki we shall return. To Havaiki the homeland—"

There was echo again. The magical word was on a hundred tongues. The undying vision of a race rose bright before watching eyes.

But there were eyes, too, that saw differently; tongues for which the old magic was gone. "Nonsense!" said Fahoai, his voice cutting through the general murmur. "In all my years I have never heard such foolishness." And several others among the councilmen quickly joined him in his protest.

"I for one will not go," said the first.

"Only madmen would go," said a second.

189

"Tiara is our home."

"Why should we run from it?"

"Like cowards."

"Like fools."

Then others came back at them. . . .

"It is the cowards and fools who would stay here."

"To be the slaves of the *papalagi*."

"On Maniloa we can be our own masters."

"We can live our own life."

"Yes, we will go. We will sail—"

"Across the seas, as our ancestors sailed—"

"To Maniloa—"

"To Havaiki—"

"And if you are insane enough to want to do this," said Fahoai, gaining the floor again, "how, may I ask, do you propose to live when you get to this Maniloa?"

"As we have always lived," replied Tafutimo. "*Fa'a Manaia*. On the fruits of the earth and the fish of the sea."

"On the fruits? What fruits? I have been to Maniloa—when I was a young man, on a copra schooner—and there is only sand and scrub and coconut trees."

"We will bring the rest with us. Taro and yams, breadfruit and mangoes, our chickens and our pigs. And we will plant and work and make the earth grow green."

"Green with what? With sea water? With urine? It is an atoll, not a high island. There are no hills, no streams."

"Perhaps you forget that I too have been to Maniloa," said Tafutimo. "There are springs beneath the earth there. And more rain than here."

"And so, even if we kept alive," said one of Fahoai's cohorts, "—what then? What sort of life would we have?"

"A life of freedom, of decency."

"In the old way."

"*Fa'a Manaia*."

"Rather *fa'a pua'a*, I would say. Like pigs. Like savages."

"No, we would build homes—as good as here."

"And what of a church?" Pastor Solomona demanded in his resonant voice. "I can give my blessing to no such enterprise unless I am assured that there will be a proper place of worship. First things must come first, and these are glory and honor to the Lord."

"Yes, of course," said one of the *matai*. "When we get there we will all kneel and pray—while we starve to death."

"If first things come first," said another, "we will build the church last."

"For the women and children."

"Why build a church at all? If we are leaving the *papalagi* world, what do we want with a *papalagi* god?"

"*Ai, ai,*" croaked old Kalamakoa. "In Havaiki we will have the old gods. Great Takaroa, who rules sky and sea; Tamanuitera, golden son of the sun; wild Tahiri-matea, who makes the wind blow—"

"Quiet, old one!" roared the pastor. "You are a heathen blasphemer. You are owned by the devil."

"And you," said a *matai*, "*you* are owned by the *papalagi*."

"Stop, all of you!" Tafutimo commanded. "We are not pagans but Christians." He glared at Kalamakoa and his supporters. "And we will have a church, there as here."

"Even so," said Solomona, only partially mollified, "I shall have to communicate with the Mission Board and the authorities in Apingo, before I can—"

"You will communicate with no one." The high chief's voice was hard and strong. "And that is to be understood by everyone," he added, looking around the assemblage. "This is a thing among ourselves and ourselves alone, and no one else is to know of it until it happens. . . . *No one,* I say. And least of all the Government."

There was a moment of surprised silence; then a chorus of voices.

"But why?"

"Why not the Government?"

"What can the Government do to stop us?"

"They cannot stop us," said Tafutimo. "But they will not approve. They will make it difficult."

"Yes, they are always telling us what to do."

"They treat us like children."

"Because you *are* children," said Fahoai, "with foolishness of this sort. . . . But even if you go ahead with this crazy thing, how, please tell me, do you propose to get to Maniloa without the Government knowing? To begin with, you would have to go in their boat."

"No, not in their boat," Tafutimo said.

"How then?"

"In our own."

"Our own? What are you saying? Our canoes can barely go as far as the reef, let alone into the open sea."

"We will build a different sort of canoe." The high chief's eyes moved from Fahoai to the circle of *matai* and the crowd beyond. "We will build a great one," he said. "We will build a canoe like those of our forefathers, in which they crossed the widest of oceans."

Again a murmur rose: a murmur not unlike the sound of the sea itself.

And again Fahoai tried to speak. "It is impossible," he protested. "We do not know how. Such canoes have not been built for generations—"

But his voice was overwhelmed as the murmuring swelled.

"Like our forefathers," cried Tafutimo, "we will sail the great ocean. Like them, we will go on until we reach our new homeland."

"Ai! Ai!" came the reply from a hundred voices. And then, from among them, rose one voice, higher and more compelling than all the rest. The withered old man, Kalamakoa, was standing erect. His head was thrown back, his eyes were closed, and from his lips, wild and free, flowed an unforgotten chant of old Polynesia:

> *... Blow, blow, O Tahiri-matea,*
> *God of Winds,*
> *Raise the west wind, the great wind,*
> *To carry us true*
> *By the sea road to the homeland,*
> *To Havaiki. ...*

Other voices joined in. The sea no longer murmured but thundered, and from its crest, high and bright, like the sail of a great canoe, rose the soaring pride of an ancient race.

In the last row of villagers, beyond the encircling pillars of the council house, John Koa sang with the others. He did not make the mistake of thrusting forward, as he had once before. But his heart was pounding. His eyes were shining.

14

NOW THE SHELL of the hotel's main building stood pink and gleaming above the lagoon. The frames of the bungalows were up. Terrace and dance floor, pool and tennis court were in the last stages of construction. What remained to be done was in the realm of carpentry, plumbing, wiring, interior furnishing, and there was no further work—even "made" work—for an enginner.

Still, Mitchell Carr stayed on.

He sat alone on the soft slope beneath the palms. He swam in the green crystal of the lagoon. Leaving the hotel, he walked out on the coast road, along the beaches, up valley and ridge toward where Tiara's cloud cap hung white on its pinnacle, and looked out at the immense peace of sea and sky. This was the world that had lived in his memory for eighteen years, that he had traveled thousands of miles to reknow, to reclaim. The work for the hotel had been merely the flimsiest of pretexts. *This* was what he had come for: this peace, this clarity. And now he strove with all his will to make it part of himself.

It was no use. It was no part of him, nor he of it. He was an interloper on a stage against a painted backdrop, and his very striving made him even more a misfit and an alien. He had spoken to Carol Loftus about the baggage travelers carried; and now his own baggage was piled so high it shut out everything around him. He walked the paths and roads, but did not know where he was going. Encountering the people of the island, he answered their greetings with an abstracted *"Talofa,"* but he scarcely saw their brown gentle faces. He saw only one face: a boy's face jerking back from him with blood dripping from the mouth.

He had sought here detachment and perspective. What he had found was new involvement, new problems—and the burden of guilt.

Over and over he struggled with the alternatives that faced him. But he was even farther from an answer than before that night on which John Koa had burst into his hut. A dozen times, on impulse, he had started for the village—only to turn back in the realization that beyond impulse there was nothing. The boy was not of his world, he told himself, but of this other, into which he could not enter; and he had returned to his own people; and it was better so. Anything he, Mitchell Carr, could say or do would only cause more trouble, more wounds, of mouth or mind or heart. He was a man who could do many things. He could blast a lagoon, survey a tract of land, read a blueprint, fly a plane, build a skyscraper. He could make money, make friends, make his way in the world—at least outwardly. But each time he had been involved in an inward human relationship it had crumbled into ruins. With his wife, Margaret. With his wife, Helen. Now with his son, his only son, John Koa.

A son who was a stranger. A barefoot brown boy in a tree. . . .

The *Harold L. Ickes* came and went: bringing in the hotel's furnishings, taking off the construction machinery. And one day when it came, Captain Stack stepped down onto the jetty and handed him a letter. It was the first he had received since he had been in Manaia.

On the front was a San Francisco address, penciled out. A Hawaiian address, penciled out. And in a corner was written: *Try TB Hotel, Manaia.* On the back was the return address:

Swanson, Bromley, Inc.
600 Fifth Avenue
New York 19, N.Y.

Back in the quonset, he opened it. He read the beginning: *Still nuts? Well, so are we. We're still hoping. . . .* He read the ending: *Call or wire us. Best, George.*

And the next morning he watched the *Ickes* sail away again to Apingo.

Frank Lavery, still busy with work in progress, took time off now and then to eye him quizzically or make grinning comments on his continued presence. "Enjoying your rest cure, Mitch?" he would say. Or—"That Va'ina gal's sure got you, boy." Or—"Guess the only way you'll get off this rock is to ship her home f.o.b." And the other Hawaiians, too, had ponderous fun with him over the clicking chips of the nightly poker game.

For he had now taken to playing with them: at first for only a few hands each evening, before restlessness drove him out; then, finding that restlessness led him nowhere, for as long as the games lasted. In the haze of smoke and the glare of the light bulbs the image that haunted him faded. He could as well have been in a construction camp in Peru or Libya, a hotel room in Pittsburgh or Detroit. "Beer, Mitch?" the others asked, as the cans made the rounds. And at first he shook his head. But then he stopped shaking it; he drank two and then four and then six beers in an evening; and then, tiring of beer, switched to whisky and sat through the games with a bottle beside him.

"Well, off that old wagon at last," said Lavery.

"Off but good," he said later.

"It's part of the rest cure," Carr told him.

After weeks of no drinking at all—except for the one night of the feast—he felt what he drank. And he wanted to feel it. By the time the games were over (and he had paid up his invariable losings) he was in a blur that carried him even beyond glare and smoke and chatter, into the darkness outside, to his hut and his room and the aloneness of the night. For, contrary to what the others thought, Va'ina no longer came to him; he had told her not to; and it was alone that he sat on his cot, having another blurring drink, or two, or three, before at last he slept.

. . . And dreamed. . . .

For always, no matter how much he had drunk, there were the dreams, there were two of them, and they were both different and the same. In the first, the "staying" dream, he went to the village. He went not in a jeep but in a bulldozer, rumbling down the road, entering the village, looking up and seeing a brown boy perched high on a palm tree. Thrusting the 'dozer forward, he struck the tree, he cracked it, he brought it down; and as it fell, the boy fell with it and lay on the ground beside him with a bloody mouth. . . . In the second, the "going" dream, there was also, at first, a tree, but now it was he who was climbing, and presently it was no longer a tree but the scaffolding of a great building, and he had built it. High above on the pinnacle there was a roaring, the roar of a riveting drill held by a brown boy. But then it was not a drill, it was a plane that roared; and the boy was in the plane, he was taking off from the pinnacle; but the plane dipped, it failed, it fell. It lay broken on the earth at the foot of the building, and beside it lay the boy—with a bloody mouth.

As the dreams blended and faded, there were others there too. There were two figures in shadow, watching, and they had no faces, but they were Margaret and Helen. Then another figure came, also a woman, and faceless, but dressed in white, and moving forward, she knelt beside the boy and put a hand to his bloody mouth. And

195

that was all. The dreams dissolved and were gone. Figures and dreams and sleep were all gone, and he was lying on his cot in the hot darkness, and his hands were fists, and the fists were trembling.

He walked up valley and ridge and sat by the pool in the forest. Above him the breadfruit tree spread bland and serene against the gentle sky.

Then there was a movement in the glade and Va'ina was sitting beside him. She was wearing a lava-lava, and her hair fell long and black from the two gardenias she wore at her ears.

"So we are back at the tree," she said, "where the Old Man stands quiet."

He nodded but did not answer, and after a moment she said:

"A cigarette, please."

He lighted one for each of them, and they smoked in silence. Then she spoke again, saying, "What is it, Meesh? You tell me, please—what is wrong?"

"Nothing," he said.

"Yes, there is much wrong. I come to you in your place at night, and you say go away. I follow you now here, and you do not want me."

He touched her hand lightly. "I'm sorry," he said.

"You are not angry then?"

"No."

"So touch me more."

She leaned toward him, her eyes on his face, her lips close to his. But he did not touch her again, and suddenly, holding his hand, she got to her feet. "Come," she said. "We swim now. Like before, yes? We swim and laugh and make splash in the fall, and then we lie here happy, under the tree, in the place of *fia fia*."

She pulled, but he did not rise; and her smile changed to a pout as she looked down at him.

"I'm sorry," he said again.

"So yes, you are angry."

"No."

"You do not like me any more."

"It isn't that."

"For three weeks you do not like me. I come to you and you do not want me. I live close by the hotel, to be with you, and you do not see me. It is like—"

He pulled her gently down, but when she was again beside him he let her go. "Look, Va'ina," he said, "you should go back to the village."

"The village?"

"Yes, to your home. Where you belong."

"No, I do not belong. I hate. It is—how you say—a dopey place. And besides—" She paused.

"Besides, what?"

"—I cannot go. They are mad at me."

"Mad?"

"My uncle, Tafutimo, everyone. I am the *taupou* of the village, who is prettiest and dances best. But there is also stupidness for a *taupou*, with no fun, they say, no *fia fia*, but only to marry a jerk like this Patali. And so now they are mad; they have bad names for me."

"Because of us—"

"Yes, us. But I do not care. I say to them they should drop coconuts on their heads and find another *taupou*. I will go anyhow. With Mr. Meesh Carr. To the hotel, to dance—for Mr. Melnick, for the *papalagi* who come—and soon the big shots will come, from Hawaii, Hollywood, New York, and they will clap and say *'Malo!'* and then I go to America, and I am rich and famous."

"So I've fouled you up too," he said.

She came back from her dreams of glory. "Fouled—what is that?" she asked. "How do you mean?"

"First your cousin. Now you."

She looked at him uncomprehendingly. "My cousin? That is John. But what has he to do with—"

Then she understood.

"Yes, it is right," she said. "Before, I do not think of it, but yes, it is since that night, since he came when we were together, that you do not see me any more. That you make like I am not there."

Puzzlement returned to her face.

"But still I do not see—"

"I've made things very hard for your cousin," said Carr quietly. "And now for you. . . . That isn't why I came here: to make things hard for people."

"Hard—for me? I tell you I do not care about the village. Or that I was a *taupou*. I care only that you and I we have been very happy, we have had much *fia fia*, much love; and now it is not the same. Now it is all trouble, all *pilikia*."

He said nothing.

"Why, Meesh?" she asked. "You tell me why, please. . . . I have done something wrong? You tell me and I stop. . . . It is because my cousin comes? He will not come again. . . . Only say why you have now the *pilikia*, and I will fix. I will make it go."

As she spoke she had moved closer to him, and now, with a lithe movement, she turned and lay back with her head in his lap. Her eyes, smiling, looked up into his, and her hair flowed in a dark wave over his thighs and knees.

"You see," she murmured. "It is nice now, no? We are again under the breadfruit tree, in the happiness place."

He looked down at her. He looked at her face, her body, her loveliness; at the island girl in her lava-lava, in his arms, smiling, waiting for love. And he thought: yes, this is how it is in the books: Gauguin with his Tehura, Melville with his Fayaway, Loti with his Rarahu. This is how it is on tin-pan alley, with the tune of the moon on the tropic lagoon. . . . And more than that; more than dream or fantasy. . . . This was how it *had been,* in fact, in truth, for him, Mitchell Carr. With a girl called Lovana, long ago. Even, briefly, with this girl, this Va'ina, a few weeks past.

"Meesh—"

"Yes?" he said.

"You kiss me, please."

Bending his head, he kissed her lightly on the lips; but when her arms rose to circle his neck he held them gently, and then, rising, drew her also to her feet.

"I must go now," he said.

"Go?"

He nodded.

Anger flashed in her eyes . . . but for an instant only. Then they filled with tears. They were not tragic tears: he knew that. They were the soft, easy tears of the islands that would soon be gone: perhaps again in anger—perhaps in laughter. But still he could not watch them. He turned away. For what he knew was the last time, he looked about him at this place of enchantment: at the pool, the waterfall, the banks of moss and blossom, the breadfruit tree. The tree stood against the shining sky—serene, flawless. The Old Man's arms were spread in wisdom and love.

There was the sound of the fall, and for a while the soft sound of sobbing. Then the sobbing stopped, and he turned back to Va'ina.

"Come, we'll go down together," he said.

And leaving the tree of *fia fia* behind, they walked back into the world that was.

He sat on his cot in the quonset, a bottle of bourbon on the table and a glass in his hand, and watched the fading light beyond the window. Then there was a knock on the door, he rose and opened it, and there was Carol Loftus.

"I don't mean to disturb you—" she said.

His initial surprise over, he smiled. "No, the timing's just right," he said. "The sour hour. Welcome."

Stepping back, he opened the door all the way, and after a moment's hesitation she came in. "With a place reserved," he added, removing a shirt and pair of trousers from the single chair. And after another brief hesitation she sat down. In her white uniform and cap she looked, at the same time, both trimly professional and ill at ease.

"I just finished at the infirmary," she said. "And it's been so long since I've seen you—"

"I've been busy," he said.

"Yes, of course." She seemed about to go on, but didn't, and opening a cupboard he took out a second glass.

"I can offer bourbon and water," he said, "or bourbon and bourbon."

"Oh no, thanks—nothing," she said.

He smiled again. "No more missteps?"

She looked at him, not understanding.

"Like the night of the revels—"

"Oh."

"—when the dedicated daughter of Dr. Loftus almost forgot herself."

He did not urge the drink on her, but, instead, replenished his own glass. "The department of self-forgetting can be very complicated," he said. "This, for example" —he raised his glass—"is one of the classical components. But it's not always foolproof."

He took a drink and set the glass down, and there was a brief silence.

Then she said: "As I was saying, it's been a while since I've seen you. I've come over every other day or so, the same as always; but you've not been around, and I thought that perhaps—"

"I was gone?"

"No, I knew you weren't gone. Mr. Lavery and the others would speak of you."

"And what did they say?"

"Nothing, really. Just that you were still here, and—"

"—how busy I was?"

She shook her head. "No, just that you—well—talked about leaving, but didn't. And I couldn't help having the feeling that something was wrong."

He took another drink and looked past her and out the window, to where the sun was setting into the lagoon.

"Is it something to do with John?" she asked.

His eyes met hers.

"John?"

"I've been thinking of when he was here in the infirmary. That was the last time I saw you—the day after his accident—and you were there with him; you were there most of the time. I wanted him to stay in bed at least another day, and you said you'd look in on him during the night, when I went back to the village. But then the next morning when I came, he was gone; and you seemed to be gone too—I couldn't find you. And I still don't know what could have happened."

"He didn't come to you?"

"Come to me?"

"In the village. When he went back there. You didn't—treat him again?"

"No. I looked for him, of course. And he was there; people told me so. But you know how it's been since *that* night. He just can't bear to be near me, and wherever I'd go, he'd manage to be somewhere else."

"You haven't seen him, then?"

"Just once, really. I was coming around a corner—past Asimo's store, I think—and there he was, and I tried to talk to him. I asked him how he was, and he said all right. And then I asked why he'd run away from the infirmary, and he wouldn't answer; he turned and went off."

"How did he look?" Carr asked.

"He'd taken off the head bandage and shoulder strap, and—"

"I mean his face. Did you notice anything"—he paused—"about his mouth or teeth?"

The girl's eyes studied him curiously. "You mean—he had another accident?" she asked.

"Yes, another accident."

She still watched him, waiting. But he said no more.

"No," she said, "I didn't notice anything. But I saw him close up for just that moment, and since then hardly at all."

"Do you know what he's doing with himself?"

"Mostly, I think, he's out in the woods."

"The woods? You mean alone?"

"No. A lot of the men have been working out there. They're building a big boat, for fishing."

Carr nodded slowly. "That's best for him," he said. "To be with them—with his own kind." He had again been looking out the window, at the red sky from which the sun had gone; but now his eyes returned to Carol. "With us—from outside—there's only trouble for him."

"He did something foolish again, didn't he?"

"Foolish?"

"That night at the infirmary. Besides just leaving. He had this other—accident, you say—"

Carr took a drink.

"That involved you, somehow." She waited. "Didn't it?"

He rose from the cot. "There's no use rehashing it," he said. "He's back where he belongs, and that's the main thing."

"Is it? I wonder. Or is it what's going on inside him? . . . First from what happened with me; then from something with you—whatever it was." Carol paused, her thoughts turned inward. Then she said: "It's strange, you know. Back then, you told me not to worry about John; that I was too involved with him in my own emotions. And now—"

She paused again. His glass was empty and he refilled it.

"Mitch—" she said.

"Yes?"

"You said I should call you Mitch—"

He took a drink and put the glass down.

"What happened with you and John, I don't know," she said. "Or even if it's that that's bothering you; I'm just guessing. But I do know that something's wrong. That you're upset, unhappy—"

Now she too rose. She took a few steps toward him. "That night on the beach, when I talked to you—it helped me a lot. You helped me a lot. I was all tied up inside, tight and frozen, and you began to unfreeze me. . . . At the dance, too. Each time I've been with you. . . . And now it's the other way. This thing, whatever it is, that's bothering you; that has *you* frozen. And *I'd* like to help. Truly, Mitch. If you'll let me—"

There was pleading in her voice. In her eyes. Extending her hand, she touched his, and for a moment they stood there unmoving, close together.

He looked at her steadily, and the whisky made only a slight blur behind his eyes. Then he said:

"A while back I told you you were a foolish girl. I'll tell you something else now. You're a damn nice one."

There was a pause. She waited. But he turned away.

"Mitch, please—" she said.

But he shook his head.

"What does that mean?"

"It means that's it," he said. "It means I've made enough of a mess already."

"A mess?"

"There once was a woman called Margaret, and another woman called Helen, who could tell you. There are a lot of engineers and architects and contractors who could tell you. There are a lot of bartenders who could tell you." Now he looked at her again, but there was no softness in his eye, no response to the touch of the hand that she again reached out to him. "I came back to this place, this Tiara," he said, "because it had meaning for me; because I thought I might find here again something I had once had and lost. I found a lagoon, and I blew it up. I found hibiscus and frangipani, and put in holes for toilet pipes. I found a boy who needed me, and brought him grief; a girl who gave herself to me, and brought her grief. And I'm not adding you to the list of the good works of Mitchell Carr."

"But I'm only asking—"

"—for trouble," he said. "And I'm not going to give it to you."

He went to the door and opened it, and watched her walk slowly across the slope toward the road and her waiting jeep. Then, with bottle and glass, he sat again on his cot in the darkening quonset, waiting for the supper bell and the evening poker game.

On the far side of the island, above the village, the *fau* and the *fetau* tree stood high on the hillside. Here, for generations past, the Tiarans had come to fell timber for their *fales*. And here, now, they came again—but for a different purpose.

Axes thudded. Saws rasped. Two great *fau* trees toppled to earth and were stripped of their branches; then were slid, dragged, and levered down the slopes to the shore. And on the shore, in a grove hidden from both the village and the road, there was again the sound and movement of men at work. Men working on a project the like of which had not been seen on the island within living memory.

Through long days and nights there had been discussions in the village councils. As to who would and would not go to Maniloa. As to how the project would be kept secret. Finally, as to the actual building of the craft that would carry them. Tafutimo's influence was strong among his people, and it was soon apparent that more than half the village—over a hundred persons—would be going. So a great boat, at least a hundred feet long, would be needed. The *matai* debated the procedure. The village carpenters submitted plans. The young men went to work on the hillside and the shore.

They had no sawmill, no machine tools. Such tools would have been procurable, if at all, only through the Government—which they did not want to know of their plans. And besides, Tafutimo and the council were resolved to make the venture wholly *fa'a Manaia*.

202

"It is from the *papalagi* world we go," they said. "Why then should we use the things of the *papalagi*?"

They would build as their ancestors had built. Except for axes and saws, which they already had, no Western tools or materials would be used. The planks for the hulls would be shaped by adzes, lashed together by strands of sennit, caulked with coconut husk and breadfruit gum. In all possible ways they would do things as in the times of the great migrations.

Pride filled them. And excitement. And a will to work such as had never been seen on the island before. . . . But more than these would be needed, it soon became apparent, before their craft could be built and launched. For with the beginning of construction they were beset by all manner of problems and trouble. . . . First came that with the timber itself; for the wood of the *fau* tree, which had been selected for use, proved too hard and splintery to be manageable. And, after much frustration and argument, this was abandoned, while two *fetau* were felled and brought down to the shore. . . . Yet still there was trouble. . . . No boat larger than a fishing canoe had been built in Tiara for generations. The carpenters, who could fashion a *fale* equal to any in Polynesia, had had no experience with the curves and joints of a hull. The huge planks that they cut would not fit together. Seams gaped. Ends jutted out. The sennit bindings snapped. Soon the men, too, were snapping at each other. And then standing in silence: depressed, morose.

"It is too big a boat we are trying to build," a voice said.

And the voice was John Koa's.

"We do not know how to build a big boat, like our ancestors'," he went on. "We must build two smaller ones, like the whaleboats of the *papalagi*."

This was the first time during the work that he had spoken. But every day, from dawn to dusk, he had been with the men in the forest and on the shore. From the moment of his return, beaten and bitter, from his job at the hotel, he had been resolved that he would make himself a place in the life of his own people. From the moment when Tafutimo broached it, he had been all for the plan of leaving Tiara for Maniloa, and had sought to help in every way he could. But after what had happened, it had not been easy. In his own family, Fahoai, already angry and shamed at what had happened, found it the last straw that he now sided with those who would leave Tiara. Tafutimo and the council of *matai* eyed him with cold disapproval. The younger men—with Patali first and foremost—never stopped their jibes and taunts about his misadventures.

For the boatbuilding every available hand was needed, and he had been allowed to work. But only among the youngest and least experienced apprentices, with no use made of his knowledge and skills. Though it had been bitter medicine, he had swallowed it. He had bided his time. He had kept his mouth shut. . . .

But now he opened it.

"In Apingo, at the dockyards," he said, "I have seen many boats built. And if you will listen to me, I can show you what should be done."

The others looked at him.

"Go chase a blonde," Patali told him.

"Go wreck a bulldozer," said another.

The older men turned away, seeming not even to have heard him. They went on working, arguing—but mostly arguing—and that evening there was a special meeting in the village at which it was decided to build two smaller boats instead of one large one.

John was not thanked. When he offered further suggestions he was not listened to. But he knew now that soon he would be, for the men were still trying to build in the ancient fashion. And there were still problems and trouble. True, he himself, like the others, had had experience with nothing bigger than a fishing canoe; but at least he understood a few principles of construction. At high school he had worked at mechanics and learned something of carpentry beyond the *fale*-building variety. At the docks, as he had said, he had watched boats being built by modern methods. And he knew that, with the old skills lost, a boat could not be built without these methods; without plan and measurement; without wrench and hammer and nail and screw and bolt.

Again he opened his mouth. And was told to shut it.

And again the next day . . .

And the next . . .

But at last the time came, as he had known it would, when the others had no choice but to listen; when the two half-built hulls lay warped and spavined under unskilled hands, and all the builders could do was to shake their heads disconsolately. And then, suddenly, it was no longer he who came to them with suggestions, but they who approached him—who sought his judgment, his advice. They nodded when he said what should be done with a joint, a rib, a strake that they could not manage. They studied the simple drawings he prepared. At his urging, they requisitioned tools and ironware from the stock in Asimo's store; what Asimo did not have they filched from the storehouse at the hotel site. And slowly the two hulks in the palm grove by the beach took on the semblance of seaworthy craft.

Even now, recognition came to him grudgingly. The younger men, his erstwhile taunters, were now jealous; the old ones reluctant to acknowledge help from a mere boy—and a pariah at that. But, bit by bit, come it did—until, by the time the boats were nearing completion, he was, in fact if not in theory, one of the inner circle who took counsel and made decisions. There were now no more jibes from his peers, no more harsh glances from his elders. Even Tafutimo treated him with a certain respect. For the first time since his return from high school, months before, he was at peace with himself—he had found a life for himself—a life of work, of purpose, of relationship to his own people.

The hotel, the events there, the man called Mitchell Carr, were remote, forgotten. As forgotten as his dreams of flying. Of that other world, only Carol Loftus remained—a white shadow moving through the village, whom he carefully, at all times, avoided. And soon she too would be remote, forgotten, beyond miles of sea.

A senior *matai,* Vaoti, was in charge of the building site. Except for periodic visits of inspection, Tafutimo stayed in his *fale* in the village, for there was much to do in the venture at hand other than with wood and tool. Here, and by him, the final decision had been made to build two boats instead of one. Here John's urging of modern methods had at last received official approval, and John himself had won his nod of recognition. Around the high chief, their backs against the pillars of the *fale,* the old men of the tribe sat through the days, rolling strands of sennit against their tattooed thighs. And when it was decreed that nails, not sennit, would be used to hold the boats together, their protests were strong and anguished.

"Is this *fa'a Manaia,*" croaked aged Kalamakoa, holding up his woven strands, "that our work be rejected for the things of the *papalagi?*" And the others joined in his plaint. But Tafutimo, though not pleased, was firm in his decision. "Everyone has agreed," he said, "that without nails the boats will leak and sink." And so it stood, to the old men's sorrow. Until then, each morning, the boys of the village had taken their sennit and carried it out to the builders in the grove by the shore. Now the boys no longer came. They went instead to the store, for nails from Asimo. But still the oldsters rolled their strands, from ancient habit, laying them sadly beside them on the pebbled floor when they were done.

The old of the village, almost without exception, were for going to Maniloa. The rest were split up and down—through families, sexes, generations—and into the high chief's *fale* came an endless procession: with questions, problems, protests, arguments. A chief of the ancient days, Tafutimo well knew, would simply have said, "We go. Make ready," and that would have been all; no one would have dreamt of raising a voice in opposition. But the ancient days were gone: in

205

this too, as with nails and sennit. And deep as it went against the grain of his pride, he had to listen, to explain, to coax, to compromise.

Foremost among those who would have no part of going was the talking chief, Fahoai. For hours on end the two village leaders debated the issue: now in the formal phrases prescribed for chiefly discourse, now heatedly, angrily, as commoners would argue. But in the end it was the same as in the beginning—except that Tafutimo had won from Fahoai the promise that he would not go to the *papalagi* with word of what was afoot.

As had been said in council, the Government could not stop them by order. They were free men in their own homeland. But it could make everything awkward, difficult, perhaps even impossible, and Tafutimo was resolved that they should know nothing until the thing was done. One circumstance that helped greatly was the continued absence of Leonard Shafter, who had now not been to the village since the night of the feast. Twice, messages came over on the *Ickes* from Apingo, regretting that he was held there by other duties and inquiring as to possible problems. And each time the high chief replied blandly that there were no problems, that all went smoothly and well.

About the people at the hotel there was little cause for concern: they lived in their own alien world, scarcely conscious that the village existed. And the villagers, for their part, had small contact with anyone beyond. Pastor Solomona was among those who were not going. (He could not, without the sanction of his church, he said; and besides, with the opening of the hotel, the devil would be far more active in Tiara than on deserted Maniloa.) But, like Fahoai, he had agreed to temporary silence. Asimo the storekeeper, though he mocked the venture and predicted dire things for it, had an audience no wider than those who came to his store. And Malele the policeman, who, as a hireling of the *papalagi,* was potentially the most dangerous, was fortunately conceiving it as his duty to spend most of his time at the hotel site (where there was much to steal, as he pointed out . . . and much free beer, as he did not) and was as yet unaware of what was going on.

Then too—and also dangerous—there were the two *papalagi* in the village: the women *papalagi*, Mrs. Mundy and Carol Loftus. But though they were of course aware of new things happening, great care was taken that they did not learn the true reason. The boats, they had been told, were being built for fishing. The food that the women were assembling was for a second feast that would celebrate the opening of the hotel. And they had accepted the explanations without question. They went about their work as usual. They knew nothing of what was being planned.

Or so it seemed . . .

Until the day when Mrs. Mundy appeared, small and birdlike, at the high chief's *fale* and said, quietly but firmly: "Tafutimo, I must speak with you."

Later, it seemed incredible to Mitchell Carr that he—not to mention the other "outsiders"—could have been there on an island a mere three miles across, with no intimation of what was happening on its far side. Yet there it was: the fact. The fact accomplished. By the time they heard of the exodus from Tiara the voyagers were already out at sea.

The beginning of knowledge came early one morning when only a handful of the Tiarans at the hotel site reported for work. And those who did were abuzz with the news that had already reached them over the coconut radio.

"Where are the others?" demanded Lavery and the "Hawaiians."

"They have gone to the village," was the answer.

"Why? What's going on?"

"It is not going. It is gone. A boat—two boats. Before the sun is up this morning."

"Gone where?"

"To Maniloa."

"Maniloa?"

"What's that?"

Lavery swore. The "Hawaiians" swore with him, or opened a beer, or went swimming, according to temperament. Mitchell Carr went to one of the jeeps, got in, and drove off down the road.

Only a few women and children were about in the "new village" by the hotel site. Apparently most of these, too, had gone off across the island (including Va'ina, for he saw no sign of her). Swinging onto the coast road, he drove as fast as he could over ruts and potholes, rounding the curves, skirting the beaches . . . and then, suddenly, pulling up as another jeep appeared, coming toward him. At the wheel was Carol Loftus, and beside her Malele the policeman.

She was tense but controlled as the two cars drew up side by side; but Malele was all but bursting with agitation and outrage. . . . Yes, two boats had put off that morning, she confirmed, led by Tafutimo, carrying perhaps half the villagers. Or so she gathered. She had not actually seen them go, for she had been confined to the bungalow.

Confined?

"Yes," Malele broke in. "And I too. I am in jail. I, the police! . . . Yesterday I find out what is happening; that these boats they built they are not for fishing but to go away. So I say I must send radio, tell Apingo. They say no, they break no law. And I say yes, that is so, but Government must know. So they say no again, and I say yes, and they put me in the jail and I am out only now."

"I'd have come too, last night, when I found out—" Carol began.

But Malele interrupted again. "And to put the police in jail, that *is* to break the law—in the book it says so. This I say in my report. It is not my fault. They resist an officer—"

He glanced off down the road, then impatiently at Carol. But she hesitated, looking at Carr. And Carr said, "Let him take your jeep. There's nothing you can do at that end."

She nodded and got out of her car, and Malele slid over into the driver's seat. "I send the radio," he declared. "Then I write the report. I tell what they do; how they put the police in jail. And how the jail is no good. It is dirty. There are rats—"

Flinging the car into gear, he jounced off down the road in a cloud of dust and indignation. Carol got into Carr's jeep and for a few moments sat in silence, fighting down her agitation.

"Oh, Mitch," she murmured, "I'm so glad you're here. I haven't known what to do. It's been so sudden—so crazy—"

Her voice trailed off. She was close to tears.

"Easy does it," he said.

And pulling herself together, she began to tell him what had happened. Or at least what she knew of it. For the first she had known about anything was on the previous night, and since then, until a few minutes before, she had politely but firmly been kept from leaving her house.

She hadn't been harmed?

No.

Or threatened?

No.

And Mrs. Mundy? Was she all right?

"Mrs. Mundy has gone with them," Carol said.

"With them? You mean they forced her?"

"No," she said. "She chose to go."

And she went on to tell how it had been from the old lady herself, the night before, that she had learned of what was going on; that the boats had been built not for fishing but to take half the village to another island; that departure would be the next morning—*this* morning—

—and that she herself, Mrs. Mundy, was going along.

"To this—"

"Maniloa. A place called Maniloa."

"But why?" Carr demanded. "Why she? Why all of them?"

"With the people, she said, it had been developing a long time. Because of the hotel, the trucks, the child that was killed. The new things and people they didn't want here. . . . And for herself, she felt it was her duty. That those who were going would need her more than those who stayed. . . . She said she'd known of the plan for some time, and at first she'd argued against it. But when she saw their minds were made up, she agreed to keep their secret—even from me. And then she made up *her* mind to go with them."

"She must be quite an old girl in her way, this Mrs. M."

"Oh yes—incredible. So frail and tiny—like a little bird—but inside all firm as iron. I found that out when I tried to reason with her. I was so surprised and confused I'm not sure just what I said. Everything that came into my head, I suppose: how hard it would be for her—how dangerous. I was so astonished at what *she* was doing I hardly thought about all the others, but just talked about her, and how she mustn't do it. I even said I'd go myself, instead; that I was younger, stronger. But I knew it made no sense. Even if she'd agreed, which I knew she wouldn't, the others wouldn't have taken me."

"All this was just last night?"

"Yes. First I found her packing. Then she asked for things from the dispensary. And it all came out. . . . Oh, I must have argued for hours. Then she went to bed, and I sat there, I paced around, I simply *had* to do something, tell someone; and I decided to get in the jeep and drive over to you; but they must have expected something like that, because there were two men outside who wouldn't let me go."

"And this morning?"

"I didn't go to bed. I just sat there. And as it was getting light Mrs. Mundy was up, and a boy came for her bag and the medical kit, and she gave me a quick little kiss and went off, just like that. Two men were still outside and wouldn't let me follow. I still had to stay there: another hour, maybe two—I don't know. And then they left. The boats were gone. I got the jeep and started off, and when I passed the jail they were just letting Malele out, and he jumped in, and—well—there it is."

Carol paused. And now her control crumbled. Her eyes were distraught, her lips trembled, and her voice, when she spoke again, was low and close to breaking. "Oh, I've been so helpless, so stupid," she said. "Not knowing anything. Not doing anything. . . . Oh Mitch, what should I have done? What *could* I have done?"

"Easy—easy," he said. He was as disquieted as she, his thoughts fumbling ahead through questions, guesses, premonitions. But he fitted his tone to the words. "What's happened has happened. I'll take you back and we'll see where things are at now."

He drove on along the coast road, and in a few minutes they were in the village. At first sight it appeared no different from before, with as many people as usual in evidence. But then he realized that many were those who had come over from the hotel site, and also that they were not spread about in the usual casual pattern, but gathered in groups at certain of the huts. Other huts—long lines of them fringing the *malae* under the palm trees—stood still and deserted, hollow shells of beam and thatch from which all life had gone.

Around the *fale* of the talking chief, Fahoai, there were more people than at any other; and Carr pulled up close beside it. A garble of voices filled the air, but died away as he and Carol got out, and curious eyes followed them as they stepped between the pillars into the hut's interior. Fahoai, together with Pastor Solomona and a few *matai*, sat cross-legged on mats near the center of the pebbled floor. Off to one side was his wife, Polu; beyond her, the niece, tall big-boned Mena. And on the other side, conspicuously apart, was Va'ina (whose curiosity, Carr thought, had obviously outweighed her fears about her home reception). At their entrance—with curiosity presumably satisfied—she had been gazing off into a space with a bored, above-it-all expression; but now her eyes were fixed on Carr, with Carol Loftus beside him, and the glint in her eyes had little to do with cordial welcome.

Fahoai's greeting was polite but formal. And his round brown face was somber.

"It is a sad day for our village," he said. "A day of things I would wish not to have seen." He shook his head slowly. "Do not think I approve of what has happened. Of your being kept in your house, Miss Loftus. Or of you gentlemen at the hotel, Mr. Carr, being told nothing. . . . But what could I do? . . . Half the village here wished to leave. They wished no one to know of it. I thought them wrong; I argued, pleaded with them. But they were determined. And we who have remained, though disagreeing, could not find it in our conscience to traduce those who are our own people—

"—or *were*—"

He paused.

"By now, I suppose," he said, "Malele the policeman has sent his message?"

"He was on his way when I saw him," Carr answered.

"It will surprise them in Apingo, I imagine. They will come soon with questions and opinions." Fahoai shook his head again. "It is too bad Mr. Shafter has not been here these past days. He would have made Tafutimo see his foolishness and stop."

"But now it is too late," said one of the *matai*.

"It is God's will," said Pastor Solomona.

"The thing is done."

"They are gone."

"How many are gone?" Carr asked.

"More than a hundred," said Fahoai. "But I do not know exactly. This morning there were some who changed their minds both ways."

"But there are many—many," said a *matai*.

"Almost half of us."

"And it is not only the numbers," Fahoai said. "It is which ones they were, and what has happened to our families. Always in Tiara, whatever has happened, families have stood together, and that has been our strength. But now, no. Now they are split. A father goes, a son stays. One brother chooses this, the other that. The families are broken."

He sighed and, for a moment, closed his eyes.

"My own is broken," he said. "I am here, and my wife, and the girl, Mena. And this one"—he indicated Va'ina—"well, she is half here; who can tell with her? . . . But the others are gone. The old one, Kalamakoa. The young one, Ioane."

"You mean John," said Carr.

It was not a question. He knew the answer.

"Yes, John Koa," said Fahoai. "He who, of everyone, should have stayed; who could have made something fine of himself in the world of the *papalagi*."

"No, with that one it is better he went," said a *matai*. "For you and everyone he brought only trouble."

"And this one—" said Pastor Solomona, pointing suddenly at Va'ina. "She too should have gone. She who was our honored *taupou* and has brought us shame."

Carr stiffened. He felt the eyes fixed now on the girl—and on himself.

But before the pastor could continue, Fahoai broke in with an angry shout.

"Stop!" he commanded. "I will not have this talk in my house."

"You yourself have said—"

"What I say of my own is one thing. But for another—"

"I am not another," said Solomona. "I am a servant of the Lord. And I say this woman is evil. She is a Jezebel, a Whore of Babylon."

Now there were voices raised everywhere. The pastor's and Fahoai's. The *matai's*. The onlookers'. Polu rocked her fat body back and forth, emitting a high-pitched wail. And Va'ina, leaping to her feet, confronted Solomona with eyes ablaze and returned his abuse in a torrent of Manaian.

"Stop! Stop!" Fahoai shouted. But his voice was lost in the uproar.

And now another woman was on her feet—Va'ina's sister, tall, lumbering Mena. She had flung herself between Va'ina and Solomona, and she too was shouting, she was berating: "—You cannot speak so to the pastor. You are Godless, wicked—"

"And you are Jesus's little lamb," Va'ina spat back. "You are a lump, a fool—"

"You shut your mouth."

"No, it's yours I'll shut."

"Try it—"

"You think I won't?"

And in the next instant they were locked together, wrestling, kicking, clawing wildly at each other's hair. Solomona had stepped back in consternation. Fahoai moved ponderously in, trying to separate them. The *matai* were shouting. The crowd was shouting. And above it all, Polu's wail rose and held in a sustained, piercing scream.

Carr took Carol's arm and led her quickly from the *fale*. No one noticed them go. In a moment he was walking her off through the palm grove; and her arm was trembling, her whole body was trembling; and they did not speak, they simply walked on, as the din in Fahoai's house faded behind them. The *fales* they passed were empty and bare. There was no life, no movement. They were alone.

—And then not alone. For a face looked up at them. It was the face of Asimo the storekeeper, who sat propped against the pillar of a deserted hut, holding a calabash, and as they passed he watched and grinned.

"Good party, folks?" he asked.

They didn't answer.

"You oughtn't to leave so soon, though. It'll get better," Asimo said. "Hell yes, it's going to be a gay dump around here from now on, wait 'n see. Just like good ol' stateside, by God. The li'l ol' tropic isle that's got civ-il-i-za-shun—"

He laughed.

Then he, too, was behind them. They came out of the grove, out of the village, onto the beach; and they stood on the beach looking out across the tidal flat to the line of the reef and the sea beyond. The sea gleamed in sunlight. The sky was bare. Only at the horizon, at the far hinge of air and water, was there a break in the emptiness— a break that was two specks, rising, falling in blue distance.

Abruptly, Carol turned away. A half-stifled sob shook her, and with a convulsive movement she clung to Carr and hid her face against his chest. Holding her, he saw over her shoulder that Asimo had followed them and was standing a short way off, watching them, still grinning. As their eyes met, he raised his calabash and winked and drank.

15

IN THE BEGINNING there was Havaiki.

Anthropologists have placed it in Malaya, India, Persia, as far west as the shores of the Red Sea and the coasts of Africa. Myth makers have identified it with Israel and its people with the Lost Tribes. The people themselves—the brown migrant people who have become the Polynesians—do not know. They know only that in all their legends, all their tradition, the place of their ancient origin is called Havaiki.

Driven by forces that can only be guessed at, they pushed out into the Pacific Ocean: first from the mainland shores of Asia, then from the large islands along its rim. And their journeys extended over thousands of miles, in the greatest sequence of migrations that men have ever made. With them in their canoes they brought their women and children, their plants and animals, their folkways and gods. And they brought, too, the name, if not the memory, of Havaiki, making it not only their place of origin but of destination, the name of the new homes they sought and found. Raiatea, near Tahiti, was once known as Havaiki. So was Savaii, the largest of the Samoan Islands. And so—with the least change through the centuries—was America's Hawaii.

When the first migrants arrived, fire and ocean, coral and seed, had already done their work. The myriad islands were green and fruitful. To them the brown men brought their Stone Age culture— fire and shelter and crops and idols—and there they lived for many centuries. From the rest of the world, with its nations and faiths, its arts and sciences and wars and convulsions, they were as remote as if they had lived on another planet. And when the first white men in their tall ships came up over the horizon, it was more unimaginable than if their own gods had descended from the sky to walk among them.

The first of the invaders merely came and went. The captains and navigators: Magellan and Medana, Schouten and Tasman, Cook and Wallis, Bougainville and La Pérouse and Kotzebue and Wilkes. But they came from—and returned to—all parts of the Western World, and in that world they told the story of the marvelous new one they had found. A world in which volcanoes rose in fiery cones from the ocean depths. Where coral atolls were flung like wreaths of flowers on blue lagoons. Where, in a stainless sky, a single sunstruck cloud could crown an island summit with the white radiance of a tiara.

. . . Where the air was soft, the earth fertile, the souls heathen, the women fair and fond . . .

And others came. And many stayed. There were seamen, soldiers, merchants, missionaries, officials, tramps, saints, villains. They came to explore, exploit, govern, teach, convert, rob, rape, murder. They brought clothing, law, guns, knowledge, liquor, machinery, God, disease. Spread a map and touch your fingers to the islands. Here is the Island of Horror, from which slavers once carried off the entire population. Here is the Island of Piety, where young men and women cannot walk on the road together after dark, under pain of imprisonment. Here is the Island of Love, to which a wanderer came, bringing pure dreams of the life of nature—and with them the spirochete of syphilis.

Men have made war in the islands. Men have made money. Men have made love. They have been the multimillion-square-mile arena of the struggle for world power, and the last retreat of the romantic escapist. Some have said, "Here is beauty, peace, paradise." Others have said, "Here is hell." For the islander it is neither hell nor heaven—it is home—but a home so transformed from the time of his ancestors, so altered from year to year, from day to day, that he is almost a stranger within it. He looks into the sky at the roaring jets, across the lagoon at the liners and yachts, down the street at the banks and stores, through the palm grove at the bulldozers and cement mixers; and he asks, with Gauguin's Tahitians, *Where do we come from? What are we? Where are we going?*

Some go to the town, the office, the mill, the hotel. They become clerks, policemen, laborers, waiters, beach boys. Some, turning their backs, go inland, if theirs are large islands, or, if they are small, to still smaller, remoter islands, resolved at all costs to keep the remaining shreds of the ways of their ancestors. In the archipelago of Manaia there is such an island: a tiny sea-ringed atoll, uninhabited for cen-

214

turies, lying some two hundred miles to the east of Tiara. And toward it, one day, moved two boats and a hundred and eighteen travelers, in still another of the immemorial Polynesian migrations.

On Government maps and nautical charts this island was known as Maniloa.

But its name was also Havaiki.

"Aiii-ah. Aiii-ah—"

Standing in the stern of the boat called *Wind of Morning,* the young helmsman, Afa, chanted the ancient cry. Until a few moments before he had not chanted but counted. Coming out through the opening in the reef, he had held his twenty oarsmen to their task by the sharp barking of the beat, and beside him a young boy, too small for rowing, had thumped in accompanying rhythm on an empty biscuit tin. But now there was no longer need for count or thump. Beyond the reef the sea was wide, the wind blew free, and the sail of pandanus matting bellied full from the mast. The only oar now in use was the long sweep of Afa the helmsman plowing the foamy wake. *"Aiii-ah, aiii-ah!"* he cried, his head thrown back, his body tall and proud against the ocean sky. And from the second boat, *Star of Evening,* off to starboard, came the echo of its helmsman, Ta'ua: *"Aiii-ah, aiii-ah!"*

In one boat there were sixty people, in the other fifty-eight: men, women, and children, from old Kalamakoa, whose age no one knew, to an infant that Carol Loftus had delivered less than two weeks before. There were pigs and fowl. There were kegs of water, of salted beef and pork, of sugar and rice and tapioca, and great mounds of ripe taro ready for cooking, and bundles of green taro shoots for planting in the soil of the new homeland. There were coconuts, breadfruit, mangoes, papayas; piles of tools and utensils, chests of cloth and clothing; cookpots, fishhooks, brooms, pillows, bottles, stools, axes, sewing machines. Lining the bottom of the boats against the seepage of the sea were layers of woven mats, and atop the cargo were other layers, as protection from rain and spray. Amidships of each boat, close to the mast, these had been angled up on wooden props to form rude shelters from the weather; but in these first hours they were occupied only by a few women, already seasick, and the very youngest of the children.

The rest were ranged along the gunwales, perched everywhere where there was room to stand, sit, or squat. Some stared aft, past stern and helmsman, toward where the hills of Tiara receded, fading from green to blue to hazy violet; others ahead into the void of sea and sky.

The high chief Tafutimo stared ahead. Seated on a platform of mats forward of the mast of the *Wind of Morning,* he was rigid as a carved figure, his lion's face heavy and brooding, and not once since they had set off at dawn that morning had he looked back toward the old home from which he was leading his people. Around him were other elders and *matai;* to either side the younger men, the rowers, with their oars now shipped; and fore and aft, from bow to stern, the women and children and oldsters of their families. There was little talk, little movement. The bright morning sun shone on huddled quietness, on brown immobile bodies, brown staring faces—and on one face that was not brown, not staring: the face of Birdie Mundy, white and thin and old, with glinting glasses, bending over a sleeping child whose head she held in her lap.

In the other boat, *Star of Evening,* the elder *matai,* Vaoti, held the place of command. Close beside him was old Kalamakoa, his skull-head bowed, his lips moving soundlessly; and to both sides and fore and aft, as in the *Wind of Morning,* were the other *matai,* the resting oarsmen, the women and children. Among the rowers here, forward on the port side, was young Patali, son of Tafutimo. And nearby, but to starboard, was John Koa. Patali, like most of the others, was gazing motionlessly, fixedly into distance. But John's head and eyes kept moving: to the sun above, the horizon ahead, the white wake of the boats streaming back toward Tiara. He was studying their course. They had no sextant—and if they had had, no one could have read it. For compasses, they had two fifty-cent toys from Asimo's store; for a chart, a one-page map of the Pacific torn from a book in Mrs. Mundy's schoolroom. If they were to find their way to Maniloa, it would be in the old fashion, by the signs of sea and sky—and by these alone.

John held no position of rank or authority. He was simply a rower, one of the crew. This did not bother him, however, for he had the precious knowledge that he had at last won acceptance and respect among his people. Without him, without his part in the boatbuilding, they would not have been where they were now—and from Tafutimo down, they knew it. He had made his mark, his contribution. When the time came, he would make it again. And meanwhile he was content.

No, more than content, he was filled with excitement, with exultation.

Until the boatbuilding—straight through from his return from high school—his life had been one blunder, one misery, after another. The waiting for the Air Force letter that never came. The drinking with Asimo—the night of the feast—the jail. Every hand had seemed raised against him, except only that of the strange American, the engineer,

Carr; and then that too had been raised, in a fist. . . . But from the time of the decision to leave Tiara, everything had been different. . . . He had seen clearly, at last, what he must do, and he had done it: abandoning his lonely, hopeless rebellion: embracing the life, the work, the purpose of his people. And in doing so—slowly, often painfully, but still surely—he had in turn won their respect and acceptance. He was no longer an outcast. No longer alone.

In those last days in the village there had been only one who was truly against him: his uncle Fahoai. For Fahoai not only refused to leave Tiara himself; he could not see why anyone else should choose to leave—and, least of all, John. "First there is the disgrace," he had said over and over. "And now, worse than disgrace, this madness. That you—you of all people—who have the education, the ways, even the blood of the *papalagi,* should throw your life away on a desert island." He, John, however, had scarcely listened. He ignored his uncle, avoided him—as he avoided Carol Loftus. For his mind was made up and he had cast his lot. He was not "throwing his life away" but dedicating it; turning his back on an alien, hostile world for what he was now convinced was his only possible way of existence.

The path of the generations had come full circle. The old man, Kalamakoa, would go. He, the young man, would go. Fahoai, the one in the middle—the straddler, the compromiser—would stay behind.

For him, the *papalagi* way. For John, *fa'a Manaia.*

In the dark of a moonless night, a week past, he had sat alone on his old perch on the cliffs and looked out again at the sea and stars. He had no God to pray to: neither the dark dead ones of his ancestors nor the remote white one of Pastor Solomona and his sister Mena. But he had prayed nevertheless: to whatever *was,* whatever listened. He had renewed his dedication. And it had remained bright within him during the days that followed: until the boats were finished; until they were launched, tested, loaded; until at last *the day* came, and in the still grayness of dawn they pushed off on their journey, while those who were to stay behind watched sad and silent from the shore. It burned bright now, in the sweep of the sea, the blaze of the sun, as the two boats, sails spread, moved on in their appointed course. The course of ancient days. To the new island. The new home. The eternal home called Havaiki.

High and proud in the stern, the helmsman Ta'ua raised his voice in song:

> She stirs, she moves, she sails,
> Our brave ship, our Star of Evening.

The handle of my sweep is a thing alive,
My steering sweep named Kautu-ki-te-rangi.
It guides to the horizon,
The horizon that lifts before us,
That ever recedes,
That ever draws near—

Others joined in. Soon all in the boat were singing. And from the other boat, *Wind of Morning,* came an answering song. In the fresh breeze the sails still bellied full; the sun beamed; the boats moved steadily on. Behind them the silhouette of Tiara grew smaller, fainter, until it was no more than a tiny shadow beneath its gleaming cloud cap. But now there were few, even of the women, who looked back at it. It was forward that they looked, their faces bright with hope and expectancy.

Open, open, horizon, they chanted.
Open our way to land,
The new homeland,
Havaiki—

So the hours flowed. The sea flowed. The sun climbed over the mast tops, and passed them, and slanted away behind. Then it was evening, and where there had been blue and gold there was grayness; where there had been breeze there was stillness, and the pandanus sails hung limp in the thickening dusk. Out came the oars again. The helmsmen counted. The biscuit tins thumped. Then night came, with the stars of the evening, and in the boat called *Star of Evening* the rowers shipped their oars and prepared to rest.

Throughout the day, John Koa had had no part in discussions or decisions. He had scarcely spoken a word. . . . But now he raised his voice.

"No, we cannot do this," he said. "We must row on."

Eyes fixed on him.

"Row on?"

"If we drift, we will lose our course and the other boat."

"But we must rest. We must sleep."

"We can take turns sleeping. Half can row at a time."

There was talk, argument. Vaoti, the senior *matai,* thought it over and then ordered the boat to be brought over toward the *Wind* for consultation with Tafutimo; and the high chief, thinking it over in turn, decided that yes, it was best to row on. The boats moved apart again. The oarsmen were split into shifts, one to row, one to rest, and alternate helmsmen were chosen to spell Afa and Ta'ua. Through the windless night they moved on, oars creaking, and at intervals, in each boat, a long hooting note was blown on a conch shell, so that they would not lose track of each other in the dark.

The men were not good rowers. Indeed, most of them had not so much as held an oar in their hands before (for in their canoes they used only paddles), and even when they were being cut and fashioned there had been much complaint about them.

"These are *papalagi* things," they had said. "Our ancestors did not know them. They made their great trips with paddles, *fa'a Manaia.*"

As with the design of the boats, John Koa had been responsible for the oars. And he had explained that craft of their bulk and height of freeboard could not be propelled by paddles.

"Then we should have built the boats differently. As the old ones built them."

"We tried," John reminded them. "But we couldn't."

So grumblingly they had accepted the oars; and grumblingly, now, they manned them through the night. Two slipped from careless hands and were lost in the dark. The rest jerked, jammed, caught crabs. And as the hours wore on almost everyone complained of blistered hands and aching backs. . . . "When day comes we will have wind again," the less gloomy assured the others. . . . But they were wrong. When at last dawn came, then sunrise, there was no wisp of wind, but only a vast heavy stillness and a sea thick as oil.

And they rowed on.

Tiara was now only a white cloud on the horizon far astern.

The rise and fall of the boats on the long swell was scarcely perceptible, yet most of the women were sick. In the *Wind of Morning,* Mrs. Mundy, with the help of the few still able to function, prepared a taro mash for the younger children, then did what she could for the sick and passed breakfast around to the men. When, first among them, she served Tafutimo, the high chief nodded and murmured, "*Manuia*—my blessings."

They were scarcely words that would have come from him two weeks before, for in the beginning he had been strongly opposed to her coming. Indeed, it was he who, over the protests of many villagers, had insisted that she, despite her years among them, was still a *papalagi,* an outsider, and must be kept ignorant of their plans. Like Carol Loftus, she had been told, when she asked questions, that the new boats were for fishing, the assembled food was for a feast. But she was too close to the life of the people to be thus taken in. From the start, she had suspected the truth. In time it had been confirmed by the excitement and whispering of the children in school. And it was then that she had confronted Tafutimo. At first she had argued against the plan as wild, foolhardy, impractical. But when she saw that argument was hopeless she had accepted the inevitable; she had kept the secret; and in the end she had returned to the chief and announced that she too would go to Maniloa.

No, he had said. But she had been persistent, adamant. She did not work for the Government, she reminded him. She worked for the people of Tiara, and where they went, so too must she go. As teacher. As nurse (for she had been that too in days past). Surely he did not propose to let the children of his people grow up without teaching, without medical care? . . . Yes, she understood that half the village would be staying on. But for them things would be different. Or, rather, not different, but as before. Miss Loftus would be there as nurse, and when she left there would be a replacement. A new teacher would be sent. Such things would continue as in the past. . . . It was on the new island, in Maniloa, that there must be someone to teach the young, care for the ill. . . .

It had been the children themselves, and their mothers, who had won the day. They had pleaded. They had cried. Some of the women, among them Tafutimo's own wife, had gone so far as to declare that they themselves would not go unless Miz Mundy went too. And at last Tafutimo had looked long at her and said quietly, "Yes, it will be so. You will come. It is from the *papalagi* we go, but you are no *papalagi* like the others. You are of Tiara. Now you will be of Maniloa. With us, always, is your place and your home."

Behind her glasses, the old lady's eyes had misted over. Then she had said briskly: "Yes, it is best so. For a while it will not be much of a school on Maniloa, but we will do the best we can."

She had made her simple preparations, packing her books and pads and pencils and few personal belongings. She had, until the last moment (when she had had to assemble a medical kit) said nothing to Carol Loftus. She had listened to the protests of Fahoai and the others who were staying behind; but in the end she had shaken her head. . . . And she had shaken it, too, when some of the villagers spoke of her selflessness, of the sacrifice she was making. For she knew that what she was doing was not selflessness, not sacrifice. . . . Her husband was gone. Her sons were gone. The world beyond Manaia was remote and lost. For twelve years these people and their world had been her life—its circumference, its totality—and to have lost them, failed them, now in their time of need, would have left her with a nothingness past bearing.

In the crude boat, in the wide ocean, she again sat with the head of a sleeping child in her lap. The sick mother, lying nearby, extended a hand and touched hers gently. Then Tafutimo stirred, leaving his high place before the mast, coming close, bending over her.

"You are all right, Miz Mundy?" he asked.

"Oh yes," she answered. "Quite all right. I'm a good sailor."

"There is nothing you want?"

"No. No, thank you," she said gently. "I have all I want."

Astern, Tiara had now vanished. In the *Star of Evening* a lookout climbed to the masthead, but even from there it was no longer visible. With no rear bearing to help in the calculations, an argument developed as to the proper course.

"We should be heading due east," said Vaoti, the senior *matai*.

"That is how we *are* heading," replied Ta'ua the helmsman.

"No, we are veering south." Vaoti was studying one of the compasses from Asimo's store. "The arrow says so."

"Then the arrow is wrong."

Others entered the discussion, some taking one side and some the other. They squinted at the sun and studied the surface of the sea. In years past their forefathers had done much of their navigation by reading the pattern of ocean swells and currents; but their secret lore had long been lost, and all had their different opinions and theories.

"What does the grandfather think?" someone asked, indicating Kalamakoa. "He is always saying he remembers the old things."

But when Vaoti put the question to him the ancient's eyes were sunken and empty.

> *Blow, blow,* he answered,
> *O Tahiri-matea god of winds—*

"What does he say?" called Ta'ua.

"He says nothing. He only mumbles."

"He cannot help us, the old one."

"He has grown dim in his wits."

"If I may say so," said John Koa, "I think we are going too far to the north."

"The north?" said Ta'ua.

"No, the south," said Vaoti.

"With the sun's angle—" John began.

"What do you know about it, boy?"

"In Apingo I saw books on navigation and—"

"Books!"

"*Papalagi* books."

"—and at this time of year and day, with the sun where it is—"

"Because you've read some stupid books," said Patali, the son of Tafutimo, "you think you know everything."

"Because you put a few nails in the boats—"

"Quiet, all of you!" Vaoti commanded.

In the end, the conch shell was blown to attract the attention of the *Wind of Morning,* and when the two boats had drawn together the discussion continued. The compass of the *Star* was compared with that of the *Wind,* and one pointed astern and the other athwartships. Then *matai* and helmsmen bent over the school map, but with no more enlightenment.

"Here is China," said one.

"And Australia."

"And California."

But when at last they found Manaia, the whole of it was a single dot—with no Tiara, no Maniloa. And they threw the map, in disgust, into the sea.

"We will follow the present course until dark," said Tafutimo, making the final pronouncement, "and then take a bearing from the stars."

Even that, however, was not to be. For as they rowed on through the afternoon, clouds moved in across the blue of sky, and when night came there were no stars but only darkness. Yet out of bad came good, at least of a sort, for at the same time the stillness broke, a wind rose, and for the first time that day they pressed forward under sail.

> *Blow, blow,* the chant rose again,
> *O Tahiri-matea, god of winds*—

But it did not last long, for soon the wind blew stronger. In the *Star of Evening* the mast swayed and creaked, the sail strained, the hull rolled in the heaving sea; and presently not only the women and children but most of the men as well were in the grip of sickness. Vaoti, from his perch amidships, tried to shout encouragement and instructions, but his words were lost in the sound of his own retchings. In the stern, the tall figure of Ta'ua slumped and crumpled, and his place at the helm was taken by his alternate, a younger man named Sega. But then Sega, too, sickened, lying limp and strengthless against the heavy sweep, and John Koa, one of the handful who were not sick, was in turn his replacement. In the scudding blackness there was no question of proper course, but only of struggling to keep the bow into the wind. At intervals, when he could free a hand from the sweep, he picked up the conch shell and blew a long ululating note, trying at least not to lose touch with the invisible *Wind of Morning.* For a while an answer came back, but growing steadily fainter, and at last it was wholly gone in the welter of wind and darkness.

Hours later Ta'ua had regained enough strength to take over again, and John stumbled forward among sprawled bodies, found a cranny of matting that would hold him, and fell instantly asleep. When he awoke the sky was gray with dawn, but it was not the sky he saw, it was the sail against it; for the wind was now stronger than ever, and the sail strained and flapped wildly from the lurching mast. With a cry he got to his feet. Others rose too. They hurried toward the mast. But they slipped and staggered; legs and arms were weak; and by the time they reached it and grasped the sennit halyards, the sail was ripped and shredded and streaming in the wind.

It blew until noon. Then air and sea grew calm, the sun appeared, the ocean lay in shining splendor. From bow to stern, however, and from gunwale to gunwale, the *Star* was drenched and bedraggled. The lowered sail and protective deck mats were a pulp of limp fibers. Much of the fresh taro was ruined; the firewood was useless; a dozen chickens had been drowned or otherwise killed, and one of the larger hogs had somehow slipped its tethering and vanished overboard. Of the human cargo, perhaps half were still violently sick, and of those who weren't, many were still too weak from lack of food and sleep to do more than look dully about them. From the all-but-collapsed fronded shelter amidships came the singsong wail of women pleading for a return to Tiara.

Eventually, however, some bestirred themselves. Food was unearthed from the protected places. The sail was spread out to dry, and the stronger of the women set about reweaving its torn matting. The younger men took up the oars and rowed as best they could with swollen, blistered hands. A boy was again sent up to the masthead to keep a lookout for the *Wind of Morning,* which had now not been seen since darkness the day before.

Then the leakage was discovered. At first it had been assumed that the water sloshing about in the bottom was merely the residue of the seas that had been shipped during the blow; but when an hour's bailing had failed to lower its level it was realized that there was steady seepage through the seams. There was no pump. There was no dry wood to heat gums for caulking. All that could be done was to go on bailing with gourds and buckets, and for this half the rowers had to abandon their oars.

"Ha, we are lucky ones, we are," said Patali, snarling at John Koa, "to have had you to tell us how to build a boat. If you'd had it all to yourself, we'd be at the bottom of the ocean."

Others joined in the accusation. There were complaints, shaking of heads, renewed wailings from the women.

Then at last one good thing happened. In the late afternoon there was a cry from the masthead; the boy called down that the *Wind* was off to starboard; and an hour later the boats were side by side. Notes were compared. In the *Wind,* Tafutimo reported, it had been much the same as in the *Star,* with torn sail, leaking seams, spoiled food and much sickness. But now, he declared, the worst was over. True, they must go on bailing. They must work harder than ever. But the weather was good again. The boats would stay together. They would sail true on their course.

Doubters raised their voices:

"What course?"

"We have none."

"We are lost."

"Maniloa is lost."

"We cannot find it."

"Where is it?"

But even as they spoke, dusk was falling; the evening star winked in the east; and Tafutimo, as if he himself had conjured it up, swung his arm, proudly pointing, "There is our course," he said. "There is the way."

And from the other boat, low and quavering, but still clear in the twilit stillness, came the answering chant of old Kalamakoa:

> *This is the way,*
> *The way ahead,*
> *The way of the sea,*
> *The way of the star,*
> *To Havaiki—*

John Koa had been peering at the star, gauging its distance from the horizon and trying to recall the charts and tables he had seen in Government navigation manuals. Now, rising in his place, he said, "If I may suggest, sir—"

"No, you may not," the high chief told him. "You have suggested enough already—with your *papalagi* boats that have almost drowned us."

"But the star is not due east, you see. At this time of year—"

Tafutimo waved him off. Others began talking. Then, as darkness fell, the boats moved on, keeping close together and sounding their conch shells, so that they would not again become separated during the night. In the *Star of Evening* it was still necessary to bail, steadily, grimly; but the sails were now up once more, patched and rewoven, and a wind carried them on without the need of rowing. With the other men, John took his turn with gourd and bucket. Then he rested. Lying on his strip of matting, he watched the blaze of stars—still trying to read them, to estimate the error of their course. But he could only guess.

He dozed and woke, and the stars had moved, but wind and sea were the same. At intervals there was the hoot of the conch shells, and between them the creak of the mast, the swish of water, the slow hum of a voice. It was the voice of Kalamakoa, still chanting. Hour by hour, since they had been at sea, he had seemed to withdraw ever farther into himself; speaking to no one, hearing no one; his sunken eyes veiled by a secret vision, his lips ceaselessly moving in the ancient litanies. And now they still moved, still chanted

—there is the way,
the way ahead,
the way of the sea,
the way of the star—

while the frail body rocked gently and the thin voice spun out into night and wind. And the thought came to John that the voice would never stop. That it was not merely the voice of one old man, but of a whole people—*his* people; that it was their memory, their hope; that it would sing on forever. . . .

But he was wrong.

For when he had slept and awakened again the voice had stopped, and there was only the creak of the mast and the swish of the sea. The skeletal figure still sat erect, outlined in starlight, among the sleeping ones around it. But it no longer swayed. The mouth was open, but it no longer moved. The eyes were open, but they no longer saw.

In the dawn, again, the boats were hove to, side by side. The old man's body had been wrapped in tapa cloth and matting and bound with strands of sennit, and the whole made so slight a bulk it seemed it could contain no more than a bundle of sticks. There were no stones in either boat, and the iron legs and treadle of one of the sewing machines had, over the protests of its owner, been requisitioned as weights. The shrouded body, with weights attached, was now propped on the gunwale of the *Star of Evening,* while in the *Wind of Morning* Tafutimo had risen to intone the phrases of ancient ritual.

When he had finished there was a silence. The men at the gunwale looked for the signal to push the body into the sea.

"A prayer—" someone cried.

"Yes, a prayer. There must be a prayer."

"Prayers are for pastors," said Tafutimo. "And we have no pastor."

"Our pastor abandoned us," a *matai* said.

"He was afraid to come."

"He was a slave of the *papalagi.*"

"He was not afraid. He was no slave," cried one of the women. "He knew God did not want us to come."

"And we defied God."

"Quiet!" shouted a *matai*. "We need no chatter about God."

"The old one was not a Christian anyhow," said another.

"It is a lie. We are all Christians."

Most of the women and a few of the men began to sing a hymn: some in Manaian, some in English. The nonsingers stood by sullenly.

"So, are you satisfied?" asked Tafutimo, when it was over.

"No—no," came the answer. "There must still be a prayer."

"Without a prayer we will not go on. His soul will be damned. And we too—all of us."

The high chief stood silent. He looked at the grim-faced men around him; at the angry, all-but-hysterical women; then beyond them, across the waste of waters, to where the sun was lifting above the far horizon. Finally he turned back to the shrouded form on the gunwale and raised his hand.

"We commend this body to the deep," he said, "and this soul to the hereafter. We do so in the name of Jesus Christ Our Lord and of the gods of our fathers, *fa'a Manaia*."

Then he gave the signal. The remains of Kalamakoa were pushed into the sea, and the iron weights on the shroud pulled it down.

Ai—ai—my sewing machine!" a woman's voice wailed. "Now I will have to sew like a savage squatting on the earth."

And an answering *"Ai—ai"* came from many others, though whether for machine or dead man was not clear.

Tafutimo had turned abruptly away. "Make sail!" he ordered. And in both boats men crowded to the masts.

Before them, the sun rose higher, huge and golden. Astern, on the ocean's surface, a black fin glinted briefly and vanished downward.

The sun climbed the sky. It became the hub of the sky, spitted on the masthead. Then it sloped away, sank, vanished. It was night again, with wheeling stars, a sickle moon. And then day again, but now without sun; with, instead, gray scudding cloud and heaving sea.

This was the fourth day. According to plan and estimate, they had hoped to reach Maniloa on the third, but there had been no sign of land—nor was there now. Maniloa was an atoll; they knew that. It would not, like Tiara, bulk high out of the sea with a shining cloud cap; but still, like all islands, it should have clouds above it, visible for many miles. On the bright third day, however, there had been no sign of it. And now, on the fourth, there were clouds everywhere. The sharpest-eyed boys and young men perched in shifts through the hours on the mastheads, but no shout came down from them. The only sound was the swish of sea and the hum of wind in the sails.

Sometimes the wind was fresh enough for them to move by sail alone. Sometimes they had to row. Always they had to bail—dully, wearily, endlessly—while backs and arms stiffened and feet swelled and burned in the sloshing bilges, Like the lookouts, the helmsmen were silent. There were no more exultant cries as their sweeps furrowed the sea, for they no longer knew if the furrows were steering them true or out into wastes of emptiness. With old Kalamakoa gone, there was no more chanting. Almost the only talk was when the two boats moved close together (for at least they had not again become separated) and there was discussion of how, if at all, their course should be altered. Sometimes they veered one way, sometimes another, always with objections from some who disagreed. Even John Koa was now grudgingly asked for his opinion; but with sun and stars hidden by cloud, he was no more able than the others to take bearings.

Even after four days, many were still sick, or strengthless from lack of food that their stomachs would not hold. And of those not sick in body, most were sick in mind and heart. In flesh and spirit, as in shipbuilding and navigation, these were no longer people of the sea. They did not understand it. They feared it. They were lost in its immensity.

"Lost—lost—" a woman whimpered in the *Star of Evening*.

"It is the old one's dying," said another. "It was a sign, an omen."

"He alone knew the way."

"He knew the old secrets."

"And now he is gone."

"The sea took him."

"The sharks took him."

"And we are doomed."

"We are lost."

The voices faded. For a while there was stillness, and then, in the stillness, another whimpering—a child's. The child cried through the rest of the day, and through the night, and in the morning it lay limp and sweating in its mother's arms, while the mother rocked it, moaning, and stared with glazed eyes out to sea.

"It is dying—dying—" she murmured.

"First the old one goes. Now a young one."

"Dying—dying—"

Other women took the child. They bathed it. They coddled it. But its fever mounted until it was a bit of burning flesh in their arms. It was now too weak to cry. The mother sat rigid and silent, as if in stupor. But the other women begin to wail. The men—those who were not bailing or sleeping—stood by, dull-eyed and helpless.

"We should get Mrs. Mundy," said John Koa presently.

"Miz Mundy?"

"She is not a Miz Nurse," someone said.

"She once was," John said. "She will know what to do. And she has medicines."

"No, we do not need her."

"Nor *papalagi* medicines."

"You would rather the child died?"

"It will die anyhow."

"It is the will of God."

"Of Takaroa."

"We will all die."

The wailing swelled. The men argued. "Quiet! Quiet!" commanded Vaoti, the senior *matai*. And then he reached his decision. The conch shell was blown; a signal was made to the *Star of Morning* to heave to; and with sail down and rowers at the oars, Ta'ua the helmsman brought the boat about until the two craft were alongside each other. Again there was discussion of the sick child—this time back and forth—but with the first words Mrs. Mundy rose from her place and began making her way to the point where the two boats almost touched. With her, at her bidding, came a young man called Atoe, whom she had been training as an orderly, carrying the small medical kit she had assembled from Carol Loftus's dispensary.

Atoe was the first into the other boat, leaping lightly across the yard of water between *Wind* and *Star*. Then the old lady was lifted up onto the *Wind*'s gunwale, and hands reached out to her from the *Star*. There was a surface swell on the sea, and the boats swung up and down, toward and away from each other; but the helmsmen heaved at their sweeps, and the rowers levered and fended with their oars, bringing the two craft even closer together, maneuvering for the right moment, the right juxtaposition. . . . "Now!" someone cried. And the hands behind pushed; the hands ahead grasped. . . . But there had been a miscalculation, for just then the gunwale of the *Star* veered down and away. Mrs. Mundy's body swung forward, but her feet slipped, the hands holding her slipped, and in that instant she was down between the boats. The hands did not lose her altogether. Even as she went into the water there was one gripping her wrist, pulling her upward. But as it did so, the boats yawed back together. In each, a dozen men were pushing, straining, with arms and oars. But still the two hulls swung closer; somewhere along their length they nudged and scraped; and at the point where Mrs. Mundy was being held they flared out above her like bulging walls.

She made no cry. There was only that faint scraping sound of wood on wood. And then the instant was over. Arms and oars swung the boats apart, and Mrs. Mundy was pulled aboard the *Star*. She was lifted over the gunwale and set gently down, and she sat with her hand pressed to her side against her dripping dress.

Figures crowded around her. Voices chattered. But for a while she herself did not speak. With her other hand she felt at her face for the glasses that were no longer there, and then at last she spoke, saying, "I can't see too well. Show me the child."

Something was wrong with her speech, too, for she had lost her dentures. A small boy, watching, giggled and nudged another. "Look— look how she talks," he said. "Her nose touches her chin."

"Please, bring me the child," Mrs. Mundy said, as well as she could.

During the day the child's fever dropped, and it slept peacefully in its mother's arms. Mrs. Mundy seemed to sleep too, lying on the pile of mats on which the people of the *Star* had made her as comfortable as they could. Now and then she stirred, and looking about vaguely, asked to see the child. Several times she made as if to rise, but each time lay back on the mats again, her hand pressed to her side.

The women sat close beside her, and the men came between their bouts of bailing and sail-trimming. "You are all right, Miz Mundy?" they asked over and over. "We can do something? You are all right?"

"No, nothing, thanks," she murmured, trying to control her tongue against her toothless gums. "I must just rest. I'll be all right."

Toward evening she asked Atoe to bring her the medical kit; but, without glasses, she could not find what she wanted, and Atoe, when she told him, could not read the labels. Finally it was John Koa who came and gave her a half-grain of morphine with water and later, during the night, he came again to give her another.

"Thank you, Haskell," she murmured to him. "Now you and the boys must go and get some rest." But he did not know who Haskell was, or what boys she referred to.

In the morning she seemed to be sleeping peacefully. The sick child was well. When the sun rose, it was bright and golden; the wind was fresh; and in spite of tiredness and weakness, in spite of doubt and fear, the spirit of the voyagers brightened, and all eyes strained forward toward the shining horizon. Presently a voice rose among them—not wailing, but chanting—and one by one, others joined in, until they were all chanting: the chant of old Kalamakoa, and of their ancestors:

> *Blow, blow, O Tahiri-matea,*
> *God of winds,*
> *Raise the west wind, the great wind,*
> *To carry us true,*
> *By the sea road to the homeland,*
> *To Havaiki—*

16

IT HAD BEEN one of those days for Mel Melnick. Indeed, one of those weeks (or two, or three), and he had already twice replenished his stock of Relaxo.

True, the hotel's kitchen and housewares had at last been extricated from their Apingo storage shed and transshipped to Tiara.

But—

1. There was still no supervisory staff (i.e., maître d'hôtel, chef, housekeeper) to see to their proper installation.

2. He himself was tied down in Apingo by (a) governmental red tape, (b) the training school for native help, and (c) waiting for the nonarriving staff.

3. The No. 1 member of the staff—one Bruce Plimpton, manager-to-be—*did,* by God, arrive. . . . But. . . . Where his wisdom tooth had been was now a hole—and an ache. A "dry socket," said the dentist at the Apingo Hospital. And through the days that followed, Mr. Plimpton nursed his socket, while he, Mel Melnick, nursed the trainees.

4. Socket O.K. Plimpton takes over trainees. He himself will (would) go to Tiara. . . . But. . . . The *Mariposa* is arriving. He has scheduled conference with Matson Line cruise director. Also, aboard *Mariposa* is the pride of the Pacific Hotel and Development Company, the long-awaited Catalina flying boat. At least he will now be able to go back and forth to Tiara in civilized fashion, instead of in that heaving hellhole of an *Ickes.*

5. He waits. *Mariposa* arrives; conference held; plane unloaded. . . . But. . . . No pilot, no copilot. Cable to aircraft company in Los

Angeles brings answer they will arrive on next Pan Am plane; but one week and three flights later they have yet to appear.

There were also Items 6, 7, 8, and, roughly, through to 100, but they tended to fade out in a general blur of frustration. . . . And rain. . . . For the deluge that had flooded the storage shed had been only the first of a relentless procession. It was, theoretically, the middle of the dry season. The schedule for the hotel's construction and opening had been carefully timed to fit in with it. But the Weather Bureau was obviously staffed by cretins, for it rained. And rained. It was raining on this particular afternoon when a boy arrived from the radio office with a garbled message that some (or half, or all) the local labor over at the hotel had, as of that morning, quit the job.

Mel Melnick's first impulse was to take the next plane to Turkey, where he would apply for work as bus boy at the Istanbul Hilton. His next was to go at once to Tiara; but the *Ickes* was now over there and would not be back until the following day. He took two Relaxos, lighted a cigar, and in the resultant semicalm decided that the only solution was to get more labor here in Utoia. He had been told that those who had gone over with Tom Taki were the only men available. Beyond them, Public Works had turned him down in everything. . . . Well, if they turned him down now, Mel Melnick decided, they could take their goddam hotel and—

Only it wasn't *their* hotel. It was *his*.

He tried to phone Russell Gorman, but the line was drowned and dead in the rain. The town's three taxis never stirred in bad weather, and Plimpton, the manager, was off somewhere in the company jeep. So he walked the half mile from the Nimitz Hotel to the Government Administration Building. The rain poured down on him. Off to the right, moored to a buoy in the shrouded harbor, he could see the dim shape of the pilotless pride of the Pacific Hotel and Development Company.

At the Administration Building he was told that Gorman was at a conference at the Governor's, but was expected back soon. . . . Would he wait in Mr. Gorman's office? He would. And did. . . . In the time it had taken him to reach it, the rain had stopped, the sun had come out, and it gleamed on the windshields of Apingo's three taxis cruising by. Also, it flooded through the window, turning the damp room into a steam bath, and Melnick pressed the switch for the air conditioner. He pressed it several times. He shook the machine. He kicked the machine. Going to the outer office, he spoke to the Manaian clerk, and the clerk assured him that it would be fixed in two months.

Back in Gorman's office, he examined his sopping cigar. He took

231

a Relaxo. He waited. And at last Gorman appeared. He was not alone, however, but accompanied by Leonard Shafter, and the two were in earnest and agitated conversation.

"You must forgive us," said Gorman, seeing his visitor, "but there's a sudden emergency."

"You're damn right there is," Melnick concurred. "I've just heard from Tiara—"

"Yes, so have we."

"—that half my men have quit work."

"It's not just work they've quit. It's the island too."

"The island?"

Gorman told him what little he knew, by way of the also-garbled message from Malele the policeman. "Apparently at least a hundred of them," he said, "have taken off for a little atoll called Maniloa."

This was beyond Melnick's depth. . . . "A little which? Called what?" . . . Then, as he found himself, for a rare moment, wordless, the others plunged back into their conversation.

"—And as the Governor damn well knows," said Gorman heatedly, "I've prophesied something like this all along. It was in the cards, and by God, here it is."

"I knew Tafutimo was steamed up," Shafter said. "But the others—that many others—"

"What about Fahoai—did he go?"

"The message didn't say. But no, I'm sure not; he wouldn't."

"Then why didn't *he* let us know?"

"Or Mrs. Mundy? Or Carol Loftus?"

Gorman sat down heavily at his desk, while Shafter paced up and down. "It's those damn congressmen," said the younger man. "If I hadn't had to wetnurse them—if I'd been over there more, as I should have—"

"Well, it's spilt milk now. All over the Pacific Ocean."

"When the *Ickes* comes in tomorrow—"

"When that *Ickes* comes in," said Mel Melnick, remarshaling his forces, "I've got to have thirty men on the dock, ready to go."

Gorman glanced at him, as if just noticing his presence. "What do you mean, thirty men?" he said.

"To work on the hotel."

Gorman shook his head. "I'm afraid that will have to wait."

"Wait? Why? You tell that Public Works of yours that—"

"It's not a matter of Public Works. It's that the *Ickes* will be busy."

"Busy?"

"We've got to look for these people."

"Don't you understand, man?" said Shafter. "A hundred or more of them are out there in the ocean in two homemade boats. Not just men, but women, children, half the village. They don't know the ocean. They don't know navigation. And they're heading for an island about the size of a grain of sand."

"You mean—"

"I'm taking the *Ickes* out as soon as it gets here. To find those fools and bring them back."

"But—"

"It's all been discussed with the Governor," said Gorman, "and that's the decision. These are free people, yes. They can do what they want—up to a point—but beyond that the Government has a responsibility." His face was grim, his voice rasping, as he eyed Melnick across the desk. "One responsibility we've already got,, and that's allowing this hotel to be built on their island. Fouling up their way of living, until now we have the result . . . plus *more* responsibility. . . . To do what we can, at least, to straighten them out."

"By tearing the hotel down, I suppose?"

"By God, I half wish we could." Gorman spat the words out; then, with an effort, controlled himself. "Anyhow," he said, "we have to find these people. Two to one, they're lost out there already. And even if they get to this Maniloa—"

"It couldn't support a half-dozen people," Shafter put in, "let alone a community."

"Besides, the weather's turning bad."

"Yeah, what about *that,* too?" Melnick demanded. "I thought this was supposed to be—"

The phone rang and Gorman picked it up. "Yes?" he said, then listened silently; and when he hung up his face was grimmer than ever.

"There's been another message," he said to Shafter. "The count's a hundred and eighteen gone, and the old lady is one of them."

"The old lady?"

"Mrs. Mundy."

"Good God! Are they sure?"

"How the hell do I know if they're sure? That's what the message said."

"What about Carol?"

"Carol?"

"Miss Loftus. the nurse."

"It didn't mention her. I guess she's still there."

"Look, gentlemen—" said Melnick, with preternatural calm.

"This means we'll have to send over a teacher."

"I'll talk to Education."

"Right. But first let's get Maritime. We'll need extra crew on the *Ickes* for this job, and—"

"I am just trying to point out—" said Melnick.

"—and they should be lined up today, so that—"

"—that there's a hotel, remember? In three weeks it's supposed to open. I've got contracts with Pan Am, with Matson, with travel agents, and three weeks from Tuesday there are going to be ninety tourists dumped down here with deposit-paid reservations." The calm, preternatural or otherwise, was crumbling. It *had* crumbled. "What the hell am I supposed to do with them?" Melnick yelled. "Tell 'em to sleep on the beach and eat seaweed?"

Shafter had picked up the phone. "Get me Mr. McCown at Maritime," he said. "And then Mr. Lebolt at Education."

When he put it down it rang, and Gorman, answering, said, "Yes, come over. Right away, it's important."

"I was promised full co-operation," Melnick shouted. "All the labor I needed. First priority on the *Ickes.* . . . How can I open the damn hotel if I can't even get to it?"

"You've got your plane now, haven't you?" said Gorman.

"Yeah, sure I've got a plane. But no one to fly it."

"I thought you cabled."

"Sure I cabled. But they can't cable them back."

"Then you'll just have to wait. We've got this emergency."

"And *I've* got an emergency. By God, I've been putting up hotels for fifteen years, and in all that time—"

The phone rang again. A clerk appeared. After him came two agitated Manaians, and after them three stateside Government officials. In a moment they were all talking. And Melnick too—but no one listened.

As he started back toward the Nimitz Hotel it began to rain again. And on reaching it he was handed two cablegrams. The first, from the Los Angeles company that had sold him the Catalina, stated that it had unfortunately been unable to find anyone qualified to fly it, and suggested that he try Australia or New Zealand, where flying boats were more common. The second, from the New York office of the American Express Company, advised that among the arrivals for the hotel opening would be a party of twelve from the Maccabee Brotherhood of Far Rockaway, Long Island, and that it was assumed that kosher food would be available.

In Tiara it had rained during the night, but with early morning the sun was golden. The high white cloud-cap shone. Green slopes and groves glittered with their billion drops of moisture. The lagoon was a swathe of silk under a silken sky, as the *Harold L. Ickes* moved slowly across toward the opening in the reef.

Mitchell Carr did not look back. Hunched at the rail, he looked

234

down into the gleaming water: at its crystal depths, its jeweled hues, its darting shapes of shade and light. It was for this—the lagoon—that he had come to Tiara. It was why Mel Melnick had brought him, with his engineering skills. With his dynamite. He had peered into these depths, picked his places, placed his dynamite, done his job. There had been the fountains of fish, and now a seaplane could touch down. He had done his job, and he was leaving.

The other engineers—the coral engineers—had taken over again. But it would take them a while to rebuild what he had unbuilt.

Straightening, he looked ahead, and there was the reef and the passage. On either side, the white fangs of the breakers; dead before the bow, the narrow lane of clear water. They were close now, and the tide was coming in, flowing fullbodied against the *Ickes* as it pushed toward the open sea. On the bridge a bell clanked, signaling full speed ahead, and Captain Joe Stack jockeyed the wheel with practiced hand.

Other than answering clanks, however, there was no response from the engine room. The tide grew stronger, but the ship's drive remained the same; and now it was losing headway, its bow was yawing, and Stack was no longer merely jockeying the wheel, but spinning, grappling with it, in a struggle to keep on course. . . . "More! More!" he shouted into the speaking tube. . . . And now there was a response, of sorts. The engine thumped louder. The ship trembled and groaned. But added power, if any, was negligible. The bow still yawed. The reef to starboard angled closer, surging, booming; they were almost upon it . . . almost, but not quite . . . for in the end Stack mastered the wheel. The bow swung back on course. It held. The reef angled away. And now they were through it, they were in the sea beyond, and Stack, turning the wheel over to a Manaian sailor, stomped down toward the engine room.

"Sonofabitching tub," he said, as he passed Carr on the deck. "I could get more go out of a one-oared rowboat."

Then he vanished below. Carr was alone again. And now the sea was around them, and he looked at the sea. At first downward, as he had before on the lagoon; but now the water was dark and opaque, and what lay below was hidden. Then out, across the surface, across the miles; and here there was no darkness, there was space and sunlight, but here too was opaqueness, for what lay beyond was hidden. Out there, somewhere in blue distance, were two tiny boats, invisible and lost. Even if their course was true, they were still out there, with their loads of men, women, children: the refugees, the exiles. With one particular exile, half boy, half man, who happened to be his son.

Oh yes, he had done his job well, with his skills and his dynamite.

With his job for the brown boy, his bedding down with the brown boy's cousin. . . . And he was good not just with dynamite, but with his fists too. Yes, indeed. Really quite impressive for an old-timer of forty-three.

He rubbed the knuckles of his right hand with the fingers of his left.

Then he looked at Tiara.

Goodbye again, Tiara. . . .

He thought of the other goodbye—the goodbye of eighteen years past—and then too he had been on a ship; no, not a ship—a boat—a forty-foot native-owned fishing boat, creaking, heaving its way through the sea, as the island faded astern. A few days before, his flight squadron had got its movement orders. At week's end they would go on toward Fiji, the Ellice Islands, the Jap-held Gilberts. And he had resolved that he must, that he *would,* see Lovana once more. He had rented the fishing boat for a hundred dollars, and in the dark of night (for he had no leave) it had left Utoia for Tiara. It had got him there, then waited, and he had found Lovana, and together they had gone into the hills, to the hidden pool, and had their last hour beneath the breadfruit tree. It had been an hour exactly: that was all. Then he had told her it was the last, holding her while she cried and saying goodbye; and he had gone down alone to the shore. She had wanted to come too, but he had said no, goodbye was better here. Here was where they had had their happiness, where he would always remember her—under the arms of the Old Man, in the place of *fia fia.*

Then he had been back in the boat, bound for Utoia. Bound for the war, the world, the future. Looking back at Tiara, he had told himself: "Wherever they take you, whatever they hold, there will be nothing like this ever again." And he had been right: there hadn't. Not with Margaret (*Oh Mitch, please, I want a home, a child—*). Not with Helen (*No, no, Mitch: I'm afraid, afraid—*). Surely not with any other woman he had known before or since.

Until Va'ina?

Well, yes and no. Yes—or almost yes (allowing for those eighteen years) for a few recaptured moments under the tree. But then, no. Then recapture gone, lost, self-devoured in cold reality. In place of magic, the fact of memory, of knowledge: this was the niece of Lovana, the cousin of John Koa. In place of the breadfruit tree, a frowzy hut, a rumpled cot, a brown boy wild and anguished. . . . And a striking fist.

No, not that again—

He wrenched his mind away. He brought it back to leaving, to the dock in the lagoon an hour before. Frank Lavery had been there, and most of the "Hawaiians," and there had been quick handshakes, a few jokes, a batch of reports and complaints for Mel Melnick. But this was simply the routine goodbye to men he had worked with. Not to Tiara. There had been none to Tiara. None to Va'ina. She did not even know he was going, and it was just as well; for what could he have said to her?

One thing he could have said. . . . "I'm sorry." . . . For he had brought trouble to her, no less than to John Koa. "What is it? What is wrong, Meesh?" she had asked in her rejection. And he could not tell her. Their affair, he now knew, had caused a scandal in the village. But what could he have done? Or do now? With Lovana, it had all been natural, simple. Even the grief of parting had been simple: the grief of return from one world into another. But now there was no such division of worlds. They were mingled, embroiled. Even the arms of the Old Man of the Tree could not give protection. Into the sanctuary came conflict and turmoil.

Into *fia fia* came . . . what was it? . . . *pilikia*.

In spite of himself, he smiled. You could not think long of Va'ina without smiling. And whatever grief he had brought her would, he knew, soon pass. For Va'ina could take care of herself. He, Mitchell Carr, had come, and now he had gone, and there might be a few moments of sadness, a soft island tear or two. And then: " 'Allo there; you are nice, yes, Meester Melnick. . . . 'Allo, you other meesters: from Honolulu, Hollywood, New York. You are nice too. I dance for you. Like so—and so—"

The image of the brown girl danced off: smiling, teasing. Where she had been was the sea, and beyond the sea, Tiara. It had receded now. Its fringe of reef was gone; its hills had turned from green to blue; and as Carr watched, its cloud cap was changing too—from dazzling white to gray, from gray to violet, then to spectral purple, as, in another of its sudden storms, rain veiled its peaks and moved out swiftly across the water.

In a moment it had swallowed the sun. In the next, a gust of wind struck the *Ickes* and rain was pattering on its slanted deck. From the covered bridge Captain Stack called down, and, ascending the companionway, Carr joined him in its shelter.

"Just a squall," the captain said. "But by God we're sure gettin' 'em."

Together they stood beside the Manaian helmsman, peering out into the scud, with Stack's glance, at intervals, moving to the compass in the binnacle. He was a small but rugged man of perhaps fifty, with a creased face, sunken blue eyes, and arms that displayed the tattooed names of what seemed to be half the ships in the U.S. Navy. Now and then, when the *Ickes* laid over in Tiara, he had sat in on the evening poker games, holding his own in both winning and swearing (which took some doing against the "Hawaiians"). But Carr knew little about him, save what the tattooing proclaimed—and that he had been in the islands for many years.

"Takin' off, eh?" he asked, after a silence.

And Carr nodded.

"Back to the Big Time?"

"Is that the name for it?"

"It's my name. Back there's the Big Time. Out here's the Small Time." Stack looked at him quizzically. "I'd had the idea you might be around a while."

"It's been longer than I'd planned, already."

"I mean really around. Sort of diggin' in."

"What made you think that?"

"I dunno. Just had the feelin'. Most guys who come here they're like the ones with the hotel. Or the Government ones—they're the same. They come out to do a job. They do it. Then they clear the hell out. It's just once in a while you find one that's different. That sort of—well, the place gets 'em."

"Like you."

"Yeah, like me, I guess."

"How long have *you* been here?"

"Twelve years now. Not countin' the war, that is. Back there I was in and out maybe four or five times. Then back stateside. Then— well, it's a long story. A cruddy life, cruddy jobs, a bum marriage. 'Hell, what am I doin' this for,' I asked myself, 'when out there there's everythin' a guy could want?' So out I came again. And here I am."

"And you haven't been home since?"

"Home—hah." Stack was about to go on, but his attention was taken by the stronger lashing of wind and rain against the wheelhouse window. His eye went again to the compass, then to the Manaian steersman, who was heaving at the wheel. "Still ten points more to port," he told him.

"Yeah, boss, I know," said the steersman. "But she no go. She slip."

"Slip?" Stack took the wheel and jockeyed it. Then he called into the speaking tube. "Give her more," he said. "Rev her up."

He turned back to Carr. "This is home, mister," he went on. "Know what I got in Apingo? I got a brown woman and seven kids. If that ain't home I don't know what the hell is."

The wind screamed. The *Ickes* heaved and pitched, losing headway, and again he concentrated on wheel and compass. "More! More, damn it!" he yelled into the tube. But if "more" was forthcoming it was not perceptible, and the compass showed that sea and wind were pushing them ever farther off course.

Stack struggled and swore. Then he listened while squawking

238

noises came up the tube. "What?" he demanded. "What?" he listened. "The pistons? The shaft?"

More squawking came from below, but he turned his back on it. "That, for Christ's sake, settles it," he rasped. "This tub gets a dry-dock overhaul before I take it ten yards out of Apingo again."

"Bad trouble?" asked Carr.

"Bad? She's a wreck, that's what. Four worn-out pistons. A cracked prop shaft. Half the shellfish in the Pacific playin' house on the bottom. For three months I been tellin' 'em she's got to have an overhaul. But they say no, wait—there's the hotel stuff's got to go over; there's this, there's that. Well, I don't give a damn what's still to go over. This ship ain't movin' again till it's fixed and fixed right."

He worked the wheel angrily, scowling out into the storm. "Look at that compass. Twenty points off course," he said. "You saw what went on back there at the reef? And that was without a squall. Know where we'd be if somethin' like this hit us there?" He jerked a thumb down. "Right there—shark food—that's where we'd be, the lot of us. Anyone tells me to take this crate out again before it's fixed, I'll spit right in their eye."

The deck swayed. Bow and compass veered wildly. For perhaps another five minutes the squall beat at them, and then, as suddenly as it had borne in, it moved on past them. Ahead the sky was clear, the sea calm, and the sun was bright on the streaming glass of the wheelhouse. Back on course again, the *Ickes* thumped and wallowed on its weary way.

"Yeah," Stack said, as if there had been no interruption, "—woman and seven kids, that's all. We'd have a high old time back stateside." He gave a grunting laugh. "Couldn't even marry her, on account of my first wife never give me a divorce. And for the kids—oh, it'd be neat. Seven little half-caste bastards floatin' around in some slum."

Carr looked at him curiously. "And here?" he said. "How's it been for them here?"

"The kids? O.K., mostly. There's not much dough, of course, but you don't need much here. And nobody cares if they're brown, white, or green. There's plenty of their kind around."

"And mostly with no father at all?"

Stack nodded. "That's right. Especially the ones from back in the war—the place is full of 'em." He shrugged. "Hell, that's what's been goin' on here since Captain Cook. 'Hiya, honey—so long, honey.' And when the kid comes the guy's in Sioux City. . . . Don't matter much, though. It's the regular thing, and the folks out here are used to it. It's a guy like me, one who hangs around, that's the queer one. . . . So all right, I'm queer. Like I said, you can have your Big Time. Me, I like it small."

He gave another grunting laugh and waved his arm at the sweep of ocean. "Sure—some small," he said. "Small like a relief check, eh? Like a strap in a subway car. Like a furnished room on Beat Street."

The squall was now only a purplish bruise on the horizon. They moved through a rain-washed vault of shining blue.

"Know what I mean?" said Stack.

"Yes," Carr said, "I know what you mean."

"I thought you would. That's why I said before—"

"That you thought I'd stay?"

"Yeah."

"What would *I* have to stay for?"

Again Stack gave him the quizzical glance. "Well now," he said, "it ain't my business exactly, but you weren't doin' too bad with that chick of yours."

"Chick?"

"That dancin' gal. Don't put on you never heard of her. Most of the hotel boys thought you were hooked but good."

Carr smiled a little. "No, it didn't work out," he said.

"Hmm—well, that's how it is: you can't tell. How it'll go with a dame. How it'll go with anyone. . . . You, for instance—with or without this cookie. Right from the first time I saw you comin' over on this tub, I thought I had you pegged. I remember you standin' at the rail there, lookin' at the island, and I said there's a guy that's hungry for this place—who's gonna be around a while. . . . Then—here's goin' wrong for fair—I look at that gal who's along. Whatsername, the nurse. The blonde tomato—"

"Miss Loftus," said Carr.

"Yeah, Loftus."

"What about her?"

"—And I tell myself, *there's* a little number that'll last about two days out here."

"It's two months now," Carr said.

"That's my point: how wrong can you get? Here's a guy with that look in his eye, and I say he'll stay. But he don't. Here's a dame who belongs on an out-island the way I belong in the Waldorf. She'll scram fast. So she stays."

Stack rubbed an ear meditatively. "You seen her more than I have," he said. "How you figure a dame like that?"

It was a moment before Carr answered. Then he said, "Well, she's a pretty serious girl. She has a great need to be of service."

"Service—" Stack grinned. "With looks like that, there's one service a dame should be givin', and that's. . . . Hey, what's up now?"

At the same time, Carr had noticed something: a change of sound or of vibration. Again the *Ickes* was losing headway, and an instant

240

later there were more squawks from the speaking tube. . . . "The what? The condenser?" Stack barked back. . . . "Okay, then: half speed. For Chrissake don't blow the whole works out." . . . Then, turning back to Carr: "Hope there's no rush, pal. The old tub'll get us there, I guess, but it sure ain't in no hurry."

The *Ickes* crept on. Stack, satisfied that it was at least keeping on course, took off again for the engine room; and presently Carr returned to the deck. All trace of the squall was gone now. Ahead, the horizon showed only bare blue, for Utoia was not yet in sight. And behind was more blue—for Tiara was gone.

John Koa was gone.

Va'ina was gone.

And another one, too. Another girl—called Carol Loftus. He had tried not to think of her during the past hours, and had almost succeeded, until Stack spoke of her; but now she was *there* again—a memory, a presence—no less than the others.

He had not said goodbye to her, either. The last he had seen of her was on the beach by the village, with the sea beyond, and, far at sea, the two receding boats. With a face watching them—the grinning, drunken face of Asimo the storekeeper. And there, suddenly, it had been, all at once: the hopelessness, the bitterness: the sobbing girl, the leering face, the fading specks—and the girl had held him, clung to him, asking for comfort, but he had had no comfort to give. He had held her for a few moments, his eyes on Asimo, his eyes on the sea. And then another figure had appeared—a small boy saying his mother had stomach cramps and would Miz Nurse please come— and he had walked with her into the village and got in his jeep and driven back to the hotel. In the quonset there had been a half-filled bottle of whisky on the table, and he had reached for it, and then pushed it away. And he had thought, no, that was no answer; there was only one answer; and he had looked from the window down the slope at the jetty and the *Ickes,* and then pulled his bag out from under the cot.

No—no goodbye. For to her, too, what was there to say? . . . "Happy nursing," perhaps? Or "Find a man"? . . . Yes, a man her own age. Not another father. Not a man she was grateful to because he didn't make a pass at her; because he accepted her in the image she had chosen for herself.

Or—what else? . . . Ah yes, he could have sung his song again; sung his *tune-'neath-the-moon-on-the-tropic-lagoon.* With Asimo added. With the two specks added: receding, fading, on the sea beyond.

The shell of Nurse Carol Loftus had cracked. The baggage she had brought with her had spilled open, and there she was—a girl, a woman. And that was another reason why he, Mitchell Carr, was on the *Harold L. Ickes,* outward bound. It was not only comfort she had asked of him. It was love. She had love to give. And he in return could only turn away. With his memory of Margaret, of Helen. With the knowledge of his emptiness. If he was still capable of love at all, it was not the love a woman such as Carol Loftus needed. The best he was capable of was love in escape, in hiding; love under the breadfruit tree. And even there, when he found it, he could no longer hold it—because of the baggage *he* carried with him. "This is the happiness time—the time of *fia fia,*" Va'ina had said to him. But he had made it the trouble time—the time of *pilikia.*

—As, with John Koa, his son, he had put out his hand. And the hand was a fist.

Again he looked out from his own emptiness to that of the sea. But now it was no longer empty. Ahead, above the bow, was the dim shape of Utoia, and he projected himself toward it—beyond it. For he would spend no more time there, he had decided, than it would take him to collect his pay from Mel Melnick and catch a plane. A plane out and away. A plane to . . .

There it was again. . . . To where?

In one direction, they flew up to Hawaii and beyond. To Joe Stack's Big Time. To Swanson, Bromley & Carr, Inc., of 600 Fifth Avenue, New York 19, N.Y. If that was the way he chose, it would be back to where he had come from. He would resume his profession, his function, living his life in the only way in which it had a function. To the thrust of steel. To the roar of drills. . . . A roar loud enough to fill the emptiness.

George Swanson's letter was in his pocket. A coin was in his pocket, too, and he took it out and held it on his thumbnail.

There were planes in other directions as well. Planes to Fiji, Samoa, Tahiti. And beyond these, though there were no more planes, there were more islands, an ocean of islands. There was no Pahukahuka, but yet a hundred Pahukahukas—by whatever name, or nameless—remote and lost beyond the miles. He could find a schooner, a trade boat, whatever offered, and go on to them. Always on to another island, farther, deeper—another outpost, another refuge—as even now, in the ocean behind him, two boats were beating their way toward an island called Maniloa.

He heard the roar of the drills. He heard the silence of the sea. Holding the coin, he thought: heads this way—tails that way.

And if it stood on edge. . . .

He flipped and caught the coin and put it back in his pocket without opening his hand; and now he could hear neither roar nor silence, but only the thump and wheeze of the *Harold L. Ickes.* At least a plane, wherever it took him, would make a better sound than that.

17

... A<small>ND IT DID.</small>

The engines were old and reconditioned, but they hummed smoothly. The power came when it was needed—driving, lifting; the harbor slanted away; the plane climbed and soared. It bore to the west (toward Fiji). It bore to the east (toward Samoa). But each time it arced back, swooping, circling, above the harbor, the sea, the hills of Utoia. For this was no transocean liner, outward bound. It was the Catalina flying boat of the Pacific Hotel and Development Company. And it had no passengers aboard, but only a pilot. A pilot who was he, Mitchell Carr.

The years had rolled back for him when he returned to Manaia. Now again they rolled back as he held the wheel, kicked the rudders, watched the serried dials of the instrument board. For in time gone by, during the years of the war, he had flown this plane through half the skies of the Pacific. Then it had been called not a Catalina but a PBY. Then there had been a copilot beside him, an engineer up behind in his "tower" between the wings, still farther back the fighting crew with its welter of armament and equipment. But it was the same plane nonetheless. Lumbering, potbellied; seeming now, in the age of jets, even fatter and slower than before; yet still able, miraculously, to surge up out of the sea; to roar, to soar, to cleave the air.

It could still fly.

And he could fly it.

He was still a pilot.

And here he was. . . .

It had begun when the *Ickes* limped into the harbor of Apingo the afternoon before, with Russell Gorman and Leonard Shafter waiting on the wharf; and they had plunged at once into an earnest, and presently vehement, conversation with Joe Stack. Carr, however, had paid little attention. Hoisting his bag, he had gone ashore, hailed a taxi (for it wasn't raining), and ridden to the Nimitz Hotel. And from there he had been about to call the airfield for the word on outgoing planes, when Gorman and Shafter had reappeared—this time with Mel Melnick. Their coming was no happenstance. It was he they wanted to talk to. (Or at least the two Government men did; Melnick, for once, was moodily silent.) And after a few questions about Tiara they got to the point.

"As you can no doubt understand," said Gorman, taking the lead, "we feel that what has happened there is wholly deplorable. And we're determined to find these people and bring them back."

"Against their will?" Carr asked.

"No, not against their will. These are free people, in their own country. But we're sure we can convince them that what they've done is foolish and impractical."

"If they're not convinced already," said Shafter.

"We don't know at the moment," Gorman continued, "whether they've reached this atoll of Maniloa or are still at sea; but in either case they're almost surely in trouble, and very possibly in danger. It was our plan to requisition the *Ickes* to go after them. But, as you're aware, the *Ickes* is in bad shape. In fact, Captain Stack says it's unseaworthy and refuses to take it out."

"And there's no other ship available," Shafter added.

"There is, however, now a plane available: a flying boat belonging to the hotel company. I imagine you saw it when you came into the harbor."

Carr nodded.

"And Mr. Melnick here has been kind enough to offer—"

Melnick's dark gaze had been turned to the floor; but now, rising, it fixed on Gorman, and the latter paused and cleared his throat.

"—has been kind enough," he amended, "to consent to its use. Unfortunately, however, there's no pilot on hand. At least none, anywhere in Manaia, who's familiar with seaplanes."

He paused.

"Except you," said Shafter.

"Yes," Gorman said. "I understand from Mr. Shafter that you flew for the Navy. The same plane, a PBY—is that right?"

"That was a while back," said Carr.

"But it's the sort of thing you don't forget, isn't it? Like—well—driving a car—"

244

"And once you got the feel of it—" said Shafter.

There was another pause.

Then Carr said, "I have no license."

"Under the circumstances, that can be handled, I think. Bill Kelly—he's the FAA man here—could issue a special permit."

"It's a question of an emergency," Shafter put in earnestly. "Maybe even of life and death."

"And the Governor himself has agreed that—"

They talked on. Melnick looked at the floor. Carr looked at the window. Beyond the window was a strip of lawn, beyond that the harbor, and in the harbor, at its mooring, rode the Catalina, with the evening sun bright on its silver wings.

. . . As now the morning sun was bright (after the rain at dawn), with, below, the green island, the blue harbor, and around, as far as eye could see, the sweep of sky and ocean, transfixed in the web of space, the magic of flight. It was a magic he had not known for a long time. It did not penetrate into the great airliners; into the pressurized, sealed-off passenger-world of paneled cabins, midget pillows, and stewardesses with toothpaste smiles and trays of cocktails. But here he was no passenger, and it was back in full potency. Doubly so, after all the years. Doubly so in his aloneness.

Nor—Gorman was right—had he forgotten what he had known. He had not lost his skill. In the beginning, to be sure, he had had his moments of doubt, and the moments had multiplied into an hour of tension, as he sat in the cockpit in the harbor waters, testing, retesting the two engines, reacquainting himself slowly, deliberately, with every instrument, every control. The tension had mounted when he put the plane into motion: taxiing, revving, cruising back and forth across the harbor, maneuvering at last to the head of the long takeoff channel. But once he let it out, it was all right. His hands were steady on the wheel, and his feet on the rudders. Surely, steadily, he had lifted the Cat out of the deep clutch of the water—through the plumes of foam, the roar of sea—until only the keel was slapping the surface; then only the step of the keel; he was poised on the step, he was off it, he was airborne. And it was still all right. He had the touch of it, the feel of it. He was a flier again.

He circled Utoia; then cut across its rugged spine. He climbed, dipped, banked, eased down to a landing, and the landing was good. He taxied once more, took off once more. And still the engines hummed evenly; still wheel and rudder and throttle responded properly to his touch. In the old days of the wartime PBYs he had never flown alone. Apart from Navy rules, it would have been almost impossible to fly one alone, with all the engine and fuel controls up in the engineer's tower. But here, as in many rebuilt civilian jobs, the major controls had been transferred to the cockpit—to save crew, and hence money—and on a short-range flight there was nothing one man could not do on his own . . . provided he knew *what* he was doing. And he did.

Now, high in the air on his second circuit of the island, the plane all but flew itself, and while his reflexes remained with it, his thoughts turned inward. They turned back to the previous night at the Nimitz; to Gordon and Shafter and their earnest plea to him: "We need you." To the smile that had faintly touched his lips, as he listened, as at last he nodded—and now touched them again as he drove the plane through the sky.

He was needed. . . .

And not for the first time, on this trip of his: this escape, this flight, this quest for the past. (Or whatever it was.) First he had been needed to blast a lagoon. Then to survey a slope. Now to fly a plane. . . . Oh yes, he was an important fellow, all right. A man of skills, of talents. Mitchell Carr, B.Sc., C.E., USNR, no less: the Mr. Fixit of the Seven Seas, developer of backward areas, rescuer of distressed indigenes. Rescuer-elect of a boy called John Koa—a brown, half-caste island boy—who had dreamed of flying a plane, like a white man; like his unknown father. And whose dream was dead. . . .

Again he brought the plane down. Again, an hour later, he took off. But now he was no longer alone. Beside him, in the copilot's seat, but taking care to touch nothing, was Leonard Shafter. Behind and above, in the now functionless engineer's perch, sat Mel Melnick, with his manager, Bruce Plimpton, near the foot of the ladder below. And beyond the forward bulkhead, in the main compartment, were eight Utoian workmen, as reinforcements for the depleted labor force at the hotel. Melnick had wanted to take more. He had had some twenty lined up and ready to go. But for the flight—or flights—beyond Manaia the plane had also to carry several drums of spare fuel, and Carr had set an over-all human limit of a dozen.

Their ultimate goal, the atoll of Maniloa, lay on the far side of Tiara. And it had been decided that it was to the latter they would go first—both to drop off Melnick & Company (for, after all, it *was* his plane), and so that Shafter could talk with the islanders who were still there. Utoia to Tiara was only eighty-odd miles: a mere forty to fifty minutes' passage in the Catalina. And at their cruising height of fifteen hundred feet, the two islands would, at mid-flight, be visible simultaneously. Carr had with him all the charts that were available in Apingo; but once the course had been set, little navigation would be needed on this stage of the journey.

Up from the harbor they soared. Over the town, the palm groves, the hills. And out to sea. Two squalls hung dark on the horizon—one to the north, one to the southeast—but they were far away, and the sky above them beamed blue and gold.

Carr's eyes moved from the instrument panel to the face of the compass at his feet. Shafter, beside him, was gazing into the distance. And Melnick, down from the tower, was now standing behind them, nervously watching Carr's handling of the plane. At intervals, he asked Carr questions. . . . Was this all right? Was that? Was *he*? . . . And each time Carr nodded.

"Good. . . . Good," said Melnick. And then, his confidence waxing: "Hell, do somersaults, boy, if you want to. So long as I don't have to ride again on that goddamn *Ickes*."

Moving away, he hovered over the seat where Plimpton sat immersed in sheaves of notes and memos. He took out a cigar and lit it. But Carr, noticing the spurt of the lighter, turned and shook his head. "Better not," he said, "with all that gas back there."

Melnick snubbed out the cigar. He took a Relaxo instead. He paced back and forth through the vestibule that connected cockpit and cabin, until he bumped his head on the frame of the forward bulkhead, and then sat down in the seat beside Plimpton.

The manager-elect of the Tiara Beach Hotel was a youngish man with trim features and an habitually urbane mien, who had served his apprenticeship in resort hotels from Sarasota to Waikiki. But under the dual impact of dry socket and new job, the urbanity had worn paper-thin, and his age—if appearance could be trusted—was increasing at the rate of a year per diem. Now, running a febrile hand across a gaunt cheek, he looked up from his mass of papers and said, "No. Absolutely no."

"No, what?" said Melnick wearily. (For they had been through this before.)

"The schedule, the equipment, everything. Why, the kitchen—and tableware alone—"

"At least that's there now."

"There? And what's *there* mean? Sitting in crates on some dock." Plimpton all but moaned. "And who'll get them opened, will you tell me that? Who'll get them cleaned, sorted, inventoried?"

"That's the maître d's and chef's department."

"Of course it's their department. But where are they?" This time Plimpton *did* moan. "Truly, Mr. Melnick—I've had experience; I'm used to emergencies. In Florida, I saw a hotel through a hurricane and—"

"They'll come—they'll come, goddammit," Melnick rasped. "Anyhow, what good would they be now when we couldn't even get 'em

247

to the island?" He jerked his head toward the Manaians in the main cabin. "I can't even get half the workmen Lavery needs, and you sure as hell can't start setting tables until you got a floor for 'em to stand on."

"If we could only—"

"Sure, if—if. If there was labor, materials, transportation, anything. Even when I get my own transportation"—Melnick thumped the floor of the cabin—"they take it away from me to go on some damn snipe hunt. And when that's over, then what? Then I got a plane but no pilot. Three weeks I got to wait for two jokers from New Zealand, and then—"

A thought struck him. "Hey, I got it!" he said.

He leapt to his feet, bumped his head again, swore, and moved up behind Carr's seat.

"You!" he said. "You, Mitch."

Carr glanced around.

"You'll stay on—right?"

"Stay on?"

"To fly this thing. Just three weeks—four maybe—till these guys from New Zealand—" Melnick's eyes went from Carr to Shafter, who had turned to listen and was now shaking his head. "What does *that* mean?" he asked.

"I'm afraid it wouldn't be possible," Shafter said.

"Not possible? He's flying it, isn't he? He's doing fine."

"It's not a question of that. It's a matter of a license and—"

"He's flying now without a license."

"This is special—an emergency."

"And me, *I* don't have an emergency? There's nothing special about the hotel? You open one out here twice a week?"

Shafter sighed. "It's not my decision. It's regulations. I had to make a strong case to Bill Kelly of FAA to issue an interim permit even for this, and—"

"And you can make another strong case—you know damn well you can—and this Kelly will do what you tell him to." Melnick threw his hands up. "Hell's bells, what do you think I'm trying to do out here: commit crimes or something? I'm building a hotel, that's what—bringing in tourists—putting these crumbum islands on the map. And if you stuffed shirts would give me a break for once—"

Shafter was staring ahead, noncommittally. From the rear Plimpton's voice cut into Melnick's with a high bleating sound. "Kosher food! What in God's name is this about kosher food?"

Melnick groaned. He seemed on the point of going on with Shafter; then changed his mind and, muttering darkly, went back to his manager. In the cockpit, for a while, there was silence, except for the hum of the engines.

Then Carr said: "Problems in paradise—"

Sighing again, Shafter nodded. Then, after a few moments he murmured: "At least his will get solved, I guess—one way or another."

He was still peering ahead, toward where the faint outline of Tiara had appeared on the horizon.

"Meaning," said Carr, "that some other people's won't? . . . The people we're going after, for instance?"

"Yes, the people we're going after. What's *their* solution?" Again there was silence for a bit; then he went on. "Say we find them, as we hope to. We persuade them. We bring them back to Tiara. . . . And then what? . . . The hotel's still going to be there. The tourists are coming. The world will be pushing in."

"So they'll have to learn to live with it."

"Yes, they'll have to learn. But it will take time. And it will hurt. As things stand now with them, it's hard to imagine a worse case of anomie."

"Come again?" said Carr.

"Anomie: it's a sociologists' word. It means formlessness, breakdown, social chaos. And here it is—all around us." Shafter's voice had changed. The quiet, bland manner he had assumed with Melnick was gone, and he spoke now with deep intensity. "I have another name for it too," he said. "Waking sickness. Not sleeping—*waking*. Waking up to a world they never made but will have to live in. And they're sick with it—yes. As sick as if they were eaten up by yaws or cancer."

"The waking's been going on a long time, though, hasn't it?"

"On the big islands, yes. There you have a different sort of situation—almost like Asia and Africa—where they've been living in the white man's world for years. They want self-government—even independence—and some of them, like Western Samoa, are getting it. But the only outsiders a place like Tiara has known until now are a few administrators, teachers, doctors. And even Manaia as a whole—a few dots of islands scattered all over the ocean—couldn't run its own show: politically, economically, or any which way. Not unless it went back to the Stone Age—and the world won't let it. Someone from outside has to run it for them."

"So it's we who get stuck with it."

"Stuck—that's exactly it. And that's the ironic part, the damn-shame part. Take the other so-called powers in the Pacific: the British, the French, even the Japs when they were in. They haven't three million square miles of their own, like the U.S.A. They *need* places like this. I'm not saying it's right that they've got them; I'm not hurraying for

249

colonialism. But at least, in pragmatic terms, it makes some sense. If you *need* something—if you want to take something out of it— you have to put something in. Just plain money, for one thing. Buildings, industries, plantations, transport. And these others have. . . . We haven't. . . . Sixty years ago we picked Manaia up in some power-politics deal, and for a while, at least, we used it as a naval base and coaling station. Now—no Navy, no coal, no anything."

"Except a resort hotel."

"Yes—suddenly a resort hotel. And that on an out-island that's about as ready for it as a skating rink."

"You think Apingo would have been all right?"

"No place is all right, the way things are. Apingo's a slum. The rest is for picture postcards. And handouts. Once in a while, when we make enough noise about the problems and what's needed to handle them, a few congressmen come out for a look. And what are they interested in? Grass skirts; more missionaries; how much we're costing the taxpayers in Keokuk."

Carr smiled a little. "So now it's Mel Melnick to the rescue," he said.

"Yes, Melnick. And his hotel. Out of nothing, the Tiara Beach Hotel. With swimming pool, tennis court, dance floor, dry martinis. . . . You may not think so, but damn it, we're doing the best we can with things. But there's no sense to it; no development; no step-by-step. It's all crazy and haphazard."

Shafter brooded a moment. "And I'll tell you one of the worst things," he said. "With the administration, I mean—and that's that nobody stays here. They appoint a Governor, and he's around a year or two, and then he's gone and there's a new one. And it's the same all the way down the line. No one digs in, gets to know the place, or really gives a damn."

"*You* give a damn," Carr said.

"Well . . . All right, yes, that's true. I like my work, I like the islands, and these are wonderful people I want to help. . . . But what does it add up to? Damn little. I'll be like the rest: back to the States when my contract's up. And even while I'm here, how much can I do? Here's an island and a batch of people"—he waved a hand ahead—"that are going through a hell of a convulsion; that need all the attention and help that can possibly be given. And what am I doing? Looking for red hula skirts for congressmen. With matching brassieres. . . ."

Shafter lapsed into brooding silence. Then he said: "Well, by God, when we get these people back it's going to be different. I don't care what Gorman says, or the Governor, or the U.S. Congress. I'm spending half my time in Tiara until things are straightened out, and if they don't like it they can whistle."

"Quite a swimmer, eh, boy?"

This time it was not Carr who spoke, but a voice behind them. And turning, they saw that Melnick had again come forward.

"Swimmer?" said Shafter.

"Getting back and forth from Tiara, with the *Ickes* in drydock."

"I don't mean in the *Ickes*. I mean in—"

Shafter stopped.

"You mean *you* got a pilot's license?" said Melnick. "All tied up in ribbons for friend Kelly?"

Shafter said nothing. He seemed to be studying the instrument panel. There was a silence, and the silence stretched, and then Carr, pointing ahead, said, "Look, it's getting close now." And, still silently, they watched, as the island of Tiara climbed swiftly from the sea.

Then Carr said, "How long will we be staying?"

Shafter did not answer at once; and when Carr repeated the question he broke out of his own thoughts with an almost visible effort. "How long?" he said. "On Tiara?" Then, again his usual self: "I want to talk with Fahoai—Malele—perhaps a few others. I'd say an hour should do it."

Carr looked at his watch "Ten forty," he said. "Right. If we get off by noon, that'll give us six hours of full daylight. On a straight course we should reach Maniloa in less than two."

Each moment now the island loomed larger before them: its white cloud cap gleaming, its hills brightening from purple to vivid green. Melnick put a hand on Shafter's shoulder and said, "We'll talk some more later, eh, Lenny boy? There's nothing I'd like better than to have you as guest in my lil' ole plane, with friend Mitch here steering it." Then he went back to his seat.

Shafter, neither answering nor turning, had taken out a batch of notes and papers and was glancing through them. "Yes, Fahoai and Malele," he said. "And Carol Loftus. She's the one who'll know most about Mrs. Mundy."

He came to a yellow envelope. "And—oh God—this," he said.

Carr looked at him questioningly.

"John Koa—" said Shafter. "You know, the one who—"

"Yes, I know him," Carr said.

"I guess I'll have to see him too, while we're here." Shafter sighed. "He'll probably be right there again, waiting for us."

"No he won't."

It was Shafter's turn for a questioning look.

"He went to Maniloa," Carr said.

"John? To Maniloa?" Shafter was incredulous. "Are you sure?"

"Yes, I'm sure."

"I can hardly believe it. He, of all people. . . . He was the educated one, remember? The ambitious one who wanted to fly; who applied to the Air Force."

Carr nodded. He looked at the envelope in Shafter's hands. "And this is the answer?" he said.

"Yes."

"And the answer's no?"

"That's right."

Carr said nothing. His eyes returned to the instrument board, then to the windshield and what lay beyond. Tiara was very close now; he could see the white line of its reef; and he eased the wheel forward for the descent.

"I could have told him," said Shafter. "In fact, I tried to prepare him. But no, he wouldn't have it. He was so eager, so sure."

He shook his head. Carr peered forward: first at Tiara's hills, now above them; then at the reef, the beaches, the palm groves, the lagoon. With the lagoon as hub, he banked into a wide arc, easing the throttle, slowly settling.

"Better fasten your belt," he said. (He had kept his own on through the trip.) Then, calling over his shoulder to Melnick and Plimpton: "Seat belts on. And tell the men in back."

"Well, now he'll know," said Shafter grimly, putting the yellow slip and the other papers back in his pocket. "I'll have to let him have it."

"When we find him," Carr said.

"You're absolutely *certain* about that? That he's one of those who took off?"

"Yes."

Again Shafter shook his head. "It doesn't sound like him at all. Everything about him was"—he searched for the words—*"in the other direction.* Out—ahead—toward the big world. All he could think of was this dream of flying."

He was silent a moment.

"And now this," he said. "Taking off; running away from it. . . . But why?"

"He's probably given up," said Carr. "He probably won't care now."

"He'll care. Whatever he pretends, he'll care. . . . Goddammit," Shafter broke out suddenly, with unaccustomed vehemence, "that's what causes half the misery in the world. Caring—wanting—and not getting. It's the ones who don't give a damn who have it good—"

Carr made no comment. He seemed not to have heard. For now, again, he was all pilot, all airman—hands and feet and eyes and nerves and mind—bringing the plane in, down, around, toward landing. They were over the island: crossing reef and beach, above the palms, above the lagoon. The wind was the normal trade, from the southeast, and he came in against it, toward the "A" channel he had blasted (with the boy Tuti and his "fountains of fish") and then marked with red-painted old fuel tins; and now he was out of his turn, he was headed straight; they were sinking—sinking. The floats were down, under the wings. The props were feathering. The Cat's nose was level—then tilted up; up just a little, just enough—and they skimmed the water, and the water slapped them. They bounced, but not too much; again just enough. And then they hit again, but more softly, more gently; and the water took them, held them, slowed them. And they were down, they were there, they were all right.

Yes, all right. . . . He had made the channel, he had flown the plane, and both jobs were all right, and there they were. . . . By courtesy of Mitchell Carr, BSc., C.E., USNR, etc. The man of skills and talents, the man who was needed. . . .

There was the jetty, the crowd, the staring eyes, the shouting voices. As he swung open the forward hatch, he could hear one voice louder and shriller than the others, and there was Va'ina at the edge of the jetty, waving and jumping with excitement.

"Meesh!" she cried. "Meesh, you come back!"

Then his attention was taken by what was going on around him. He had brought the plane to rest perhaps fifty yards from shore; no sooner had he cut the engines than dozens of men and boys were swarming out to it—some swimming, some in skiffs and outriggers; and now, suddenly, it was all he could do to keep them from bumping it with their craft or clambering aboard. Behind him, his passengers were standing, waiting impatiently to get out. But it took several minutes before a large rowboat could be maneuvered alongside to receive them. The shouting continued. Oars waved and thumped. Two of the new Utoian workmen fell in the water.

Then at last all but Carr were off, ferrying across to the jetty. And he stood alone in the hatch, watching. Lavery and most of the "Hawaiians" were there, waiting for Melnick and Plimpton. Malele the policeman was there, waiting for Shafter. But, though his eyes searched the crowd, he could not find Fahoai. . . . Nor Carol Loftus.

"Meesh!" came the shrill cry again. "Meesh, you come, no? I wait—"

Then it was cut off. She had seen the approaching boat—and in the boat, Mel Melnick—and she was no longer waving at the plane. She was waving at him. She was at the edge of jetty, waiting, smiling, her hands and hips moving in the suggestion of a dance. And then the boat was alongside; the men were climbing up—Melnick was climbing up; he was on the jetty, and she threw her arms around him, she kissed him on both cheeks, she looked up at him, glowing, smiling. . . . And Carr, watching across the water, smiled too—inwardly— thinking, "Yes, she'll get along, she'll do all right." And if the smile was a little sad, a little rueful, it was not bitter; for what he and Va'ina had had was already gone. It was back in the quiet place under the breadfruit tree; lost, remote; as remote as another girl, the long-dead girl, Lovana. . . . And still he smiled as he watched her take Melnick's arm and walk with him, laughing, chattering, along the jetty and up the slope toward the hotel.

Plimpton and the "Hawaiians" followed them, with the new workers from Utoia straggling behind. Shafter walked slowly away, in conversation with Malele. "Hey, boss, you no come too?" a Tiaran called to Carr from one of the outriggers. But he shook his head. The Cat's anchor was down, its mooring calm and protected; but with the crowd all around he was not going to leave it untended. . . . And besides, what was there for him to do in Tiara?

He glanced at his watch. An hour, Shafter had said, and a quarter of it was already gone. Enlisting several of the watching men as helpers, he did the jobs that needed doing: first topping off the plane's tanks with gas from one of the drums in the cabin; then getting the other drums ashore by skiff and outrigger and storing them in a shack near the jetty. The fuel in the two full tanks would be more than enough for that afternoon's flying, whether to Maniloa and back or on a sea-ranging search. The rest was available for what—if anything—would follow.

The last drum had been stored, and he was on the jetty, about to return to the plane, when there was a sound from the road behind him, and turning, he saw a jeep approach and pull up. There was only one person in it—Carol Loftus, in her white nurse's uniform— and as he waited, she got out and approached him.

"Hello," she said, stopping.

"Hello," he answered.

And there was a pause.

"You're back," she said.

"Yes."

"I didn't even know you'd left—until just now, back on the road—"

"You've seen Shafter, then?"

She nodded. "As I was leaving the village. When I heard the plane I wanted to come over right away, but I was in the middle of a class."

"A class?"

"I've taken over at the school for Mrs. Mundy. Well, sort of—the little I can."

254

"That's what he wanted to ask about—Mrs. Mundy."

"Yes—he did. I couldn't tell him much, of course. We talked only a minute or two, and then he went on to see Fahoai."

"He should be back soon. He has to be, if we're going on today."

"He told me." Carol paused, her eyes on his face. "At least *someone* tells me things," she added. "If not that you're gone, at least that you're back."

"I—I left suddenly," he said.

She let it go. Her eyes moved past him to the moored plane.

"And you hadn't told me you flew," she said.

"It never came up. . . . And I haven't for a long while."

"Leonard said you did wonderfully. And that they couldn't have done anything without you."

Carr smiled thinly. "Didn't you know?" he said. "I'm the Indispensable Man."

The smile was not returned. There was another silence, and he half turned, as if to step down into the skiff that was waiting for him.

Then—"Mitch," she said.

"Yes?"

"Aren't you ever going to tell me anything?"

"Tell you—?"

"About why you left. Why you've come back."

"I came back to fly the plane. To go out to Maniloa."

"Yes, I know. But why *that*?" He started to speak, but she forestalled him. "Don't tell me it's because they asked you to. That isn't the whole of it."

"These people have done something foolish. They may be in trouble."

"And that's all? That's enough to make you do this?"

"It's enough for Shafter. It would be enough for you, wouldn't it?"

"That's different. We work here. We've an obligation."

"So have I."

"To these people—these strangers?"

He didn't answer.

"Or to John?" she said.

Again her eyes were fixed on his, and for an instant he met them, and then looked away.

"It was because of John you stayed on here," she said. "Wasn't it? . . . When he left, you left. And now that there's a chance to go after him, you've come back."

"What makes you think—"

"What else should I think." Now it was her turn to smile thinly. "That you came back for *me*—whom you hadn't even bothered to say goodbye to?" . . . She fought down the bitterness that came suddenly into her voice, and when she spoke again it was soft and gentle. "Oh Mitch," she said, "you helped me so much while you were here. I've told you that. And that I want to help you too, if I can—if you'll let me." Again, as on that evening in the quonset, she put out her hand and touched his lightly. "You're so alone; so awfully alone. As I was. . . . Then you made me talk to you. . . . Why won't you talk to me? About what's bothering you; what's gone wrong for you. With Tiara—with John—"

The idlers around them were staring, listening; but she paid no attention. She was very close to him now. Her face was raised, pleading.

"Mitch—"

Then, again, there was a sound from the road. Again a jeep appeared and stopped, and in this one were Leonard Shafter, Malele, and Fahoai. The policeman, who had been driving, remained in the car, but the other two got out and came toward them along the jetty.

Shafter was all business. "Ready?" he asked Carr.

"Yes."

"Fahoai is going to come along. If these people have reached their island, and we can land there and talk with them, I think he can be of a lot of help. With Tafutimo, especially."

The talking chief had greeted Carr and Carol with his usual formal courtesy. Now his eyes were fixed on the moored plane, but if he felt any apprehension at what lay ahead, it did not show in his round bland features.

Carol turned quickly to Shafter. "And I too," she said. "Yes, I'll come too."

"You?"

"Some of them are sure to be sick—or hurt. I've my bag here in the jeep, and—"

Shafter was shaking his head.

"Why not?" she demanded. "If I can help—be of use—"

"No, you'll be of more use here. We don't know what we'll find out there—or even if we'll find them. If they're still at sea, we won't be able to get to them anyhow. If they're on the atoll—" He shrugged and glanced at Carr.

"We'll see," Carr said.

"You mean it may be dangerous, and—"

"No, no—not dangerous." Shafter's voice carried perhaps a shade too much conviction. "It's just that it's better this way. Not too many in the plane. You getting your things ready here. And if we get them back and anyone needs attention—"

He let his voice trail off. Then looked at his watch. "Past twelve," he said. Then to Carr and Fahoai: "Come on—let's go."

"If it's just because I'm a woman—" Carol persisted.

But Shafter was already stepping from the jetty into a skiff, and now the two other men followed. Carol did not speak again; there was only the creak of oars as they were rowed out to the plane. And then they were in the plane; Carr was back at the wheel, with Shafter beside him and Fahoai in a seat behind; and Carr told the chief how to fasten his seat belt.

He turned the switch, started the engines, checked the dials on the panel. Through the windscreen he could see the skiffs and outriggers, now moving away from the plane, and beyond them the jetty, lined with brown figures—and one white figure—watching. Then the figures were gone. Jetty and boats were gone. He pushed the throttle forward, working wheel and rudders, and the Cat swung about and moved slowly out across the lagoon.

18

Now THE COURSE was the important thing. Maniloa was
only two hundred miles distant, some ninety minutes straight flying.
But it was less than a tenth the size of Tiara; it had no hills; it was
the merest speck in the wastes of the sea; and finding it would take
more than look-see navigation. Carr had studied the charts carefully.
Rising above Tiara, he swung until the compass showed eighty-seven
degrees, three points north of due east. Then the hills were behind
them. Beach, lagoon, and reef were behind them. Ahead, in the blaze
of noon, was sky and ocean.

It had been decided to fly straight to Maniloa, and only then, if
the refugees were not there, to range out in a pattern of search. If
they *were* there—and after five days it was to be hoped that they
were—it would, on so small a place, be quickly apparent. And the
next problem would be that of landing. Maniloa was a classic coral
atoll—a ring of narrow islets surrounding a central lagoon—and,
according to the chart, the lagoon was both big and deep enough for
the Cat to land. But no plane had ever done so; and there was more
to bringing one down in virgin waters than reading forty-year-old
figures on a sketchy chart. The decision could not be made until they
got there and looked it over. And the yes or no would be up to Carr.

For the present, he kept his eyes on compass and instruments.
Course: 87. Altitude: 1500. Shafter, in the copilot's seat, and Fahoai,
now standing behind them, surveyed the sea ahead and to either side,
but without expectation of seeing anything; for whether or not the
two boats had reached Maniloa, they were by now, surely, far out
from Tiara.

258

The engines throbbed smoothly. As before, squalls showed as purple smudges on the distant horizon, but the sky above them was clear, and the air quiet.

"Ah, it is fine. It is beautiful," said Fahoai.

"It's your first time in a plane?" Carr asked.

"Yes, my first. And I have waited long. In the war, when I was in Utoia, there were many planes—hundreds, thousands—and I hoped always that I would fly, but it did not happen." The talking chief paused and chuckled reminiscently. "It is funny how it happens," he said. "I, who am a man, who work for the Air Force, do not fly. But my sister—*she* flies. My little sister who is only a girl and stays home in Tiara: she goes in a plane with a crazy Navy *lutenanti*. And I hear. I am jealous. I too will go in a plane, I say; but still it does not happen. Not until now, today, after so many years."

Carr's eyes were on the compass.

"And this sister of yours," he said, "was named Lovana?"

"Yes, Lovana." Then surprise came into Fahoai's voice. "But how do you—"

"Va'ina told me."

"Ah, yes. She was the aunt of Va'ina."

"And the mother of John Koa."

"Yes, his mother. By the Navy *lutenanti*." Fahoai laughed. "Maybe I should have found a lady *lutenanti* and . . ."

He was talking on, but Carr no longer heard him. The compass needle had swung past 90; he brought it back to 87.

And—*so there it was,* he thought.

Just like that. Out of the air; up in the air. The last piece of the jigsaw.

True, he had, for weeks now, been sure that John Koa was his son. So sure that it had passed for knowing. . . . But still it had not *quite* been knowing. It had not been a spelled-out fact. . . . And now it was. John was his son, the child of Lovana. The years and the miles had brought them together. They had stood at last face to face—the son unaware, the father half-aware; wanting, yet reluctant, to be sure. He had tried to speak, but his voice had faltered; to put out his hand, but the hand had wavered. All he had brought to the boy was more of what he already had in full measure: self-doubt, ambivalence, confusion, frustration. Until at last the wavering hand became a fist. The boy's torment became flight. Flight from his unknown father; from the world of his father.

But even flight was denied him. . . .

For now that world was reaching out to fetch him back. "No," it told him, "you cannot run away. You cannot retreat to a simpler

259

world, the world of your mother and her ancestors. It no longer exists. It is gone. You must come back."

Back—to what?

From the moment, the night before, when he had been asked to fly the plane to Maniloa, he had known that he would do it. That he must do it. Partly, to be sure, it had been a simple response to an appeal; the obligation to contribute his help when it was needed. But, far more than that, it had been a grasping of the chance to follow John Koa. He still did not know what he would do when, and if, he found him. If anything, indeed, he knew less than before, because now, to all the rest, there had been added a bitter irony. He, Mitchell Carr, guided the instrument of return. He was the man of skills— the flier. But John Koa Carr, his son, who dreamed of flying, could not fly. "No, not you," said the world that both reclaimed and rejected him. "Not you," said the United States Air Force on official stationery; on the folded sheet in the envelope in Shafter's pocket. And that was the heart of the irony, the last blow of the fist: that this was the final mission of the Long-Lost Father, the Indispensable Man. To seek out his son in the plane he could not fly. To bring the message that would kill his dream forever.

". . . and that, too, of course, is why the boy thinks of planes," Fahoai was saying. "Only he is foolish and stubborn about it, for he thinks he can fly himself. As if he were not an island boy, but himself, like his father, a *papalagi*."

Carr didn't speak. The compass had strayed again, and he brought it back. . . . "So now you *know*," he thought. . . . It was no longer guessing, feeling, surmising. He knew.

But the knowledge added nothing, resolved nothing. He was still where he had been before. As was his son.

Wherever that was.

A few minutes later Shafter suddenly stiffened and pointed to a dark shape in the water off to their right; but when he had got out his binoculars and focused them it proved to be only a drifting log. After that, nothing more appeared. On all the sweep of ocean only one thing moved and had a separate entity of its own: the shadow of the plane, that now crept slowly ahead as the sun westered behind them. In the distance the storm clouds still loomed. But they came no nearer.

They ate the sandwiches and drank the coffee they had brought from Apingo. And Shafter again reviewed the plans they had laid out before leaving. If the two boats were still at sea, there would be nothing they could do but show them the proper course to Maniloa, and then return when they had reached it. If they were already there, it would be the question of landing; and after landing (if they could) . . . well, of many things. It was about Chief Tafutimo's pride and stubbornness that Shafter was most concerned. And in Mrs. Mundy that he put his best hope. He still could not understand why she had chosen to go with them (for he could not believe that she had been forced). But whatever the cause, she was a reasonable woman. The Tiarans loved her. They would listen to her. . . .

He talked on for a bit and fell silent. Carr followed his own thoughts.

Then suddenly he said, "That letter—"

Shafter glanced at him. "Letter?"

"The one from the Air Force. About John Koa."

"Oh."

"You still have it?"

"Yes."

"What are you going to do about it?"

Shafter sighed. "What can I do? Tell him about it—sooner or later."

"Not right away—when we find them?"

"No."

There was another pause. Then Carr said, "Let me have it, will you?"

"You?" said Shafter.

"Yes. I've gotten pretty close to the kid, you know. Let me handle it."

Shafter looked dubious. "He'll come to me anyhow, eventually."

"I suppose so. But I'll tell him first. Break it to him."

"Well—it's hardly something I'm looking forward to."

Shafter took the yellow envelope from his pocket, looked at it a moment, then at Carr—curiously. Then he handed it to him, and Carr opened the door of a compartment beneath the instrument board before him, and put it in, and closed the door.

"Thanks," he said.

"Thank *you*," said Shafter.

Then, again, they were silent. Within the plane now there was only the drone of the engines. Beyond it, stillness and space. Presently an hour had passed since their takeoff, then eighty minutes, then ninety; and they knew that they were rapidly closing in on Maniloa. But still it was hard to believe, hard to convince mind and senses that they would not fly on forever through blue emptiness.

Emptiness was all there was, with themselves at its core. There was no land in it anywhere. No atoll. No Maniloa. . . .

And then there was.

They saw it first not as land, but as a change of light, of color, in the sea ahead. In the vast wheel of ocean there was a glint of lighter blue; of cobalt turned to azure, of azure to emerald green. Then the glint grew. It became a node, a surface, a circle, itself a wheel within a wheel—a gleaming patch of incandescence—as, out of the depths of ocean, the sea floor rose, and the sun struck on the shallow waters of a lagoon. It shone. It dazzled. And for a time that was all there was—a dazzle of light and prismed brilliance—until slowly, from the world of water, there emerged a thread, a hint, of land.

It was not land such as Tiara's or Utoia's. It was without height, depth, or bulk: a mere line of demarkation between cobalt ocean and green lagoon. Nor was it even a continuous line, but rather a series of dots and dashes, the merest jottings of land on the sweep of waters. In itself it was nothing; no more than an outline, frail and broken, of a shining oval. The lap of a wavelet, one felt—or a patter of rain-drops—could wipe it away. Yet, though they could, they had not; not in a hundred or a thousand centuries. And that was the wonder, the miracle: that it was there at all: that out of the ocean deep, out of a world of water without imaginable end, this thread of land could rise and endure.

The plane moved closer. Carr eased the wheel forward. The three men stared downward in silence. Fahoai had never before seen an atoll from above; Shafter had seen several; Carr uncounted hundreds, back in the days of the war. But all were held in the same fascination, the same spell. For of all sights on his earth that airborne man has been granted to see, none can compare, in purity, in radiance, in glory of light and color, to a ring of coral islands in a tropic sea.

Fahoai was the first to speak, and his voice was an awed whisper. "It is Havaiki," he said. "Yes, the homeland—Havaiki."

Then Shafter cried, "Look!" He was pointing again. And from one of the threads of land they saw another, vertical thread arising—a thread of smoke. "They're here!" said Shafter. "They made it. They're here!"

The plane nosed down, propellors feathering. Lagoon and islets rose to meet them. The latter were now no longer threads but strips of land, with texture and detail, with palms and scrub and rock and sandy beaches. And on the strip from which the smoke rose they could see, near the seaward beach, the dark shapes of shelters and human figures. Shafter had opened the window on his side of the cockpit and was peering down through his binoculars. And Fahoai, forgetful of both awe and chiefly dignity, was all but climbing up his back to peer over his shoulder.

Then smoke and figures passed beneath them. They were over another islet, over the sea beyond. Carr's eyes flicked across the dials on the panel; then, banking and descending steeply, he brought the plane back across the islets to the lagoon.

They were low now, a mere five hundred feet above the water, and its reflection filled the cabin with a rainbow glow. But it was no longer of such things that he was thinking. It was only of landing—landing them safely; and his eyes stared down, searching, appraising, as he eased the throttle back to minimal speed. The lagoon was large enough: there was no question of that. The figures on the chart showed ample depth. But still no plane had ever landed here. There had been no dynamiter, no planter of red fuel tins.

It was with submerged coral heads that he was chiefly concerned, but he could detect none beneath the crystal waters. Reaching the far side of the lagoon, he turned and recrossed it in a second dry run—now at a height of only a hundred feet; but still he found none. Nor did Shafter and Fahoai, peering down beside him.

"Well?" he said, and glanced at them.

But they said nothing. Nor had he expected them to; for the decision was up to him.

He made it. Again banking out over the sea, he lowered the floats beneath the wings. Following his instructions, Shafter and Fahoai got out the drogues—two canvas bags designed to slow the plane once it hit the water—and attached them on either side of the fuselage beneath the cabin windows. Then they strapped themselves into their seats. And he came in again. There was scarcely any wind. (He wished there were more.) But he came in low and slow against what there was; as slowly as he conceivably could without losing headway and stalling. They seemed to hang in the air, not to be moving at all, and it was only the water that was moving, bright and rushing beneath them. And then the water rose, and they hit it. They bounced, as in the landing at Tiara—but harder—and the plane shuddered—and for a dreadful instant it seemed it had not been water they hit, but coral rock, and that they were ripped and shattered. But then the shuddering passed. They hit again, and the impact was softer. They stayed on the water; they sank into the water; and now the engines were reversed, the drogues were braking, and they wallowed deep and slow and quiet in Maniloa's lagoon.

Carr leaned back into his seat and flexed his stiffened fingers against the wheel. "Part Two of mission accomplished," he thought.

And all that remained was what they had come for.

From the lagoon's surface, the pattern of the atoll, so clearly defined from above, was wholly gone, and each of the surrounding islets appeared identical to the other. But above one of them they could still see the column of smoke. Carr taxied toward it, moving very slowly, his eyes probing the water ahead; and when they had come within perhaps a quarter of a mile of the shore he stopped, for now, in the shimmering clearness, he could see the outlines of the dreaded coral heads. From the Cat's nose he lowered its two anchors, and felt them catch and hold.

No boats came out to meet them, as at Tiara. Nor was there anyone on the shore. The smoke, indicating the site of the settlement, rose from the far side of the islet, and all that confronted them was bare beach and, behind it, scrub and palms. A life raft, already inflated, was in the cabin, and now they got it out and into the water. Shafter and Fahoai climbed down, and then Shafter turned and looked questioningly at Carr.

Carr, too, had asked the question of himself, and made his decision. The anchors were down firmly. The wind was no more than a zephyr. There was no one about. Nodding, he followed the others into the raft, and they paddled ashore.

When they reached it, the beach was no longer deserted. A half-dozen small, almost naked boys had appeared from the brush and now stood a short distance off, watching them silently. But that was all. No one else came. As the three men advanced they seemed on the point of running; but then Fahoai called to them, speaking their names, and they held their ground.

"Your people are on the other side?" he asked, pointing to the still visible smoke.

"Yes."

"Then take us to them," he said.

And the boys led the way along the beach.

To one side, the lagoon shone in rainbow splendor; but the strip of land that had, too, seemed so magically lovely from the air was now wholly transformed. The beach itself lay bare, desolate, glaring in sunlight. At intervals were black patches of rotting seaweed. Here and there was a creeping snail, a scuttling crab. The rest was sand, gravel, broken shells, jagged coral. Inland, flanking the beach, stretched a belt of sparse, reedy grass, and beyond it the scrub and palms they had seen from the plane. The palms were not tall and richly crowned, like those of Tiara and Utoia, but dwarfed and warped, with ragged fronds and slanting boles. Here on land, there was now no breeze at all. The trees, like the beach, were transfixed in a glare of heat and stillness. But they showed, as clearly as if a storm were now raging, what happened when the stillness broke. How the breeze, when it rose, became a wind—and the wind a gale—blowing for days on end, pouring in over miles of ocean, scouring, battering the thread of land, while every growing thing bent before it: straining, cowering, literally clutching for its life.

As they moved down the beach, shards of coral ripped at their feet. A cloud of black flies closed in. Then the boys, ahead, cut inland through the grass and brush; and they—and the flies—followed. There was, of course, no path; the refugees could have been on the island for, at most, a couple of days. And they soon found that, besides the standing palms, there were many fallen ones, through whose moldering rubble they had to pick their way.

"You'd think they'd have settled on the lagoon side," said Carr, panting and swatting flies.

But Fahoai shook his head. "No, that is where the storms come," he pointed out. "You can see by the trees. On the ocean side would be better—if anything is better in such a place."

At least the islet, as they had seen from the air, was narrow, and presently, ahead, they could again see beach and water—this time the open sea. Before reaching it, however, they came suddenly into a small clearing, where a group of women were at work planting taro shoots; and here they paused while Fahoai spoke again.

"*Talofa*," he said, and a few responded in the traditional greeting. But most merely stared up at him from their squatting postures with dark, lusterless eyes.

"And how does it go? he asked them.

But now no one answered. And stooping, Fahoai picked up a clod of coarse, gravelly earth and rubbed it in his hands, slowly shaking his head.

Then they came out of the brush, across another belt of grass bordering the beach. And before them was the village—or, rather, the encampment, for it consisted only of a few crude lean-tos made of logs and fronds. Close by was the fire they had first seen from the plane; and now they saw, too, why its smoke had been so clearly visible. For it was smoke alone: a white steamlike column, with no flame at the base, but only smoldering ash and rotted wood. A few men were squatting beside it, poking with sticks. Others, roundabout, were simply squatting, doing nothing. And beyond them, in the shade of the largest lean-to, seated on mats on the sand, were the High Chief Tafutimo and three elder *matai*.

In the fashion of Manaia, they did not rise as the newcomers approached. Nor did their faces express surprise, or any other emotion. Fahoai, as both visitor and talking chief, spoke first, in the elaborate set phrases reserved for persons of high rank; and when he had done, Tafutimo responded in kind, speaking slowly in singsong cadence. Then he gestured to one of the men beyond the shelter. Three more mats, torn and ragged, were brought and spread in the shade. And the visitors sat down.

"I regret that we cannot offer better hospitality," said the high chief.

"It is understood," Shafter replied.

"And that we can offer no kava. There has not yet been time to prepare it."

"It is understood."

The conversation continued—formal, ritualistic, *fa'a Manaia*—with the administrator, no less than the chief, playing his appointed role. In that decrepit shelter, on the harsh, glaring, flyblown beach, it was to Western eyes and ears an absurd performance. . . . Yes, absurd, Carr thought. And pathetic, too. But, at the same time, something else besides; at the same time, strangely gallant and moving. . . . For Tafutimo, beneath his trappings of chiefdom, was a sorry sight, less man than scarecrow. His lion's face was peaked and ravaged; his body skeletal; his lava-lava a tattered rag about his loins. And even more than this, Carr saw, he was a crippled scarecrow. For he was not seated in the usual cross-legged fashion, but with one leg out before him, and the leg was ugly and stiff and swollen with infection.

The three *matai* beside him sat normally, but seemed otherwise no better off. Nor did the crowd that had surrounded the shelter and were now watching and listening, gaunt and somber in their rags. Moment by moment their numbers were augmented, until, Carr judged, there were at least a hundred in the encompassing circle. The boys who had led them across the island were there, the women from the taro patch, the men who had been by the fire—plus scores of others who seemed to have appeared from nowhere. But still, as his eyes moved over them, carefully searching, he could not see, he could not find, the *one* he sought.

John Koa was not there.

. . . Nor, he then realized, was another. The one Shafter sought. . . .

A moment later, the formal colloquy had ended. Shafter, too, was looking out at the crowd: searching—not finding. And now, turning back to Tafutimo, he asked:

"Where is Mrs. Mundy?"

"She is dead," the high chief said.

There was a silence.

"Dead?"

"There was an accident in the boats. She fell into the water. And the next day she died."

Another silence followed. Words formed on Shafter's lips, but he held them back. Whatever emotion he felt, he fought it down; and when he did speak it was quietly, coolly—still as the official in his official role.

"She was buried at sea?" he asked.

Tafutimo shook his grizzled head. "When she died we were already here. She is buried on the other side of the island."

"When we are through here I should like to see the grave. And of course a report and certificate will have to be sent to Apingo."

"We did all we could," said the *matai*, Vaoti. "It was a great shame. A great sorrow."

"We can talk of that later," said Shafter. His eyes returned to Tafutimo. "Who else has died?" he asked.

The chief answered: "The old man Kalamakoa, of the family of Fahoai, has died. Him we buried at sea."

Fahoai said nothing.

"Any others?" said Shafter.

"No, no others," said the chief.

"How many are sick or injured?"

Tafutimo was silent, his eyes veiled and withdrawn. All his chief-hood, all his pride of rank and office, rejected the ordeal of the catechism.

"How many?" Shafter persisted. "We must know, so that we can help you."

"We do not need help," said Tafutimo. "We are strong and well."

"*You* are not well," Shafter indicated the chief's swollen leg. "You have a bad infection."

"It is nothing. A small sore from salt water."

Shafter looked about him at the tatterdemalion crowd. "And I see others, too," he said, "who look unwell. There are many, aren't there?"

Again Tafutimo did not answer. His head was bowed, his face grim and brooding. . . . But now, abruptly, one of the *matai* spoke.

"Yes, many—many," he said.

"Twenty, thirty," said another. "Half the women. Half the children."

"Yes." . . . "Yes." . . .

These were voices from the crowd around them.

"We have sores on our bodies."

"We have fever."

"We have no food."

"And no homes."

The ring was pressing closer. And now a torrent of voices, mostly women's broke through the pall of sullen apathy.

"The taro will not take root."

"Our fires will not burn."

"The animals sicken."

"And we too."

"It is an evil place we have come to."

"With evil earth."

"And evil spirits."

"Pastor Solomona is not here to drive the spirits away. And they come at night."

"The ghost of Miz Mundy comes."

"And of Kalamakoa."

"There was no pastor to bless them. They are both in hell."

Tafutimo had raised his head; then a pre-emptory hand. Back in Tiara, the gesture would have reduced the interrupters to instant silence, but now no one paid attention. When at last the chorus died away it was of its own accord; and it was Shafter, not the chief, who resumed their direct conversation.

"I take it then," he said, "that most things have gone badly."

There was no reply.

"And that you are willing to come home."

"Home?" At last Tafutimo spoke again. "*This* is our home," he said.

"Your people don't seem to feel that."

"The people are easily discouraged. Especially the women."

"*Easily?* Are you sure you would say that?"

"There have been troubles," Tafutimo conceded. "In the boats it was hard, yes. And it is bad and sad about Miz Mundy. From the start I said she should not come, but—"

"There's no use going into that now," said Shafter. "The important thing now is your present situation." Again his eyes moved out to the circle of scarecrow watchers, and beyond them to the desolation of sand and scrub. "And that too is bad, isn't it? Very bad. In fact, hopeless."

Tafutimo's face was hard with stubborn pride. This, for him, was no mere matter of practicalities, but of *mana*—the immemorial prestige of an island chief. "No, not hopeless," he said. "We will make it go."

"How? What will you do for food?"

"We will fish, gather coconuts, plant taro."

"Taro?" It was Fahoai who now spoke. "We have seen the women scratching the rocks for a taro patch, but it will not grow here in a thousand years."

"And shelter," said Shafter. He looked about at the makeshift lean-tos. "What will you do for that when the winds and rains come?"

"There is wood here," said Tafutimo.

"Wood, hah!" This was Fahoai again. "It is as rotten as old seaweed. You cannot even build a fire with it, let alone a proper *fale.*"

"We will find better wood. Even now, some of our young men have gone to the far end of the island to see what is there."

It was now, for the first time, that Carr spoke.

"Is John Koa with them?" he asked.

"Yes, John Koa, my son Patali, and others. "And when they return—"

"—there will still be no good wood," said Fahoai.

"And no taro," said a *matai*.

"No meat."

"No anything."

Again voices joined in from the surrounding crowd. Then they faded away, as Shafter leaned forward and spoke earnestly to the chief.

"I am your friend, and you know it," he said. "The Government is your friend, and the friend of your people, and we want only to help you. But first you must help yourselves. You must recognize that what you've done is a mistake—that a life for you here is impossible—and come back home to Tiara."

"Tiara is no longer home," said Tafutimo. "It is the home of *papalagi*."

"No, it is yours—still yours. We will see to that. The hotel has caused trouble, I know. There are many things that have to be taken care of. But we will work them out. The Governor himself is deeply concerned; and when you return to Tiara he will come there himself to discuss your problems."

Shafter paused. The chief was shaking his head.

"You will not agree?"

"It is not simply a matter of agreeing," said Tafutimo. "Even if we wished to go, it is impossible."

"Why?"

"We have destroyed our boats."

"The boats aren't needed. Even if you still had them, it would be crazy to make such a trip again. . . . We will take you back in the plane."

"The plane?"

"Yes. That's why we're here. There are a hundred and eighteen of you, right?" Shafter caught himself. "I mean a hundred and sixteen—"

He paused, drawing a breath. Tafutimo sat impassively. But a buzz of excitement had risen among the others.

"Anyhow," said Shafter, "the plane can carry more than sixty for a short flight. We can take the sick ones and the women and children today, and come back for the rest tomorrow."

Again he paused, this time waiting for the chief's response. But at that moment there was an interruption, as a group of young men emerged from the nearby brush and joined the surrounding crowd at the edge of the shelter. "Come. Come forward," Tafutimo said, beckoning. And they complied—meanwhile staring at the visitors. There were nine of them, Carr counted, and among them he recognized the chief's son Patali, and a few others he had seen back in Tiara . . . But there was still no John Koa.

"And how did it go?" Tafutimo asked.

There was a shaking of heads. The young men, the pick of the village, were, plainly, as defeated as the others. Their eyes were dull, their shoulders stooped, their bodies wasted and covered with sores.

"You found no wood?" said Tafutimo.

"No," said Patali. "At least no good wood. It is all the same as here—rotten."

"You see," said Fahoai, with smug satisfaction.

"There is none anywhere here," said a *matai*.

"No wood, no soil, no anything."

"It is an accursed place."

Again the crowd joined in, raising its chorus of lament. Some of the young men joined in, while others stood silent, their heads bent. As the murmur continued, Carr rose and approached Patali.

"Where is John Koa?" he asked.

The chief's son had been one of the silent ones. Now, raising his head, he jerked it slightly. "Back there," he said.

"Back where?"

"At the other end of the island."

"He was with you?"

"Yes."

"Why didn't he come back with you?"

"He is still looking for wood."

"When there isn't any?"

Patali made a grunting sound. "He is a know-it-all, that one. In the boat he is the great pilot. Now he is the great woodsman. Any fool can see there is no good wood anywhere; but he says yes there is, he will stay and find it."

Carr said nothing. Turning, he saw that Shafter was again talking earnestly to Tafutimo. The crowd was watching, listening. Passing unnoticed through the circle, he headed up the beach in the direction Patali had indicated.

The islet was perhaps a mile long and nowhere more than a few hundred yards wide. For most of the way he could see straight across from the ocean to the lagoon side, and he watched closely for a sign of movement. He saw none, however. And when, at intervals, he called out, there was no answer.

Approaching the far end, he cut into the brush, zigzagging his way

270

through scrub and fallen palms, until it petered out into a sandpit and blue water. Then he worked his way back, this time keeping close to the lagoon shore; and still he peered about, still he shouted—but with no result. Presently the plane came into view, framed between two standing palms and riding motionless on the still lagoon. Like a travel poster in an airline office, he thought, pausing to watch it. . . . And only then did he become aware that he was not the only watcher. . . . That, seated with his back against one of the palms, and still unconscious of his presence, was John Koa.

He moved up until he was almost beside him. But even now the boy's eyes remained fixed on the plane.

"There's no wood in it," Carr said.

And the boy looked up, startled.

"I said there's no wood in it. Just steel and aluminum."

John got to his feet.

"No damn wood anywhere, I guess. At least that's what your friend Patali says."

"Patali?" John was confused, fumbling.

"He and the others came back to the camp. Mr. Shafter's there now, and your uncle Fahoai. They're talking to Tafutimo."

John said nothing. For a moment his eyes met Carr's, and then moved away. Like the others on the island, he was thin—but he had been thin before. There were a few sores on his arms and legs; his lava-lava was soiled and torn; but otherwise he looked the same as . . . As when? No, not as the *last* time he had seen him, Carr reminded himself. . . . The last time he had been sprawled on the floor of a quonset hut with blood seeping from his mouth.

Carr looked at the mouth, but it was closed and tight. The boy had spoken only one word, and that had not been enough for him to see what he had to see. To know what he had to know.

"Are you all right?" he asked.

"All right?" said the boy. "Why shouldn't I be?"

—And yes, it *was* all right. The teeth were there. . . . Thank God, Carr thought. . . . But what he said was, "Most of the others, it seems, are having their troubles."

"They are easily discouraged."

"It sounds as if you, not Patali, were Tafutimo's son."

"What do you mean?"

"That's what he said about the others."

"It is true."

"You feel things aren't so bad?"

"No."

"They're going well?"

"Well enough."

"As with Mrs. Mundy, for instance?"

John didn't answer.

"As with no fire, no shelter, no taro. With the infections and the fevers?"

Again no answer.

"Anyhow," Carr said, "it's over now."

"Over?"

"You'll all be coming back to Tiara."

For another long moment the boy was silent. Then he shook his head slowly. "No," he murmured. "No."

"I think you'll find it's yes. All the others want to go."

"No, not all. Tafutimo doesn't."

"His pride doesn't like it. But he sees the truth. And that he has no choice."

The boy tried to speak, but found no words. Again he looked away: head bent, face thin and tight.

"John, listen—" Carr said quietly.

The head came up. "My name is Ioane."

Carr regarded him for a moment. He looked at him again as he had that day in the jeep near the Tiaran village, when he had not yet been sure, but still *knew,* that this was his son. He saw the brown silk skin, the liquid eyes: the skin and eyes of Lovana. He saw the frame, the bones, the lineaments that were his own.

Ioane Koa, he thought. . . . John Carr. . . . Which was he?

Both.

"All right—Ioane," he said. "Anyhow, listen. You're proud too: I know that. As proud as Tafutimo. But you've good sense, too, and you can see as well as he that you can't make a go of it here. There are all sorts of reasons, and you know it. Food, shelters, sickness, storms—almost everything you can think of. And even more than outside things, it's what's inside: in the head. In *your* head most of all, because you know more; you've had an education. This isn't a thousand years ago, or even a hundred. Whether you like it or not, it's the second half of the twentieth century, and you can't climb out of it. The world has moved in on you, and you can't live outside it."

"Or in it," John flung back.

"Yes, I know: it's been hard. For all of you. And for *you* most of all." Carr's voice, as he argued, had risen; but now it was again quiet and gentle. "I did my share to make it hard," he said. "I didn't mean to, but I did, and for that I'm sorry."

He was again looking at John's mouth.

"With all my heart," he said.

272

The boy was looking at him, but his face was closed. What he thought or felt did not show.

"And Miss Loftus is sorry too," Carr said.

"Miss Loftus?"

"For her part in—what happened. She's written to the proper people in Apingo, and I can promise you the case will be dropped." Carr paused. Then he smiled a little. "Even though you jumped bail," he added, "and I'm not too sure about my fifty dollars."

"I will pay it to you," John said stiffly.

"That would be quite a trick—with the money you'd earn here."

John said nothing, and Carr touched his shoulder lightly. "I wouldn't worry too much about it," he said. Then he glanced at his watch. "Come on. We'd better go."

"Go?"

"The plane has to be back in Tiara before dark. The people will be coming to board it soon."

"No."

"Yes they will. You'll see."

"All right, let them then. . . . But *I* won't."

"You'd rather stay here alone?"

"Yes. At least it's better than the other."

"John—Ioane—listen . . ." Again Carr put out his hand, but the boy jerked away. For a moment it seemed as if he were about to bolt off into the brush, but then he held his ground. His body was tense, almost trembling; his eyes wild and defiant.

"Better than back in the village," he said bitterly. "Mending fish nets—cleaning latrines."

"No, it won't be like that for you."

"Working at the hotel then. Washing dishes. And I'll get tattooed, like the old ones, to make better pictures for the tourists."

"Not like that either."

"What else is there?" Carr tried to speak, but John plunged on. "The world you talk of—it is a world for white men. Our island, Tiara, will be an island for white men. The *papalagi* is king, and we are natives—gooks."

"John!"

"Not John. *Ioane.*"

"No—John too. As much as the other. You're half white yourself. Have you forgotten?"

"Half!" The word was spat out. "Half is worse than nothing. It is a mongrel, a bastard. Without a home, a place—belonging nowhere."

Now the boy's thin frame *was* trembling. His chest heaved. It seemed almost that he would burst with the anguish that filled him.

And to Carr, watching him, there came suddenly a recollection and an image. The recollection of a moment in the house of the now-dead Mrs. Mundy; the image of a painting she had described—a painting by Gauguin—of a group of somber and mystical brown figures, imprisoned by life. . . . "And in the center of these figures," she had said, "is John. John asking, *Where do I come from? What am I? Where am I going?*"

Then the voice was gone. The image was gone. There was only the boy alone, a boy of flesh and blood, standing before him. And he was silent now; he had asked no question.

But Carr answered him.

"You are going with me," he said.

John struggled for control. He neither spoke nor moved.

"With me, now. To the others. To Tiara."

Still John said nothing.

"I know what you're thinking. I came to you before, in the jail, and you went with me, and it was bad. This time it won't be bad. You must believe me."

The boy looked at him steadily. "Why do you come again?" he asked.

"For the same reason as before. I want to help you."

"Like your son—"

"Yes, like my son."

"Why? What do you care about me? About any of us? Gooks on an island. . . . You're not with the Government; you're with the hotel. Why don't you stay there? Or go? . . . Why do you come with Mr. Shafter and my uncle?"

"I didn't just come with them," Carr said. "I brought them."

"Brought them?"

"I happen to be a pilot. I flew the plane."

John stared at him.

"*You* flew it?"

"Yes. It was in Apingo, for the hotel, but without a pilot. No one else could fly it. So I did."

"You never said—"

"No. It didn't come up. Lots of things haven't." Carr returned the boy's steady gaze. "Such as that I was a flier in the war," he said. "Like your father."

There was no response.

"In fact"—Carr pointed off between the palms—"this is probably the sort of plane your father flew. A Catalina. Back then they called it a PBY, but it's the same thing. . . . Come on, I'll show it to you."

Still no response.

274

"You're not interested?"

"No."

"Planes mean nothing to you?"

"No."

"When I found you here, staring at it, you were thinking of fire-wood?"

"I was only—"

"Only being yourself, because you were alone. Thinking of what you care about; of what's in your heart."

John shook his head. "That was before, when I was still a child. Now I am not a child. I know I will never fly."

"Yes you will. Today. To Tiara."

"No."

"Yes."

"To Tiara—for what? To be a gook—a dishwasher?"

"Neither."

"What then?"

"To go on from Tiara. *To be a flier yourself.*"

There was a pause. . . . So, he had said it, Carr thought. . . . He had not planned to. It had simply come out. Exactly what he meant, what he had in mind, he did not know. But this he did know: that, if it was the last thing he did in his lifetime, he was going to make it come true.

"A flier—?" It was John's lips that said it. There was no voice.

"Yes."

"You—you mean—there's been word? That Mr. Shafter—"

Still the words were the merest whisper, but the boy was rigid with inner excitement. And Carr saw at once that they were on dangerous ground.

"*—has heard from the Air Force?*"

The dark eyes were shining.

For an awful instant, Carr groped, fumbled. To tell him the easy lie was unthinkable; when he learned the truth, he would never forgive him. But to tell him the truth himself—here, now—might be to lose him forever.

"No—not that. Not yet," he said. . . . "But it will be all right. Believe me, John. You *must* believe me. It will work out; it will happen; you'll be a flier. I promise that. So help me God. . . ."

Still the eyes were on him. But they had changed. Where the gleam had been was doubt and puzzlement.

"You—you mean—you can—"

"Yes, I can. And I *will.*"

Carr came closer. He put his hands on the boy's shoulders. But

275

before he could speak again there was the sound, from the distance, of another voice—the voice of Shafter, calling his name. And raising his eyes, he saw, between the palms, a ragged procession emerging from the brush onto the beach, near where the plane was moored.

"He called back, "Here! Coming!"

Then to John: "You see—they've agreed. They're leaving. . . . And we too. . . . Come on."

John stood still as the palm trees.

"Believe me. Trust me."

Carr started toward the beach.

"Come on," he said again.

And when, a few moments later, he looked back, he saw that his son was following him slowly.

19

A LITTLE WAY down the beach, set back a few yards in the bordering scrub, there stood a cross. It was perhaps three feet high. The two sticks that formed it were, like all the wood on the island, warped and rotted, and were lashed roughly together with a strand of sennit.

Shafter and Carr had been led to it by the *matai,* Vaoti, with a straggle of other Tiarans following; and now, for a few moments, they stood in silence.

"It is only sand," said Vaoti. "We could find no proper earth."

And then: "With the wood so bad, we could also not put her name."

"Was there a service?" Shafter asked.

"There was no pastor, no Bible. Tafutimo spoke some words. . . . You will take her to Tiara?" Vaoti asked.

"Later, probably," Shafter answered. "Not now."

They stood for another moment in the harsh scrub, by the blazing sand. Then he said, half to Carr, half to himself: "You can almost forgive what the rest of us have done out here for two hundred years, so long as, every so often, there's one like her."

On the shore, close by the plane's mooring, the crowd waited. Only half of them—the women and children, the sick and injured—would be going on the first flight; but every human being on the island was there. The children ran about, waded out into the water, clustered around the beached life raft, by which Fahoai was posted to fend them off. The men and women stood or squatted on the sand and stared at the plane, Indeed, there was only one among them all whose

277

eyes were not hypnotically fixed on it—and that was the chief, Tafutimo. He had been carried across the island by a few of the younger men, working in relays, and now sat on the beach, his swollen leg still extended before him, staring, silent and motionless, into the distance.

Returning from Mrs. Mundy's grave, Shafter approached him. "We're ready now," he said. "The boys will put you on the raft and take you out."

Back at the camp site, even after he had capitulated, Tafutimo had held out stubbornly against being himself in the first plane load. He had been deaf to the argument that he, perhaps more than anyone, needed medical attention. And Shafter at last had had to change the approach. "It's not so much for yourself that it's important," he had said, "but for the others. Many of your people are afraid of flying. Especially the women. If they see you hold back, they will think you are afraid too, and there will be much trouble. But if you go first, you will give them confidence; you will be their leader." And this, in the end, had satisfied the chief's pride.

Now, on the beach, he made no further objection, but allowed himself to be lifted and carried to the raft. Carr followed; for it was essential that he be in the plane before the crowd swarmed aboard. And as the raft was readied for launching he looked around for John.

The boy was at the far edge of the crowd, watching silently.

"Come on!" Carr called.

But still John stood still. And he went to him.

"Come on. We're going," he said.

John shook his head. "I—I will go tomorrow," he murmured.

"No, now—with me."

"Only the women and children go now. And the sick ones."

"You're not coming as a passenger. You're coming to help me."

"Help?"

"Yes. There's too much for one man to do. Especially with a full load."

"Mr. Shafter can help. Or my uncle Fahaoi."

"They're staying here until tomorrow. They don't feel they should leave until everyone else does."

"But—"

"Come on," Carr said. "I need you. And they're waiting." And while a hundred eyes watched them curiously, he led the boy to the raft.

Tafutimo was already in it, as were another disabled man, a girl with high fever, and two mothers with infants. Carr and John stepped in. Two young men, assigned as paddlers, followed, and

278

with a few quick strokes took them out to the plane. The chief and other passengers were helped aboard and established in the main cabin. The paddlers returned to shore. Standing in the plane's doorway, Carr showed John the two drogues, still dangling in the water beside the fuselage, and told him to get them up.

"But keep them handy," he added. "We may want them for coming in at Tiara."

Then, for a half-hour, the loading operation continued. The raft moved back and forth, bringing the sick, the halt, the very young and very old. A few of the younger women and older girls swam out and were hauled aboard, with long black hair and lava-lavas dripping. But most who were scheduled to go hung back, and had to be urged or led or even pushed into the raft. Among these were some who, back at the settlement had been the loudest in their pleas to be taken home. But now they stared at the plane with fear-struck eyes; in the raft, they sat rigid and moaning. And when at last they came in through the open hatch, it was as if into the jaws of a waiting monster.

Standing by, Carr kept count. He tried to soothe and reassure them, helping the infirm ones up and in; and then John, now finished with the drogues, took over and led them on into the cabin. There were seats for less than a third, and they were given to those who seemed to have the greatest need for comfort. The rest sat or squatted at their feet, in the aisle, in the fore and aft vestibules: anywhere where a human body could fit. Under Carr's supervision, John fastened the belts of those in the seats and secured the others as best he could with lengths of clothesline that had been brought along for this purpose.

"See, you're a steward already," Carr told him. "You rate half a wing, and the other half will come soon."

He smiled. And for the first time the boy smiled back. His hostility seemed wholly gone; even his diffidence; with a function to fulfill, he was no longer ill at ease under the stares of his own people. Finding an empty oil tin, he set it in the aisle as a prop for Tafutimo's bad leg. He held a crying baby, brought a paper bag for a woman who was suddenly sick with fear and tension. And Carr, watching, felt within himself a glow of warmth, of satisfaction; and he thought, "Yes, it will be all right. It takes so little—of what he needs, what he's starved for. We've made a start. It will be all right."

Then the raft was alongside again. But this time there were no more passengers aboard. Only the paddlers and Leonard Shafter.

"Sixty?" Shafter said.

"Sixty," said Carr.

"That's it?"

"That's it."

279

"See you tomorrow then."

"By eight, if I can make it."

The two men waved. Then John was beside Carr in the open hatch, and waving too.

"Look—I am the crew!" he said.

"Good boy," said Shafter.

"By the time I go with the Air Force, I will already know all about flying."

Shafter's glance went back to Carr. Their eyes met. But neither spoke.

"Mr. Carr is a flier; he knows the Air Force," John said. "He is sure it will happen right. He has promised."

A wail came from within the plane, and with another wave he disappeared. Shafter's paddlers were easing the raft away. Carr closed and bolted the hatch. In the cabin, John was bent over one of the older women, quieting her, and as her crying subsided Carr raised a hand. "There is nothing to be afraid of," he said, speaking slowly and quietly. "You are tied in to make it easier for you if there is a little bump when we take off or land. It will take only about an hour and a half to reach Tiara, and you will all be home for supper."

From the seats, from the floor, along the length of the cabin, dark eyes stared up at him. For a moment there seemed to be only eyes: a screen, a tube of eyes. Then a few individuals emerged. He saw the propped-up leg of Tafutimo, so huge and bloated that it appeared to fill the aisle. Closer, huddled on the floor before him, two of the younger women who had swum out to the plane sat soaked and dripping, their long hair in matted strands. Farther back, in the aisle seat, another woman had bared a breast and was nursing her child.

Turning, Carr went into the cockpit and took his seat at the wheel. The time was all right—four thirty—meaning another two hours of daylight. He turned the ignition switch, checked his instruments, started the engines. But at first he could scarcely hear them, for now, again, there was sound from the cabin. It was no longer a single voice, but a chorus—a chorus of women. And no longer a wail, but a chant, a hymn.

Then he revved up the engines, and the voices faded. While the plane trembled and roared, he went briefly back to the cabin and summoned John. "Haul up the anchors," he told him. And back in the cockpit, he shouted instructions while the boy clambered into the nose and got them aboard.

"Now strap yourself in," he said, as John came back.

The boy stared at the copilot's seat.

"There?" he said.

"Yes, there."

John sat down and fastened the belt.

"Now watch what I do," Carr said, fastening his own. "No questions while I'm busy. But watch. Keep watching."

It was all right. The plane was heavy. The lagoon, in the windless calm, was heavy, with no surface rise and fall to thrust them loose. But still it was all right. He got the Cat up—onto its keel, onto the step, up and out of the clinging water—and there was still a half mile of freeway ahead when it rose, clear, into the air. An islet flowed away beneath. Then the plane climbed, banked, and the whole atoll flowed. It wheeled, receded, diminished, until the islets were threads, and the threads dissolved, and it was again a node of light, a gleaming spectrum. Then it was a speck, it was nothing, and there was only sea and sky.

The engines' roar had now subsided to a drone, and from the cabin there came again the chorus of women's voices singing a hymn. "They sound all right, but you'd best have a look," Carr said to John, and the boy unstrapped himself and went aft. Alone, Carr occupied himself with the business of flying. He watched sky, horizon, sea. On the sea there was now no shadow of the plane to be seen, for it was following them, invisible, and ahead was only the westering sun. In the sky, to the south, storm clouds were still massed, tall and purple; but they were little closer than before, and the air was quiet. Routinely, he checked course and altitude. Then his eye moved over the other dials on the panel before him; over the closed compartment beneath the panel, in which were his folded charts, a flashlight, binoculars— and a yellow envelope.

Perhaps ten minutes passed. Then John reappeared.

"Some are sick," he reported, "but I have given them paper bags. Tafutimo sits with eyes closed. The rest sing."

"Have any unfastened themselves?" Carr asked.

"A few, on the floor; but they aren't moving around. Should I go back and tie them?"

"No, let them be—until we come in."

Carr pointed to the seat beside him, and John sat down again. For a while he stared silently out through the windshield.

"Not much to see." Carr said.

"No."

The boy's glance shifted to the dials on the instrument board.

"*There*," Carr said, "there's plenty to see."

"Yes."

"Do you understand them?"

"Some, I think."

"This"—Carr pointed at the compass at his feet—"is the most important one. What does it say?"

John leaned over, peering.

"West by—"

"In figures."

"Two hundred and—sixty-seven."

Carr pointed at the altimeter. "This shows our height," he said. "What is it?"

"Fifteen hundred."

"Fifteen hundred what?"

"Feet."

"This one shows RPM's. Do you know what RPM's are?"

"Yes."

"What?"

. . . They went on across the board, and back again. Sometimes Carr asked questions. Sometimes he explained. "These are the things you must know—and watch," he said. "When you're in the air, in good weather, actual steering is the least of it."

He took both hands from his wheel.

"Hold yours," he said.

John held it.

"You see?"

He let the boy have it for a minute or so. Then he took over again. "—Although there's more to it than that, of course. I'll show you some of it tomorrow."

"Tomorrow?"

"When we fly back to Maniloa."

John stared. "You mean, I—I'll be—" The words would not come out.

"I'll need your help then too," Carr said. "We'll take off as soon as it's light.'

The plane droned on. From the cabin still came the voices of singing women. . . . And now, in the cockpit, high in the ocean sky, there was a boy called John Koa who was singing too. . . . But his song was secret and it made no sound.

The jetty in the lagoon had been crowded enough for the plane's first arrival, but now it was almost invisible under a mass of humanity. Voices shouted; arms waved; figures leapt or were shoved into the water and became bobbing heads among the skiffs and canoes that were swarming out from the shore. Carr had cut the engines. John had secured the lines to the mooring buoy. Now they stood outside on the plane's wing, trying to keep order in the fleet that was closing in.

From the nearest craft men sprang aboard, and there was more shouting, more gesticulating. Then they entered the cabin, to reappear presently carrying Tafutimo and the few others who were too lame or weak to walk. While these were transfered to the boats, the rest of the passengers pressed forward at the open hatch, impatient for their turn. And as on the jetty, several jumped or were pushed overboard. Of these, some swam to shore—one a woman carrying her baby on her shoulder. Others were pulled into boats, to be joined presently by the crowd flowing from the hatch. And soon all were being ferried off to add to the crush on the jetty.

Clambering down, Carr inspected the cabin; but there was no one left. Then he returned to the wing and watched the chaos ashore. The crowd was now so great that only part of it could fit on the jetty, with the rest spilled out along the nearby shore. Back a way, out of the crush, he saw the hotel contingent: Melnick, Plimpton, Lavery, the "Hawaiians." And near them, standing beside a parked truck on the road, was Carol Loftus.

"You will not go ashore?" John asked.

Carr shook his head. "I'd better stay with the plane."

"No, I will stay with it. I will take good care."

Carr hesitated.

"You go see your friends," John said.

"You have friends too—and family."

"I will see them later. The cabin is dirty, and I will clean it up." The boy smiled. "I am the steward, aren't I—and it is my job."

Carr smiled back. "O.K., it's your job," he agreed. "But I'll be back soon." And he climbed down into a skiff that was still standing by.

The jetty, when he reached it, was more jammed than ever, and it was all he could do to edge his way through the crowd. Everyone was in motion. Everyone was babbling, laughing, weeping, embracing. Malele the policeman was shouting orders; Solomona the pastor was making a speech; but no one listened. From somewhere, suddenly, a drum thumped. A guitar strummed. A voice was singing. Then everyone was singing. And this time it was no hymn, but a feast song, a joy song, wild and jubilant. The welcomers, the returnees—men, women, children—all joined in. Even those from the plane who, during the trip, had been the most somber and fearful, were now caught up in a frenzy of celebration.

Off the jetty at last, Carr came to Melnick and Company. And here the prevailing mood was notably different. The proprietor of the

Tiara Beach Hotel managed a nod and a grudging "Well you made it. Good going." But it was quickly followed by a dour "Well, where *are* they?"

"They?" said Carr.

"The men, for God's sake. The ones we're waiting for, to go back to work. There's not an able-bodied one in the lot."

"We took the sick ones first. And the women and kids."

"Women! Kids! What good do they do us?" Melnick groaned. "I got forty crates of furniture waiting to be opened. I got the kitchen equipment to set up, two tons of trash to move, and—"

There was an interruption: sudden, explosive. . . . "Meesh! Meesh!" . . . And out from among the "Hawaiians" flew Va'ina. "You are back again!" she cried. "My Meesh—my sweetie!" And she flung her arms about Carr, kissing him, looking up at him, smiling, glowing. "I am so happy," she said. "You are back. They all come back. I am so happy I dance—"

Then she *was* dancing. First with her eyes; then with her head, her feet, her hips, the whole of her. "Look, I show you. It is the new dance that I practice. That I will do for the hotel—"

She stamped. She whirled. She spun before him, and then away. She picked up the beat of the drum and guitar on the jetty. The drum and guitar came closer. The crowd came closer, streaming off the jetty. And voices were shouting, hands were clapping. A circle had formed, and Va'ina was dancing at its center—at first alone, but soon not alone—soon with others, with five, ten, twenty—until everyone in sight seemed to be dancing, clapping, shouting, whirling, except the hotel men, who stood by, watching . . . and Carr, who now moved on toward the road and the waiting truck.

It was different here. Here were the sick and halt, and the few who were tending them. Tafutimo had been carried up from the jetty, and now sat on a mattress in the back of the truck. Two of the other cripples were beside him; the girl with fever and a woman with a wailing infant were being helped in; and Carol, kneeling on the truck's floorboard under the canvas top, was settling them in as best she could. It was not until she had finished and got out that she was aware of Carr's presence. And then he saw at once, from her face, that she had already been told about Mrs. Mundy.

As he approached, she bent her head and let her forehead rest for a moment against his shoulder. "I should have stopped her," she said, her voice the barest murmur. "Somehow, some way, I should have stopped her."

That was all. She raised her head. She had things to do. "Are there any more?" she asked the men who had brought her patients, looking down toward the jetty.

But if there were, they weren't distinguishable. At least not now. They were part of the crowd, of the celebration: dancing, shouting, rejoicing.

"The mourners—" said Carr, watching.

Carol looked at the tight line of his mouth and shook her head. "No, don't feel that," she said gently. "They loved her. I know it; I saw it. This is just—the way they are. And she would have understood it better than anyone."

Abruptly, she was a nurse again, regarding him with a professional eye. "You, Mitch—you're all right?" she asked.

"Yes," he said.

"And—John?"

"All right, too."

"He's still on the island?"

"No, on the plane."

"The plane?"

"He's become my assistant," Carr said. "My steward." He smiled. "He's flying back with me tomorrow."

"Oh, Mitch—I'm so glad." For a moment Carol's eyes held his. "For him," she said, "—and for you."

She turned back to the truck. No other patients were being brought, and one of her helpers had climbed into the driver's seat. "All right, we'll go now," she told him. "Straight to the dispensary—and watch the bumps."

She got in beside him; then turned to Carr.

"Take care," she said.

He nodded.

"It's important," she said.

Then the truck drove off.

Carr watched it go. Then, turning, he faced the crowd on the shore and jetty, and they were starting to go too—still singing, shouting, in a triumphal parade. Malele, looking stooped and weary, rode off on his bicycle. Melnick and Company were walking toward the hotel. The sun had set while the plane was still being unloaded, and it was now quickly growing dark.

He started back toward the jetty; then changed his mind and veered off toward the hotel. He had already decided that he would spend the night on the plane. Here, with so many people about, he could not leave it unguarded, and he could sleep all right on a tilted-back seat. But there was no food aboard. He would go to the mess hut, get something for himself and John, and then return to the plane. They would eat together (the boy must be really hungry by now), and then John could either stay or leave for the night.

. . . No, he would leave. He would urge him. Make him. Flying the plane with him—having something to *do* with him—was one thing. But to be alone with him—just the two of them together, through the night—was something else. He was not ready for it. Not yet. . . .

In the mess-hut kitchen the cook greeted him cheerfully. The evening meal, soon to be served, was on the stove, and he got two helpings—a huge one for John and a normal one for himself.

"Whisky too, boss?" The cook nodded toward the dining room. "Some good stuff there now."

Carr smiled. "No thanks," he said.

"Then beer?"

"No thanks."

Carrying the plates, he left the hut and descended the path to the now deserted jetty. He had shown John the switches for the plane's electrical system, and the cabin ports now glowed yellow in the thickening dusk. But, although the hatch was still open, he received no answer when he called across the intervening strip of water.

He called again—louder: "Hey, there's no one here. Bring the raft in!"

But still there was no reply. The boy did not appear.

He's making noise cleaning, Carr thought. Or he's fallen asleep.

After a brief search he found a skiff tied up under the jetty. He got it out, set the plates in it, and rowed out to the plane. As he came alongside he called once more, but with the same result; and then, securing the skiff, he went aboard. The lighted cabin was empty. He looked in the vestibules, the lavatory, the storage space aft, and they were empty too. So, when he reached it, was the cockpit. But standing in a corner was a broom, and on the floor were a dustpan and a wad of rags.

Then his eyes moved to the instrument panel. . . . To the compartment below the panel in front of the pilot's seat. . . . The compartment door was open. Bending forward, he saw that the folded charts, the flashlight, the binoculars were still as they had been when he had last opened the door on the flight to Maniloa. But the yellow envelope he had laid on top of them was gone.

In the dispensary in the village, Carol Loftus went about her work. The first task was to get her five patients to at least a semblance of cleanliness. Then she examined and treated them. The girl with fever had a temperature of 104°, and she put her to bed in the single cot in the "hospital" room. The wailing baby also had fever, and she settled it for the night in a bassinet (there was just one of these, too), with its mother, who refused to leave, keeping vigil beside it. For the two men other than Tafutimo who were suffering from infections she provided wet dressings and shots of antibiotic; then allowed them to be taken off by their families—to be seen again in the morning. Tafutimo himself she wanted to stay, for his infection was more serious; and for such a contingency she had readied the bed in the adjoining dwelling house that had, until a few days before, been Mrs. Mundy's. But the high chief refused. No argument would budge him. And in the end, dosed with penicillin and swathed in dressings, he too was taken off to his *fale*.

Meanwhile, with the crowd straggling into the village, a half-dozen other patients had appeared—those who had forgotten their ailments, or been overlooked, in the earlier excitement—and for some time she was busy with these. Then came an emergency: a report of a woman, just returned, who had been seized by convulsions in her home, but had fought off all efforts to bring her to the dispensary. And Carol went there in her jeep. As it turned out, it was only a case of hysteria, requiring simple sedation; but she remained with the woman until she fell asleep.

As she drove back toward her house, the village was quiet. The flame of excitement and jubilation at the dramatic homecoming had by now burnt itself out. Inevitably it would rise again the next day when the rest of the Maniloans were flown in; but, as of now, both returnees and welcomers had subsided in near-exhaustion. Only a few lights showed, yellow, flickering, in the pillared *fales*. Few figures stirred in them. The sweep of the *malae* was empty.

. . . Or, rather, almost empty. For now, as Carol passed along the road beside it, she became aware, in the darkness, of a single moving figure. There was no reason to pay attention to it; no reason why anyone in the village, other than a few invalids, should not be moving about. Yet, for some reason, she found herself watching. It was a male figure: she could tell that. It was crossing the *malae* toward Asimo's store. But the store was dark. And it was not Asimo himself. It was a figure taller, more angular than Asimo. Somehow younger . . . more familiar. . . .

Then it was gone, lost in shadow. And she drove on home. Going first to the dispensary, she found her two patients, the young girl and the baby, asleep, their fevers obviously down; and the baby's mother was asleep too, curled on the floor beside the bassinet. Then she went through to the house proper, made herself a cup of coffee and a sandwich (for she had eaten nothing since noon), and sat down with them in the small living room. She was not hungry, however. She was too tired to be hungry. And too depressed. Mrs. Mundy, to be sure, had been on her mind since the moment, by the jetty, when

287

she had learned of her death. But while she had been working, it had been only in the mind's corner; she had been too busy to face the fact full on. *Now* she faced it. She felt it. She looked about: at Mrs. Mundy's room; at her furniture, her books, her knickknacks; at the Indian rug she had brought from Fiji, the wooden carvings from Tahiti, the photographs of her long-dead husband, of her two sons, gone longer still. . . . And suddenly the lonely sadness of the room crushed in on her, unbearably.

She rose. She moved around. She went back to the dispensary, half hoping one of the patients had wakened and needed attention. But they were still asleep, and she returned to the living room. She wanted to go out again; to be with someone, talk with someone. . . . But where? With whom? . . . In the same instant she asked it, she knew with whom. She wanted to be with Mitchell Carr. With him, and him only, she could find a way out of the sadness, the loneliness. But he was—where? At the far end of the island. Perhaps with Melnick and the others at the hotel. Or with his girl, Va'ina. (She shut the image out quickly.) Or— most likely—on the plane. Yes, of course, on the plane. He would be flying off again at dawn, and he was aboard now, readying it. Or sleeping. He and John Koa. . . .

And now, suddenly, her mind veered again. Mrs. Mundy was gone; Mitchell Carr was gone; and in their place was another —a figure tall, thin, and angular, half seen in darkness, moving alone across the empty *malae*. It had been John: she knew that now. John Koa— here in the village.

She considered. "Well, why not?" she thought. John was helping Carr with the plane. He would fly with him tomorrow. But that didn't mean he couldn't have the night off to do as he wished. To visit the village, his family.

No.

But—another *but*—when she had seen him, it had not been toward his family house that he was going. It had been in exactly the opposite direction: across the *malae,* toward Asimo's store. Asimo's, where he had gone before, on another night. Now, as then, alone, half seen, a furtive shadow. . . .

She sat down again. Beside her were the almost full cup of coffee, the uneaten sandwich, but she did not touch them. She did not even see them. She saw the shadow. She tried to follow it. For perhaps five minutes she sat there. Then, rising, she crossed to the door, went out, and walked down the road under the palms.

As before, everything was dark. The road. The *malae*. Beyond the *malae,* the old shed that was the store. Or at least it was dark in front, on the road side; but at the rear, in the rickety annex that was

Asimo's living quarters, a dim light showed behind the tapa-screened window. Approaching the door, Carol stopped and listened, but heard nothing. Then she knocked.

There was no answer.

And she knocked again.

"The store's closed," said Asimo's voice.

"I'm looking for John Koa," she said.

"He's not here."

"Yes he is. And I have to see him, please. It's important."

There was another silence. Then, after she had knocked again, the sound of slow footsteps, and the storekeeper opened the door. His squat, fleshy body was clad, as usual, only in a pair of ragged shorts, and he held a calabash in his hand.

"No pills tonight, sister," he said. He raised the calabash. "We got our own medicine."

"Please, I must see John," Carol said.

Asimo belched, and with his free hand patted his stomach.

"John!" she called.

"He don't want—"

"John! I must talk to you. *Please*—"

"What about?" John's voice came from within the room.

"About—your aunt, Polu."

"Polu?"

"She's been taken sick. I need your help, right away."

John at last came up beside Asimo, and peered out at her with hostile eyes. "What do you mean?" he said. "What kind of sick?"

"She's having convulsions. I can't handle her. Please help me."

"I can't help. I'm drunk."

"No you're not."

"Well, I will be."

"If you give him a chance," said Asimo. "Every time two pals sit down for a drink, there's some goddam interruption."

"John!" Carol's voice was no longer pleading, but sharp and hard. "Come with me. Now. Do you hear? If you don't, you'll regret it the rest of your life."

Asimo started to speak again, but she cut him off. "Be quiet," she snapped. Then to John: "Now come. Before it's too late."

He hesitated; then came slowly through the door.

"The boy scout to the rescue," said Asimo.

"I'll be back," John said.

"Yeah, sure—with your merit badge."

"Come," Carol said. And, with John reluctantly following, she walked away across the *malae*.

She did not go far, however. On the far side, in the palm grove, she stopped suddenly and turned. "Now I have to talk to you," she said.

"Talk?" John eyed her suspiciously. "What about? You said my aunt—"

"I made that up."

"You *what?*"

"Your aunt's not sick. I said that just to get you away."

The boy was staring at her, eyes narrowed, lips tight. "You mean you lied," he said.

"All right, I lied. I had to get you, to see you alone, and—"

"*You* lie. *He* lies. There's nothing but lies in the whole damn world."

"John, listen—"

He was going.

"John—"

Her voice was not loud, but it seemed to fill the quiet grove. In it there was command, there was plea, there was the whole intensity of her being.

"*John—*"

If he went now, she had lost him. Mitchell Carr had lost him. Only if he heeded her cry—if, for at least a moment, it held him—would there be hope for them. Or for him.

It held him. He half stopped, half turned, looked at her. And in an instant she was at his side.

"You said *he* lied to you," she said. "Who lied? About what?"

He didn't answer.

"Why are you here, John? Why are you running away again?"

"I'm not running."

"Yes you are. From Mr. Carr again. From the plane."

"I came back in the plane. That's all."

"No, it's not all. You're to fly back with him tomorrow. He told me."

"He lies. All he says are lies."

Carol's voice had remained low, but John's was high and strident; and now she became aware of movement in a nearby *fale* and realized they were being watched.

She took his arm. "Come," she said.

"Where?"

"To my place. We can talk there."

"There's nothing to talk about. I'm going back to Asimo."

"No." She held his arm tight. "That's when I knew there was something wrong: when I saw you going to Asimo's. . . . And you're not going back, John. No, you're not!"

290

The boy said nothing. In the next instant, it seemed, he would break away and run off. . . . But he didn't. . . . Stiffly, slowly, with eyes fixed on her curiously, he allowed her to lead him on through the palm grove.

Then they reached the road and walked along it. And Carol was on the point of speaking again—but he spoke first.

"There is no Malele tonight," he said.

"Malele?"

"He is not in the village. He is at the hotel with the Utoians, drinking beer."

Now it was Carol who said nothing.

"And if I do now as I did here after the feast, he will not come to help you."

"John please—"

"No one will come. The others are asleep. And even if they wake and hear you, they won't care."

He moved in front of her, so as to block her way. And they stopped, facing each other.

"You are afraid?" he asked.

She shook her head.

"I'm drunk."

"No."

"I'm a savage."

"No."

"Yes. And you've read in books what a savage does with a white woman. You saw it that other night, on this road."

Again she shook her head, gently.

"What does that mean?"

"That you're wrong about me." Reaching out, she put a hand on his arm. "Does that look as if I'm afraid?" she asked.

In the boy's face were bitterness, bravado—and now, beneath them, confusion. With a jerk, he flung her hand away.

"*Why* aren't you afraid?" he demanded.

"Of you, John?"

"You were afraid before."

"I was surprised then. Shocked. But now I know you better."

"I could take hold of you now, the same as then. Put my hand on your mouth. Pull you into the bushes."

"You could, perhaps. But you won't."

"Why not?"

"Because of what you are."

"What I am? . . . And what's that?" He was very close to her now, looking down at her. His body was rigid, his face harsh. But his lips trembled. "Tell me!" he cried, his voice wild and high. "Tell me, tell me—you know so much. *What am I?*"

"A decent human—"

"Human!" He spat the word. "Human is for *papalagi*. Like you. Like Carr. Like the United States Air Force." Carol tried to speak, but he wouldn't let her. "Humans are white. Or they're black, brown, red, yellow. At least they're something. Not nothing—"

His voice was close to breaking.

"Not mongrel bastards—" he cried.

Then it did break. He too, his face, his body, seemed to break. Like his lips, they were trembling, and the trembling swelled into a sob.

"John—" said Carol.

He had turned away.

"John—" Her voice was soft. She took his hand. "Come on," she said.

He did not resist, he said nothing, going with her dumbly, blindly, down the road. Presently they reached her house. They went in. They were in the living room, and she had turned on the light, and he stood there. He was no longer sobbing. The spasm had passed as quickly as it had come, and he stood silent and stiff, his face stiff, looking neither at her nor at anything.

He would not run now. She knew that. And saying "I'll be right back," she went through to the dispensary. The girl, the baby, and the mother were all still asleep. And when she returned to the living room, John was exactly as she had left him.

"Sit down," she said.

He didn't move.

"John, sit down." She sat herself. "Here, facing me."

This time he obeyed, moving slowly, numbly. But he still did not look at her.

Her eyes went to the untouched sandwich on the table beside him. "Are you hungry?" she asked.

He shook his head.

"Would you like something to drink?"

He shook it again.

"All right. . . . Now tell me: what's the matter?"

He didn't answer.

"John, tell me." Her voice was stronger. "What is it? What's happened?"

"Nothing."

"You were talking of lies before. You said *he* had lied. What did you mean?"

John met her eyes for an instant and looked away.

292

"You meant Mr. Carr, didn't you?"

"Yes."

"How did he lie to you?"

There was a pause. Then at last John answered. His voice was low and toneless.

"He said he could get me into the Air Force."

"Well?"

"On the island—on Maniloa—he came after me. He made me come back. He said it would be all right—promised it would—that the Air Force would take me. And all the time he was lying. He knew it wouldn't."

"Wouldn't?"

"The Air Force had said no. There was a letter, and he knew it. It was in the plane, in a private place by the pilot's seat. When I was cleaning the plane, I found it. I read it."

"But—"

"He lied. He lied." John's voice was still low, but now it quavered. His hands were tight, white-knuckled, on his knees. "He was saying these things—that it would be all right, I would be a flier—and I asked him, was there word from the Air Force—and he said no. *No, he said!* And there it was. He had it. He knew it."

"John, I'm sure—"

Carol paused.

What was she sure of?

"—I'm sure," she said, "that he must have had a reason. A good reason. . . . He didn't think it was the right time yet. Or he felt there was something he could do."

"Do? Do what? Tell the Air Force to change its mind?"

Carol floundered. Then she pulled herself up. "John, listen," she said. She leaned forward. Her voice was filled with urgency. "I said before that you were wrong about me. And you're wrong about Mr. Carr too. Whatever he's said, whatever he's done, it's to help you; it's for your sake. Believe me."

For the first time, John looked at her full on.

"What do *you* know about it?" he asked.

"I've seen it. I've felt it. . . . Yes, I know there was trouble back there when you had the accident. And now, again. . . . But still it's true. He cares about you: truly, deeply."

"Why? *Why* should he care?"

"Because—"

She didn't know.

"Why does he come after me: here—in Maniloa. Why is he always looking at me, asking questions, telling me things?"

"Haven't you asked him yourself?" said Carol.

"Yes, I've asked him. But the answers are crazy. . . . Because he was in the war, like my father, he says. Because he has a son like me. . . . So he wants to help he, he says. But instead he lies. Instead, he—"

John stopped. His eyes fixed on her. "What is it?" he said. "Why do you look at me so?"

A long moment passed before she spoke.

Then she said, very quietly: "A son, John? He said he had a son?"

"Yes."

"Like you?"

"Yes. But what does that—"

And now he was speaking again. But she did not hear him. She only saw him . . . saw the long bony hands on the up-jutting knees; saw the line of his shoulder, his neck, his chin, his cheekbones . . . saw the whole of him, plain, clear before her, as if a caul of blindness had been swept from her eyes. She saw. She knew. She saw the boy before her; and beyond him, the other, the man who sought the boy; who had stayed on in the village, come again and again to the village, returned to fly a plane to Maniloa. . . .

And she rose. She went to the boy. She knelt beside him, took his hands in hers, and looked up into his face.

"You must trust him, John," she said. "And you must trust me when I say it."

There was a silence. (And she thought: yes, the head was the same; its lines, its bones, its set on the shoulders.)

She pressed his hands.

"John—" she murmured.

He was looking down at her. (Even the eyes were the same.)

"Dear John—"

20

IN THE CATALINA, close by the jetty, Mitchell Carr sat alone in the cockpit. Beside him, on the copilot's seat, the two plates of food he had brought with him lay unnoticed. Beyond the windscreen, the new moon, setting early, threw a thread of golden light across the lagoon. But he did not notice this either.

He sat, and he thought.

He did not muse. He did not brood. He thought. He struggled, step by step, toward decision.

At first he had felt disappointment and anger at the boy for having left his post—whatever the reason. But not after he had pondered the reason. To begin with, in finding the Air Force letter, John had been at no fault. He had not pried, but come across it in his routine cleaning of the plane. It had been himself who was to blame there; who had been careless, stupid, in leaving it in the compartment.

And beyond that? . . . The fault had been even more his own. He had lied, and been caught in the lie; and that he had meant it well made no difference. John had not known that. He knew only that the letter had come, that the hope of his life had been snuffed out, crushed. And that he, Carr, had lied to him about it.

God knows, the boy owed him nothing.

His quick impulse had been to go after him. But it was only impulse; it was no good. For one thing, he must stay with the plane. For another, how would he find him, on the sleeping island, in the dark? . . . But, bigger than these, there was the further question, the old question: If he did find him, what then? . . . Twice already he had

295

gone after him: once to the village jail, once to Maniloa. And what had come of it? First, an accident, a scene, a blow in the face. Now, another blow—harder, deeper. The third time there must be something better than that. Or there could be no third time.

It was hot and airless in the cockpit. Back in the cabin it was hotter. And presently he went out and sat on the wing of the plane. Even here there seemed to be no air; the darkness was heavy and still. But at least there was space around him: the space of darkness: of earth, sky, water. The moon was down now, and the lagoon was black. And so too was the land, for the lights were out on the hotel grounds. The only sounds were the honk of frogs and the occasional flop of a fish breaking water.

> . . . *Croon a tune*
> *with no moon*
> *on a tropic la . . .*

He didn't sing the jingle. It made no sound. It was deep inside him —with a wry, bitter smile. With his thoughts.

And what he thought was: this was why he was here. Not to dynamite a lagoon, build a hotel, fly a plane. But for this. For the stillness, the darkness. For the darkness that would break with the morning in the glory of sunrise—or the fury of storm. It didn't matter which, for, if it was storm it would pass; the sun would come again; it would shine on the sea, the beach, the grove, the hillside—on the pure white cloud that was Tiara's tiara—on the still leaves of a bread-fruit tree in the place of *fia fia*. This was why he had come, what he had sought, what he had needed. And the hell with the rest, he had said. The hell with the big world, the big shapes, the big noises. The hell with success—whatever that was. With money. With involvement.

The inward smile deepened. (Or perhaps it was no longer a smile.)

For what had he found instead? . . . Just that. Involvement. . . . He had found a son

John owed him nothing. It was he who owed John. If he had not come back to Tiara it would have been different; one is not involved in what one doesn't know exists. But he had come. He knew. John existed, all right. Margaret had yearned for a child, and they had had none. Helen had dreaded a child, and they had had none. The child had been by Lovana, who hadn't thought about it one way or another. And here he was. His son. John Koa.

John Carr.

If it had been a Carr, not a Koa, who had made application to the

296

Air Force, would the answer have been different? And if . . . but what good were the *ifs?* . . . The answer to John Koa had been no, and he knew it. He knew he had been lied to. He, Mitchell Carr, had done the lying.

And then?

Then he had said, *It will be all right. Believe me, John. It will work out; it will happen; you'll be a flier. I promise that. So help me God.*

For a long time he sat there on the plane's wing, in the dark stillness. It was too still—the stillness of threatening storm—and though the sky above was clear, the stars huge and bright, he knew that the clouds he had seen to the south, above the open sea, must still be moving closer. If the storm came before daylight, there would be no choice: he would have to wait until it was over. If it did not, he would take off as soon as he could fly around or above it to Maniloa.

First, the flight. The return.

Then John. For the third time he would seek out John. But this time it would be different, for he knew at last what he must do.

Lying back, he watched the stars. On and off, he dozed. And the night passed. At intervals he looked at his watch, and when the dial showed four he rose, climbed down into the moored skiff, and rowed to the jetty. He would go to the hotel hut where Tom Taki and his Utoian crew were quartered and get two or three of them to help with the drums for refueling. They would grumble, but they would come, and the job would be done, and the rest he could handle alone. It would have been easier with John, of course: the preparations, the flight, all of it. Easier both as work and—more importantly—in his mind. For, though he had tried throughout the night to push the thought away (since there was nothing he could do about it), there was still the unanswered question of where the boy was and what he was doing.

In his resentment, his misery. . . .

He pushed it away again. He had a job to do, a plane to fly. Reaching the jetty, he secured the skiff, climbed and walked toward the shore. But he did not reach it, for a shadow was moving out from the shore end, toward him. And the shadow was John.

"Are you coming with me?" he asked

"Yes," John answered.

And they went to work, rolling the fuel drums from the storage shed to the end of the jetty, then ferrying them out to the plane. The Utoians weren't needed now. The two of them managed alone. And their only talk was of the job at hand.

With the gas aboard, they filled the tanks. Then John rowed the empty drums ashore, while Carr checked over the plane; and by the time they were through it was past five.

"Have you eaten?" Carr asked.

John shook his head.

And they ate the cold stew from the plates in the cockpit.

At about five thirty the darkness began to break. The air was still quiet, the sky clear; and Carr started the engines. For a few minutes he warmed them up; then turning to John said, "Moorings," and the boy, clambering down into the nose, released the buoy lines.

"Drogues up?"

"Yes," said John.

"Hatch closed and bolted?"

"Yes."

They fastened their seat straps. Carr advanced the throttles, listening, watching the instrument board, and the hum of the engines grew louder, deeper. Beyond the windshield, the sky was gray, the lagoon grayish green, a sweep of silk drawn smooth and tight, untouched by crease or ripple. Wisps of mist hung briefly above it; thinned, rose, and vanished. On the shore a few figures had appeared and were standing motionless, watching the plane.

The plane moved now. Carr brought it about and headed it out, and they pointed toward the red line of buoys, cleaving the stillness. Reaching it, they followed the line to its end; then followed it back; moving slowly, the plane wallowing, rumbling in its throat. Then, briefly, they had stopped. The red line stretched ahead . . . and leapt at them. The buoys were streaming by. Where the rumbling had been was a roaring; there was the rush, the surge, the trembling of metal, the beat of water; and the water was heavy but the plane was light; and now it was up, on the keel, on the step; it was off, it was clear. Tiara wheeled below. The lagoon, the groves, the hills and valleys streamed past. And beyond them was the sea.

"What's the course?" said Carr.

John was caught by surprise. "I—I don't—"

"Yes you do. What was it coming in from Maniloa?"

The boy thought. "Two hundred and—sixty-seven."

"So what is it going back?"

He thought some more. "Eighty-seven?"

"Right." The compass needle swung and stopped. Tiara's cloud cap drifted past. Then it was gone—and the island too.

"The bearings come from charts," he said. He indicated the panel compartment. "The charts are kept here. Maybe you noticed when you were cleaning up."

John didn't answer.

298

"Did you?"

"Yes," said John.

"Did you look at them?"

"No."

Carr opened the compartment, took out the topmost chart and two plexiglass triangles, and handed them to John. "This is the one for where we are now," he said. "Get the line between Tiara and Maniloa on one of the triangles. Then move the triangles around to transfer it to the compass face in the corner of the chart; and you get the bearing."

The boy unfolded the chart and propped it against the copilot's wheel.

"Or at least you almost get it," Carr added. "There's a thing called magnetic variation that effects the real compass"—he nodded at the instrument between his feet—"and you have to make allowance for that. It's a matter of your position in relation to the magnetic pole, and for where we are it's minus five degrees. That shows on the chart too. If you get that line over accurately, it will show a bearing of ninety-two degrees, Tiara to Maniloa, and that's the true bearing. But because the real compass is magnetically affected, you have to take that five off; and then you've got eighty-seven, which is what we're on."

John maneuvered the triangles. Carr looked out through the windshield. The dawn was full now—no longer somber gray, but pearly, shining—and in the east, dead ahead, the sky glowed pink and gold, as the earth rolled toward sunrise. It was not with the east that he was concerned, however, but with the south, where the clouds had been ranged the day before. And they were still there—still tall and livid—no longer a series of disconnected squalls, but a complex of squalls, a storm front, rising in a wall from the horizon. They were there. And they were closer—unquestionably closer. But still not so near as to be imminently menacing. The air around them was quiet. The wind within the storm was principally from the east, and might carry it past them entirely. Carr kept on his course. The plane seemed almost to float, weightless, in the heart of the dawn.

John had looked up from the chart.

"Got it?" Carr asked.

"I think so."

"Eighty-seven?"

"Yes, eighty-seven."

The boy refolded the chart and, leaning over, put it, with the triangles, back in the panel compartment.

"Nothing else?" Carr said.

John looked at him.

"To put back. Like—a letter."

There was no answer.

"What did you do with the letter?"

John was no longer looking at him.

"Did you throw it away?"

"Yes."

"That was the best thing to do."

There was silence for a moment. Then Carr said: "I'm sorry about that. Damned sorry. About the no from the Air Force—and that I didn't tell you the truth."

John's eyes were fixed on the instrument board.

"I meant well—but that's beside the point. You were hurt and angry: I understand that. In fact, I didn't think you'd come back."

He looked at the boy.

"*Why* did you come back?" he asked.

Again there was no answer.

"Why? Tell me."

He waited.

"Where did you go when you left?"

"To the village," John murmured.

"To your home?"

"No."

"Where then?"

"To—Asimo's."

"And what did you do there?"

Carr waited.

"You talked?"

"Yes."

"And drank?"

"No."

"No?"

"I was going to. But—" John hesitated. "But there wasn't time."

"Why? What happened?"

"Nothing."

"What happened, John?"

"I—I said I wouldn't tell."

"Said to whom? Whom did you see then?"

The boy struggled. "She didn't want me to—"

"She?"

"Miss Loftus," he said.

"You went to see Miss Loftus?"

"No."

"What then?"

"She came to Asimo's, looking for me."

300

"How did she know you were there?"

"I don't know. But she came."

"And you went with her?"

"Yes—to her house."

"And you talked?"

"Yes."

"About what?"

"About coming back to the plane."

"You told her why you'd left?"

"Yes."

"And what did she say?"

"She said I must come back. That—well—that I was wrong about you, she said. That you must have had some reason. She knew it—"

"And you believed her?"

"Yes."

"Why?"

"Because—" John paused. He searched for the reason. "Because she would not lie. Because she is good," he said.

"And when you'd talked, she sent you back?"

"She didn't send me. She brought me."

"Brought you?"

"Yes. In the jeep. She took me to the jetty and left me, and then I waited until you came ashore."

The sun had risen, lying round and huge on the horizon ahead, and the plane droned on into its golden eye. To the south, the storm clouds glittered darkly—a range of brooding mountains. But they were no closer; still perhaps ten miles distant, moving past them toward the west. And if he kept on course it would be all right.

He checked the compass. Eighty-seven. Then he squinted ahead.

"Miss Loftus was right," he said. "I had a reason. I've told you I want to help you. I told you you'd be a flier—and you will be."

He paused. The boy was watching him now.

"The Air Force isn't the only way of becoming a flier," he said.

"Not the only—"

"No. There are such things as flying schools. Have you heard of them?"

John shook his head.

"There are hundreds of them. In Hawaii, California, all over. Most fliers, even the professional ones, didn't learn in the Air Force."

"But how—"

"How do you get in? You go, that's all. Just like that."

"For money?"

"Yes, for money."

"I have no—"

"No. But I do. Or at least I will." Carr looked at John for a long moment. "And I'm going to send you to Hawaii, to flying school," he said.

Just what he expected from the boy he didn't know. But it was not what happened. For John's face remained closed and somber, and then again, slowly, he shook his head.

"What does that mean?" said Carr.

"It is good of you," John said. "It is the best anyone has ever been to me. . . . But no, it is no use. It would not work."

"Not work?"

"The school, yes: they would take me, I suppose—if they are paid. But after that? I am a flier, but what do I fly?"

"You said you didn't plan to stay with the Air Force anyhow. That you just wanted to learn there and then go with an airline."

"What I wanted, yes. But what would happen is something else, and that I know now. If the Air Force will not take me, what would an airline do? Have you ever seen a pilot who was not white? In America, I mean. Is there a black one, a brown one?" Carr tried to speak, but John went on, his voice low but intense. "I have thought of this much. For many months I waited. And now, with the letter here—all last night—I have thought; I have seen how foolish I was—"

"You talked about this with Miss Loftus?"

"No, not with her. . . . But still she has to do with it. She too was part of my foolishness. . . . The night of the feast, when I made the trouble, I was drunk, yes, but it wasn't only that. I am saying to myself I am a man, like any other. Not a brown island boy but a man—as good as a white man, a *papalagi*."

He paused, then went on. And his voice, though still taut with emotion, was quiet, controlled, with neither wildness in it nor self-pity.

"But I was wrong," he said. "Miss Loftus is good; she is kind. She does not look down on me because I am brown. But still I *am* brown, I am an island boy, and she is white, and we are different. . . . That I know now. And from Asimo, too, I know it. . . . Yes, he is drunk, he is hard and bitter, but still I have learned from him, for *why* is he so? Because he went to the *papalagi* world; he tried to live as a *papalagi*; and he could not. He tried to be a lawyer, but he could not. The same as I cannot be a pilot for an airline."

He stopped. There was silence and the droning engines. Then Carr said:

"Why did you come back, then?"

"Back?"

"If you've given up on being a flier, why are you here now, in this plane?"

"Because—"

"Miss Loftus made you come?"

"No, she didn't make me. She showed me why I *should* come."

"Why?"

"To help you."

"Oh."

"And to help my people."

"Your people?"

"The ones still on Maniloa. To help get them aboard. To see they are all right aboard. And if the storm comes—"

"Since when," said Carr, "are you so concerned about your people?"

"That is another thing I have learned. That I am part of them, and must stay so. If I cannot be one thing, I must be another. If not a man of the big world, then a man of the islands."

Carr shook his head. "Things aren't that simple any more. . . . 'I'm this. I'm that.' . . . Sometimes one has to be both."

He looked squarely at John.

"You *are* both," he said. "In your blood. In your bones."

Now it was the boy who tried to speak and he who overrode him. "And you can live as both," he said. "Staying here—flying—the two of them. . . . You're in a plane now, aren't you? Do you think it's the only one in the South Pacific? The only one there'll ever be in Manaia? If your people are going to be part of the world, God help them, planes are exactly what are going to do it. And they're coming; you'll have them. You'll fly them yourselves. *You*—not outsiders. You, and others like you, because you've learned, you know how. . . . You want to help your people, you say. How? By running away to a desert island? By picking coconuts, chopping wood? How can you help them more than by flying? *Right here*. The first Manaian pilot. In Manaia. For Manaia. . . ."

The engines droned. Whatever it was that John had been going to say, he did not say it now.

"You're going to go to Hawaii," Carr said. "You're going to flying school and get your licenses: private, commercial, transport. And then you're coming back here to be the best goddamned pilot in Polynesia."

As on the previous day, he took his hands from the wheel.

"Now we go on with the kindergarten," he said. "Take over. It's yours."

John stared at him, words trembling on his lips. But they made no sound. And slowly his hands moved, taking the copilot's wheel.

"Only this time we do more," said Carr. "If you make a mistake, there's just two of us, not sixty."

Unstrapping himself, he rose and moved around behind John's seat.

"But you won't make one," he said.

John held the wheel. The plane flew itself.

"Now take it up a little. Ease the wheel back gently."

John eased it back. The plane's nose lifted.

"Now level off. Ease forward."

They leveled off.

"All right—down. Farther forward. Don't jerk it."

The plane responded.

"Good. . . . Now back, easy."

They went through it again; then flew level for a while. The sun, higher now, filled the cockpit with gleaming light.

"The turns are harder," Carr said, "because you bank and use both the wheel and the rudders. We'll try that later. Now I'm going to the head."

He waited to see what John's reaction would be. But the boy remained as he had been: motionless, concentrated.

"Not too tight with the hands. Easy does it," he said, and went aft.

But he did not go to the head. Entering the main cabin, he sat on the arm of an aisle seat and remained there. Through the vestibule and open door beyond, he watched the cockpit. But there was nothing to watch except the back of John's head and the sky beyond. The plane flew smoothly, the same as before.

. . . The same, yet not the same—not all the same—Carr thought; for now it was not he who was there in the cockpit. He was in the cabin, watching. In the cockpit was a brown island boy named John Koa: a boy who was also John Carr, his son. And there John would remain: in this plane, in others to come; for come they would, by the hundred, the thousand, as surely as the ships of the sea had come before them. It was not he, Mitchell Carr, who had put him there. It was the turning of the earth—and the boy's own dream. But at least he had helped. At least, and at last, after all his fumblings, all his false moves, he had put out a hand that had neither shaken nor been a fist; a hand raised, quiet, steady, from the wheel of a plane, saying, *Here—take it—it is yours.*

It had been during the long night that he had reached his decision. This must be. No matter what—this must be. He himself would teach the boy what he could. He would send him through school. And then. . . . Then, John was right: he must come back to Manaia. The time was not yet when an island boy, however skilled, would be taken as a pilot by a stateside airline. The leap was still too great, the big and little worlds too far apart. . . . John would return. He would fly the airways of his own world. Good or not, bad or not, that world would have its planes—as it would its Tiara Beach Hotels. And he, John Koa, would be a pioneer among his people.

"My people. . . ."

304

The boy had said it not once but many times. And he had not meant the people of his father, but of his mother, the people of the islands whom he knew and had grown up with. He was John Koa, and he was John Carr, but, of the two, the Koa was stronger. That was the essence of it. . . . And the irony. . . . For in the beginning he had clung to his half-whiteness; he had sought to reject his own people and enter the white world; and it had been precisely this seeking, this striving, that now had led him back to them. His experience with the Air Force, with Carol Loftus, even—ultimate irony—with his own father, had all made him less a *papalagi,* more a Manaian. And it would be as a Manaian that he would lead his life.

An image flashed into Carr's mind: the image of John on the atoll the previous day—trembling and anguished. Crying out in his anguish (though his own words had been different): *Where do I come from? What am I? Where am I going?* . . . Now, if all the answers had not been given (when are they? and to whom?) there was at least a beginning. He was John Koa, student pilot. He was going to Hawaii, to flying school. And then . . .

Carr's head jerked up.

There was something wrong. With the sound of the plane. With its movement.

He sprang to his feet; but at the same instant it tilted, sideslipped, and he was thrown across the aisle onto the seat on the far side. Picking himself up, he started forward, grasping the backs of the seats, thrusting himself on, while the floor swayed beneath them. As he reached the forward vestibule, the sway became a second slip, a wild lurch to starboard, and he went down again, with cups and plates from the galley cupboard raining around him. Then once more he was up. He was through the bulkhead. He was in the cockpit.

In the copilot's seat John sat rigid, straining at the wheel. If he had called out, Carr had not heard him. And if he spoke now, he did not hear him either, for as he moved toward his own seat the plane slipped again, tilting downward, and sent him reeling against the instrument panel.

"Pull back!" he yelled. "Nose up—up!"

The boy heaved back, and with a shudder the plane leveled off. Carr lunged for his seat, reached it, strapped himself in. And now it was he who was again the pilot, working wheel and rudders. John was shouting at him. He was pointing off through the window on the copilot's side. But Carr already knew what was wrong. He had heard and felt it even while back in the cabin; he had seen it the instant he reached the cockpit; he did not need John to tell him that the starboard propeller was motionless, its engine silent. Bracing against the wheel with his left arm, he put his right hand out. To the switch. To the throttles. But with no response. His eyes flickered over the dials for the starboard engine, and none was registering. . . . To the fuel gauge. . . . It showed empty.

There was a leak in its tank: it could be nothing else. Both tanks had been full when they left Tiara, still almost full when he had gone back to the cabin, and even now the dial for the port tank showed a scarcely perceptible fall. There was a leak—and a big one. In a few minutes they had lost some seven hundred gallons. Where and why he did not know. Except that the Cat was old, and there always *something* wrong with old planes.

. . . And old pilots.

The plane lurched, yawed, slipped a little. But he held it. They were not going down yet. They were not going down at all; for there was still more than enough gas in the port tank to get them to Maniloa and back, and he could make an adjustment in the lines so that it fed both engines. . . . Or could he? . . . The valves were not in the cockpit. They were up in the engineer's tower. The need for a switch in feed lines, once a plane was airborne, was a one-in-a-thousand contingency, and they had not been moved down with the other engineering controls. He would have to go up. . . . But he couldn't.

He had to stay at the wheel.

All this, in his thoughts, had taken only an instant. His eyes had been on the fuel dials. But now they had moved. They were on the compass. And the compass showed, not eighty-seven degrees, but one hundred and fifty.

John was watching him. Now he spoke. "I tried to hold it, but—"

No explanation was needed. What had happened was obvious. With the starboard engine out, he had been unable to keep on course. The unbalanced thrust from portside had pushed them to starboard.

Toward the south. And the storm.

This, too, Carr had been aware of, as he jockeyed the wheel, scanned the instruments. . . . The sun was gone: no longer before them, but off to portside, fading, receding. The light in the cockpit was greenish gray. And ahead—dark, huge, close—was the wall of the storm front. Already shreds of cloud were streaming by. Rain was spattering the glass. Wind rolled at them like an angry sea. . . . He was trying to bank, to turn. But it was no go. On a straight course he had been able to keep the plane in control; but the moment he sought to veer off, it lost speed, shivered, sideslipped. In still air, he might have managed. But it wasn't still. Each moment it was wilder, more turbulent. On the one engine, all the Cat could do was limp on—into the storm.

They *had* to have the other engine.

"John—" he said.

But that was all he said. For even as he spoke, the storm took them.

306

An instant before there had still been sky above, sea below, but now there was only wind, cloud, rain, streaming against the cockpit. The storm sucked them in, closed behind them, enveloped them. In the opaque depths, lightning was flashing, thunder was booming, drowning the sound of the engine. The wind rolled them, shook them, lifted them up, smashed them down. John, unstrapped and trying to reach the tower, could not have taken two steps before being himself smashed against the walls of the cockpit.

Carr fought the wheel and rudders. He was no longer trying to turn; only to keep going, to keep up. Straining every sense, he tried to gauge the wind, to fly the wind, so it would lift them, not beat them down. It was not one wind, however, but a dozen: a tangled web of winds striking from all sides at random. They were not only sideslipping. They were yawing, bucking, tossing—the engine thrusting one way, the wings another, the tail still another—while they jerked and trembled in their metal bones.

John had turned when his name was spoken. Carr did not look at the boy. His eyes were busy elsewhere, everywhere. But still he saw him, felt his presence: his body rigid, his face tight and stricken: not with fear, he knew, but with shame, with guilt, that he had taken them off course.

"It wasn't your fault," Carr shouted through the din.

And then: "Sit tight. We'll make it. It's not the end of the world."

But it seemed like the end. Or that the end had already been— for the world was gone. Sky and ocean were gone. There was only space and storm, and themselves at the heart of it; only a roaring and tossing in a frail shell in the void. What he wanted to do was to climb. In a storm of unknown dimension, up was usually the shortest way out. But he could not gain an inch. Each time he pulled the plane's nose higher, a tide of wind struck down, slamming it back, all but ripping the wheel from his grasp. He heaved it toward him, held it by main force, fought to keep the nose at least level. But even this was increasingly hard. Again and again, in spite of his efforts, it dipped down. Again and again, they lurched, veered, slipped. And each time they lost altitude. Before the trouble they had been at the usual fifteen hundred feet. Soon the altimeter showed thirteen hundred. Then twelve.

Even before the storm hit, he had been unable to turn, to change course. There was even less chance now. But still he tried it, hoping he might find a headwind, an updraft, that would sustain them. The answer was no. At each attempt they lurched, slipped, losing more height. They were at eleven hundred feet. . . . Ten fifty. . . . With the port engine at full throttle, he made one more try at climbing. And for a moment there was a response; the nose went up. It held.

But the plane would not follow it. It seemed a thing separate from the nose: a tail, an anchor, dragging down from it. Body and wings and engines dragged: the starboard engine a dead weight, the port one coughing, stuttering. The plane hung there. It hung, swayed, trembled, ready to stall; ready to be swept away, end over end, like a chip in a torrent. . . . And then Carr had lurched forward again. The nose came down. They were flying again. The port engine rumbled; the storm roared; the void shimmered with lightning. The plane bucked and quivered. The port wing shot up, and they slipped to starboard. Leveling off, they dropped. They were under a thousand feet.

There was no choice now.

"John—" This time he had to shout.

And faintly he heard the boy's voice answering.

"Can you hear me?"

"Yes."

"We have to get the other engine going. It's out of gas. We have to switch the tanks."

This time he heard no answer. But John was moving, unstrapping his belt.

"The valves are in the tower. You'll see them—three of them—as you come up. It's the one in the middle. Turn it to the left, all the way."

John was out of his seat.

"And hold on. Hold on tight," Carr said.

The boy nodded; but even as he moved, a new lurch sent him crashing against the side of the cockpit. Recovering, he edged out between the seat, was thrown again, and then on all fours moved out of Carr's range of vision. Carr no longer tried to climb or turn. Even when the plane slipped or nosed down, he did not try to regain the lost height, but only to hold its tossing to a minimum. They still had a margin of nine hundred feet. . . . No. Eight fifty. . . . Then a downdraft hit, an enormous one, smashing them down into a quivering dive, and when he caught it they were at seven hundred.

They couldn't afford many more like that, he thought grimly. And what the last plunge had done to John he didn't know. He shouted, but no answer came back. Then, for an instant, he turned—and there was John on the tower ladder. How he had hung on he didn't know. But there he was: halfway up, still climbing. . . . The brown island boy climbing his coconut tree.

There was another lurch, another slip, and the altimeter showed six fifty. From cockpit to tower was ordinarily a matter of ten seconds, but already it seemed minutes since John had left. He fought the impulse to turn again. The wheel was his job, and he stayed with the wheel. With the strength of both hands, it was all he could do to hold it to a semblance of steadiness; but now he needed one hand free, and he held it with one hand, one arm, against his chest. With the other, he reached for the starboard switch. He turned it, held it. But nothing happened.

A blaze of lightning lit the cockpit. The altimeter seemed to leap at him. . . . Six hundred. . . . He tried the switch again. Nothing. He turned again. And John was gone. He was in the tower, at the valve, turning it. But why then—

A sickening thought struck him. The valve wouldn't turn. It hadn't been used in years; it was stuck, rusted; John needed a wrench. . . . He shouted, but could scarcely hear his own voice. The plane trembled, slipped, and he clung to the wheel. . . . Then once more he tried the switch. And the starboard engine turned over. It caught, rumbled—then faded. But it was getting fuel; its dials had come alive. *It* was alive. It was rumbling again. Its propeller was turning. He was working the throttle, the choke, and the engine was roaring. Two engines were roaring. He was pulling back on the wheel, and the wheel responded. The plane responded. The nose was up—and the altimeter. It showed six fifty, seven hundred, seven fifty. . . .

Carr kicked the rudders. The Cat banked, turned, still climbing.

And beyond the windshield, suddenly, something happened. At first he thought it was a flash of lightning—nearer, brighter than the others. But it wasn't lightning. It was light: pure light, in a flash of its own—in a wave, in a tide—pouring toward them through the cloud and rain. Above, a streak of blue appeared; below, a darker streak, lengthening, widening, becoming the blue sweep of ocean. And now the sky was spread above them. The last pelt of rain hit the shield. The last clouds streamed past. As abruptly as they had entered it, they were out of the storm, into the clear; and though the wind still blew, it was smoothly—they rode it smoothly, boring on to the east with humming engines—and the sun blazed before them in the rain-washed sky.

Then the wind had dropped. The storm was lost behind them. Only the humming broke the stillness of mid-ocean.

"Better then, at least," said Carr, "than with a load of sixty."

But John, beside him, made no response.

"What's the matter? Cheer up. It's all over."

"I am ashamed," the boy murmured.

"Ashamed?"

"For going off course. For being so—"

"Nonsense."

"If it hadn't been for me—"

309

"If it hadn't been for you, we couldn't have switched tanks either. That's what flying is, boy. The good and the bad. The foul-ups—and then this—"

Carr nodded forward into the shining stillness. At the sweep of blues: above, below. At the node of light, brighter than either, that now gleamed far ahead in the blue of the sea.

John stared. "It is Maniloa?"

"Yes, Maniloa."

They were silent again. The plane hummed. And in the humming stillness the atoll drew nearer. It became a ring, a necklace, a blaze of jewels on blue velvet: a thing of light so pure, so crystalline, that it seemed eye and mind must have imagined it.

The boy's lips moved. The word he spoke was barely audible. But the word was "Havaiki—"

"That's what your uncle said," said Carr.

"My uncle?"

"Fahoai. When we flew in yesterday."

"It is beautiful."

"Yes."

"And sad."

"Sad?"

"That a place so beautiful from far off is so hard, so cruel, when one is there."

They flew on. Soon the atoll was not so far off. But still it was beautiful. Still it shone with magic brightness.

Carr gauged the distance. "All right," he said presently, "start taking it down."

John looked at him.

"You," Carr said. "It's yours again. Take the wheel."

"You mean—you'll let me—after—"

"Especially *after*. That's the important time: after trouble." Carr took his hands from his own wheel. "Go on—down easily—you know how. You don't need the compass here. Just your eyes and the seat of your pants."

John took the copilot's wheel. He eased it forward. The plane's nose went down, and Maniloa was dead ahead through the windshield.

"I'll do the landing; it takes some practice," Carr said. "But you'll be doing that too, soon enough."

The plane sloped down at a gentle gradient. The atoll was no longer a jewel, a prism—but an atoll. They saw the lagoon, the islets; on the islets the sand and scrub; the whole of it, each moment, nearer, larger. John's hands were light but firm on the wheel; his eyes were fixed ahead. But not Carr's eyes. His were fixed on the boy. Watching him, he could almost physically feel his concentration; and beneath that, something else besides—something stronger, deeper—his joy, his exultation, in doing at last what he had so long dreamed of.

Carr smiled.

"It's in the family," he said.

"The family?" John kept his eyes ahead.

"Flying," said Carr.

"You mean Fahoai, yesterday?

"No, not Fahoai. I mean closer family." He paused. Then he said it. . . . "Like, for instance, your father,"

John said nothing.

"Your father was a flier, you told me."

"Yes."

"And your mother. She flew once, too, didn't she? *With* your father."

John's eyes moved, met his—but for just an instant. "I didn't—"

"No, you didn't tell me. Fahoai did." Carr paused. "And I know a little about it myself," he added, looking out through the windshield.

John seemed about to speak again, but he forestalled him. "Down a bit more now," he said. . . . "That's it. . . . And now with the throttles. Here—" He pointed. "Ease down with them too."

Their angle was steeper. The hum of engines was softer.

"She was as crazy about planes as you are," Carr said. "Every time I came over from Utoia she begged me to take her up, and finally I did; and I never saw anyone get as big a bang out of flying."

He stopped, listened. "Off a little more with the port engine. . . .

". . . But she wouldn't have made a pilot, I'm afraid. She got too excited, too distracted. . . ."

The plane's nose had gone up.

"Hey!"

The nose came down.

"Because good pilots *don't* get distracted," Carr said. "No matter what. . . . And you're a good one."

They were over the atoll now. The reflected green of the lagoon tinged the windshield, filled the cockpit.

"In fact, so good," he said, "that I'm going to have you try a turn. Watch now—with the wheel, over like this. With the pedal, like this. That's for starboard—the right. . . . O.K., try it now. Easy."

The plane jerked, began to sideslip, and he caught it with his own controls.

"That was too much," he said. "Now easier. Real easy. . . . That's it. Don't be nervous. You're a pilot, goddammit. . . ."

The plane banked. This time there was no jerk, no slip.

"That's it," he said. "That's it, son. Easy. Easy . . ."

21

THE RAINS were gone. Sun and ocean smiled. Even Mel Melnick smiled, using almost atrophied facial muscles, on the opening day of the Tiara Beach Hotel.

"—And tonight a full moon," he assured the guests sipping their late-afternoon drinks on the poolside terrace.

At seven that morning, precisely on schedule, the *Mariposa* had arrived at Apingo. Three jet planes had followed: two from Hawaii, one from Fiji. And through the rest of the day the Catalina had shuttled back and forth between Utoia and Tiara, with all eighteen seats filled on each outward flight. By 5 P.M. the total was five flights— ninety guests. Which, at thirty-per-day-minimum per guest (not counting plane fares, drinks, and beach cabanas) came to . . .

Mel Melnick's smile was not forced.

To be sure, a few things had gone wrong. Kosher food products to the amount of $514.63 (plus air freight charges) now filled the kitchen storage bins, to the vociferous annoyance of Chef Freddy Hoapola, late of Don Beachcomber's of Waikiki; whereas the Maccabbee Brotherhood of Far Rockaway, Long Island, had changed its plans and gone to Tahiti. A Mrs. Althea Lundgren of Spokane, Washington, had cut her foot on a shard of coral rock on the beach (where there was no rock—the folder said so). Four guests had requested Metrecal for lunch, in lieu of the gala buffet, and had had to be regretfully told that there was none on hand. ("Goddammit, you goofed that one," Melnick told his manager, Bruce Plimpton, in a pro tem lapse from euphoria.)

But in general things had gone well. The president and executive director of the Pacific Hotel and Development Company had not required a Relaxo since breakfast. And he was at his urbane best as, late in the day, he welcomed to his domain the Governor of Manaia and his party.

On the tour that followed, the group proceeded in two ranks of three each: in the first, Melnick with the Governor and his wife; in the second, Plimpton with Russell Gorman and Leonard Shafter. And all continued to go well. The hotel buildings stood white and bright against the green slope. The paths were trim, the lawns smooth, and the Governor's wife particularly admired the new plantings of hibiscus and gardenia. They inspected the beach, the pool, the tennis court, the terraces. And in the main building they viewed the lobby, restaurant, and kitchen (though the last only briefly, for Freddy Hoapola still had lox and matzos on his mind).

Then they visited the Model Village. This was on the site where the construction quonsets had formerly stood, but now, in their place, was a group of newly built Manaian *fales*. In and roundabout them were islanders wearing bright new lava-lavas with the monogram TBH. And as the visitors approached, a tall, plump Manaian in the regalia of a talking chief advanced to greet them.

"Ah, Fahoai," said the Governor genially.

And Fahoai replied in ceremonial phrases.

"My compliments to you for the fine work you did in going out to Maniloa."

"It was only my duty, sir," said the talking chief.

"Chief Fahooley here is manager of the Model Village," Mel Melnick put in. "Costumes, handicrafts, stuff like that. And then Sunday nights there's a native feast and show, and for that he's the M.C."

"I beg your pardon?" said Fahoai.

"You run it. You're in charge."

"Yes, that is right." Fahoai nodded and smiled. "I am in charge at this end of the island."

He led the party through the largest of the *fales*, in which a variety of merchandise was displayed for sale. There were shells, kava bowls, lava-lavas, headdresses, grass skirts, lengths of tapa cloth. And the Governor, eyeing the skirts, said, "Say, these red ones are pretty."

He glanced at Gorman. Gorman glanced at Shafter. Shafter took pen and notebook from his pocket and made an entry.

"We expect the red ones to be very popular," Melnick said, as Fahoai held one up for inspection. "You've sold several already, haven't you?" he asked the chief.

"Yes, six," said Fahoai. "Very popular. Very nice."

He handed the skirt to his wife, Polu, who was standing by as chief saleslady. Polu handed it to their niece, Mena, the stock girl.

313

And Mena, after refolding it neatly, went on with her work of unpacking other identical skirts from a carton marked WAIKIKI MODES—HONOLULU 16. As she did so, she softly hummed "Rock of Ages," for she was happy in her new vocation. It was much pleasanter than cleaning fish or shredding taro; and on her wages she could afford two O. Henry bars a day from Asimo's store, and still have enough left for Sunday church offerings that won her special praise from Pastor Solomona.

Meanwhile, the official party moved on. At the edge of the Model Village Fahoai bade them a ceremonious goodbye, and they returned across the grounds to the main building. Here, on the Talofa Terrace, outside the Breadfruit Bar, they sipped Paradise Punches, as the sun sank toward the lagoon.

The Governor's wife raised her eyes from her glass to the scene beyond. "It really is, you know," she murmured.

"Is what?" her husband inquired.

"Paradise."

"It's not bad," he conceded.

"When we get the cabanas set up," said Mel Melnick.

"I'm so envious of you, Leonard," the Governor's wife told Shafter. "Spending half your time here. But still—" She had a happy thought. "Still, we'll be coming often ourseves, now, won't we, Albert?" she asked of her husband. "With the plane and all. And so much to take care of. . . ."

An hour later the guests of the Tiara Beach Hotel were dressing for dinner; but at the Admiral Nimitz Hotel, in Apingo, dinner was already over. There had been a total of three diners, of whom one was Mitchell Carr. The others were Bert Windrow and Nigel Lawn, late of New Zealand's TEAL Airways, currently pilot and copilot of the TBH's Catalina. And now the three sat by an open window, inhaling the stench of low tide in the harbor.

"Bet it's a bloody good binge they'll be having over there," said Windrow. "And here we're stuck in this dump."

"If they had buoy lights on that lagoon—" Lawn groused.

"They will soon," Carr said.

"Much good that does us tonight."

The two New Zealanders had arrived the previous evening, and through the day Carr had flown with them while they familiarized themselves with the Cat. Now the five round trips were behind them. They would spend the night in Apingo, while the plane was serviced, and in the morning, with more tourists coming, they would resume their shuttling—on their own.

The three men smoked. They talked desultory fliers' talk. Then

314

the horn of one of Apingo's taxis sounded outside, and Carr got to his feet.

"Well—" he said.

Windrow looked at his watch. "Going Qantas or Pan Am?" he asked.

"Pan Am."

"It doesn't leave until nine."

"I've some things to do first."

They shook hands, said their goodbyes and good lucks, and he left. The taxi driver took his bag, which stood by the Nimitz's front door, and then he got into the cab himself and told the man where to go. It was a clear night, filled with stars. But the moon had not yet risen, and it was dark and quiet as they drove along the harbor road.

"—things to do," he had said.

Well, one thing.

One more goodbye.

The goodbye to John had already been said: late that afternoon, on the jetty in Tiara's lagoon. And it had been brief, almost casual. And unreal.

For three weeks, since the completion of Operation Maniloa, he and the boy had flown together. Back and forth, on hotel business, between Tiara and Apingo; once again to Maniloa—with a group of Tiarans—to bring back the body of Mrs. Mundy; and, many times, simply over and around Tiara on practice flights. John had learned quickly. Takeoffs, landings, navigation, all of it. Toward the end, indeed, Carr had done little more than sit by while he flew on his own; and he had all but reached the point where, in a small plane, he would be ready to solo.

That would not be until Hawaii. As of today, with the New Zealanders taking over, he was temporarily grounded, and for a while he would be their one-man servicing crew in Tiara. But it would not be long. Carr would see to that. During those three weeks he had been carefully planning the future.

"My first stop out of Manaia will be Honolulu," he had told John. "I'll find the best school. Then I'll write and send money."

And a few days later:

"I've spoken to Mr. Melnick. He owes me something for flying this plane of his; he owes *you* something for helping me; and when you come back you won't be ground crew any longer. He's promised me that. You'll fly. You'll be second copilot. And the New Zealanders won't stay forever."

John's eyes had shone.

"And beyond that," Carr had added, "wait and see. It's a few years yet before you can rate as a full pilot, and by that time . . . remember what I said . . . flying is just beginning out here. You've got it all ahead of you. The jets, the big flights, the new routes. The whole damn Pacific Ocean."

They had talked planes, planes, planes.

And that was all.

For there they were on common ground. On firm ground. But beyond it there was . . . what? He didn't know. It was beyond words, beyond communication. He had come to this far place and found a brown boy who was a stranger. In time he had come to know who he was—what he was. And now the boy knew too; they both knew; it was a fact accepted between them. But in spite of this—no, *because* of this—they were more strangers than ever.

There had been planes, planes, planes. And beyond that, constraint, silence. Carr had told the truth because it had to be told; for John's sake and for his own. But since that moment on the Cat, flying in to Maniloa, he had not spoken of it again. Nor had the boy. They had let the truth lie quiet, knowing it, but not touching it. . . . Until this day, three hours past, on Tiara's jetty, as the Cat lay ready for its last return trip to Apingo.

Windrow and Lawn were already aboard, warming it up. There were no other passengers. And John rowed him out in a skiff. As they came alongside the hatch, Carr rose, heaved his bag aboard, and then, with a quick, almost awkward, movement, turned and put out his hand.

"Happy landings," he said. "Watch those cross winds. Easy does it."

And then it was John who spoke. Whose face changed. Whose eyes changed. And whose voice, when at last he found it, was barely audible.

"Will—will you—I mean will we—"

He left the question hanging. But Carr knew what it was. It was the question he had asked himself a hundred times over in the days and weeks past.

He gave the only answer he had:

"I don't know, John."

Then, after a pause: "It will be a while, I suppose. Perhaps a long while. . . . You'll be here, with your life. I'll be there, with mine. . . . But it won't be like before. No. You'll know I'm there; I'll know you're here. Remember that. Where it counts, I'm with you. Remember that."

They had shaken hands. Their hands were at their sides. Windrow was gesturing from the cockpit, and Carr stepped from the skiff into the plane.

"Goodbye, son," he said, turning.

316

John swallowed. His lips moved. He struggled for the words. And at last he found them.

"Goodbye—Father," he said.

And Carr closed the hatch.

Then the flight . . . Apingo . . . the Nimitz . . .

From the Nimitz he had called the airfield and the cable office. He had sent a cable to George Swanson, Swanson, Bromley, Inc., 600 Fifth Avenue, New York 19, N.Y.

And now the taxi bumped along Apingo's harbor road.

To the left were the shore line, the wharf (from which the *Mariposa* had gone), and, on the dark water beyond, the mooring lights of the Catalina. To the right were closed shops, the Apingo Bar, a warehouse, an open market, the high school. And then the hospital. Beyond the hospital stood a smaller white frame building, in war days an NCO club, now the quarters for stateside nurses, and here he stopped the cab and got out. Telling the driver to wait, he walked up a short path and rang the doorbell. He waited. A plump, middle-aged nurse he had not seen before opened the door. He waited again.

And then he was alone on the steps of the house with Carol Loftus.

"I'm leaving tonight," he said.

Carol smiled a little. "Again?" she asked.

"Yes, again. But this time really."

"I'm honored, then."

"Honored?"

"That you've come to say goodbye. . . . Or perhaps you just need a pill."

"Thanks, I have a pill."

She had sat down on the steps, and now he too sat—at their farther edge—and for a few moments they were silent. In the past three weeks he had seen almost nothing of her. The day after he had brought Mrs. Mundy back to Tiara, they had stood together, with a crowd of others, while she was reburied beside her husband in the village churchyard. A few days after that, he had flown a native nurse from Apingo to Tiara, along with a Government teacher to replace Mrs. Mundy; and on the return trip he had flown Carol out. But on the same flight there had been a load of departing "Hawaiians," and she had been simply another passenger back in the cabin. Since then, he had not seen her at all. For she had been here at the Apingo Hospital, and he had been shuttling back and forth between the islands.

Now she was looking out across the road at the darkness of the harbor. And he was looking at her. A streak of light from a window behind them touched her hair and the curve of her shoulder above

317

the line of her cotton dress. It was the first time since the night of the feast that he had seen her out of uniform.

"I came also to thank you," he said.

Her eyes returned to him. "Thank me?"

"For what you did that night when John returned from Maniloa. When he ran away again and you brought him back."

"Oh. He wasn't supposed to—"

"I know he wasn't. But he did. I got it out of him."

"It was the least I could do."

"No, the most. The most anyone could have done. For him—or for me."

"Is he with you now?" she asked. "Here in Apingo?"

"No, he's in Tiara." He was on the point of going on—but didn't. "Will you be going back?" he asked instead.

She shook her head. "I'll be here at the hospital a few more weeks. Dr. Friede has asked me to help train the student nurses."

"And then?"

"Then I go to Karangi."

"Karangi?"

"It's an out-island, up to the northwest. Like Tiara, only farther."

Carr smiled. "And with no hotel."

"No, no hotel."

"I'd have thought they wanted you to stay in Tiara. The people, I mean. They liked you so."

"Some did; some wanted a Manaian nurse. It's always that way. . . . But it was just a fill-in assignment."

"And this new place? How long will you be there?"

"A few months, I guess."

"And after that?"

"I don't know. I've only a one-year contract. It will be almost up by then."

"But you could renew it?"

"Yes, I could renew it. If they want me."

"They'll want you," said Carr.

She made no reply, and again they were silent. Across the harbor, a greenish glow showed above the hills from which the moon would soon be rising.

"Karangi—" he murmured.

"It's a nice place, they say."

"It's a nice name. Almost as nice as Pahukahuka."

She looked at him. "What's that, Mitch? Where *you're* going?"

He shook his head.

"Where *are* you going?"

"To another island. Even farther than yours. It's called Manhattan."

"Oh."

"You're surprised?"

"I'm not sure."

"But you approve?"

She didn't answer. "You mean you're going back to work?" she asked.

"Yes."

She nodded slightly.

"So you approve," he said.

"It's not for me to—"

"Of course you approve. You're the Job Girl, aren't you? The Pull-Your-Weight Girl. The world's work must be done; the wheels must turn." He paused, then added: "Not to mention that Beachcomber Carr must make some money."

Carol said nothing.

"Of that you *don't* approve, of course. Too crass, materialistic. . . . But there are extenuating circumstances. . . . For instance, flying schools cost money."

"Flying schools?"

"That's where our friend John Koa is going. To Hawaii. To flying school."

"You mean—"

"Yes, that's what I mean. He's going. I'm sending him. Or at least I'm sending him when I've something to pay with."

"Oh, Mitch—" Her voice changed. Before, it had been dull, almost toneless, but now suddenly it came alive. "How wonderful," she said. "I'm so glad for him."

"I knew you'd be."

"—And for *you.*"

It wasn't only her voice. It was her face, too, that had changed. The rim of the moon was edging up over the hills; the darkness was thinning. And for a long moment he looked at her without speaking.

Then he said:

"There's something I must tell you about John and me. He's my son."

"I know that," she said.

He stared.

"You—you *know*—?"

"Yes."

"How? Since when?"

"I'm not quite sure."

"What do you mean?"

"Looking back, I think I must have felt it for a long time. I'm not blind, you know. I've seen how much you cared for him—wanted to

319

help him." Carol paused. "But that was only—well—feeling. When it really happened was that last night: when you came back and he ran away. I found him, and he came with me, and we talked. And all of a sudden—there it was. I saw. I knew."

She stopped. He was still staring, saying nothing.

"And John—" she said. "You've told him? *He* knows?"

Carr nodded.

"I'm glad of that, too. . . . And if you want it a secret between you, don't worry; I've told no one."

"You didn't even tell him."

"No."

"Or hint at it."

"How could I have? If he was going to know, it had to come from you."

She paused.

"The same as here, now, with me. It had to come from you," she said. "And do you know, Mitch—it's the first time you've told me anything."

For another moment he looked at her silently. "No, I've told you things," he said. "I've told you you were a foolish girl. I've told you you were a nice girl. Now I'm going to tell you one more thing. You're a wonderful girl."

The moon was full up now. It shone on the harbor, the road—and on the taxi that stood waiting at the side of the road. Carol looked at the taxi. And Carr looked at his watch.

"It's taking you to the plane?" she said.

"Yes."

"And you'll be in Honolulu—"

"In five hours."

"And in New York?"

"In a few days."

"It will be different for you this time," she said. "I don't know much about it, of course, but I do know you were unhappy before—when you came here." She was still looking away. "It's strange, isn't it? So strange. There you were, on Tiara, talking to me about my being on my own—being lonely—and it was really you who was the lonely one. . . . But now—from now on—you'll have John. Not there, with you; but still you'll *have* him. Someone that means something to you. That you care about. . . . And I think that's, most of all, what you need, Mitch. And what you want."

He was looking up and out into the moonlight.

"So—happy ending," he said.

She said nothing.

"John gets his planes. I get a son. You get another island. . . . Happy

320

ending, nice and tidy. . . . Just croon that tune 'neath the moon on the tropic lagoon, where

no

one

has

a . . ."

He got up.

"Goodbye," he said.

"Goodbye."

Her voice was firm, quiet. But the moonlight was bright now. It gleamed in her eyes, and in the tears that filled them.

For a long moment he stood watching her. Then—

"Carol," he said.

"Yes?" She did not look at him.

"That's the way it is?"

"Yes."

"You're *sure* it's the way it is?"

"Yes."

Still he looked down at her. Then, extending a hand, he touched the wetness of her cheek.

"It's not in character," he said. "Not for the daughter of Dr. John Normal Loftus."

"I—I can't help it," she murmured. Her head was bent. "And I don't give a damn."

He smiled. "I've been pretty fatherly myself. You haven't got me mixed up with your father?"

She shook her head.

"Because I'm not, you know. Not your father—just John's. For you, I'm a piece of shopworn goods called Mitchell Carr."

There was a sound from the road. The sound of the taxi's horn.

"Mitchell Carr, C.E.," he said, "expert on dynamite and family relations, of Swanson, Bromley and Carr, Inc., Six Hundred Fifth Avenue, New York Nineteen, New York. And when you're through with Pahukahuka—"

"Karangi."

"All right, when you're through with Karangi—and if you're still out of your senses—"

Now her face was raised to him. Bending, he kissed her: quickly, lightly.

"—then maybe I'll do better than that," he said. "There's a lagoon just a few blocks from the office, in front of the Seagram Building. And when the moon comes up over East Fifty-second Street—"

The horn sounded again. For a last long moment he stood before her. He looked down into her face, her eyes, into all there was of her.

Then he smiled again. "You know, all those men you keep running away from are right," he said. "You *are* a cute tomato."

The moon rose higher. It shone on the wings of the jet plane soaring up over Utoia, and on the girl who sat, watching it, on the steps of a house in Apingo. It shone on the hills, the beaches, the bays, the ocean. Eighty miles across the ocean, it shone on the terrace of the Tiara Beach Hotel.

"Mel Melnick's moon, by God," said Stanley Kupferberg (*the* Stanley Kupferberg) of New York and Beverly Hills, vice president in charge of production for Premier Pictures and thirty per cent stockholder in the Pacific Hotel and Development Company. "You're doing all right, pal. Turned it on like a kleig light."

"It's just organization, Stan—organization," Melnick explained, as he lighted a fresh cigar and surveyed his domain.

And there was plenty to survey, for the terrace was full. Tables and dance floor were full. Mel Melnick's moon gleamed brightly on linen and silverware; on white evening jackets, bare shoulders, and the horns and saxes of Jackie Jackson's Aloha Troubadors. True, Jackie— as his employer well knew—was not in the best of moods. His working schedule called for a neat jigger of Jack Daniels after every third number, and it had developed (more goofing by Plimpton) that there wasn't a Daniels in the house. But at least Jackie was not letting it interfere with his professional competence. The crowd loved him. His music was soft, sweet, throbbing in the tropic night.

The table next to Melnick's was that of the Governor and his party. The Governor was in fine humor. His drink was not Jack Daniels but gin and tonic, and there was plenty of gin and tonic. And his wife was dancing with Russell Gorman.

Leonard Shafter was dancing with a Mrs. Wilbur Orthley—off the *Mariposa*—who had political connections in Wisconsin. In the eyes of both there was a faraway look. In Mrs. Orthley's case, presumably, it was the effect of music and shining lagoon. But for Shafter it was because the next morning he had an appointment in the village with Tafutimo and his council of *matai*.

There came a pause in the music. The dancers returned to their tables. There was stillness, drumbeat, then a single dancer—Va'ina dancing—the *taupou* of Tiara in her glittering headdress, her body golden as the Tiaran moon. There was no sound but the drumming. No movement but hers. Her audience sat rigid, enthralled. . . . Until at last her dance was ended, and she stood bowing, smiling, blowing kisses, and then applause swept over the terrace like the booming of the sea on a reef. . . . Protocol was observed. There was a special smile, a special kiss, for the Governor's table; then the same for Mel

Melnick's. And the proprietor of the Tiara Beach Hotel responded with his own smile and a *"Malo! Malo!"*

"What's that mean, pal?" asked Stanley Kupferberg, v.p. in charge of p. for Premier Pictures, over the din.

"It means the kid's something—I really got something here—what say, Stan?" said Melnick, beaming.

What Stanley Kupferberg said, thumping his hands, was *"Malo! Malo!"*

And from the *taupou* of Tiara came a smile, a kiss, a moonlit wink.

The lagoon was moonlit too. Its blackness gleamed. Beneath the gleaming, in dark stillness, the coral engineers built on.

The beaches gleamed; the palm groves and the hills. In a valley between the hills the moon shone on a waterfall, a pool, a breadfruit tree. There were now no lovers beneath the arms of the breadfruit tree. But they would come. As long as the island rose from the sea, they would come: to the place of peace—of refuge—of *fia fia*.

The moon shone on Tiara's village. On the open *malae,* the road and paths, the pillared *fales*. On the faces of sleeping children, of women spreading mats of pandanus, of old men rolling strands of sennit against tatooed thighs.

It shone on the dispensary, the school, the church, and on the two crosses of *toa* wood, one old and one new, that stood side by side in the churchyard.

It shone on the shed that was Asimo's store, on the shack behind it, and, through the torn tapa curtain on the shack's window, on a sprawled, snoring figure and an empty calabash.

It shone on the bony frame and lion's head of the high chief, Tafutimo, as he looked out from his *fale* and saw another figure passing by. He spoke and gestured, and the figure approached, and the chief asked, "What are you doing here?"

"I have come to visit my aunt Polu and cousin Mena," said John Koa. "I have now not seen them in some time."

"You have been flying with the plane, they say."

"Yes."

"And soon will be leaving Tiara."

"Yes. For a while."

"So what do you care about an aunt and cousin? About this village, and its people? You have turned your back on them."

"No," John said, "these are still my people."

The high chief shook his head. "We are not one people now; we are two. There are those who live *fa'a Manaia* and those who go the way of the *papalagi*. To the hotel. To ships and planes. To another world. . . . You are one of those."

"It is my hope I can be of both worlds," said John. "It is, I think, the only way I can live."

"It is not possible. It will tear you, destroy you. As it destroys our people."

"It will not be easy, that I know. For me—or for anyone. But still it is what we must do."

"Until we are nothing."

"Until we are part of the world. Until there are not two worlds, or many worlds, but only one."

The chief looked at the boy long and searchingly; and, searching, he saw that he was not a boy. He was a man. . . . And the two men were silent. . . . Around the *fale* there was the rustling of palm fronds. From the distance there came the sound of the sea. And then, presently, there was another sound—from greater distance, from the night above —and the lights of a plane streaked high across the moonlit sky.

"It is not the hotel plane," said Tafutimo.

"No," John said. "It is the plane to Hawaii."

The chief's dark eyes brooded. "It all changes. All that was is dead and gone," he murmured. "Once it was Havaiki, our promised land, that was beyond the ocean. Now it is a place of the white men that they call Hawaii."

"The name is not so different," said John.

He watched the plane's lights, winking, receding. . . .

. . . And, from the plane, Mitchell Carr watched the island.

For a few moments, flying past, he could see the splash of light that was the Tiara Beach Hotel. He could see the black of the lagoon, the silver of the beaches, the soft billows of the hills rising still into the moonlight. Then they were gone. Looking back, he could see only a white cloud gleaming in the ocean night.

The plane hummed on.

He had taken a coin from his pocket and was holding it on his thumbnail; but he did not flip it. In the bar in Waikiki he had flipped a coin and dropped it. On the harbor road of Utoia he had flipped ten heads and ten tails. On the foredeck of the *Harold L. Ickes* he had flipped and not looked.

Now he looked without flipping. The folding table on which he had been served his dinner was still open before him, and, shifting the coin in his hand, he held it upright on the flat surface. He took his hand away. The coin stood on edge. A stewardess, coming down the aisle, paused, smiling, and said, "You see—how smooth the flight is."

Carr smiled back at her.

"Just like in the ads," he said.

324

JAMES RAMSEY ULLMAN is, on his own words, "a New Yorker by birth and, subsequently, by choice—the fact that I now live in Boston being irrelevant, except in its indication of my difficulty in staying put."

Indeed, moving about—along with writing—has been very much the mainstream of Mr. Ullman's life since his graduation from Princeton in 1929. While working as a young newspaper reporter, he made his first venture into the theater as a playwright, and from 1933 to 1939 was producer or coproducer of some dozen plays on Broadway (among them Sidney Kingsley's *Men in White,* which won the Pulitzer Prize for 1934). Since 1939, excepting a wartime interlude with the American Field Service in Africa, he has been a full-time writer—and roughly half-time traveler.

Two trips to the Amazon jungle of South America resulted in the writing of *The Other Side of the Mountain* and *River of the Sun,* the latter a Book-of-the-Month Club choice. *Windom's Way,* a Literary Guild selection, is the story of an American doctor in Southeast Asia; and *The Sands of Karakorum* tells of a missionary's disappearance in the interior of Communist China. Between novels, Mr. Ullman has written two histories of mountaineering, plus many short stories and articles for national magazines. And five of his books have been bought for motion picture production.

Travel, and particularly mountaineering (of which he himself has done a fair share), has provided both the physical background and spiritual core of most of Mr. Ullman's books. Two of his novels, *The White Tower,* a Book-of-the-Month Club choice, and *Banner in the Sky,* a novel for young readers, are set in the Alps. *Tiger of the Snows* took him to India and Nepal to work with Tenzing Norgay, the great Sherpa who shared in the conquest of Everest. And for his most recent novel, *The Day on Fire,* which was suggested by the life of Arthur Rimbaud, he followed the poet's tracks from France to Ethiopia.

Now Mr. Ullman is recently back from more than a year of wanderings in the South Pacific—"a journey I have long wanted to make, but which I deferred until I could make it slowly and fully." The first fruit of this is *Fia Fia.* And he is currently at work on a nonfiction book with the same background.

THIS BOOK WAS SET IN

GRANJON AND ELIZABETH ROMAN TYPES BY

V AND M TYPOGRAPHERS.

IT WAS PRINTED AND BOUND AT THE PRESS OF

THE WORLD PUBLISHING COMPANY.

DESIGN IS BY LARRY KAMP.